Wes stepped closer, and without thinking, Thea let her head tip forward until her forehead rested on his chest. She was too weak to fight the pull she felt to him. Or maybe she was strong enough to act on it in this moment.

After a second, Wes's arms came around her, enveloping Thea in a warmth and closeness she hadn't let herself experience for so long. For a lifetime. Her heart pounded harder and her knees softened. She raised her head to peek up at him, to see into his eyes again. They drew her in, so full of something she'd never seen before—scars and regret but also a flicker of hope that kindled hers. Thea couldn't look away. She couldn't step away. The hammering of her heart pushed her to move, to touch her lips to his. The contact knocked the wind out of her, bringing a small whimper hurtling up her throat.

Wes startled, pulling away from her. But then his gaze locked on hers and everything paused. A year seemed to pass between them all at once, and her chest burned with each shallow breath. What had she done? What was she doing?

Thea didn't know, but she needed more.

PRAISE FOR
SARA RICHARDSON

A COWBOY FOR CHRISTMAS

"Tight plotting and a sweet surprise ending make for a delightful Christmas treat. Readers will be sad to see the series end."

—*Publishers Weekly*

COLORADO COWBOY

"Readers who love tear-jerking small-town romances with minimal sex scenes and maximum emotional intimacy will quickly devour this charming installment."

—*Publishers Weekly*

RENEGADE COWBOY

"Top Pick! An amazing story about finding a second chance to be with the one that you love."

—Harlequin Junkie

"A beautifully honest and heartwarming tale about forgiveness and growing up that will win the hearts of fans and newcomers alike."

—*RT Book Reviews*

HOMETOWN COWBOY

"Filled with humor, heart, and love, this page-turner is one wild ride."

—Jennifer Ryan, *New York Times* bestselling author

NO BETTER MAN

"Charming, witty, and fun. There's no better read. I enjoyed every word!"

—Debbie Macomber, #1 *New York Times* bestselling author

One Night with
a Cowboy

One Night with a Cowboy

A SILVERADO LAKE NOVEL

SARA RICHARDSON

FOREVER
New York Boston

Copyright © 2021 by Sara Richardson
Bonus novella *It's All about That Cowboy* copyright © 2019 by Carol Pavliska

Cover design by Daniela Medina
Cover photographs © Rob Lang Photography; Shutterstock
Cover copyright © 2021 by Hachette Book Group, Inc.

Forever
Hachette Book Group
1290 Avenue of the Americas, New York, NY 10104
read-forever.com
twitter.com/readforeverpub

First edition: March 2021

Forever is an imprint of Grand Central Publishing. The Forever name and logo are trademarks of Hachette Book Group, Inc.

The publisher is not responsible for websites (or their content) that are not owned by the publisher.

ISBNs: 978-1-5387-1716-5 (mass market), 978-1-5387-1717-2 (ebook)

Printed in the United States of America

CW

10 9 8 7 6 5 4 3 2 1

ATTENTION CORPORATIONS AND ORGANIZATIONS:

Most Hachette Book Group books are available at quantity discounts with bulk purchase for educational, business, or sales promotional use. For information, please call or write:

Special Markets Department, Hachette Book Group
1290 Avenue of the Americas, New York, NY 10104
Telephone: 1-800-222-6747 Fax: 1-800-477-5925

To Clover

Chapter One

Garth Brooks had it all wrong. The best sound at the rodeo wasn't the roar of a *Sunday* crowd. It was the roar of the *hometown* crowd.

Weston Harding jogged into the arena at the Silverado Lake rodeo grounds, the familiar faces from his childhood serenading him with rowdy cheers. The way the audience carried on, someone might've assumed he was the main attraction instead of the bull riders who were getting ready to test their luck. He was no bull rider, though if you asked him, his job wasn't any less important.

Wes took his position on the inside of the south fence, his eyes trained on the chute. It was time to tune out everything—including the loud, succinct chant of his name, which seemed to rebound off the metal roof. He'd always been popular in Silverado Lake—a hometown boy, born and raised. To hear the locals tell it, he'd overcome a lot—the grief of losing his father in such a tragic accident, the learning disability he'd struggled with since the day he'd opened his first book.

He'd had a hard time at school, and he'd had an even worse time after his father's death, but now here he was, one of the most well-known rodeo clowns—aka bullfighters—in the world. Little did his friends and fans know, he hadn't overcome the past so much as he'd ignored it. He'd escaped this town and the memories it held exactly one month after graduating from high school, intent on proving himself to the world—intent on living up to his father's good name and making something of himself. And now he was finally back with something to show for all the blood, sweat, and injuries this gig had brought.

Once again, he wondered if his dad knew—if he was watching from some other world. It didn't matter how many times he stood in arenas like this, he always wondered if he'd made his dad proud.

Wondering wouldn't get the job done, though. Wondering brought on too many memories.

Shutting out everything else, Wes refocused on the arena. Adrenaline simmered along with the anticipation, but it wouldn't fully spike until that chute opened and he approached the champion bull named Tantrum. Most people said you had to be one crazy SOB to provoke a lethal bull into a good foot chase, but Wes was there to protect the rider, bottom line. Once the rider hit the dirt, Wes and the rest of his team had a responsibility to protect the cowboy by keeping the bull as far away from him as they could. He took his duty seriously. Chalk it up to the fact that he felt a responsibility to protect these riders the way he hadn't been able to protect his own father.

A hush finally fell over the crowd. Mikey Ruiz happened to be the first rider up, and Wes estimated it would take Tantrum T-minus two seconds to whip the man off into the dirt. For Ruiz—who was still pretty green—Wes always had to move extra fast.

The rider climbed up onto the fence and slid onto the bull's back. Tantrum hardly flinched, though the animal's powerful, sleek brown body did tense. Wes had learned to read the bulls, to detect how their muscles moved so he could anticipate how to move with them—and how to get away from them.

From the other side of the arena, Gabe—their team leader—gave the thumbs-up. Wes returned the gesture, retraining his eyes on Tantrum. The bull had given him more close calls than any of the others, but that's what made him Wes's favorite. You never knew what to expect; you didn't have time to think, only to react; and nothing brought on the adrenaline rush like the thrill of the unknown.

The countdown went quick, and then the gate swung wide open. Wes closed in on the rider, along with Gabe and their other teammate Colin, confining the bull to the corner. Sure enough, Ruiz had hardly raised his arm in the air before he went sprawling off Tantrum's back sideways.

Wes lurched into action, the cheers roaring in his ears. The bull jolted toward Ruiz, who still lay in the dirt, but Wes jumped between them, raising his arms and yelling who the hell knew what to distract Tantrum. The diversion worked. Instead of going after Ruiz, the bull lunged at Wes. He was ready for it, though. He jumped sideways and jogged backward while the bull charged him.

The cheers became deafening. Wes dodged the bull twice with his best moves and then turned and sprinted in the direction of Tantrum's exit gate.

But instead of leaving the arena, the bull stayed hot on his tail.

Damn. Tantrum was extra feisty today.

Wes evaded him again and flung himself onto the fence, finding his balance with his boots positioned on the second rung so he could raise his arms and whoop for the crowd.

They indulged the dramatics, hopping to their feet to give him a standing ovation.

Seeming to give up on him, Tantrum did a lap around the arena before trotting through the exit gate for his postgame snack.

Wes did a backflip off the fence and landed on his feet in the dirt—a move he'd only recently perfected. If the crowd noise got any louder, it would shake those mountains outside.

"Thanks, man. You're the best." Ruiz walked over and swatted him on the shoulder. "You saved my ass again."

"That's what I'm here for." Maybe one of these days, saving someone's ass would make him feel something. Hell, he didn't know what he should feel when the rider came to thank him. A sense of accomplishment maybe? As it was, he only felt something when he was running from the bull—the instinct, the adrenaline, the rush he'd come to live for. It didn't matter how many saves he made, how many close calls he'd survived, nothing ever managed to fill the hole his dad's death had left in his life.

The rest of the afternoon flew by in the same blur it always did. Wes stayed focused, diverting the bulls, joking around with the bull riders when he got the chance, and adding in some flair with more backflips off the fence for the hometown crowd.

After the last ride, he removed his protective gear and made his way down one of the chutes that led underneath the bleachers, high-fiving the fans who'd lingered until the end to say hello. All in all, it had been a perfect day—no serious injuries, a good solid lineup of riders. Hell, Wes wasn't even as sore as he usually was.

And yet…he couldn't quite shake the emptiness. Damn. What was up with him, anyway? All these thoughts creating noise in his head. He usually didn't allow himself the time to think—to reflect on what he was feeling. All that self-introspection bullshit was dangerous territory. It had to be because he'd come back home. Being here was messing with his head.

"That was quite the show you put on out there." Jane, his younger sister, stood at the end of the hallway. Every time he saw her lately, he had to do a double take. It still caught him off guard that his little sister was around seven months pregnant…if he remembered correctly.

"Gotta give the crowd what they want." He leaned in to hug her, careful of her baby bump. "Thanks for hanging out all day. I know it's not usually your thing." Jane had always detested anything that involved danger. But then she'd gone and married a bull rider. Go figure.

"It was fun." His sister's smile brightened. "You're really good at what you do, Wes. I'm impressed."

"I'm impressed too." He eyed her belly. "You sure you're not carrying twins in there?"

Jane gasped in mock outrage and swatted him while he laughed.

He'd always loved teasing her. "Kidding, of course. You look as gorgeous as always, sis." Not only gorgeous, she looked...happy. There was a light in her eyes that hadn't been there when she was younger.

"I don't know about gorgeous, but I'll take it." His sister rested her hand on her belly and smirked up at him. "Keep the compliments coming if you want to stay in the running to become the baby's godfather."

"Oh, come on. I'm a shoo-in." He slipped his arm around her and they walked side by side out into the concessions area. "Of course you're going to pick me. We hardly ever see August." Their eldest brother had been managing a winery out in Napa for the last several years and rarely made it home. Though Wes didn't know what he had to offer as a godfather. Advice and wisdom weren't exactly his specialty. Fun, on the other hand? That he could do.

"How's Tobster?" he asked his sister as they passed the BBQ food truck and ice cream vendor parked in line on the outside of the arena. His sister's husband had made it past the pro rodeos all the way to the Professional Bull Riders circuit and was away at some big event in Texas this weekend.

"Doing great," she said dreamily. "He calls me about every hour to check in. Speaking of..." She dug her phone out of her back pocket and grinned at the screen. "Right on time. Give me a sec." Bringing the phone to her ear, she backed away as though she didn't want Wes to hear their lovey-dovey newlywed talk. Fine by him. He'd never been one for all that sugary sentimental crap. Though he couldn't deny something about seeing his sister so happy—so fulfilled—made him wonder if he could make room in his life for something like what Jane and Toby had...

And there he went, thinking again. He didn't have room in his life for a family. Not with the constant traveling. And then there was the fact that he faced off with bucking bulls on a regular basis. One wrong move and an animal like Tantrum could end him.

"Yo, Wes." His boss, Craig, strode over from the line of trailers parked along the perimeter of the bleachers. "Hey, awesome job out there today." The man took Wes's hand in a firm shake.

"Thanks." As Wes was the most junior member of the team, it used to be that Craig never acknowledged him, but lately he'd made a point to find him after each event. "I figure it's always a success when the riders walk away." There'd only been a few times on his watch that hadn't happened.

"You got that right." Craig removed his black cowboy hat and mopped sweat from his forehead. "You've got one of the best records of anyone out there these days. In fact, I want you on team lead next week."

Team lead. Wes tightened his jaw so his mouth wouldn't fall open. "Really?" That was a huge step. He'd started working in the rodeo world as an assistant handler for the bovine athletes, and it had taken him years to find himself in the arena, only to realize that each new position was like starting all over in the chain of command.

"Yeah." Craig slipped his hat back on. "You're hot right now, Harding. Careful, but also entertaining for the crowd. You're exactly what they want out there. It's time to put you at the top."

"Great." Wes made sure to punctuate the words with a casual shrug. No big deal. He was just getting a huge promotion. Maybe this was it—the step that would finally give him more than the fleeting rush of adrenaline. He was ready for this—for something bigger.

Of course, he had to play it cool with Craig. "I'm ready. Whatever you need."

"I knew you would be." Craig gave him a businesslike nod. "I have to go catch up with Gabe, but we'll talk soon."

Wes let him walk away before he grinned.

"Wow. Team lead, huh?" Jane walked back over. She must've been within earshot the whole time. "Look at you—" A gasp cut her off. His sister's eyes widened with the sudden intake of air, and both of her hands cradled her belly.

"What is it?" Wes studied her face. She didn't look so good. "You okay?"

Instead of answering, his sister hunched over and exhaled with a whimper.

"Jane?" Wes moved in front of her. Her face had paled. "Is it the baby?"

"Not sure." She inhaled deeply and straightened back up. "That was a weird pain, but it's going away now."

Thank God for that. Pain during pregnancy couldn't be good. "Where's the pain?"

"My stomach." She massaged her belly. "I've felt it a few times on and off today, but it always goes away." She peered up at him with mild concern in her eyes. "Maybe it's Braxton Hicks."

Braxton what? He shot her a look. What the hell did that mean? He knew nothing about this stuff—about pregnancy and babies...

"False contractions." She seemed to shrug it off. "From everything I've read, they're no big deal."

"I sure hope they're no big deal." He wasn't equipped to deal with anything like contractions, and with Toby out of town, Wes was all she had. Lucky her. "Maybe we should go to the doctor—"

His sister's squeal cut him off. She doubled over again, clutching at her stomach. "Oh God, oh God, oh, it hurts..."

Whoa. Wes's heart bucked around his chest like one of those bulls back there. Panic brought on a totally different kind of rush. "Okay, okay." He put his arm around her to support her. "Can you make it to my truck? We need to get you to the doctor. Now." She wasn't supposed to be in pain. She wasn't supposed to be having any kind of contractions right now. Not for a few more months...

"I don't need the clinic." Jane stood and pushed him away. "It's probably just Braxton—" She gasped again, and that was it. Enough messing around. Wes scooped her up into his arms and ran her to his truck in the parking lot. As carefully as possible he got her settled in the passenger's seat and sprinted to the driver's side. "Call your doctor."

"I'm sure everything's fine," Jane said as he slid behind the wheel, but she was still breathing hard.

"We can't take any chances." Not with his niece or nephew. He shoved the keys into the ignition and gunned the engine. "Call your doc. We'll get everything checked out to be safe." It was either that or he was taking her to the closest emergency room.

"Fine," Jane grumbled, but at least she took out her phone.

While he sped out of the parking lot and turned onto the main road, his sister explained the situation to the doctor.

"Okay. Sure. Sounds good. We can be there in about forty-five minutes." She hung up and pocketed the phone. "We have to go to her clinic in Steamboat. She'll meet us there."

"Got it." Wes made a quick left and maneuvered through town as fast as he dared, given the number of people out and about for the town's annual Gold Rush Days. The weeklong festival was only just getting started with the rodeo kickoff, but the crowds had already come.

"Oh no." Jane's hands flew to her stomach again. She seemed to fold in on herself, her lips twisting with pain. "What's happening?" She raised her head and peeked over at him. The fear in her eyes locked up his chest.

"I don't know, but everything will be okay." Panic gripped him by the throat. She couldn't lose this baby. Their family had already lost too much. Images from his dad's funeral flashed in front of him—the way he'd sat frozen in his chair during the graveside service, that final moment when the casket had been lowered into a hole in the ground. The back-bending grief came again, as heavy as it had been then.

He wouldn't let his family endure another loss. Everything had to be okay. He took the exit to get on the highway that led out of town and increased his pressure on the gas pedal. Screw forty-five minutes. He'd have her there in twenty. "Maybe we should keep track of how far apart the contractions are." Wasn't that what you were supposed to do when someone was in labor?

"I can't be in labor." Jane raised her voice. "I can't be! It's too early! I'm only thirty weeks. The baby's not big enough!"

"Okay. Shh. Everything's fine." He rested his hand on her

shoulder but also glanced at the clock to note the time. "Maybe we should call Toby."

"No." Jane swung her head and shot down the idea with a glare. "He's already worried enough. It has to be Braxton Hicks. It has to be."

Growing up with one tough mother and sister, Wes knew when to argue and when to keep his mouth shut. He flicked on the radio, but the music didn't take the edge off the adrenaline coursing through him. Nothing could happen to his sister. Or the baby. That was all there was to it. He had to make sure nothing bad happened to them.

"Ow. Ow, ow, ow, ow." Jane's whole body tensed again, flooding Wes with a sense of helplessness. He glanced at the clock. Only five minutes had passed since the last round of pain.

"It's okay," he murmured while his sister gasped and whimpered. "You're okay."

The rest of the drive went the same—with Jane writhing in pain every five to eight minutes while he tried to comfort her. Finally, Wes swung the truck into the empty parking lot outside the clinic. He ripped the keys out of the ignition and raced to the passenger's side to help Jane out. Thankfully the waiting room wasn't busy. The receptionist took one look at his sister and beckoned them both back. "I'll get the doctor," she said, leading them into a small room before hurrying off.

"I think I'm fine now." Jane sat on the exam table while Wes paced.

He glanced at his watch. "The last one was ten minutes ago." Not enough time to declare everything was fine, in his estimation.

Within a few more seconds, the door opened, and the doctor rushed in. "Jane." She greeted his sister with a concerned frown. "You're having pain? Can you tell me more?"

"She's been having contractions every five to eight minutes for the last hour." Wes butted in.

"This is my brother. Wes," his sister said with a quick nod in his direction.

The doctor gave him a terse smile but didn't greet him. He didn't like the serious expression on the woman's face.

She opened a drawer and pulled out one of those useless paper gowns. "I'll need you to get undressed so we can check things out right away."

"Of course." Jane took the gown and raised her eyebrows at Wes, nodding toward the door.

Oh. Right. This would be a good time for him to take a walk. "Um...I'll wait outside."

Jane laughed, the sound a welcome relief in comparison to the gasps of pain. "That's probably best."

Wes led the way out of the room and the doctor skirted past him. She was definitely moving fast.

He paced up and down the hallway a few times and pulled out his phone. Should he call Toby? Their mother? Mara was currently on a monthlong cruise in Europe with some friends, so she wouldn't be able to offer much help...

A nurse rushed past him, pushing a small cart with a computer. Maybe an ultrasound machine? The doctor followed behind, and they both disappeared into Jane's room.

Shit. Things definitely didn't look good. What was he supposed to do? Not knowing the answer, he clicked on Toby's phone number, but the call went right to voice mail. "Hey. Uh...this is Wes." As if he wouldn't already know that. "You should give me a call when you can. I brought Jane to the clinic—"

The door opened and the doctor hurried out.

"What is it?" Wes hung up the phone. "Is everything okay?"

He could see the answer in her eyes. No. Everything was not okay.

"She's in active labor," the woman reported. "She's already dilated. I'm having the nurse start an IV of terbutaline and I'm calling for an immediate ambulance transfer to Denver."

Ambulance. The floor seemed to shift under Wes's boots. "What does that mean? Will Jane be okay? Is the baby okay?" He'd promised her...

"She needs to be at a full-service hospital with a level four NICU," the doctor said instead of answering his question directly.

"She's having the baby? Now?" Every breath he took seemed to sear his lungs. This couldn't be happening.

"We're trying to stop the labor." The doctor started down the hall. "Hopefully we can hold her off for a few more weeks at least. But she'll likely be on bed rest while she's monitored at the hospital."

A few weeks? Jane would have to stay in the hospital for a few weeks? He plowed into the exam room, everything around him seeming to blur. Jane was on the phone.

"They're bringing me to Denver," she said. She was lying on the table still dressed in that gown, but they'd also given her a blanket. Wes surveyed the IV line a nurse was setting up. How could Jane sound so calm?

"Yes. I'm fine, honey. Please don't worry. Just get to the hospital whenever you can." She must've gotten hold of Toby. "I will. I promise. I'll see you soon." She hung up the phone and directed an earnest stare at Wes. "I need you to go back to the ranch ASAP."

"No." He crossed his arms over his chest. "Hell no. I'm staying with you." He'd ride in the ambulance with her. "You can't be alone." His dad had been alone the day he'd died. Because of him...

Determination tightened his sister's frown. "I need you to go back to the ranch. Please. I have that Project Sanctuary group coming to stay in two days."

Right. The group of veterans and their families the ranch hosted for a week every summer. "You have to go back to the ranch and get things ready," Jane went on. "I can't let Thea down."

His confused expression must've spoken for him.

"Thea is my friend from college," his sister said with exasperation. "Don't you remember her? She visited the ranch a few times. You met her way back in college. And you probably saw her at the wedding too."

"Well, I'm sorry if I can't think clearly right now." Keeping Jane safe. And the baby. That was his focus. How was he supposed to protect his sister if he went back to the ranch?

"Thea lost her husband in Afghanistan three years ago," Jane reminded him. "She's the group leader. They're coming for a ten-day retreat, and I refuse to let them down. They've all been through so much. You'll have to host them at the ranch for me. Take my place."

He was supposed to head out to Oklahoma for an event in three days.

"Oh, wait." His sister's head fell back to the pillow. "You can't stay. Your boss made you the team leader—"

"No, it's fine." He might not be able to stop her labor or promise her that the baby would be okay, but he could take this stress away from her. "I'll stay. I can take over at the ranch for you." Craig wouldn't like it, but this was a family emergency. "You just focus on keeping that baby in place as long as you can." He would take care of everything else.

Chapter Two

She should've never gone with the soufflé.

Thea Davis paced in front of her polished stainless steel double oven, resisting the urge to open the door so she could peek. She'd turned the oven off approximately eighteen minutes ago, and opening the oven door to let colder air in before the soufflé had set could result in a catastrophic collapse. Twenty to twenty-five minutes was the optimal time to wait before pulling the confection out of the oven, according to *Fine Foods* magazine. So she had at least two more long, painstaking minutes to see if this dessert she'd tackled for the group's last meeting just before their Colorado retreat would totally bomb.

"Is someone giving birth in there or what?" At thirteen, her daughter, Olivia, had recently perfected the art of sarcasm. "You look like you're waiting for bad news." Olivia reached for the handle on the oven door.

"No!" Thea stepped in front of her. "We can't open it yet. It's not time." They needed between one and five more minutes…

"Sheesh." Her daughter walked to the refrigerator and pulled out a sparkling water. "You'd think the president was coming for dessert or something."

"I want everything to be perfect." She winced at the word. No matter how hard she tried, nothing ever seemed perfect enough. Her eyes focused in on a smudge on the oven's sparkling stainless exterior. *Don't do it. Do not grab the rag...*

Oh, who was she kidding? Thea snatched the cloth she'd used to polish the oven not thirty minutes ago and worked at blotting out the smudge while her daughter shook her head.

"This is an important night for our group." She'd started volunteering for Project Sanctuary during Dylan's first deployment. She knew the strain that army life put on a marriage firsthand, and she'd figured leading retreats for military families was one small way she could help. Most of the families they served were still intact—soldiers coming back from long deployments, doing their best to integrate back into their families, who had learned to function without them. Planning these retreats at Silverado Lake Ranch each year had been a highlight of her life. Even after losing Dylan.

"No one's gonna care if the soufflé turns out more like fudge," her wise daughter insisted. "Chocolate is chocolate."

Thea had to smile at that. "Well, I'm glad you've listened to something I've taught you." She walked over and ruffled her daughter's gorgeous black hair. She looked so much like her dad. "But still. I want this dessert to come out perfect. You know me."

"Yes. I know you." Her daughter smirked while she sipped her bubbly water. "The hostess with the mostest." She pulled out a stool and sat down. "Do I have to stay for the soirée? I was going to meet Dallas and Casey at the park."

Don't frown. Whatever you do, don't frown. Dallas and Casey were most certainly not her favorite thirteen-year-old boys, but she couldn't let Olivia know that, or all her daughter would want to do was hang out with them. As a social worker, she'd witnessed all too often how kids felt the need to rebel when their parents overreacted, but reining in her emotions was still a challenge when it came to her own kids. "I need you to stay, sweet pea." Not only because Dallas and Casey were obnoxious and disrespectful toward most adults, but also because... "We're going to be spending ten days with these families, and it would be good for you to meet them." Though the adults had gathered twice a month for the last three months, none of their kids had met yet.

"I don't see why we're still doing this stupid retreat when Dad is dead." Lately, her daughter had seemed to latch onto blunt statements. Thea wasn't sure if she wanted attention or if she really felt so matter-of-fact about Dylan's death.

"I still volunteer with the organization." She managed to say the words without a tremble in her voice. "And this is important to me." Every year, she led a new group of families on the retreat, and she'd stayed in touch with each one. If she could help these families, maybe they wouldn't walk down the road she and Dylan had been walking right before his death.

Guilt lodged itself painfully in her throat, bringing on the ache of regret. If she'd known he was going to die, maybe she would've tried harder to save their marriage. Maybe she would've found a solution. Instead, the last conversation she'd had with her husband before his ultimate sacrifice had been about divorce. No one knew that, though. No one could ever know that. Not her children, not her friends. She and Dylan had managed to hide their problems from everyone for years.

"What's that smell?" Ryan, her ten-year-old son, came bounding into the kitchen.

"The soufflé!" Thea lurched to the oven and threw open the door, holding her breath. The fluffy confection had risen from the dish like a chocolate miracle. She slipped on her oven mitts and carefully pulled the dish out of the oven. "It's so pretty."

"Crisis averted," her daughter muttered.

"What is it?" Ryan came over to inspect the dessert, wrinkling his nose.

"A soufflé." Thea set the dish on a hot pad on the counter. Dust on a little powdered sugar, and it would look exactly like the one on Pinterest.

"It smells soooo good." Her son leaned in closer, and she resisted the urge to back him up. She was really working on toning down her perfectionistic tendencies in front of her children. "We'll all get to taste it soon." She glanced at the clock. The rest of the families would arrive in ten minutes.

"I can't wait to go to Colorado again." Her son climbed up onto the stool next to his sister.

"I can't either." She loved her job as a social worker for the school district, but the last semester, her caseload had nearly doubled. She needed some time off, and there was no place here in Texas quite like Silverado Lake Ranch. Her friend Jane's father had built the place on the shores of a glacier-fed lake decades ago, and it was the perfect place to escape. Thea snuck a glance at her daughter, who was busy tapping away on the screen of her phone. Now more than ever, she needed to reconnect with her kids. Olivia was getting older—and lately she'd felt more distant. And Ryan... well, he was too much like Thea. Her son always put on a smile, a good front, but she often saw glimpses of sadness and grief in him.

You'd think her career would've made her the perfect person to talk him through those feelings, but Ryan never mentioned his father. And if she did, he often changed the subject.

That didn't mean he didn't miss Dylan, though. Just the other day, she'd found him in his room looking through the picture album she'd made for him and Liv after the funeral. Tears were still stuck in his eyelashes, but when she'd asked if he wanted to talk, he'd insisted he was fine. Ryan was a brave boy, but she didn't want him to grow up denying his pain and always pretending to be okay.

The doorbell rang. Ten minutes early. That had to be the Hershbergers. Though Calvin had recently retired from active duty, he still ran a tight ship. "Olivia, will you please answer the door?" Thea started to fuss with the plates and napkins she'd set out, always and forever organizing.

"I will!" Before his sister could drag herself off the stool, Ryan was already racing out of the kitchen.

Thea walked over to Olivia and tilted the iPhone away from her face. "Phone down or it's mine. You know the rules when we have company."

"It's not my company," Olivia grumbled, but she slipped the phone into her pocket, obviously unwilling to risk Thea's threat.

Oh, how she longed for the days when her daughter had smiled more, bringing light into every room she entered. These days Liv entered the room more like a thunderstorm—rumbling off annoyed sighs. According to the friends who'd walked this road with teenagers before her, it was normal. But still, she missed her baby girl.

"Thea." Kelly Hershberger glided into the kitchen and hurried to give her a hug. As always, the woman wore a wide, friendly smile. She was one of those people who always seemed comfortable in their own skin. Today, her curly auburn hair was pulled up into a messy ponytail and she wore jeans and a simple T-shirt, yet she still somehow looked elegant. "Thanks for inviting us over. Your home is beautiful." She glanced around, her gaze pausing on the soufflé. "And look at that dessert! It's incredible!"

Before Thea could deflect the compliment with a humble shrug, Calvin and their two children sauntered in.

"We're so glad you could come. Aren't we, Liv?" Thea sent Olivia a pointed look to remind her she had no problem holding that phone of hers hostage in her pocket if she needed to. She'd raised the girl to be polite, no matter what.

"So glad," her daughter echoed, rising off the stool with a dazzling smile. "I'm Olivia." She shook Kelly's hand first, and then Calvin's. "It's *so* nice to meet you."

"Nice to meet you too." The man looked impressed, and Thea had to admit, even with the teenage angst, Liv still had her charm.

"This is Preston." Cal nudged his fourteen-year-old son toward Olivia. Kelly had mentioned how shy Preston was.

He happened to be pretty cute, too, Thea noted, watching Liv's eyes light with interest. "Hi, Preston. You can call me Liv." A subtle shyness softened her daughter's grin.

Sure, now she was excited. Thea should've mentioned Preston long before. Though if she had, she would've spent the last hour listening to her daughter complain about how she didn't have anything to wear...

"Look!" Ryan bounded into the kitchen, carrying his fishing pole. "I'm bringing this to Colorado." He showed it to the Hershbergers' other son, Timothy, who was only a couple of years younger than him.

"Wow." The eight-year-old's eyes lit up. "Do ya think we'll actually catch fish in Colorado?"

"I did last year," her son proudly informed the room. "A rainbow trout right out of the lake. It was this big!" He held his hands a good twenty inches apart, making Thea laugh.

"Roughly that big," she told Kelly.

"I can tell a pretty good fish story myself." Calvin chuckled. "That's the most important part of being a fisherman."

"Mom, can I show them how good I cast in the backyard?" Ryan was already halfway to the backdoor.

"Sure, that's a great idea." She glanced at Olivia. "I have some drinks set up outside. Why don't you and Preston head out too? I'll just put the finishing touches on the dessert and be right behind you."

"Okay." Her daughter had gone into full flirt mode, tossing her hair over her shoulder as she turned.

Everyone paraded through the back door, except for Kelly. Over the last several months she and Kelly had become close friends—meeting for coffee and walks when Thea wasn't at work or running the kids around. "Thanks again for inviting us over. And for leading this trip. It means a lot."

"Of course." Thea walked to the pantry and pulled out a bag of powdered sugar. "We're looking forward to getting away." If she was being honest, she would say they desperately needed this trip. All of them. But admitting that would mean admitting she didn't exactly have things together right now. Not as a mom, definitely not as a woman.

Outside of work and her two children, she had no life. She rarely met up with friends for a fun night out. And dating? Well, she couldn't even think about that. Last week, a colleague had asked if he could take her out to dinner sometime, and the invitation had made her so nauseous she'd had to escape to the restroom so she could splash some water on her face. She couldn't date. Guilt left no room in her heart for anyone else.

Thea quickly poured some powdered sugar into a sifter before her friend could see any evidence of the doubt in her eyes.

"You amaze me." Kelly leaned against the counter next to her. "I mean, you've got a great job, you keep this house immaculate, you always look so beautiful, and you still manage to volunteer leading these trips every year. Even after all you've been through." The woman let out a humorless laugh, shaking her head. "I can hardly manage to get the kids to school on time most days. I thought things would be easier with Cal home, but—"

She stopped abruptly, her eyes wide with obvious regret. "I'm so sorry. I didn't mean…I know you'd give anything to have Dylan home…"

"It's okay." Thea had gotten used to the military families she worked with walking on eggshells around her. "I understand. Every time they come home, the dynamic changes." She knew that better than she could say. When her husband had been away serving overseas, she'd have these idyllic fantasies about what things would be like when Dylan came home from a deployment. She'd picture family time and him playing with the kids in the yard and kissing her before they fell asleep in each other's arms every night.

But then when he actually got home, reality would set in. She and Dylan never seemed to know how to act together. She wanted to spend time with him. He always wanted to go out with the guys. When he was home, he would snip at them for the smallest things. Instead of playing with the kids in the yard, he would obsess over the grass, over the house. That's why everything around here was so perfect. Because it seemed to be all Dylan had cared about. Her training had told her his withdrawal from the family was more than irritation. He'd seen a lot of combat, and it had to affect him. More than once, she'd brought up the idea of counseling or getting some help to process everything he'd experienced, but he always refused and told her she didn't know what she was talking about.

When discussing his behavior hadn't worked, she'd tried to give him space, but the weeks would turn into months, and he only ever seemed to get more miserable instead of less. It had gotten to the point where she couldn't wait for his next deployment.

Guilt tightened her chest once again. She shouldn't even be thinking those things with Dylan dead, let alone saying them out loud to someone else.

"I know you understand." Kelly pulled out a stool and sat across from where Thea carefully dusted the powdered sugar over the soufflé. "How did you do it?" she asked. "How did you and Dylan manage to have such an incredible marriage with all the separation?"

The question rocked her at the very center of her being. People had seen her and Dylan's marriage the way she'd wanted them to see it—the way *she'd* wanted to see it. *We didn't have a marriage. We were on the verge of a divorce.* She couldn't bring herself to say the words. Thea turned to take the sifter to the sink and to escape Kelly's gaze. "All any of us can do is our best," she murmured. Had she done her best?

That was the question that would always haunt her.

Chapter Three

Thank. God. For. The. Mountains. Thea gazed steadily out the front windshield of her Volvo SUV, wondering what on earth had possessed her to think a road trip was a good idea.

"You got to pick the music for like an hour now," Ryan whined at Olivia from the backseat. "It's my turn! I want to play some songs!"

"I'm older." Liv gave her little brother a smug smile over her shoulder. "That means I have more privileges than you."

"You're both about to lose all kinds of privileges," Thea muttered in a tone meant to encourage a little self-reflection. Once again, her optimism had gotten the best of her. When they'd set out on the highway thirteen hours ago, she'd envisioned them playing games and singing while they took in the scenery through New Mexico and Colorado. Instead, her two angelic children had argued about everything—from where to stop and eat to how cold or how hot the car should be. When they weren't arguing, their eyes were glued to tech screens—Thea to her phone and Ryan to his iPad. So much for quality time. Next time, they were definitely flying.

"We're almost there," Thea said before Ryan or Liv could ask. After all, it had been a good eight minutes since someone had voiced that question. "The ranch is just in front of those peaks."

They couldn't see it yet, but Silverado Lake was nestled into a lush valley at the base of the mountains. She inhaled deeply, remembering the beautiful blue water that gently lapped at the shoreline, the evergreens and pines and aspens reflected on the glassy surface. "I can't wait to see Jane."

Though they'd been coming to the ranch since the year before Dylan had passed away, it had been years since she'd been able to spend any time with her college roommate. Mara, Jane's mother, had always been the one to welcome groups from Project Sanctuary, but now that Jane had taken over the ranch, she would get to spend ten whole days with her friend.

"Is she the one who got married?" Ryan asked, straining against his seat belt to lean between the seats.

"Yes, last October." It had been a beautiful ceremony, but also a quick weekend trip Thea had made by herself. Since the kids couldn't miss school, her parents had come to stay. "I can't wait for you two to meet her." Thea had roomed with Jane for only one semester before she'd gotten pregnant and had to drop out of school, but they'd hit it off right away and had managed to stay in close touch. Despite the fact that Thea was a few years older when she finally went off to college, she and Jane had bonded over the struggle to navigate a whole new world. They'd taken different paths, that was for sure. Thea had fallen into the party lifestyle, while Jane preferred to spend most of her time studying, but they'd spent every Sunday night together, eating pizza and watching rom-coms. Those were some of her best memories from her short college stint.

"Well, I can't wait to get out of this car." Liv added a hearty huff to the end of her sentence.

"You're in luck, my dear." Excitement rose through Thea. "Our turn is right up there."

Just ahead, a large banner stretched over the highway: SILVERADO LAKE WELCOMES YOU TO GOLD RUSH DAYS.

"Gold?" Her son leaned between the seats again. "Do we get to find gold while we're here?"

"No, dum-dum." Olivia rolled her eyes. "That's just the name of the festival or whatever."

"Exactly." Thea turned off the highway and slowed the car as they approached Main Street. "It wasn't a dumb question, either," she said with a stern look at her daughter. "This week, the town is celebrating their mining history with fun activities like a parade and a carnival. There might even be some gold panning too. That's why Jane and I thought this would be a good time for the trip." Every year, coordinating the trip dates for different families proved to be a challenge, but this year everyone's schedule had happened to line up with visiting the ranch during a good old small-town festival.

"I like parades." Ryan settled back into his seat. "Do you think they throw out candy?"

"I'll bet they do." Thea navigated the streets from memory. Not much ever seemed to change in Silverado Lake. There was the castle-like library—the fanciest attraction in town. The rest of the square brick buildings lined up in rows exactly like they had been back in the Old West. Thea slowed the car as they passed an antique shop, a local artisan gallery, and a bar that looked like an old saloon, complete with wooden swinging doors.

The only difference in the town now was the decorations. There seemed to be flowerpots everywhere—along with banners and gold and silver balloons tied to every lamppost.

At the end of the block, she took a right. A colony of white tents had been set up in the town's main park, which was adjacent to the local high school.

"This is going to be amazing!" Ryan had pressed his face against his window, gawking at the carnival that had been set up on the football field. "Look! A Ferris wheel! And bumper cars! And a Tilt-A-Whirl!"

Thea found his enthusiasm contagious. "Jane and I set aside a whole afternoon in the schedule to have fun at the carnival." She glanced at her daughter, who still bore the marks of a scowl. "I'm sure Preston will be going."

That perked Liv up. "He's nice."

"And he seems like a good kid too," Thea added. The entire evening he'd been at their house, Preston had been nothing but respectful and polite. Which was more than she could say for some of her daughter's other friends.

They rolled closer to the outskirts of town, where the houses grew sparse and the lot sizes grew larger. Thea had always seen Silverado Lake as a haven. She'd often dreamed of living in a place like this, but growing up near Dallas and then living near Fort Bliss, that had never been an option. Even now...she could never take the kids away from the house they'd shared with their father. She did everything she could to keep his memory alive for them.

She flicked off the air conditioner and buzzed down their windows instead. "Smell that clean mountain air." The breeze had a fresh piney scent.

"There's the ranch! There it is! I see it!" Ryan hung his head out the window as Thea turned onto the winding driveway. It looked like they'd gotten a new fancy gate. She carefully navigated the dirt road—which looked and felt more like a washboard with all the bumps—and passed beneath a new stone-and-wood welcome sign. "Wow, the place looks great."

The main lodge had always been quite a sight—a large log-and-rock structure sitting atop a small hill—but the rest of the cabins dotted around the lake had been showing their age last year when Thea came for the wedding. That was before. It seemed Jane and her husband, Toby, had made a few upgrades.

"I can smell the fish in that lake," Ryan declared, releasing himself from his seat belt and the car the second Thea parked.

"You can't smell fish," his sister insisted.

Thea got out of the car, too, inhaling deeply. "Oh, I can. Smells to me like that lake is full of big huge rainbow trout."

Her son's grin revealed his I'm-too-cute-for-my-own-good dimples. "And I'm gonna catch 'em all."

"Hold your horses there, tiger." Thea waved for Liv to get out of the car. "We need to find Jane so we know where we should unload our stuff." *And* so she could give her friend a big hug while she checked out the baby bump. "Come on." She led the way to the main lodge's entrance, feeling an extra bounce in her step. This might be her favorite building on the whole property. In addition to housing the office and a few guest rooms upstairs, the lodge had a jaw-dropping great room, complete with a floor-to-ceiling rock fireplace and a wall of windows that looked out onto the lake. The families they brought every year had spent a lot of time within these walls—sharing meals and playing games. Thea climbed the few steps up to the porch, a sense of home enveloping her.

The large wooden door creaked when she pushed it open. "Hello?" she called. "Jane? We're here." Originally, they'd planned to break up the drive into two days and arrive tomorrow morning, but Jane had told her they were welcome to come as soon as they could, and they'd made good time getting the heck out of Texas. Thea hadn't wanted to be stuck in the car for another day, so they'd pressed on. She figured that would be the perfect opportunity to catch up with her friend.

"Doesn't seem like anyone's here." Ryan pushed past her and walked fully into the entryway. Thea followed, with Liv tagging behind. Though the place had been updated with what looked to be new slate tiles and dark crown molding, it still had that wonderful woodsy scent. Beyond the foyer, they wandered into the great room, and Thea could almost hear the laughter they'd shared here.

"Heeelllloooo!" Ryan's shout echoed.

"Maybe she's outside," Liv suggested, moving closer to the window. "Oh, wow." She stopped.

Thea moved around the fireplace so she could see what her daughter was gaping at. Shirtless men and suntanned, bikini-clad women were playing a rowdy game of volleyball along the lakeside.

"I thought we got this whole place to ourselves." Ryan seemed put out that a crowd had dared to gather at his lake.

"We were supposed to." Thea scanned the group for any sign of Jane. "Maybe there's another event here tonight. We *are* a little early," she reminded her son. "Let's go out and ask if they've seen Jane."

"That's a great idea." Her daughter took the lead, obviously eager to ogle the muscular men who were currently putting more than their volleyball skills on display.

Thea followed behind, trying to straighten her rumpled Bermuda shorts and the wrinkled short-sleeved button-up that had seemed like a good idea at four o'clock this morning. The closer they got to the shore, the slower she moved. She hadn't worn a bikini since long before she'd given birth.

The group didn't even seem to notice her and the children. Most of them had a can of beer in one hand while they managed to smack the ball with the other. Play continued on while the three of them watched. Liv's jaw was hinged open, but Ryan shook his head and stubbed the toe of his shoe into the ground like he did every time he got irritated.

Finally, Thea cleared her throat. "Excuse me," she called, feeling about sixty years old compared to these people. "We're looking for Jane. Does she happen to be around?"

One of the men on the side closest to where they stood caught the ball, halting the game.

"We were supposed to get here tomorrow," Thea went on when no one said anything. "I texted her we were going to be early, but I haven't heard back..."

"You must be Thea." The man who held the ball—who she now recognized as Wes Harding—started toward her. She should've known. Of course Wes was having a party. Last fall, when Thea had come for Jane's wedding, Wes had been front and center at the reception, dancing and making toasts and charming unsuspecting women. But Thea knew to avoid him, thanks to the stories Jane had told her about Wild Wes and her remembrance of the time Thea had met him when she'd visited the ranch during college.

Oh, she knew about Wes all right. If it hadn't been for the backward ball cap and the dark aviator shades he wore now, Thea would've pegged him right away.

"Yes. I'm Thea." Her face heated. He clearly didn't remember her the way she remembered him.

Jane's brother tossed the volleyball to another man on his

way off the court, and the game resumed. "I'm Wes. Jane's older brother."

"I remember." She could feel those gorgeous women staring at her. "We've met." Had he really forgotten?

"Have we?" He flicked off his shades and seemed to give her a good once-over.

Yep, his eyes were still as blue as that glacier water. "I was at Jane and Toby's wedding." No surprise he didn't remember seeing her there. He'd been much too busy. "And I came home with Jane our first semester of school." Though it was tempting to refresh his memory, she stopped there. Her children didn't need to hear how Thea had been in awe when she'd first met Wes on that dock right over there. Her facial expression had probably looked a lot like Liv's did now. Ironic, the man had been shirtless back then too. And she'd been young and stupid.

Wes had flirted with her—telling her how shocked he was that his sister had such a hot friend, and then he'd invited her to go to a party with him later that night. She believed his exact words were *Want to be my date?* She'd spent two hours getting ready— changing her outfit about twenty times, asking Jane to help her with her hair and makeup, all the while ignoring her friend's warning about how unreliable her brother was.

At seven o'clock, she'd walked to the lake to meet him like they'd planned—her stomach a knot of nerves and anticipation—except Wes wasn't there. He'd already left for the party. Without her.

"You came home with Jane back in college?" The prompt didn't seem to spark his memory. "Huh."

"You have really big muscles." Leave it to Ryan to state the obvious. Thea, on the other hand, had been purposely not noticing how well defined his pectorals and biceps and abs and whatever else was rippling right in front of her face were.

Wes grinned at her son. "You've got some big guns yourself there, Sport."

"Really?" Ryan held up his arm and flexed his bicep. "Well, I *do* play baseball."

"I can tell," the man said as though impressed.

"I'm Ryan." *Uh-oh.* Thea had seen that smile on her son's face before. He'd just made a new best friend.

"And I'm Olivia." Her daughter nearly bumped her brother out of her way to introduce herself to shirtless Wes.

"Nice to meet you both." All he had to do was smile and her children gazed up at him as though completely captivated. Well, she wouldn't be so easily charmed. She was all too familiar with Wes's notorious reputation for being a ladies' man. And at the moment she had other things on her mind.

"So anyway…" Thea slung one arm around Ryan and the other around Liv. "Where's Jane?"

"Oh." Wes's forehead furrowed. He led them away from the party and up to the massive deck that ran the full length of the lodge. "She didn't call you? There's been a slight change of plans."

Thea stopped abruptly. "A change?" That wasn't what she wanted to hear less than twenty-four hours before the rest of the group showed up. She didn't do change well on a normal day, let alone when she had been planning something for the better part of a year.

Wes faced her, no longer smiling. "Jane went into preterm labor two days ago."

"Oh no." Dread pinched her heart. "Is she okay? What about the baby?" Only last week, they'd talked about the fact that Jane had over two months left before the baby came.

"So far so good." His eyes wouldn't meet hers. He looked… genuinely worried. "They were able to stop the contractions for the time being, but she's on bed rest in a hospital in Denver. They're hoping to hold off labor for at least a few more weeks."

"That's awful." Thea sank to a nearby bench. In a show of solidarity, Ry sat next to her and put his hand on her shoulder.

"Sorry about your friend, Mama," he murmured.

"Thanks, bud." She patted his hand and focused on Wes again. "I'll call her and check in." She couldn't imagine having to worry about the health and well-being of your unborn baby when you should be getting the nursery ready and having showers and shopping for all those adorable baby clothes...

"I know she'd love to hear from you." Wes sat on the bench across from them. "Since she can't be here, she asked me to step in as your group's host."

"You?" She hadn't meant to laugh, but seriously? Wild Wes was going to be their host? She steered her gaze back to the spectacle on the beach. He obviously knew their group was coming, and, instead of preparing, he was playing volleyball with a bunch of friends. Of course, Jane likely had no one else to put in charge in her absence. From the sound of things, their mother, Mara, was off traveling the world, and Jane had mentioned she and Toby had been handling the events at the ranch.

"Don't worry about a thing." Wes stood and put his hands on his chiseled hips, looking a lot like the daredevil god he was rumored to be and nothing like a responsible administrator. "I think I'm up to speed. Once you're settled, we can go over the schedule. I've made a few changes."

"I'm sorry? Changes?" Thea stood too. She and Jane had labored over that schedule—trying to come up with exciting activities for the kids, ways to encourage quality family time—

"I tweaked a few things." Wes winked at Ryan. "Added in more action. More time for fishing."

"Yes!" Ryan high-fived the man.

"Anyway, you all are staying in the Blue Spruce cabin." He gestured to the same cabin Thea and the kids had stayed in each year. It sat closest to the lodge and yet also right on the water's edge. "I can help you with your—"

"That won't be necessary." She gathered Ryan under her arm and started toward the parking lot, waving for Liv to follow. "I know the cabin. We'll manage just fine." She wouldn't want to interrupt his little beach party and trouble him.

"You sure?" he called as they walked away.

"I'm sure!" She waved. "I'll catch up with you later. After your party." Though she doubted she'd be up as late as his friends.

Thea hurried the children up the sidewalk that led to the parking lot.

"That's Jane's brother?" Liv trotted in front of her, stealing another look at the man over Thea's shoulder. "You didn't mention he's a total hottie."

"I hadn't noticed." Thea refused to look behind her. "Besides, he's too old for you."

Her daughter snickered. "Yeah, well, he's not too old for you."

Thea ignored the comment. Lately, Liv had taken to making jokes about her dating—mostly to be sassy—but she never indulged her daughter's comments. "I have all I need right here." She smiled at Ryan and Liv. Part of keeping Dylan's memory alive for them meant not introducing any complications into their lives. Or hers, for that matter. "Come on. We need to get our stuff." Thea stalked ahead of her children before she gave in to the temptation to steal one more glance at Wes over her shoulder. Yes, the man might be a "total hottie," but she and Wes Harding had absolutely nothing in common.

This was going to be a long ten days.

Chapter Four

Time to look official.

Wes threaded his best belt through the loops on his jeans and clasped the engraved silver buckle one of the riders had given him last summer. On his way out of his cabin, he shoved on his boots and grabbed his lucky black cowboy hat. God knew he'd need it today. When he'd taken on this assignment, he'd assumed it would be no big deal, but he'd gotten approximately ten texts from Toby in the last twenty-four hours about schedules and food allergies and individual preferences regarding activities and accommodations for each family. It was as if Jane didn't trust—

His phone buzzed from his back pocket. He paused outside the cabin and brought the phone to his ear. "Hey, sis." He didn't even have to look at the screen.

"Wes? Oh good. I didn't know if you'd be up yet." She hardly inhaled a breath before continuing. "Did you get Toby's texts? They've hardly let me be on my phone at all. The nurses are always checking me and poking me and bringing me food to eat. I haven't even had two minutes to get anything done."

"You're supposed to be resting," he reminded her. Maybe they should take her phone away altogether...

"I can't get any rest with them bugging me all the time," his sister muttered. "Anyway, what's going on there? Is Thea in town? I haven't even been able to check in with her."

"She's here." He shaded his eyes from the early morning sun and gazed at the Blue Spruce cabin. "Got here last night."

"And you helped her settle in?" Jane's voice had sure started to resemble their mother's since she'd taken over the ranch.

"She got settled." Thea hadn't wanted his help, that was for sure. The woman didn't seem to have any more confidence in him than his sister did, judging from her reaction when she'd found out he was in charge.

The party on the beach probably hadn't helped, but how was he supposed to know she would arrive early? All he'd been doing was worrying about the baby and his little sister, and so when some of his old high school friends had called to ask if they could swing by, an impromptu get-together had been the perfect distraction. He shouldn't mention all that to Jane, though. "What's the doc saying?"

His sister sighed. "That I'm going to be in here for the long haul. So far, they've been able to stop the labor. My only job now is to lie around and get as fat as I can in case she's born early."

"That's good news." The lingering tightness in his chest released. At least he didn't have to worry about her in the hospital. She would be in good hands there. "Do everything they say. And don't worry about what's happening here." Stress wouldn't be good for the baby.

"I just hate that I can't be there." Muffled voices murmured in the background. It sounded like maybe the nurse brigade was back in her room. "I can call August and ask him to come home to help you..."

"You don't have to do that." Of course she'd bring up calling August. Back when they were kids, his brother had been everything Wes wasn't—organized, well behaved, trustworthy. Somehow the differences between him and his brother had only made them closer back then. But when their father died... well, everything changed between him and his brother.

August had never said he blamed him, but Wes could take a hint. The whole family probably blamed him for their father's kayaking accident. Wes should've been with him that morning but hadn't shown up.

After that, his brother used to get in his face about the partying, the drinking. Pretty much everything. Like he'd taken over the dad role or something. But Wes hadn't needed a father replacement back then, and he didn't need one now. In the past, he hadn't been the most upstanding, responsible citizen. He'd made his fair share of stupid mistakes. But he'd been atoning for them ever since— working hard, clawing his way to the top. Only problem was, the top seemed to be getting further away instead of closer. He didn't feel any different now than he had when he was a junior out on the circuit. Wes switched the phone to his other ear. "I'm here for you guys. I promise I won't let you down."

The hum of voices grew louder.

"Thanks, Wes." He could hear a smile in her voice. "Be good to Thea. I'm not sure she likes you much after you ditched her to go to that party years ago."

Well, shit. "That was her?" Of course it was her. It all came back to him now. Perfect. One more person he had to prove himself to...

"I gotta go," his sister said. "Time for another shot."

"Okay." He wished he could take this all away from her. "Let them take care of you. And don't worry about a thing," he told her again. Maybe one of these times it would stick. "I have this under control."

They hung up, and Wes hiked the rest of the way to the lodge to get a read on what he needed to do first.

Time to get this retreat under control.

The second he stepped inside the commercial kitchen, the salty, greasy scent of bacon made his stomach groan.

"Don't you get any ideas about eating all this food." Louise came out from the pantry carrying an unopened container of maple syrup. "I made breakfast for that sweet Thea and her kids. I happened to notice their car was here." The look she gave him made it clear he should've let her know they'd arrived, but Louise couldn't stay irritated with him for long. She'd never been able to. Back when he was younger, he might've even said he was Louise's favorite Harding child. Their father had hired the woman to manage the kitchen and housekeeping right after they'd opened for business, and she'd been a fixture ever since. Louise hadn't changed all that much in those years, either. Other than a little more gray in her blondish-brown hair, she still had the same laughing brown eyes, no matter how stern her glare.

"Don't worry, I'm not going to eat all the food." Wes eyed the eggs, bacon, and waffles piled up on platters. He grinned at her. "Even though I sure do miss your breakfasts, Louise. When I'm out on the circuit, your cooking is what I crave the most."

The compliment had the intended effect.

Louise smiled back. "Well, maybe you can have a bit of the eggs and bacon." She rushed to a cupboard and pulled out a stack of plates.

"I would love to. But I'll wait until the rest of the gang is here." He moved to the silverware drawer and started pulling out the knives and forks. "I really came by to touch base with you about meals for the retreat."

Louise laughed. "Don't you worry about meals. I'm more than prepared." She pulled a pitcher of fresh-squeezed orange juice out of the industrial-sized refrigerator. "Seems to me you've got plenty on your plate, being the head honcho and all. Let me handle the food."

"It's fine." All he had to do was play the charming host. How hard could that be? "Things are totally under control."

The woman simply pursed her lips as though holding back another laugh. "Speaking of being the head honcho, do you want to text Thea and let her know breakfast is ready?"

"Well…" He didn't have her phone number. It was on a list somewhere. Maybe in the office? Or back in his cabin? "It's nice out. I think I'll walk over to the Blue Spruce to let them know."

"Mmm-hmm." Louise raised her eyebrows but said nothing more as he walked out the door.

Wes made his way across the deck, drafting a mental to-do list. First item, add Thea's phone number to his contacts so they could stay in touch during her stay. He hurried down the steps to the path by the lake before stopping dead in his boots. What the hell was the canoe doing all the way out there?

The boat bobbed in the middle of the lake, but from where he stood, he couldn't see anyone in it.

Great. One of his friends must've left it in the water last night, only adding to his to-do list for this morning. Jane had made it abundantly clear she wanted all of the canoes and kayaks available for the guests to use at all times.

Wes kept his eyes on the canoe, jogging down to the beach. Hold on. There was someone in it. Someone small. That kid...Thea's son. It had to be. He kept his gaze centered on the middle of the lake, watching while Ryan stood up, the boat wobbling beneath him.

No, no, no. "Don't stand up!" The wind seemed to steal Wes's shout.

The kid wasn't even wearing a life jacket. He hauled ass to a kayak he'd pulled up onto the beach yesterday and kicked off his boots. After yanking off his socks and tossing his phone and hat aside, he splashed into the water and jumped into the boat.

"Sit down!" He was still too far away for Ryan to hear him. Keeping his eyes trained on the canoe, he paddled across the lake's glassy surface, but he'd only made it halfway there when Ryan tried to cast a fishing pole and lost his balance.

"Ryan!" Wes yelled his name just as the kid fell overboard.

Wes didn't have time to think. Blind instinct took over, driven by a familiar surge of adrenaline. He ditched the kayak paddle, dove into the freezing water, and swam to where the boy was flailing and splashing.

"All right, you're fine. I've got you." He pulled the boy into his arms, warmed by a sudden onslaught of pure relief. "Relax, Sport. I'll get you back into the boat."

"O-o-okay," the boy sputtered, seeming to settle.

Securing him under one arm, Wes swam back to the canoe and helped the boy climb inside. "You okay?"

Ryan nodded slowly, his eyes wide and his teeth chattering. "I can swim, you know."

Even with the lower half of his body still immersed in the mind-numbingly-cold water, Wes had to chuckle at the stubborn lift to the kid's chin. "I'm sure you can, but swimming in glacier water is a little different. Isn't it?" The shock of falling in was enough to subdue even the strongest swimmer. Wes knew from personal experience. His dad had pulled him out of the frigid water a time or two.

"Thanks for helping me." Ryan stared at the floor of the boat.

"No problem." Wes kept his tone light. He didn't want the boy to be scared of him. Ryan was all right. That's the only thing that mattered in this moment. "I'm going to swim back to get the kayak and then I'll tow you into shore."

There was that remorseful nod again.

Wes gave the boy's shoulder a pat before swimming away. He returned on the kayak and hooked up the canoe's bowline to his boat. "All set, Sport?" he asked, peering at the boy over his shoulder.

"Why do you call me Sport?" At least Ryan had stopped looking down.

The question stumped him for a few seconds. The name had simply come out of his mouth when he'd met the kid. "I guess...because that's what my dad called me." His dad had called him that many times when they were sitting right there in that canoe. The memory sliced through him with razor-sharp clarity, bringing on that familiar ache.

"My dad called me Ryan," the boy said, breaking Wes out of the past. "Sometimes he called me Ry, but not very often."

"Oh." Wes rested the paddle across his wet jeans, letting the kayak gently tap the canoe. "Well...I don't have to call you Sport if you don't—"

"I like Sport." A sudden grin brightened the boy's eyes. "I've always wanted a nickname. My mom calls me Ry-ry." He made a grossed-out face. "That's such a baby name."

Wes laughed. "Well, sometimes my mom still calls me Wessy, so I feel your pain."

Ryan seemed to think that was hilarious. "Wessy?"

"Yeah." He decided not to disclose that his mother had actually sometimes called him Messy Wessy when he was little. Even back then he'd had an affinity for getting dirty.

"My mom said I should call you Mr. Harding," Ryan informed him. "That's what she calls you."

Was Thea serious? He didn't think anyone had ever called him Mr. Harding. "You can call me Wes. And so can your mom." He pointed at the kid with a serious expression. "Not Wessy. *Wes.*"

"Got it." Ryan gave him a solemn nod. "And you can call me Sport. It makes me sound tougher."

"I knew you were tough the second I met you," Wes told him. A kid would have to be tough to lose his father so young and still have that grin. "So, what're you doing out here all by yourself anyway?"

The boy lifted one shoulder in a guilty shrug. He wore an unsure expression to match. "My mom wasn't awake yet. She's been super tired and busy lately. But you know what they say—'The early worm gets the fish.'"

Man, this kid was too cute for his own good. "Right." Wes glanced across the surface of the lake. He couldn't deny this was the best time to fish—early morning when the air was cool and the flies were landing. Only problem was, Thea didn't seem like the type of parent who would be okay with her kid fishing in the middle of the lake by himself. Wes didn't know her, but he could tell that much.

"I felt a bite right before I fell in," Ryan said hopefully. "I think if I stay out here awhile, I'll probably catch a humongous fish."

Aw, hell. How did anyone ever tell this kid no? Louise's amusement with his taking over responsibilities still bugged him, though.

He was the head honcho here, and he had to act like it. "I'll bet you could catch a humongous fish," he agreed, not wanting to stomp out the hope in this kid's expression. "But we're both soaking wet. And I was coming to find you and your mom because breakfast is ready." He gave off a low whistle. "Trust me. You don't want to miss Louise's breakfast. I think I saw some chocolate chips in the waffles."

Now the boy looked truly torn. He bounced his gaze from Wes to his fishing pole to the lake.

"How about if I promise to take you to the best, supersecret fishing spot I've ever been another day?" He hadn't been up to the waterfall in years. Some of the best fishing he'd ever done with his dad had been at that spot.

"Really?" The boy had frozen. "You would show me your supersecret fishing hole?"

"You bet." Wes picked up the paddle again. "It's right here at the ranch. Not too far of a hike. We probably can't go today since everyone else will be here soon. But I promise I will find a day to take you." And catching a fish up there was pretty much a guarantee since no one else knew about that spot.

"Okay! Yes! I can't wait to see it!" Ryan sprang up and down, nearly capsizing the canoe.

"Whoa." Wes steadied the boat. "We'll make it happen. I promise. But right now, I'm going to tow you back to shore so we can go find your mom and sis and you can get changed. How does that sound?"

"Good." The boy sat back down on the small bench in the center of the canoe, eyes wide with relief. "My arms are killing me after all that paddling."

"It's tough work." Wes started them off. With the weight of the canoe dragging behind him, he didn't move nearly as fast.

"You're really good at that," Ryan observed from behind him. "Where'd you learn to paddle?"

"My dad taught me." More memories came flooding back. Usually he was able to block them or change the subject or distract himself with something else, but that was harder to do on the lake. They'd gone on many kayaking trips together. They likely still would be if Wes had shown up for his dad on the day he died...

"Where's your dad now?" Ryan asked.

Now he had nowhere to hide. Wes gritted his teeth. "He passed away."

The boy let out a gasp. "So did my dad. It's really hard."

Wes looked back at him, tempted to explain it was a long time ago, so it wasn't as hard anymore. But that wasn't the truth, and he couldn't lie to a kid. "It sure is." He turned back around and focused on the lake in front of him. They were pretty much crawling toward the shore at a snail's pace.

"My mom says when you love someone, they're never really gone." Something in Ryan's tone sounded almost...skeptical. "Do you think that's true?"

"I know it's true." The pain in his chest was all the evidence he needed. His dad wasn't gone—not from his memory, not from his heart.

The guilt wasn't gone either. As much as he tried to outrun it.

Chapter Five

Thea had forgotten how dry the mountain air could be. Moaning, she flung out her arm and blindly searched for the water bottle she'd put on the nightstand before she went to bed.

Sheesh. Her mouth was like a desert wasteland. Tomorrow she'd have to use the humidifier they provided in every cabin.

Propping herself up, she took a sip of water and let her eyes adjust to the daylight. It was awfully bright for being so early. Squinting, Thea tried to make out the clock.

No. No way. That couldn't be right. She sat up and snatched her phone off the table.

Eight thirty.

Eight thirty?

Eight thirty!

What the actual hell? She threw off the covers and sprang out of bed, trying to find her footing. She hadn't slept past six in a lifetime! How could her internal clock have failed her today of all days? The day she was supposed to welcome the other families to the ranch?

Careening out of her room, Thea checked the open-concept kitchen and living room. Her heart slowed. At least it appeared the kids had slept in too. She crept down the hallway and pushed open the other bedroom door. Liv was buried underneath blankets and pillows on the bottom bunk, but the top bunk was empty.

Great. She shook her daughter awake. "Where's Ryan?"

Liv's eyelids fluttered, but she only groaned and turned over.

"Come on!" Thea nudged her again. "Where's your brother?"

"How am I supposed to know?" Liv pulled the comforter over her head.

"Okay." Thea inhaled a deep calming breath. He had to be here somewhere. Ryan knew better than to leave the house when she wasn't awake, didn't he? Maybe not. She'd never in her life had the luxury of waking up *after* him . . .

Sprinting out into the living room, Thea resorted to calling his name. "Ry-ry! Hey, buddy, where are you?"

The kitchen sat empty, as did the small bathroom at the other end of the hallway. That meant he was outside. With thousands of acres to explore. And the lake. Oh, God. The lake!

Thea bolted out the front door and ran directly into Wes, who had been walking up the porch steps.

It was like ramming straight into a brick wall.

"Whoa." The man teetered backward before reaching for the railing, and she quickly jolted back to the top step. "What's going on?" Wes's T-shirt clung to his torso and his jeans were soaked. Her son stood behind them on the grass, sheepishly digging his toe into the dirt. "Ryan, where were you?" She didn't wait for him to answer before shifting her gaze to Wes.

As the man stared back, a few things occurred to her. First, she was still in her pajamas—tiny shorts and a tight tank top that she would never ever, under any circumstances, allow anyone to see her wearing. Second, she'd neglected to put on a bra before busting down the door to get outside. And third, Wes Harding likely thought she was a lunatic. Or a lazy lunatic, given the fact that she'd obviously only just managed to roll out of bed and discover her son was missing.

Humiliation burned hotter across her skin than any sunburn ever could. "I'm so sorry." She wasn't sure if she was apologizing to Ryan, to Wes, or to herself for the spectacle she'd created. She tried to smooth her wild bedhead waves away from her face. "I must've slept in. I can't believe I...I never sleep past six. *Never.*" She always woke before the kids and got herself ready and made them breakfast...

"Don't worry about it." To his credit, the man didn't gawk at her or back away or even raise his eyebrows. He gave a simple shrug accompanied by a smile. "It seems Ryan here wanted to do some fishing." He glanced over his shoulder at her son with a wink. "Like he said, the early worm gets the fish."

"I didn't want to wake you up," her son added, edging his way up the steps to join them on the porch. "'Cause you looked so happy sleeping, and you don't get to sleep a lot."

"You can always wake me up." Her voice got shaky. "You know that, Ry-ry." She did her best to strike a tone between stern and understanding. "Did you go out on the lake by yourself?" She could already see the answer in his downcast eyes, in his wet clothes. He knew the rules. He wasn't supposed to come within twenty feet of the lake without an adult present. Her stomach lurched. "God, did he fall in?"

"I'm sorry, Mom. I was so excited. I didn't want to wait." Ryan didn't have to try for puppy dog eyes; he simply already had them.

"I happened to be walking by and saw the canoe out," Wes said.

She couldn't quite look the man in the eyes. Oh, what he must think of her right now. As if she'd had any right to judge him last night for having a party. She couldn't even keep track of her children. Her son had almost drowned! Her heart seemed to flood with emotion, buckling her knees, but she had to keep it together. She couldn't fall apart in front of Wes.

"Everything turned out okay," the man said as though trying to comfort her.

"Thank God." Thank God Wes had walked by. She shuddered, the panic and embarrassment fading enough that she could finally feel the cool breeze against her skin. She hugged her son. That was all she wanted to do. Hold him right there forever.

He was okay.

He was okay.

He was okay.

And yet her heart was not.

"I'm real sorry, Mom." The words were muffled under her shoulder.

"I know you're sorry." She pulled away, struggling to keep the tears at bay. "And thank you for owning up to your mistake. But you're still going to have a consequence."

Wes laid his hand on her son's shoulder. "Don't go too hard on him. I'm sure it won't happen again."

Easy for him to say. Thea's cheeks flamed again. Handing down punishments had never been her favorite part of parenting. If she relied solely on her heart to raise her kids, she would've hugged her son and told him not to give it another thought. But over the years she'd taught herself to rely on logic too. This was one of those safety issues that couldn't be ignored. He had to learn a lesson. Not that Wes would understand that. She could've lost him. God, she could've lost him on the bottom of that lake. Fiery tears raged at the backs of her eyes but she blinked them back.

"I know I'll have a consequence." Her son's shoulders slouched pitifully.

"Maybe he could help me clean up the beach later," Wes suggested. "And we can scrub out the canoe."

Ryan's eyes lit up. "That's a great consequence!"

Yes, a great, fun, rewarding consequence. She drilled her gaze into Wes's so she wouldn't roll her eyes. "I was thinking something more along the lines of losing privileges, but we'll talk about it later." She kissed the top of her son's head and gave him a pat. "Now why don't you go inside for a few minutes? See if you can wake up your sister for me."

"All right." Ryan walked away but looked back over his shoulder on his slow journey through the door. "See ya soon, Wessy."

"Not if I see you first, Ry-ry," the man said through a laugh.

Thea could hear Ryan's giggle even after the door closed.

She, however, was not laughing. She was hardly breathing. When it came to her children's well-being, she seemed to feel every emotion about a hundred times more intensely—the panic, the fear, the love. And all she could seem to see right now was a vision of Ryan sinking down into dark water. That was her worst nightmare.

Thea turned away from Wes and steadied a hand on the porch rail, her legs nearly giving way.

"Hey."

She could feel the man's presence close by, but she couldn't see him through the tears. Damn it! She had to stop crying. She had to get it together. She never did this. Especially in front of a virtual stranger.

"Thea…" Strong arms came around her. "He's all right. Everything's all right."

She hadn't realized how soothing Wes's deep voice was. Or maybe this was a tone she hadn't heard from him before. "If you hadn't walked by—" The damn tears wouldn't stop. "He could've—"

"But I did walk by." Wes tightened his hold on her, and instead of fighting the gesture and piecing herself back together, she leaned into the embrace, letting him hold her. Only for a minute. His clothes were still damp, but the closeness of his body against hers brought a warmth she hadn't realized she craved.

God, she couldn't remember the last time she'd been held.

"I can't lose him," she murmured. "Liv and Ryan are my everything."

Wes said nothing. He simply kept his arms around her, letting her cry everything out as though he knew that was exactly what she needed.

Eventually the tears did their cleansing work, purging the emotions enough for her to feel the embarrassment creep back in. Who knew how long she'd been standing there crying all over the man? "I'm sorry." Thea straightened and edged away from him. "I shouldn't have unloaded on you like that." She shouldn't unload on anyone. She was the group leader, for crying out loud. She was supposed to keep everything together.

"It's okay." Wes seemed to study her closer.

She couldn't blame the man. She was losing it. She hardly recognized herself right now. Thea tried to smooth the frizz from her hair, grasping at her last strand of dignity. "Thank you again. I'm really grateful you were there. Ryan usually knows better, but he's so excited to be here."

Wes slipped off his cowboy hat. "Do you really have to punish him?"

Thea crossed her arms—partly to look stronger than she felt and partly to hide the fact that she wasn't wearing a bra. Holy moly, she'd just pressed herself up against the man and she wasn't even wearing a bra! "Would *your* dad have punished *you*?" Right after she said the words, she wanted them back. How could she bring up his dad? Jane had told her all about the kayaking accident...

Wes was quiet for a few seconds.

"I'm sorry." Damn her big mouth. It was the embarrassment of having a complete breakdown in front of a good-looking cowboy in her pajamas. It made her snarky. "I shouldn't have—"

"My dad definitely would've punished me," he interrupted. "And you don't have to keep apologizing for things you have no business being sorry for."

"Excuse me?" The intensity in his eyes pushed her back a step.

"You don't have to be sorry for sleeping in." The man ran a gaze down her pajamas. "You must've needed the rest. That's nothing to feel bad about. You're supposed to be on vacation."

She had needed the rest. Even with the embarrassment of nearly plowing the man over in a panic while wearing skimpy pajamas and then the ensuing panic when she realized what had happened, she couldn't deny she'd felt more rested when she'd woke up that morning than she had in a long time. But she still felt bad about it. Wes obviously wasn't acquainted with the high potency of mom guilt.

"And you don't need to feel bad about bringing up my father either." His crooked smile somehow made him seem more approachable than he had last night, all shirtless and hot. He was still gorgeous, of course, but the smile he wore now seemed more real somehow. "My dad was a master at finding ways to make the punishment fit the crime. I'd forgotten that. Thank you for reminding me."

She really should say no problem and then run back inside to get dressed. But she had to ask. He'd already seen the jammies anyway. "What do you think your father would've chosen for your punishment if you had snuck onto the lake by yourself at ten years old?" Because she was kind of at a loss. She couldn't fault the kid for having a passion to fish. And he never got to fish at home, so she couldn't exactly take away his fishing time during this retreat.

Wes seemed to think, clicking his tongue, gazing out over the lake. "If you want the truth, I think my old man would've climbed into that canoe with me and made me row the whole length of the lake and back all by myself while he kicked up his feet and relaxed to prove how hard it is and that I shouldn't be out there without backup."

Thea laughed. "That's kind of brilliant. I might have to borrow that."

"I'm happy to help." Wes glanced down at her pajamas, but then quickly directed his gaze back to hers. "The more weight in the boat, the harder it will be to row."

This time the heat that flashed across her face didn't have anything to do with embarrassment. Was he checking her out? Did she want him to? Thea cleared her throat. She was clearly still groggy. "Um...okay. And thanks again. I know you said not to apologize, but I am sorry. I usually keep better track of my kids."

"I'm the one who should apologize to you." His smile disappeared. "When you arrived yesterday, I should've kicked my friends out so we could've gone over the details for the retreat. This should be like a vacation for you. I'm sorry I didn't make myself available."

Thea was too stunned to speak.

"But Louise has breakfast ready for us," Wes went on. "So maybe we can talk through the details over waffles?"

"Sure. I need a few minutes, though. I should probably get dressed first." She probably should've gotten dressed a long time ago.

"Take all the time you need." There went that crooked smile again. "I'll meet you up at the lodge whenever you're ready."

* * *

Wes pulled off his shirt and tossed it into the laundry basket in the closet. The danger Ryan had put himself in had long since passed, but his heart still pounded like it was trying to break out of his chest. There were other things, too...feelings.

He quickly stripped off his boxers and jeans before pulling on new ones. He couldn't explain what had happened to him when Thea had started crying. Instinct had kicked in, and before he knew what was happening, he'd reached for her. When he'd pulled her into his arms, shock waves had coursed through him. It was different than the rush he got in the arena, but it wasn't any less powerful. Maybe the impact had come from seeing how deeply she loved her kids. He'd seen the fear in her for sure, but there was also this underlying courage in her demeanor. She would do anything for her kids; he didn't doubt that.

He didn't doubt that he'd best find a way to put out the heat the woman had generated low in his gut either. He wasn't looking for a distraction like Thea Davis. He was about to take the biggest step up in his career. Hopefully, after this short delay, he'd find himself at the top.

Feelings or no feelings, he wasn't going to get sidetracked now.

Wes bolted out the door and jogged the whole way back to the lodge. Louise didn't waste a minute scolding him when he walked back into the kitchen.

"Where've you been?" she demanded, scrubbing a dish in the sudsy sink. "I had to put everything in the warmer so it wouldn't get cold."

"Sorry." He hurried over to grab a towel so he could help dry the dishes to make amends. "I happened to see our friend Ryan out in a canoe unattended, so I had to provide a kayak rescue real quick." He decided not to mention that the kid had fallen in without a life jacket. No need to freak everyone out.

"Ryan was on the lake without Thea?" Louise stopped her scrubbing and gaped at him.

"Yep." The poor kid. All he'd wanted to do was catch a fish, and instead he caught a whole heap of trouble. "I brought him back to the cabin, and my guess is he and his mom are having a little discussion before they head up here." Maybe he shouldn't have suggested a punishment.

"Thea hardly ever lets those kids out of her sight." Louise handed him the dripping pan and plunged her hands back into the suds. "Every summer when they come out, she's with them twenty-four/seven, always watching out for them."

Wes nodded while he dried the pan but didn't say a damn word. This line of discussion wasn't helping put out the fire Thea had kindled. It was funny...last night he'd hardly given Thea a second look. She'd seemed so buttoned up, with her collared shirt and her hair pulled back into a tight, no-nonsense ponytail. And she hadn't seemed all that thrilled that he'd been put in charge of her trip. After that introduction, he'd assumed they wouldn't get along all that well.

But this morning when she ran out of the cabin completely unhinged, with her soft tawny hair all wavy and flowing and the sheer passionate concern for her son radiating from her eyes, some switch had flipped on inside him. His blood seemed to surge again, driven by an erratic heartbeat.

"Well, where was she?" Louise handed over a skillet and dunked her hands into the water again, this time working on a plate.

"Where was who?" he asked, buying time while he meticulously wiped water droplets off the Teflon. Thea had been embarrassed about oversleeping, and somehow he sensed she wouldn't want word of that getting around.

"Thea!" Louise shoved the dripping plate into his hands. "How did Ryan sneak away without her knowing?"

Yeah, he had to give it up. He was no match for Louise when she was on the hunt for information. "I think she was still sleeping." In a pair of slinky pajamas he had no business remembering with such clarity right now.

"Good. That woman needs some rest." Louise turned back to the sink. "I, for one, can't imagine doing everything she does—raising two kids all on her own, doing her job as a social worker for the school district, and volunteering to lead these trips? It's a wonder she can hold it all together."

"Yeah. That's a lot." Again, this line of conversation was not going to help the attraction he had brewing. Thea was a social worker? No wonder Ryan had said his mother doesn't get to sleep much. It was sweet the way that boy cared for Thea. It reminded Wes of how he felt after his father died. He'd suddenly taken on the burden of worrying about his mother, of protecting her. It had been a lot for an eighteen-year-old to carry. Not to mention a ten-year-old.

"Hopefully she'll be able to get at least a little rest while she's here." She deserved a break. The memory of her leaning into his embrace sparked again.

"I don't know about that." Louise handed over a mixing bowl. "That woman works like the dickens when she's here too. Not sure she knows what it means to rest."

He could relate. For him, too much downtime meant too much time to think. Right now, he had to stop thinking. About Thea. About how good it had felt to have his arms around her...

A text dinged from his back pocket. He slung the towel over his shoulder and checked his phone. Well, wasn't that just great. He hadn't expected to hear from his boss today. Craig hadn't been thrilled when Wes had told him he wouldn't be able to make the event next weekend.

Need to talk to you. Meet me at the rodeo grounds ASAP.

Perfect. This was exactly what he needed right now. "Sorry.

I gotta run to the rodeo grounds." He tossed the towel onto the counter. "Tell Thea I'll be back as soon as I can." Hopefully this wouldn't take too long, and he and Thea would be able to go over a few things before the rest of the group arrived around lunchtime. Now that he knew everything she had on her plate, it was his duty to make this week as easy on her as he could.

"I'll tell her." Louise shot him a warning look. "But I doubt she'll be happy about it."

No, probably not. Especially given the way he'd been busy when she'd arrived last night. "I'll make it up to her." But he couldn't ditch his boss. Sure, Wes couldn't make the next event, but he could get to the one after that. And the one after that. He had to be sure Craig knew he was ready for this next step. "He's leaving town later tonight, so I don't have a choice. I'll see you soon." He dodged out of the kitchen and sprinted to his truck. There was only one reason Craig wanted to talk to him right now. His boss didn't take no for an answer from anyone and would likely make one more attempt to talk him into being the team lead next week.

After mostly obeying every traffic law, Wes parked outside of the arena. Crews were still tearing down from the Friday event—rolling up banners, packing up the special sound equipment and loading it into trucks.

Wes found Craig underneath the overhang sorting through all of their promotional gear. "Hey."

"There you are. Thanks for coming." His boss walked over to meet him.

In his day, Craig Riordin had been a legend, one of the first rodeo clowns to gain any sort of notoriety. In those days, the profession was badass, with no protective equipment like the pads they wore now. And Craig still had an imposing presence. He was taller than Wes by a good couple of inches and still very much in shape, despite being in his late fifties. Since his own rodeo days, he'd become a contractor for staffing the events, and it was thanks to him that anyone gave a damn about the guys who distracted the angry bulls after a rider went flying.

Wes had always respected the man. Craig had given him his start, and he hated to let him down now. "I'm guessing you called me over here so I could tell you again that I'm not available to travel to Texas next weekend."

Craig belted out a laugh. "Wrong. I called you here to tell you you're one of my best guys, and I need you to be the team lead next week." The man's expression sobered. "If it's not you, I'll have to put one of my other guys in the lead spot, and it's not like I can demote him for the next event."

Wes got his meaning. If he didn't make it to Texas, someone else would likely get his promotion, along with the notoriety, the sponsorships, the media coverage. Basically, the team leads were the only well-known bullfighters out there. They were the ones who made it big. "My sister's in the hospital. I have to manage the guests at the ranch." What did the man want from him? "Unless you can work a miracle and guarantee me that she won't have that baby early, there's nothing I can do." He'd been in touch with his mom, and she was currently trying to make travel arrangements to get home as soon as possible, but seeing as how she was on a cruise around Europe, it would likely take her a week.

Craig nudged a box of T-shirts aside with his boot and faced Wes directly. "Find someone else to fill in at the ranch for you. It's not like I'm asking for a lot here. I only need you to lead the event on Sunday. You can head back right after."

"The group I'm helping with needs me." Yes, he wanted to do this for Jane, but those people coming to the ranch? They'd sacrificed a lot. They deserved a retreat where someone else worried about the details and made their meals and kept things running smoothly for them.

Craig's jaw tightened, a sure sign his patience had waned. "This is a big opportunity for you. Opportunities like this don't come around very often in this business."

Wes didn't remind him that this opportunity hadn't simply come around. He'd worked for it. He'd done everything they'd asked of him; he'd labored and practiced and trained. He had become one of the best. He'd earned this opportunity, and now he might not be able to take it.

"Think about it for a few days." Craig walked to a stack of boxes nearby. "I'll give you until Wednesday to make a final decision."

Temptation started to rival his sense of duty, but Wes tamped it down. If he took off, he would only be confirming what everyone else thought—that he couldn't live up to responsibilities. "You can give me all the time in the world, but that won't change what's happening with my sister." He couldn't cause Jane more stress by taking off.

"It's one day, Harding," Craig grumbled. "I'll even pay your airfare. Find a friend to cover for you for one day."

"I'll let you know if anyone comes to mind." So far, he had no ideas. He refused to put all the work at the ranch on Louise when she was already managing the kitchen. But there was no use in standing here arguing for another hour. He'd leave Craig a message later.

"Since you're here, I could use some help loading up the trailer." Without waiting for an answer, Craig handed him a box.

"I really should get back." The rest of the group would arrive in less than two hours, and he and Thea hadn't gone over his schedule changes yet . . .

"This'll only take an hour," his boss insisted.

Sure, he'd heard that before.

Chapter Six

That was the best consequence ever!" Ryan leapt out of the canoe and dragged it up on the sandy shoreline before reaching his hand out to help Thea. "Need a hand, my lady?"

Thea laughed. "Such a charmer." She let him help her climb out of the canoe. "And, yes, that was a pretty fun consequence." When she told Ryan he would have to row her across the entire lake and back, he couldn't wait, so they'd come down to the beach right after breakfast.

Liv was still laying out in her bathing suit on a lounge chair nearby. She had her phone in front of her face, but at least she was in the great outdoors, so that was something.

"I wish Wes could've gone with us." Ryan dragged the canoe all the way up onto the beach.

Ah, yes. The infamous Wes. That man was all her son had talked about during their little "consequence" excursion across the lake. Ryan had told her all about how Wes had taught him tricks for rowing. He'd also gone over how Wes showed him to pull the boat onto the beach when he was done with it.

According to her son, Wes was pretty much the coolest person he'd ever met. The one problem with that was the man didn't seem to keep his word. It hadn't taken her more than twenty minutes to get ready and show up for breakfast, but according to Louise, Wes had to run out "real quick" for some work thing. That had been over two hours ago, and now the rest of the group would arrive in a half hour.

No matter. Thea let it slide off her shoulders. She didn't need Wes's help. She was more than capable of handling the details for the retreat by herself. After all, she handled everything else by herself. This would be no problem. In fact, it might be easier for her if the man decided to make himself scarce. Especially after the scene she'd made earlier. No wonder Wes had run out. He probably was afraid she'd blubber all over him again.

"Well, *I'm* glad we had some mother-son time." She draped an arm over her son's shoulders and squeezed him into a hug. "I'm happy that I get to spend these ten days with my two favorite kids." She chose her next words carefully. "Just remember, honey . . . we're here to be together as a family and to hang out with our new friends. Wes is really busy, and he likely won't be around a whole lot." Between the man's social life and whatever work commitments had pulled him away today, she wouldn't hold any expectations.

"But he promised to take me fishing at his secret spot," her son reminded her for the tenth time. "He said I'll catch a fish there for sure. He's never been skunked."

Annoyance flared again. Why did Wes strike her as someone who only said things he knew people wanted to hear? Oh, maybe because he'd stood there and apologized to her just a few hours ago about not being available the night before and then he'd run off and been gone all morning. "We'll see about the fishing spot," Thea said, brushing off Wes's sudden absence. "We have so many other fun things—"

Somewhere deep inside her beach bag, her phone rang. Thea pulled out a towel, her sun hat, three different types of sunscreen, and a water bottle before she found it. Jane! She lifted the phone to her ear and walked a few steps away from Ryan. "I'm so happy to hear from you!"

"Thea, I'm sorry I'm not there." Jane sounded like she might be on the verge of tears.

"No way. I won't let you apologize." She almost started to cry, too, emotional mess that she was today. "Things here are great. I'm worried about *you*." She purposely hadn't called, knowing that Jane and Toby were occupied with constant checkups and preparations in case the baby came early. "How are you holding up?"

Jane sighed into the phone. "All's good with the baby. But it's hard to be here. It's hard to sit still."

"I can't imagine." Her nesting instinct had really kicked in during the last part of both her pregnancies. All she'd wanted to do was work on the nursery and organize the baby clothes. "You're a champ. Being there is the best place you could be right now."

"I know."

But that didn't make it any easier, Thea would imagine.

"I wanted to check in," Jane said, raising her voice over some unintelligible noise in the background. "Are things going okay with Wes?"

Hmm. She wasn't exactly sure how to answer that question. Thea glanced at Ryan, who had started to build a sandcastle on the beach. Gratitude washed over her again. "Wes has been amazing." It wouldn't be a stretch to say he saved the day, but she didn't want to worry Jane and tell her about Ryan's solo adventure. "Everything is going perfectly." Well, everything except the minor breakdown she'd had earlier.

"Okay." Jane paused. "Wes is great, but I know he's got a lot going on, so I have a call in to August. You might see him around there soon."

August? As in the eldest Harding brother? Thea had never met him.

"I just want to make sure everything goes as smoothly as possible for all of you," her friend went on.

Thea didn't like the concern in her voice. "I'm not worried." At least she was trying not to worry. Even if Wes didn't step up, Thea had been around the ranch before. She knew how things went.

"We'll manage fine. All you need to do is sit back and relax and prepare for that baby. I can't wait to hold her someday."

"You and me both," Jane said. "At least they're monitoring everything. They'll know if anything goes wrong."

"Nothing will go wrong," Thea assured her. "And the hospital stay will all be worth it. Soon you'll be holding a little angel in your arms." And there was no better feeling in the world. She knew that.

There was more commotion in the background. "The doctor is here and wants to chat again." Her friend's voice seemed to have perked up. Hopefully Thea had allayed her concerns about what was happening at the ranch.

"Take care of yourself and that baby," Thea said, bidding her friend a quick goodbye before she hung up.

"Mom!" Ryan waved her over. "Come help me build a sand-castle."

"Actually..." She checked her watch. "It's about time for us to head up to the lodge to greet everyone else." Who knew if Wes was around?

"Do we have to?" Her daughter groaned. "I was almost asleep."

"I guess we have a few more minutes." Thea eyed a water gun sitting in a toy bin nearby. *Hmmm...* Maybe a quick few minutes of impromptu fun would help Liv loosen up a little.

She winked at her son and crept over to the toy bin, lifting the water pistol into her hands. Her son's eyes got wide as he rushed over to take it from her.

"You relax, sweetie," Thea said to Liv, quietly pulling another squirt gun out of the bin. She joined Ryan at the shore, letting the cold water lap at her toes as she filled up the gun.

"Thank you." Liv stretched out more on her lounger and Thea almost felt bad for what was about to happen. Almost.

She shared a wide, toothy grin with her son, and he yelled, "Attack!"

Together, the two of them ran toward Liv, pulling the triggers to spray her with water just as her daughter scrambled to get up.

"Hey!" Liv squealed and ran. "No fair! I don't have a weapon!"

"That's true..." Thea turned to face Ryan. "I guess I'll have to get you instead!" She squirted her son in the forehead.

He giggled and took off in the opposite direction, leading her on a chase. Their feet splashed through the water and she gained on him, but he got in a couple of good shots over his shoulder.

"Hey, Mom," Liv called from behind her.

Thea spun just in time to take a bucket of water to the face.

"Ah!" Now she was the one squealing. "That's freezing!"

Her daughter collapsed into hysterics. "You should see your face right now! That was the best moment of my life!"

"I'm so glad." Thea mopped the water off her face with the edge of her now-damp T-shirt. Taking a bucket of snowmelt to the face was a small price to pay to see her daughter laugh like that again.

"I leave you three unattended for a few hours and look what happens."

Thea lifted her head. At some point Wes had come down to the beach and was watching them from the grass. He still had on similar jeans and a snugly fitted T-shirt like he'd worn that morning, but not his cowboy hat. A warming sensation started dead center in her chest at the sight of him, which was not a good sign. It had been a good long while since she'd felt those butterfly wings flare in her belly.

"Wes!" Ryan sprinted to the man the same way he'd run at Captain America when she'd taken the kids to Disneyland last year.

"Hey, Sport." He took a knee. "I see you found our water gun arsenal."

"It was my mom," Ryan revealed proudly. "She started the whole thing by spraying Liv while she was lying in the sun."

"But I got her back." Olivia shot Thea a smug smile.

"You sure did. Lesson learned." She pulled her wet T-shirt away from her body so the material didn't conform to every curve.

"*You* started it?" Wes stood and stared at her like a true skeptic, his brows pinched together.

"Is that so hard to believe?" she shot back. Geez, why'd she have to lose her cool in front of him earlier? Now he probably thought all she did was sit around and cry. But she could be fun. Sometimes.

"My mom is a pretty good shot," Ryan informed him. "I'll bet she could take you on any day."

"Is that so?" Wes's eyes widened, still blaring his disbelief.

That expression on his face sent a fire roaring through her. Before she could think, Thea lifted the water gun and shot him right between the eyes, making Wes turn away. "I'm a good shot," she confirmed with a sweet smile.

Ryan and Liv were both laughing. "Get him!" her son commanded, aiming for Wes again.

Oh, Thea would get him all right. She would wipe that smug disbelief off Wes's face, even if it meant she went down and lost the battle. While the kids chased him around and unleashed their water cannons, Thea refilled her gun and took cover behind the umbrella Liv had been lying under.

At some point, Wes had managed to secure a much larger water gun than hers and was returning fire at Ryan. Thea took advantage of his blindside and blasted him with a stream of water right to the back.

The man let out a howl and whirled to retaliate, but Thea lunged back behind the umbrella.

"Oh, I'm coming for you," Wes promised seconds before he grabbed the umbrella stand and tossed it out of the way.

"I need backup!" Thea started to retreat, running back toward the water.

"Come on, Liv, let's get her!" Ryan and her daughter both joined Wes's pursuit, the little ingrates.

"No!" Sprays of water seemed to come from all directions, converging on Thea as she sloshed through knee-deep water. "I can't see!" She dropped the gun and tried to move faster but ended up face-planting into the water instead. The frigid lake shocked the breath out of her, forcing her to inhale with her head under the water.

Air! She needed air! Thea flailed, trying to find her way back above the surface.

Strong hands came underneath her arms, pulling her up to her feet while she gagged and coughed.

"You good?" Wes turned her to face him, his intense blue eyes searching hers.

"I'm—" Another coughing fit took over and she couldn't be sure, but she may have spit water all over him.

"Seriously, Thea? Are you okay?" Concern growled through the man's words.

The coughing suddenly morphed into laughing. She couldn't help it. First, she'd cried all over the man, and now she'd gone and spewed water in his face.

"That was hilarious." Ryan joined her in having a good laugh about the whole thing.

"You're soaked, Mom," Liv added, grinning.

"I'm definitely soaked." Her hair was plastered to her head and neck, and her wet clothes clung to every inch of her. At least she wouldn't have to worry about Wes being attracted to her. Something told her overemotional, disheveled women weren't really his type.

"You're fine then?" Something in the man's expression seemed to loosen. He even smiled that smile at her—the one that hiked up one corner of his mouth. "So really the whole almost-drowning thing was a ploy to get us to stop shooting you."

"It worked, didn't it?" she sassed back. Better that than letting him in on the fact that she was clumsy and had tripped over her own feet.

"We still won," Ryan informed her.

"I don't know . . ." Wes seemed to be looking only at her. "Your mom might've won that battle. I believe you now. She's definitely a good shot."

Water still glistened on his tanned skin where she'd gotten him earlier. The sun seemed to catch his eyes in just the right light.

Geez-o-Pete, the man was ridiculously handsome. The butterfly wings didn't simply flutter this time . . . they beat against her ribs.

Thea realized she was staring at him. They were staring at each other. "Um...we need to go change so we can get up to the lodge." She cleared her throat, unsure if the ache had come from all the coughing or from the unexpected swell of attraction. Hello! This was Wes Harding. Wes "I'll invite you to a party then leave without you" Harding.

"Yeah. We should get up to the lodge," the man agreed, but he didn't shift his gaze away.

What did he see when he looked at her so intently? Thea was almost afraid to know. "Everyone will be here soon." She had to shift to administrator mode...and she also had to stop looking at Wes. No one would blame her for being attracted to the man, but she had no room for any kind of attraction right now—physical or otherwise. "Come on, kids." She caught Wes in a fleeting glance. "We'll meet you up at the lodge."

"Aw, Mom. I don't have to change." Ryan looked down at his T-shirt. "I'm hardly wet at all. Can I go up with Wes?"

"Sure," Wes said at the exact time Thea said, "No."

"Oh, sorry." The man gave her a sheepish grin. "I really don't mind if he comes with me, but it's your call."

"Please, Mom!" Ryan clasped his hands in front of his chest in expert begging formation.

So much for cautioning her son against idolizing Wes. Ryan was already too far gone.

"Sure, that's fine." She kept her tone light, but her son's obvious admiration rekindled her concerns. Ryan had a sensitive side, and she didn't want to see him disappointed if Wes took off and bailed on their fishing trip. "We'll see you up there." She would have to figure out how to address her son's developing relationship with Wes later.

Right now, she'd steal a few minutes alone with her daughter. She and Liv walked to the cabin, joking along the way, and quickly got changed. When Thea came out to the front porch to meet her daughter, she noticed Olivia had traded in the jean shorts she'd had on earlier for a cute sundress. "Wow, you look nice." She resisted the urge to tease her about Preston. "I love that dress on you."

"It's no big deal," her daughter insisted, moving two steps in front of her. "I just pulled it out of my suitcase."

But Thea didn't have much room to talk. Instead of putting on the standard jean shorts and old T-shirt uniform she'd had on earlier, she'd opted for a cute knit black skirt and a sleeveless hot-pink top, telling herself it was because she wanted to look nice when she greeted everyone.

In reality she was no different than a thirteen-year-old girl trying to look good in front of a boy. Which was ridiculous, seeing as how Wes drove her crazy. Or, rather, it made her crazy how easily she seemed to let down her guard in front of him. She couldn't remember the last time her children had seen her cry, and yet she'd known Wes all of twenty-four hours and she'd already sobbed on his shoulder.

"What's your deal with Wes anyway?" Her daughter paused to wait for her.

"What do you mean?" she asked, looking straight ahead while she walked alongside Olivia.

Liv snuck in front of her, calling her out with those dark eyes that reminded Thea so much of Dylan's. "We were all having fun, and then suddenly you got all weird and stopped smiling and started to glare at people."

"What?" A nervous laugh bubbled out. "I did not." Did she?

"Yes, you did," Liv argued. "Did he make you mad or something?"

"No!" Thea navigated the steps up to the lodge's back deck. "Of course I'm not mad at Wes." She was mad at herself. Did it bother her that the man drew a physical reaction out of her? Sure. Did it make her uncomfortable how quickly he'd bonded with Ryan? Yes. But...

"He seems nice enough. He's not very reliable, that's all." She needed to keep that well in mind. "And I'm worried about your brother expecting too much from a man who doesn't follow through." The same way his father hadn't followed through. She hadn't realized that was her fear before saying it out loud. But the deepening ache in her heart confirmed that worry was the root of every hesitation.

Before Dylan would leave on a deployment, he would promise Ryan that they would spend all this time together—father-and-son bonding time—when he came back. But it never happened. The fishing trips or the baseball stadium trips or even the batting practice down at the park. Dylan always came back tired and angry and too distant to spend that quality time with his son.

Dylan had always made her promises, too—that things would be different, that he would be there for her. Guilt shut down that line of thought. She had no right to hold anything against a dead man.

"I think it's too late to *adjust Ryan's expectations*." Her daughter put one of Thea's favorite phrases in air quotes. She was always talking to her kids about adjusting their expectations the way she'd learned to.

"Yeah. It would appear so." Her son had already put Wes on a pedestal, and she had no idea how to help prepare him for disappointment.

Thea held open the lodge's back door for her daughter, and they walked into the great room. It looked like everyone had already arrived. There were the Hershbergers—Cal and Kelly standing with Preston and Timothy. Then there was the Mills family—Gabe and Abby along with their five-year-old daughter, Piper. And Wes and Ryan were greeting the Garcia family—Carlos, Luciana, and their sixteen-year-old twins, Elena and Daniela.

"Hey, everyone!" Thea's face flushed. She was never late. She should've been up here an hour ago in case anyone was early. Waving at them, she hurried to the table where they'd gathered. Thank God, Louise had set out snacks and her wonderful homemade lemonade. "You all must've made good time driving up from the airport." And she'd totally lost track of time, thanks to a certain cowboy.

"We made great time." Luciana met her with a hug. "You weren't kidding. This place is beautiful." Her dark eyes glistened. "It's the perfect place to get away."

"Wes was just telling us about all of the fun things we'll be doing," Abby added.

"We get to be in a parade," Piper said, accentuating the words with an excited squeal.

"Say what?" Thea shot Wes a questioning glance and tried to hold on to her smile. They'd planned to go watch the parade, but she had no intention of being in the parade.

"I pulled some strings with the parade organizers." His eyes worked their magic, making her heart speed up. "They're friends of mine. When I told them we'd have a bunch of kids staying here, they suggested we build a float and join in."

"That is so cool!" Ryan gave his new buddy Timothy a high five.

"Um. Wow." Thea tried to muster an ounce of enthusiasm, but that sounded like a lot of work. "The parade is the day after tomorrow. And we don't have a float." Why was she the only voice of reason here? "I'm not sure we have time to—"

"That's no problem," Wes interrupted, hooking everyone in the room with his grin. "I have tomorrow afternoon all blocked off for us to spend time working on the float."

So he'd gone and changed the whole schedule around without even talking to her? Thea decided to avoid his eyes so she didn't get sucked into his charisma like she had on the beach earlier. He would not charm her into messing up the entire retreat. "Tomorrow afternoon was supposed to be our family art project." Jane had set up a local watercolor artist to come and guide them through a simple mountain scene painting.

"Painting is boring," Ryan called. "I wanna build a float!"

"Me too," Piper and Timothy both said at the same time.

The older kids added their agreement too.

"I think it's a great idea," Kelly offered. "Painting would've been fun, too, but the kids have never been in a parade before. That's something we can't do back home."

Murmurs of agreement went around the room.

"Great. Sure. Yeah." Thea managed a smile. "This time away is all about you guys, so we can change any and all plans to make it exactly what you want it to be." She genuinely meant that, but her internal concerns had started to stack up. Didn't Wes understand the logistics involved with changing all the plans they'd made? "What theme are we planning to go with for the float? What materials will we use?" She had to be the one to ask the questions so no one ended up disappointed.

"Wes said we can make their horse wagon into a *covered* wagon." Ryan had not left the man's side once since Thea had walked in.

"We could look like real prospectors headed out west!" Timothy added.

Well, that sounded easy. They basically had one afternoon to build a float and find costumes. Thea was starting to get a headache.

"Sounds like the kids have it all under control," Cal said, putting his arm around his wife. "This is gonna be great. I haven't seen them this excited in a long time."

"Perfect." Wes scrubbed his hands together as if he couldn't wait to get started. "It'll be great. I promise." Was it just her or did Wes's smile change when he glanced in her direction? His mouth seemed to soften slightly, and his eyes drew hers in and made it difficult for her to look away. Could he possibly know what that grin did to her?

Wes's grin derailed her—that's what it did. And she had put far too much time and effort into planning the perfect retreat to allow it to go off the rails now.

"As far as the rest of the schedule...today will be all about settling in." Wes addressed the group again. "I can help deliver your bags to your cabins on the golf cart for you."

"I'll come with you and help." Ryan stood a little bit taller, a little bit prouder, and once again Thea wanted to shield her son.

"Dinner will be served in the dining room at six o'clock," Thea said quickly, before Wes could change something else on her. "And then tomorrow morning we'll spend some time on the lake, kayaking and canoeing and swimming—"

"And fishing!" Ryan threw in.

"Yes, of course. How could I forget fishing?" Thea ruffled her son's hair. "On Wednesday we're planning to be in the parade..." If they finished the float on time, that was. "And that evening, we have free time scheduled for families—"

"Actually..." Wes moved to the center of the circle. "I talked to a buddy of mine who runs a wilderness camp nearby, and he's willing to put together a special overnight excursion for the kids, if they're interested."

Thea's heart dropped. "Overnight?"

"That sounds cool." Those were the first words Preston had spoken since Olivia had come in.

"It's pretty amazing," Wes said. "It's a fully accredited camp, and he said they would take you all rock climbing and on a night hike to go stargazing. They also have a swimming pool with a waterslide, and the cabins are really nice too."

"Sweet! Sounds awesome," the twins said, finishing each other's sentences.

Even Olivia seemed excited. "I've always wanted to go rock climbing," her daughter murmured to Preston.

And Thea had always wanted to walk through a pit of snakes.

"That would give the parents some alone time too," Wes added. "We have great restaurants in town. Or Louise would be happy to take requests and make individual dinners for everyone."

Individual dinners. Like dates. Wes was giving the couples a date night, which would be wonderful for Cal and Kelly, Carlos and Luciana, and Gabe and Abby. The problem was, Thea had no one to go on a date with. See? That was exactly why he shouldn't have taken liberties with the schedule. On a retreat like this, you had to make sure to consider how the plans would work for everyone. A date night most definitely did not work for her. Thea almost told him so, too, but the smiles on all of the other adults' faces made her keep her mouth shut.

"It's been forever since we've gone on a date." Abby sighed with what seemed like longing. "Thank you so much." She looked at Wes first, and then Thea. "This is going to be the best retreat. You have no idea how much we need it."

Thea had an idea. She'd been looking forward to this trip with her kids for a long time. She'd been looking forward to reconnecting with them, and now they were headed out on an overnight excursion without her.

While everyone else started to chat about the excitement of the next few days, Thea tugged on Wes's elbow. "Can I talk to you for a minute?" Without waiting for an answer, she marched to the corner of the room. They didn't need an audience for this conversation.

"You can all help yourselves to more snacks," he said to the group on his way over.

"Yes! More lemonade!" Ryan sprinted to the drinks table.

Before Thea could remind her son that he didn't need more sugar, Wes approached her, making the corner feel too small, too cramped.

"What's up?" There went the corner of his mouth again, lifting to a perfect angle to highlight a shallow dimple she hadn't noticed before.

"I'll tell you what's up." She silently commanded those damn butterflies in her belly to stand down. Right now, she didn't want to feel any fluttering. She wanted to be mad. "Jane and I had this whole retreat planned, and now you're changing everything around." That wasn't exactly *the* problem. Currently, there was a whole list of problems. He hadn't even bothered to clear the changes with her ahead of time. Everyone liked his itinerary better than they liked the one she and Jane had worked out. And she couldn't seem to keep her emotions in check when Wes was around. That was proving to be the biggest problem of them all.

"I didn't think changing things up would be a big deal." His grin finally faded so she could think straight, thank God. "When Jane told me about the families, I asked some of my friends what would be fun for the kids to do. I just thought maybe we could add in a few more events."

"Because you didn't think I could be fun?" That was what really had her in a tizzy. It was like he'd looked over the schedule and thought it was too boring.

"You're a lot more fun than I'd planned on, Thea."

She'd set herself up for that comment, but she still hadn't been prepared for it. Or for the way Wes delivered the remark, with his tone lower, almost hungry.

She blinked up at him, unable to swallow, unable to draw in a full breath. There was no stopping those butterflies now.

Wes stared at her as though waiting for her to say something.

Say something, damn it!

"You're fun too." Really? That was the best she could come up with? She blamed his grin. It had completely derailed this conversation. "What I mean is, the changes sound fun, but next time, I would appreciate a heads-up."

"Duly noted."

His gaze intensified in hers, and Thea had to walk away before she did something really stupid like walk into his arms again. "Anyway. We should get moving." They should move away from each other—away from whatever strange chemistry experiment was happening between them. She'd always hated chemistry.

Thea scurried to the other side of the room and poured herself a glass of lemonade to quench the sudden desert in her mouth.

"All right." Wes clapped his hands. "Let's get you all settled. I'll start delivering the luggage. Feel free to walk around. Any and all of the facilities are open for you to use while you're here. We want you to relax and have a great time. Don't worry about a thing."

Right. Don't worry. While everyone else dispersed, Thea hid out by the drinks table. She wasn't worried about *a* thing. Oh, no. At the moment she happened to be worried about *many* things.

Chapter Seven

Wes!" Ryan came flying up the deck steps from the beach, arms flailing, freckles shining on his wet face.

Wes couldn't help but grin. The kid reminded him of himself at that age in a lot of ways—carefree and a little wild. A spitfire, his dad had always called him.

"Hey, Sport. What's up?" He greeted the kid with a fist bump, but Ryan was so out of breath from the sprint over, he couldn't get out any intelligible words.

While Ryan inhaled, Wes searched the beach. Thea sat on a lounge chair next to another mom, chatting away. All afternoon, he'd been trying to steal a few minutes alone with her to talk about what had transpired between them in the lodge. And on the beach earlier. Something had transpired, that was for damn sure. When he stood closer to her, when her eyes locked on his, a whole lot seemed to transpire. But no matter how hard he'd tried to get her attention in between delivering luggage and helping Louise prepare, serve, and clean up after dinner, Thea had been too busy moving from one cabin to the next to make sure the families had everything they needed to even look in his direction. Either that, or she was avoiding him.

"Do you want to come swimming with us?" the boy finally uttered, gesturing to where the group of kids splashed and played on the shoreline.

"Swimming after the sun is down?" He laughed, remembering how he likely would've wanted to do the same thing at ten years old. "It'll be freezing." Already, the shadows were descending upon the lake's surface. It wouldn't be long before it was dark.

"Mom said we only have ten more minutes to play in the lake and then we have to have a fire." The boy seemed to pout.

"Sounds like your mom doesn't want you to be too tired for the rest of the retreat. Or for a special fishing trip." After their conversation in the lodge, he'd best check with Thea on the timing for a fishing excursion. "Speaking of fires, I have to go get one started for you." He'd completely forgotten about the evening campfire. He could almost hear his sister's voice in his head. *You forgot?* No doubt Jane would be on her phone calling in August right now if she could see what was happening. He hadn't thought changing the schedule would be a big deal, but he should've asked Thea first. And now he was forgetting his responsibilities because he couldn't seem to take his mind—or eyes—off one of Jane's friends.

Yeah, his sister wouldn't like how this retreat was going at all.

"No swimming for me, I'm afraid." From now on, he was going to stick to the plans, stick to the schedule. That's what his father would've done. Being here—managing the ranch—had reminded him how much he'd always wanted to be like his dad. His hero. Seeing things through may have never been Wes's strong point, but this was his chance to prove he could handle more. He'd prove it to Jane. He'd prove it to his dad. He'd prove it to Thea. "Don't worry though," he said to Ryan. "I'll help Louise bring down the s'mores stuff." So hopefully all would be forgiven.

"S'mores?" Ryan jumped at least a foot off the ground. "Yes! Yes, yes, yes. I love it here!" He turned and took off again—heading back to the beach, yelling, "We get s'mores tonight!"

All the kids cheered.

The commotion seemed to get Thea's attention. She glanced over her shoulder in his direction and Wes swore some magnetic force pulled their gazes together, even across all this distance.

For a second, he thought she might come and talk to him, but then she turned back to her friend as though she hadn't seen him. It looked like he'd have to talk to her later. Or maybe he shouldn't. What good would it do, addressing the pull he felt between them? It would likely only make things more awkward.

Wes made his way to the other side of the deck and followed the worn path to the fire pit. It was the perfect spot for a true campfire—a ring built into the earth with stones his father had found on the property. He picked up a log off the woodpile nearby. His dad had also built the comfortable log benches positioned around the fire ring. Back when he was in high school, the whole fam would sit around here together during the off-season, their father telling stories about the stars or the gold panners who had tried to make their living here years ago.

"Please tell me you're getting ready to burn that T-shirt."

The log fell from Wes's hands and hit the ground with a thud. That couldn't be...

He spun and found himself staring at his brother across the fire pit. "Auggie?" It looked like Jane had called in backup after all. He shouldn't be so surprised.

"Seriously, Wes. I think you've had that shirt since high school." His brother moved around the pile of logs looking like he'd just stepped out of one of those fancy wine catalogs. He wore a collared gray shirt that was tucked into dark jeans. It seemed he'd traded in his cowboy boots for shiny leather shoes too. Then there was his hair. It'd always been darker than Wes's, and August kept it the perfect length—not too long, not too short, not too wavy, not too straight.

Wes looked down at his tattered "Cowboy Up" T-shirt and dirty boots. Standing next to August, he looked like riffraff, but then again, that's the way it had always been.

"This isn't the same shirt I had in high school." At least he didn't think it was. "What're you doing here?" He already knew but wanted to hear August say he'd come to bail him out. Just like old times.

"I came from the hospital." His brother sat on one of the benches their father had made. "Jane thought maybe you needed some help up here, so I took a few extra days off."

"Whoa. I'd best sit down too." Wes sat across from his brother. "You took *days* off?" Well, that was a real honor. He must really have no confidence in Wes. Last summer, his brother had barely managed to take off an hour to meet him for lunch.

"I'm due for some time off." August still had the same shiny smile he'd had back when he was schmoozing people in an effort to become student body president. His brother had always been a polished charmer. "Besides, I have some business out here anyway."

And there it was. August couldn't seem to take time off and do nothing. Not that Wes could talk on that front. They were both workaholics in their own ways. "I can't even begin to guess what business you could possibly have in Silverado Lake."

"My boss is interested in expanding. So I'm investigating." He started saying something about Valentino Bella's, the small, locally owned winery in town, but Thea snagged Wes's attention. Farther down the shoreline, she'd gotten out of her chair and was standing with her feet in the water, watching Ryan on a paddleboard. Her skirt was fluttering in the breeze, and the evening light seemed to halo her with a soft glow.

Man, he wished she would smile at him like that sometime…

"Maybe this is just me, but you probably shouldn't be checking out one of the wives who's staying at the ranch." His brother leaned back and crossed his arms, eyes analyzing him.

"I'm not checking out anyone," he lied. It wasn't like he'd meant for his gaze to keep finding her. It just happened. "Even if I was…Thea isn't one of the wives. She's a widow." Not that checking out a widow was much better…

"Oh." His brother seemed to take a closer look at Thea. "I

didn't realize they did these trips for people whose spouses have passed away."

"She's leading the trip. And she's a good friend of Jane's." Yet another reason he had no business checking her out.

"That's right." August glanced at the beach again. "Jane mentioned her. Thea. She's got two kids?"

"Yeah. Ryan is ten, and Oliva is thirteen." And they both seemed well adjusted and happy, even with all they'd lost. That only proved Thea was a supermom.

"Then I know you definitely weren't checking her out." His brother's laugh bordered on condescending.

"What's that supposed to mean?" Wes stood and reached for the log he'd discarded earlier. He'd best get the fire going before Thea walked over and decided he was shirking his responsibilities.

"You with kids?" August came to stand over him as he knelt to position the kindling. "You've never wanted to be tied down like that."

How the hell would he know? Wes stood and faced his brother. Auggie had always been taller than him, but Wes was stronger. August had used wit and charisma and intellect his whole life, while Wes had relied on his sense of adventure and physical prowess. "We haven't spent more than three days together since I was eighteen years old," he told his brother. "I like to think I've changed some since then." He didn't know why he tried. His place in this family had been defined long ago. He was stuck right in the middle between two brilliant, responsible siblings who'd always done what everyone had wanted and expected.

Then there'd been him.

August tilted his head to the side as though Wes's attitude amused him. "So, you're saying you *were* checking Thea out."

"No," he muttered. "I'm not saying anything." As much as he hated to admit it, August was right. He had no business starting anything with a woman who had kids. He moved around. He had a dangerous job. And he didn't know a whole lot about keeping his word. He'd proved that the day his father died. *Why can't you be more like your brother?* It was a question his dad had asked him more than once, and God help him, he wished he was more like August. Maybe then his old man would still be here. Maybe August would've saved him if he'd shown up that day.

Wes knelt again and busied his hands, pulling out scraps of wood and paper from the metal bin and then lighting the kindling. He blew on the small flames until the scraps of paper caught.

"Jane mentioned something about you getting a promotion," August said when Wes stood back up.

"Yeah. Well, I was offered one." If he didn't show up next weekend, he had no doubt his boss would kindly rescind that offer. Craig wouldn't have a choice.

"She's worried you'll lose your chance if you don't go to that event this weekend." His brother shot him a questioning glance. It killed him how much August looked like their father. Especially with that deliberate gray-eyed gaze.

"It's fine." He bent to nestle a larger log down over the kindling. "I told her I'd stay, and I will." If only to prove to everyone else he could be a man of his word.

"You don't have to stay." August directed a glance toward the beach.

The group was starting to pack up, the kids all bundled in towels and the moms loading up their bags to head to the fire.

"I'm here," August said, settling himself back on the bench. "I'll stay so you can go to your event."

Wes found himself looking at Thea again, but he quickly tore his gaze away so Auggie wouldn't notice. His brother was right. He was free to go. He could pack up and leave tonight for the next rodeo in Texas. Craig would be thrilled. Only problem was, he didn't want to go. Not yet.

It used to be that he only felt an adrenaline rush when he walked into an arena—that's what he lived for. But then Thea had gone and leaned against his chest when he'd comforted her. She'd shot him right between the eyes with a water gun. She'd looked directly into his eyes, letting him see more of her. She made him feel something different, and now he was acquainted with a whole new kind of adrenaline addiction. "I already told Jane I would stay, and..." He wanted to see this retreat through. For Ryan, especially. And for Thea, too, if he was being honest.

"Come on, Wes," his brother pushed. "It sounds like this is your big chance. Don't screw it up."

"I'm not screwing anything up." But he appreciated his brother's confidence in him. Sure, going to the event next weekend would earn him the top spot long-term. It was tempting. He'd hardly made any money those first few years, and this promotion would likely put him in a higher income bracket. But money had never been as important to him as it was to August. "It's fine."

Voices grew louder as the group approached the fire ring. Ryan led the charge with Thea close behind. Wes checked on the fire again, wanting everything to be perfect. The log had caught and was putting out some good heat, but it would take a while for those marshmallow-roasting coals to develop.

"Let's eat some marshmallows!" Ryan went straight for the metal roasting sticks they kept on one of the benches.

"Not so fast, Sport." Wes ruffled his hair. "I have to go up and get the marshmallows and chocolate first. And we need to wait until those coals right there"—he pointed to the fire—"are glowing red."

"Aw, man." The kid looked past him and seemed to notice August for the first time. "Who're you?"

By now the rest of the group had clustered around, and August introduced himself as articulately as if he were doing one of those speeches he'd loved to give back in high school.

"And I'm here to help out with whatever you all need during your retreat," his brother finished. As if Wes wasn't enough to take care of that task. While everyone introduced themselves to August, Wes caught Thea looking at him. She quickly diverted her gaze when their eyes connected.

Yeah, he didn't know what to do with the attraction between them either.

It seemed his brother had things under control around the fire, so Wes headed up to the kitchen and found a tray of Louise's special assortment of s'mores goodies all ready to go. By the time he returned to the fire pit, everyone had settled in, and the kids were singing silly songs while August tended to the fire.

"The chocolate and marshmallows have arrived." If that didn't get the kids' attention, he didn't know what would. Wes set the tray on a nearby cedar table and the kids crowded in, clamoring for the first marshmallow.

For the next half hour Wes tried to give lessons on proper roasting technique—where to hold the marshmallow at the perfect angle above the flame to get that golden-brown crust. August, on the other hand, hung out with Carlos, Gabe, and Cal. No surprise that his brother got along so well with the dads on the trip. Even back in elementary school, his brother had always been good with adults, while Wes had always been better with kids. Still was. He liked kids better anyway. They were more real.

Helping them build their s'mores took him back to his own childhood days, and he somehow found the patience his father had always shown him, rationing out the chocolate, neutralizing arguments about who had the best marshmallow. As soon as they ran out of marshmallows and the sugar rush kicked in, they started a lively game of tag, with him as the target, as always. Wes laughed as he darted after Ryan. That kid was fast.

When the game evolved into more of a hide-and-seek situation, he took the opportunity to start collecting the trash.

Thea jumped up from her seat by the fire and retrieved an uneaten graham cracker from the grass, tossing it into the garbage bag he held.

"Nope." He moved the bag out of her reach. "You don't get to help clean up. Go sit and enjoy the evening with your friends."

A look he was beginning to recognize flashed in her eyes. They went wide with surprise for a split second before they seemed to brighten. He'd seen that same look when she glanced up at him after she'd stopped crying on the porch. And then again when he'd lifted her out of the water on the beach. It was a look that told him she felt the energy between them too.

"I can help you clean up, Wes." She masked her expression again, giving him the same attitude she'd confronted him with in the lodge.

"I know you *can*." She'd proved she could do a lot of things—including surprise him on a regular basis. "But I'm asking you to enjoy your night and let me take care of the work." Though he was just getting to know her, he could already tell she didn't often let people do things for her. That only made him more determined to give her a break.

After a lengthy hesitation, Thea nodded. "Okay. If you're sure you don't need my help."

"I think I can handle it, but I'll let you know if I need a sharp-shooter for anything." He couldn't resist teasing out her smile.

"Sounds good." Her eyes held on his. "Thanks. It'll be nice to have a break." The softness of her voice and her smile stayed with him long after she walked away and he moved along the shoreline, picking up pop cans and empty juice boxes the kids had likely discarded earlier. Tomorrow, he'd have a discussion with the kids about making sure their trash made it into the bear-safe trash cans. They didn't need old Smokey making a visit to the property later for a midnight snack.

The lampposts scattered along the path gave off just enough of a glow for him to locate a few more cans on the beach. He pulled the kayaks up all the way out of the water and put the umbrellas down while he was at it—all things his parents had made him do to help take care of the place back in the day.

Before his father died, Wes hadn't ever wanted to leave the ranch. His dad used to take him out on the canoe or on a hike so they could get a good view of the property. *This could be yours one day*, he'd told him. Wes had wanted nothing more than to do all the things his dad loved to do. While their personalities were different, they shared a love for outdoor adventures. He stopped to look out over the lake. Right up until the day his dad died, when people asked Wes what he wanted to be when he grew up, he would tell them he wanted to be the owner of the Silverado Lake Ranch.

But that dream had shattered. He didn't deserve the place his father had loved so much. He couldn't face the everyday reminders of what his failures had done to his family. So he'd followed a different path in a desperate attempt to find success and become the man his father wanted him to be. Had he though? Why did it still feel like he was chasing something he couldn't hold on to?

Maybe it was best if he didn't look for the answer to that loaded question.

Wes snatched up the half-full garbage bag and headed in the direction of the dumpster. He hadn't made it three steps past the boathouse when he heard a familiar giggle.

Uh-oh. That couldn't be good. Wes set the garbage bag against a tree and edged around the boathouse's wall until he could get a look at the front. Olivia stood there with that Preston kid, a distinct puff of smoke hovering above her head. While he watched, the girl brought what sure as hell looked like an e-cigarette to her lips and puffed again.

Damn. Wes leaned his head back against the wall and shut his eyes. Wasn't it his luck to find Thea's daughter getting herself into trouble? He was almost tempted to walk away. This wasn't his jurisdiction. The last thing he wanted to do was rat out another one of Thea's kids. And yet...if he were a parent and that was his kid, he would want to know.

He had no choice but to confront them.

"What's going on here?" he asked, stepping out of the shadows. Man, he sounded like his father.

Olivia instantly threw the vape pen onto the ground. "Nothing! I swear! Nothing is going on!"

Wes steered his gaze to Preston, who looked like he wanted to run. To the kid's credit, he didn't.

Instead of telling Olivia he wasn't as stupid as he looked, Wes knelt to pick up the vape pen. "You want to know what this crap will do to your lungs?" Hadn't they seen the commercials? "I realize I don't know either one of you, but I have to say, I expected more." Yep, that was another Dad line.

"It wasn't Preston," Olivia whimpered. "It's mine. My friend gave it to me before I left Texas. He didn't even touch it. I swear."

Wes looked at the kid for confirmation.

"My parents would bust me if I ever touched something like that," Preston muttered. "I don't even wanna know what the consequence would be."

And Thea wouldn't bust Olivia for vaping? He already knew the answer to that one. She wasn't the kind of mom who would let this go, and he didn't blame her.

"You're not gonna tell my mom, are you?" The girl turned on the waterworks. "I've never vaped before, and I'll never do it again. I swear! I had it with me, so I wanted to try it, but it'll never happen again."

He'd said the same thing to his own parents many times after making a stupid decision, and he could still hear his father's response: *I'm glad it'll never happen again, son. But you're still gonna take responsibility for your actions.* That had been the only way he'd learned anything. So, dealing with this situation may not be his jurisdiction, but he'd had the best damn father in the world, and he knew exactly how his old man would've handled this same situation.

"I'm not going to tell your mom." Wes handed the vape pen back to Olivia. "But you are."

Chapter Eight

Thea zipped up her sweatshirt and scooted to the edge of the bench to get closer to the fire.

Even with the chill, this was just about the most perfect night she could remember having in a long time. The adults were still gathered around the fire, and Kelly was telling everyone a story about their last family vacation to Mount Rushmore. Somewhere nearby in the darkness, the kids were playing—and miraculously all getting along—laughing and teasing.

And she was sitting. She couldn't remember the last time she'd sat and relaxed with a group of friends like this, trading stories and enjoying the sight of the stars and the crackling fire.

Home, along with all its stresses and responsibilities, felt a million miles away from the calm serenity of these mountains. Maybe it wasn't only the mountains and friends that made her feel more alive. She reflected on the kindness in Wes's eyes when he'd told her to simply sit and enjoy being part of the group while he took care of the mess. It had felt like a gift. Enjoying the moment was a luxury she rarely had.

A tap on her shoulder had her sitting up straight, drawing her gaze away from the fire. She peered behind her to see Wes standing outside of their circle. "Can I talk to you for a second?" he murmured as though he didn't want to interrupt. But it was too late. Kelly had stopped talking.

"You want to join us, Wes?" Cal scooted his chair back from the fire, making room next to him.

"Oh." Wes took a step forward. "No. Thank you though. I just need to borrow Thea for a minute."

The calm she'd been enjoying only seconds before seemed to go up in the campfire smoke. Something was wrong.

"Sure." She scrambled to her feet, keeping a smile intact despite the way her pulse had started to thrum.

"I'll be right back," she said, following him away from the circle. "Then we can wrap up and plan for tomorrow."

A murmur of acknowledgment went around, and the conversation started up again as though it had never paused.

Thea hurried to keep up with Wes as they left the hum of voices behind. "What's wrong?"

Wes kept walking. "Olivia needs to talk to you."

"Olivia?" She reached for his shoulder and pulled him to a stop. "Olivia is over there playing with the kids." She gestured toward the raucous noise closer to the shoreline.

"No, she's not." Wes turned and started to follow the lighted path again. "She's actually over by the boat shed."

Humiliation burned to the tips of her ears. How did she not know where her daughter was? She could've sworn she heard Liv's voice not twenty minutes ago. Thea beelined in front of him, gaze zeroed in on the boat shed's light. "What is she doing over there?"

"I promised I would let her tell you," the man said simply.

Why was he being so tight-lipped? She wasn't going to wait any longer to find out. Thea stalked the rest of the way to the boat shed and froze. Her daughter was standing on the dock with Preston. And she was crying.

"What's going on?" Her voice shook. If Preston had touched her . . . if he'd laid one hand on her—

"I'm sorry, Mom." Olivia sniffled and swiped at her nose. "Please don't be mad. I made a mistake. A stupid mistake."

Thea couldn't seem to move or speak. She turned her head to look at Wes, who stood a few feet away. He nodded toward Olivia like he wanted her to continue.

A sob bubbled out of her daughter. "I was vaping. Wes caught me, and I'm so sorry. I'll never do it again. I swear."

"Vaping?" Thea was as breathless as if she'd been the one damaging her lungs. She narrowed her stare on Preston. "You gave her a vape pen?" He had to have, because Liv would never do something so irresponsible on her own. They'd talked in depth about the dangers of vaping.

"No." Her daughter hid her face behind her hands and continued to cry. "It's my vape pen. Dallas and Casey gave it to me before I left home."

Thea closed her eyes and kept her mouth shut so she wouldn't yell. Why wasn't she surprised? But still, Olivia had been the one to bring the vape pen *here*. She'd been the one to use it. There was no one to blame but her daughter.

"Preston didn't touch it," Liv said tearfully. "He shouldn't get in trouble for something I did."

Even so, guilt seemed to be radiating off the poor kid. His eyes were wide, and he stood as though bracing himself for a good lecture.

"I'm sorry, Mrs. Davis," Preston said so quietly she almost didn't hear. "I should've tried to stop her."

"It's not your fault," she assured him, buying time to sort out her emotions and her options. "Why don't you go back to the fire with your parents?"

He nodded silently, and even Thea had to admit it was sweet how he squeezed Liv's hand before slipping away.

Instead of addressing her daughter, Thea turned to Wes. "I want to know exactly what happened." She employed the silent stress breathing techniques she'd learned in therapy sessions after Dylan had passed away.

Wes stepped closer, coming into the light from the shadows. "I was cleaning up the beach and heard voices, so I came over to check things out." His tone held a certain degree of gentleness. "When I glanced around the side, I saw Olivia holding the vape pen, and I confronted her."

Thea nodded, letting the information sit. Then she turned to her daughter, still grasping at calm. "So, if Wes hadn't caught you, you'd likely still be standing here vaping?" Right under her nose. Not even a quarter of a mile from where she'd sat at the fire relaxing and believing all was right with the world.

Liv was smart enough not to answer. "I'm so sorry," she moaned again, in her most pathetic teen-drama voice. "Please don't ground me. Oh, God, please don't take away my phone."

"Oh, that phone is mine, honey." Thea held out her hand. Liv dissolved back into sobs, but she handed over the phone. "We've talked about vaping. You know exactly what it does to a person's lungs. You want to tell me why you thought it would be a good idea to bring a vape pen on our vacation?" She held her tone under careful control. *Don't escalate the situation. Don't shame. Don't berate.* No matter how much anger had built. As a social worker, she had all the tools, but sometimes it didn't feel any easier to put them to use.

"I don't know," her daughter sobbed. "Dallas and Casey said it was fun. I wanted to impress Preston."

"Well, Preston didn't seem too impressed to me." That was one natural consequence. In fact, the boy had looked downright terrified. "You can't do things like this, Liv. We've talked about vaping. One bad choice can lead to a worse one. You have to be smart and safe." God, it was so hard to watch her kids grow. The older they got, the more the stakes would rise. The more the potential risks would increase. Why couldn't they just stay five years old forever?

"I'm tired of playing it safe!" Her daughter stepped closer, tears streaming down her cheeks. "I don't want to be careful all the time! I want to live a little. I don't want to have no life like you!"

The words came at Thea like a slap, making her flinch. That teen-girl angst still caught her off guard most days. She remembered the days when Liv would tell her she wanted to be just like her when she grew up. Things had started to change after Dylan died, though. Thea had been so careful to hide their constant arguments from the kids. She'd tried to overcompensate by making her husband's favorite meals and complimenting him in front of them. But maybe her daughter knew more than Thea wanted her to. Maybe she blamed her.

She closed her eyes, drawing in a deep enough breath to stabilize her fragile heart. "I want you to live, sweetie," she said quietly. "I want you to have the best life." She didn't want her daughter to end up like her either—alone and busy and stressed out most of the time. "I'm just trying to save you from pain." Her daughter wouldn't understand. She couldn't. Thea wouldn't have understood at thirteen either.

Her daughter let out a grunt of frustration. "This is so humiliating! Preston will probably never speak to me again, thanks to you two." She shot a glare at Wes, but it didn't seem to faze him any. He still stood a few feet away, watching the drama unfold.

"I'm going to the cabin!" Liv stalked away from them. "Wake me up when this retreat is over!"

Thea watched her dart down the lighted path along the curve of the shoreline until Liv climbed the porch steps and disappeared into their cabin. Thea rested her head against the shed wall and closed her eyes. She hated fighting with her daughter. Hated that Liv saw her as someone who didn't live life to the fullest. She hated that there was some degree of truth in her daughter's words.

"Could she really sleep for more than a week?" Wes asked in obvious disbelief.

Thea opened her eyes. She'd almost forgotten he was standing there. "No way." She stood up again, dreading the march over to her cabin to confront her daughter yet again. Sometimes in situations like these, a little bit of space was best for both of them. "She'll wake up tomorrow morning and be back to her mostly happy self." That had been the hardest thing for her to understand with her daughter's outbursts. Sometimes they hit with no warning, but after releasing her wrath, she could be giggling ten minutes later.

"I'm sorry." Wes approached her, a guilty expression tugging at one corner of his mouth. "Maybe I should've left well enough alone. Vaping one time isn't going to kill her. God knows I did a hell of a lot worse when I was a teenager."

"No." Thea stacked her shoulders back up like she'd done many times before. Even when she felt ready to crumble, that mom resolve always seemed to build her back up. She didn't know where it came from, but she was damn grateful for it all the same. "You did the right thing coming to get me. Vaping once won't kill her, but continuing to make bad decisions could really mess things up for her someday. I'd rather have her learn lessons now than when she's older." Heck, Thea's own parents had given her no freedom growing up. They'd had too many rules and regulations. They were always looking over her shoulder. On a trip like this, she wouldn't have been allowed to run around and play with the kids in the dark. Then college had come around, and she'd had no idea what to do with the freedom.

"That's true." Wes seemed to think on her words. "I'm glad I made most of my stupid mistakes when my dad was alive. He never let me off the hook for anything."

Every time Wes mentioned his father, his whole demeanor changed. His easy smile grew weighted and the light disappeared from his eyes. Thea couldn't help but wonder about his relationship with his father. To hear Jane tell it, the man was perfect—an amazing father, a devoted husband. When her friend talked about her dad, she smiled with a genuine happiness. But mentioning his father seemed to have a different impact on Wes. "What mistakes did you make?"

"You name it." The sadness in his eyes tugged at her heart. "I was always running off with my friends, getting into trouble. Partying, underage drinking, raising hell." He grinned and the look of despair was gone. "If vaping had been a thing back then, I'm sure I would've done that too."

"Why?" She knew why she'd gone a little wild in college. She'd never been allowed to date or go to parties or do what she wanted during her high school years. So she'd rebelled against everything they'd taught her and wound up pregnant and married too young. "I know maybe those things seemed fun when you were a kid, but if you knew you'd get in trouble, why would you do it?" Why would Liv bring a vape pen on this trip when the chances of getting caught were so high?

Wes didn't answer right away. Instead, he gazed out to where the water rippled on the shoreline, moonlight dancing across the surface. "I guess I was trying to figure out who I was. Or maybe who I wanted to be," he finally said. "My older brother, August, was popular and good at everything he tried—from the debate team to the football team. My sister, Jane...Well, you know Jane." He laughed a little. "She's your classic overachiever. Brilliantly smart and driven. Way more responsible than me." His eyes met Thea's again, catching the glare of the light that buzzed above them. "I wanted to be seen too. For who I was. I wasn't the smart one or the leader or the one who won every honor." He paused, as though he wasn't sure he should continue. But then he sighed. "I wanted to be important too. And getting into trouble got me a lot of attention."

His gaze drew her in, a subtle trilling deep in her heart gaining momentum. Wes wasn't smiling now. He wasn't charming her. He wasn't teasing her. He was letting her see him, pain and all. "I guess that's what we all want," she said quietly. "To be important to someone." Her job made her important—that's why she put so much of herself into it. Being a mom made her important. Those two roles defined her. But Liv was right—she had no life outside of them. No passion. No boldness. She took no risks. Had no adventures. Because all of those things would involve her heart, and that was the one thing she couldn't give. Not when it was ensnared in the guilt brought on by her tumultuous marriage, by her husband's death, by her failure to love him the way she should've.

"You're a good mom," Wes told her. He stepped closer, likely only to reassure her, based on his sympathetic tone, but without thinking, Thea let her head tip forward until her forehead rested on his chest. She was too weak to fight the pull she felt to him. Or maybe she was strong enough to act on it in this moment.

After a second, Wes's arms came around her, enveloping her in a warmth and closeness she hadn't let herself experience for so long. For a lifetime. Her heart pounded harder and her knees softened. She raised her head to peek up at him, to see into his eyes again. They drew her in, so full of something she'd never seen before—scars and regret but also a flicker of hope that kindled hers. Thea couldn't look away. She couldn't step away. The hammering of her heart pushed her to move, to touch her lips to his. The contact knocked the wind out of her, bringing a small whimper hurtling up her throat.

Wes startled, pulling away from her. But then his gaze locked on hers and everything paused. A year seemed to pass between them all at once, and her chest burned with each shallow breath. What had she done? What was she doing? She didn't know, but she needed more.

They moved at the same time—as though someone had pushed the play button again. Wes's lips met hers in the middle of a shared desperation and longing and need. *Yes, yes, yes.* She needed his lips on hers, his arms around her, his solid strength and the vulnerability she heard in his deep moan when her lips parted and her tongue grazed his.

Wes tightened his arms around her, his hands cradling her waist, and she pressed her body to his, sure this was exactly what had been missing. The kissing and the closeness and the surge of emotion. Wes filled her senses—the faint scent of campfire coming off his clothes, the sugary-sweet taste of marshmallow still in his mouth. She stood up on her tiptoes so she could get more of him, closer—

"Mooooom! Are you down here?"

Ryan's voice slammed into her, bringing an instant panic that caused her to push Wes away. What was she doing? "This shouldn't have happened," she gasped, gathering her hair in her hand to get it away from her forehead. "Oh my God, this can't happen."

"But it did," Wes murmured calmly, just as her sweet, angelic son blitzed around the corner.

"There you are!" Ryan went straight to Wes—the man he thought was a superhero. The man she'd just kissed with reckless abandon...

"Sorry!" Kelly hurried around the corner too. "Man, Ry. You are one quick ki—" Her mouth snapped shut when she caught sight of Thea's face.

Thea instantly looked away. The guilt had to be inscribed in her wide eyes, in her flushed cheeks. "We had an incident with Olivia," Thea announced, her voice both too high and too tight. "I'm so sorry. I was going to come back to the fire, but..." She'd been kissing Wes Harding. Kissing him!

"Oh, it's no problem." Kelly waved her off as though she wasn't suspicious about the two of them standing here alone together. The slight narrowing of her eyes told a different story, though. "We all decided to call it a night, so Ryan and I thought we'd come find you."

"Maybe we should go fishing," her son said to Wes, eyeing the dark water.

Wes laughed.

How did the man sound so casual? Maybe the kiss hadn't gotten his heart all revved up the way it had hers.

"We'll go fishing another time, Sport," Wes promised. "But right now, you need to get a good night's sleep so I can take you tubing on the boat tomorrow."

"Tubing? Yes!" Her son pulled on her arm. "Come on, Mom. We gotta get to bed so Wes can take us tubing."

Thea had never been more grateful for her son's exuberant persistence.

"Right." She carefully avoided looking at either Wes or Kelly. "We'll get you to bed right away." She allowed him to drag her toward the path. "Good night," she called feebly over her shoulder. "See you tomorrow." Unless she decided to sleep for the rest of the retreat along with Olivia, which sounded a lot more tempting than facing Wes again.

Chapter Nine

Dark, rich coffee spilled out from the Keurig like liquid hope, filling the ceramic mug Thea had blindly pulled out of the cupboard when she'd stumbled into the kitchen at five o'clock this morning. This would be her third cup, and she had only just started to feel human again. Three more cups and maybe those dark circles under her eyes would disappear.

Amazingly enough, neither one of her children had gotten into any trouble overnight. No running away on an unsolicited fishing trip for Ryan. No more vaping for Olivia in the last ten hours . . . well, that she knew of anyway.

Mercifully both of her children were currently sleeping in, but a good night's rest had eluded her. Every time she closed her eyes, she flashed back to the moment she'd kissed Wes. And the moment he'd stared at her before kissing her back. Despite her best efforts, she couldn't read his expression in her memories. Had he been shocked? Disgusted? The way he'd kissed her back, it sure didn't seem like it, but that was always a possibility.

"It doesn't matter," she told herself as she dumped too much vanilla-flavored creamer into the coffee. "Nothing can happen any—"

"Who are you talking to?"

Ryan's sleepy voice made her whirl, and her coffee swooshed up over the sides of the mug.

"Hey, little man." She swiped a paper towel so she could mop up the mess on the floor and hide her blazing red face. She was seriously losing it. Kissing random men, talking to herself in the kitchen. It was almost like she'd become someone else the second she stepped onto the ranch's property. You'd think she was in Vegas or something.

"Who were you talking to?" Ryan asked again, pulling himself onto a stool at the small bar on the other side of the counter. He still had his teddy dangling from one hand, and his hair was mussed over to one side.

As always, the sight of him in the morning melted her heart. "I'm talking to myself," she admitted. Might as well let the kids in on the fact that their cautious, responsible, always put-together mother had started to lose her carefully organized marbles.

"I do that sometimes too." Her son always seemed to know what to say to make her feel better. "Sometimes I listen the best to myself."

And sometimes she didn't know how to listen to herself. Or, rather, which voice to listen to. There seemed to be two different voices guiding her thoughts and actions right now—rational Thea, whom she liked the best, and then this other side of her, whom she wasn't sure what to do with.

The memory hit again. Good lord, she'd kissed Wes...

"I wonder if Wes is up yet." Her son yawned. "I want to go fishing."

Was Wes an early riser? Was he already in the shower?

She shook her head. *Nope, nope, nope.* That was not a rational thought. "You can't go fishing, sweetness." She set down her coffee and walked over to plant a kiss on that sleepy bedhead. "We've got a full schedule today." Somehow, she said the words without groaning. Had she even slept at all? "We have breakfast." Which was already in T-minus thirty-two minutes. "And then we're boating and tubing." And, if she got her way, she would be watching from the beach while she caught a nap. "Then, after lunch we have to work on the float for the parade." Because they didn't already have enough going on, Wes had added in a whole new activity.

"Yes! The parade float." Ryan hopped off the stool, all bright eyed and bushy tailed. "I'm so excited. That's gonna be fun. Maybe me and Wes can go fishing tomorrow then."

"Maybe." Thea hid her concern with a smile. "Or the next day. You have more than a week, you know." Except she hadn't forgotten how Wes had disappeared yesterday morning after promising to go over the trip details with her. He had a busy life. She didn't hold that against him, but it might be a good idea to come up with a plan B. "If Wes can't take you for some reason, I would be happy to find a special fishing hole, just the two of us."

In fact, maybe her son would want to stay back from the overnight camping experience to fish with her. Thea resisted the urge to propose the idea. He deserved to go to the camp and have a little adventure. She'd simply find something else to keep her busy. Nothing wrong with a little alone time, right? Sure, the older the kids got, the more alone time she seemed to have on her hands—that's how it was supposed to be. They'd go to sleepovers or camps or special school excursions while she missed them like crazy and roamed the house, unsure of what to do with herself.

Olivia's words came echoing back to her. *I don't want to be like you.* She didn't blame the girl one bit.

"Mom, Wes is going to take me fishing," her son announced, cutting through her internal drama. "I know he will. He promised."

It amazed her how a promise still meant so much to Ryan, even after Dylan had broken so many of them. Where did that hope come from? That resilience? She wished she could find it for herself. "Okay, honey." What else could she say? Nothing. She only had to hope Wes would follow through. She should have a conversation with the man. Of course a conversation would mean being close to him again, looking into his eyes, both of which were dangerous prospects.

A door down the hall opened, and Thea scurried back to her coffee, already bracing herself. By the time she and Ryan had made it back to the cabin last night, her daughter was pretending to be asleep, and she'd let it go. Thea had had enough scenes for one night. But she couldn't ignore the situation forever.

"Good morning," Olivia sang as she traipsed into the kitchen with her ponytail flouncing.

Thea stared at her wide-eyed. Dare she answer with a *Good morning*?

"I'm starving." Her daughter went to the empty refrigerator and pulled it open as though she expected food to magically appear. "What's for breakfast?"

It took her a few seconds to respond. At least the girl hadn't come out of her room swinging. "Something delicious, if Louise has anything to say about it." She tried to keep the surprise out of her tone. This seemed to be how things went with her teen daughter lately. One minute the whole entire world was falling apart, and the next everything was sunshine and roses. It was all she could do to keep up. "Speaking of breakfast, we should head up there." In the past, she'd always liked to arrive at the group events early so she could help Mara and Louise set up. But this year, she would have to spend that time clearing the air with Wes and denouncing that kiss as the mistake it was so things wouldn't be awkward between them for the whole retreat. She would make sure to stand a few feet away from him and avoid his magnetic eyes so he couldn't put her under his spell again.

"I hope Louise is making her French toast." Olivia pulled on a sweatshirt by the door.

"And that yummy cinnamon sauce!" Ryan bounded past Thea and bolted outside, always needing to be first everywhere. Normally, Thea would've called on him to wait up, but she could use this moment alone with Liv. As much as she'd like to pretend everything was peachy, she couldn't ignore what had happened last night, not when there was self-destructive behavior involved.

She stepped outside behind her daughter, and even she had

to admit it was hard to believe things weren't all sunshine and roses when you were being greeted by that view. Everything in Colorado seemed brighter in the mornings. The sun was already well over the eastern horizon, illuminating everything it touched—the rocky peaks, the glistening evergreens, the azure surface of the lake. The brisk chill might've been the thing she loved best about the mountains. It made everything feel fresh and new—pure and clean instead of stagnant. And she was about to ruin it all.

"Hey, Liv." She hurried to walk alongside her daughter. "We need to talk about last night."

"Do we have to?" There was the mutter she knew and loved.

"Yes." Thea moved to put her arm around her. "We have to. Because I love you and I want the best for you."

"Yeah, yeah, yeah." A small smile perked up her daughter's lips.

Thea pulled her to a stop, letting Ryan run up the hill ahead of them. "I'm still thinking of an appropriate consequence." That she likely wouldn't make her serve until they went home. "And I'm keeping your phone for the rest of the retreat."

"That's fine. You can keep my phone." Her daughter's gaze dove to the ground. Yeah, she seemed pretty embarrassed. "Preston hates me anyway. It's not like he'll be texting me anytime soon."

"Actually..." Thea paused, wondering if she should tell her. Aw, what the heck? It would make her smile. "Preston has texted you three times since last night asking if you're okay."

"Really?" Hope lit Liv's lovely eyes. God, when had her daughter grown up so much? It stunned her every time she looked into those eyes.

"Really." Thea slipped her arm around Liv and kept walking. "Seems to me you don't have to try so hard to impress him. He already likes you and wants to be your friend."

Her daughter nodded, giving her mother a timid glance. "I'm sorry."

"I know you are." She inhaled deeply, grasping at wisdom as they climbed the steps to the porch. What she said now mattered.

In the heat of the moment, Liv might not have heard her, but she was listening now. "The thing that matters most, honey, is how you see yourself. Not how other people see you."

Like Wes had said, everyone wanted to be important to someone, but you couldn't build a relationship on trying to be who someone else wanted you to be. Thea had learned that when she'd married Dylan. She'd tried to make him happy by giving him space, not giving him a hard time when he wanted to go out with his friends instead of spending an evening with her. She'd tried being more positive around him, and when that didn't work, she'd been quieter. It didn't matter what she did—how she changed—it was never good enough to fix their problems.

"It's okay to make mistakes." Lord knew she'd made plenty. In some ways, her daughter's mistakes were every bit as important as her victories. "But you need to learn from them. You are smart and fun-loving and incredibly thoughtful. Anyone would be lucky to have you as a friend just as you are."

They paused outside the lodge's main entrance, and her daughter seemed to shrink a couple of inches. "I'm sorry for what I said about you not having a life." The words came with a wobble of sincerity.

"It's okay." She'd been speaking the truth. "I can take it. And I know you didn't mean to hurt me." Despite the extra layers of attitude the teen years had added to her daughter's personality, she knew the same sweet, compassionate Olivia still lived in there, too, and she was grateful she got to see glimpses of her heart.

They passed through the lodge's grand entrance and walked through the great room into the dining area, where Louise and Ryan were putting flowers in the vases.

"Good morning, you two." The woman greeted them both with hugs, which were every bit as welcoming and cheerful as the mountain daisies on the table.

"I'm helping Louise," Ryan informed them importantly, standing three more daisies in a small glass vase.

"And you're doing a great job." Louise laid a hand on his shoulder affectionately, seeming to admire his work. "I might have to hire you on for the rest of the summer."

"Yes!" Ryan skedaddled to the next table, taking his job even more seriously with all of them watching.

"My goodness," Louise murmured, looking Olivia over. "It looks like someone got her beauty sleep. I swear, you get prettier and prettier every year."

Liv beamed at the compliment. "Thanks, Miss Louise."

"You take after your mama." She turned her attention to Thea. "You are positively glowing this morning."

That made her laugh. "That's nice of you to say." But after the vaping situation and the kiss, she would call her look haggard. Speaking of the kiss... "Is Wes—"

"Eggs, coming through."

Thea turned expecting to see Wes, but instead, his brother came hurrying into the dining room carrying a large silver basin with scrambled eggs. He set it on the buffet table and readjusted the cover before turning to them with a grin that closely resembled his younger brother's. Though their features were different, and August had much darker hair, he and Wes had the same chin, and... also the same mouth.

Oh, Wes's mouth...

Her knees softened the way they had when he'd kissed her back last night, giving her the sensation of floating.

"Thanks much, Auggie." Louise bustled to the buffet table, where the French toast and fruit were already set out. "You've been a savior in the kitchen this morning," she clucked like a proud mother hen. "I don't know how we've been managing without you around here for so long."

"And I don't know how I've been managing without your chocolate chip cookies," the man replied. Everything about August appeared polished and refined, from his styled hair to his chinos. And yet, he didn't seem pretentious or insincere, just... savvy. After what Wes had shared with her last night about the dynamics in their family, she could easily see the vast differences between the brothers.

"Everyone else will be up soon." Louise waved the kids over to the table. "So you two had best get the first serving of French toast while the getting's good." She handed each of them a plate.

"Is there anything I can help you with this morning?" August approached Thea with the ease of an old friend, even though she'd only met him last night. "I'm here to make sure your group has everything you need," he went on. "We want to make sure you all have a superb experience here at the Silverado Lake Ranch."

"That's great. Thanks." Thea tried to contain her frown. Wasn't it Wes's job to make sure they had everything they needed? She glanced around but saw no sign of August's brother. Of the man she'd kissed. Her cheeks warmed all over again. Maybe that's why he'd made himself scarce this morning. Or maybe he'd left. Maybe he didn't want to see her.

Oh, this was torture. This wondering and awkwardness. She had to fix things now. "Is Wes around?" she asked, doing her best to keep her expression even. Was he truly hiding from her?

"He's around." August glanced out the windows to their left. "Right now, he's getting the boat ready for tubing." The man chuckled. "But knowing him, he'll be out of here soon."

"Out of here?" She tried to wrangle the surprise from her tone. "Is he leaving the ranch?" Before he took Ryan fishing? She glanced at her son, who looked to be talking Louise's ear off.

"He's got work stuff going on," August told her. "But don't worry. That's why Jane asked me to stay at the ranch for a few extra days. I can take care of everything you need."

No, he couldn't. He couldn't take care of her son's disappointment. Just that morning Ryan had been so sure Wes wouldn't let him down. "I appreciate that." She hoped her smile wasn't as plastic as it felt. "I thought Wes said he was staying for the whole retreat." Somehow, she managed to make the words sound casual.

August laughed again. "You know Wes. He's all over the place. He never stays around anywhere long."

"Right." She *should've* known that. She'd experienced his disappearing act once before. But Wes wasn't a cocky kid anymore. She'd seen glimpses of his good and loyal heart, especially in the way he interacted with her son, the way he'd handled the situation with Liv last night. Surely he would've told her if he was planning to leave. And, more importantly, he should have prepared Ryan for that possibility.

"There's the rest of the group." August scooted away from her and opened the door for the Hershbergers, followed by everyone else.

"Good morning!" Kelly beelined right for Thea and linked their arms together.

She hardly had time to greet her friend back before Kelly dragged her to a quieter corner.

"So, maybe it's just me, but it sure seemed like Ryan and I might've interrupted something between you and Wes last night."

"It wasn't like that." The lie sizzled in her throat. It shouldn't have been like that. It wouldn't have been like that if she hadn't lost her ever-loving mind for those few seconds. See? This is why she'd steered clear of men. She didn't know what to think about Wes right now. When they were alone, standing close, she felt this strong connection to him. But it wasn't a guarantee. With Wes, there were no guarantees.

"Oh, come on." Kelly's frown told Thea she didn't buy one word of that explanation. "I saw the way you two were looking at each other. How long have you known him?"

"I don't really know him." She had to keep reminding herself of that, no matter what he made her feel.

"Coulda fooled me," Kelly said with a giggle.

Thea couldn't even bring herself to smile. Her stomach was turning over. Why had she let herself open up to the man? Why had she gone and kissed him? "There was an incident with Olivia, and it got a little intense, that's all." She had been the one who'd gone and turned it into more. That was her mistake.

"He's pretty good-looking," her friend prompted, elbowing her gently in the ribs.

"Mmm-hmm." Wes's good looks were no secret. But good looks didn't make a man. She'd learned that the hard way too. "He's also my good friend's brother." And he had no staying power.

She'd rather not explore why that bothered her so much.

Chapter Ten

Wes steered the boat toward the shoreline, scanning the beach where all the families had gathered. Some of the dads had started a game of volleyball with a few of the older kids, including Olivia and Preston, so all seemed to be well there. A couple of the moms were sitting on the lounge chairs, but where was—

"Wes!" Ryan caught his gaze from the other side of the boat shed. The boy jumped up and down, waving his arms, but it was Thea who captured his attention.

She looked even more gorgeous than she had last night, wearing a white gauzy swimsuit cover-up. She'd pulled her soft brown hair into a messy bun on top of her head, and some loose tendrils had escaped and were moving in the breeze.

"Can I be first on the tube?" Ryan begged. "Me and my friend Timothy want to go first!"

Wes downshifted the boat and then put it in neutral as it drifted into the shallow water near where they stood. He had to remind himself to take his eyes off of Thea, but that was difficult to do when she had been all he'd thought about for the last twelve hours. He'd hoped to make it up to breakfast so he could try to catch a minute alone with her, but getting the boat motor running had proved to be more challenging than he'd estimated. "Sure, you can go first," he finally called to the boy. None of the other kids had lined up on the shore to wait, so at least there would be no arguments.

His gaze drifted back to Thea again, but she had turned her head as though she didn't want to look back.

"I'll need a spotter to go in the boat with me." Maybe that would give them a minute alone to discuss what, exactly, had happened last night. Even though he'd been there, he was still having a hard time believing Thea Davis had kissed him. More than that, he was having a hard time forgetting what her soft lips had done to him. She might've claimed the whole thing was a mistake, but he held no regrets. No regrets about kissing her back, no regrets about wrapping his arms around her and holding her close. What he needed to know was if she truly regretted it.

"Mom'll come in the boat." Ryan grabbed his mom's hand and dragged her to wade into the water.

"My mom'll come too," Timothy said, waving Kelly over.

"Sounds good." Wes hid his disappointment behind a smile. He'd be lucky to find a few minutes alone with Thea at all with everything else going on.

"Come on, Mom," Timothy called, already wading toward the boat.

Wes hopped out where the water went up to his board shorts and pushed the boat to turn it around.

Ryan splashed his way over, and Wes easily lifted him into the boat. When he turned around, Thea stood right in front of him.

"Good morning." His gaze fell into hers, and for the life of him he couldn't tear it away from her.

"Hi." Her voice seemed to have a breathless quality he'd never noticed before. She looked like she wanted to say something more, but again they were interrupted.

"Let's go!" Ryan called behind them.

Right. He had to move. It wasn't just him and Thea standing here. "Here. Let me put the step down." He could lift her into the boat, too, but it might be best if he didn't take her in his arms right now. Instead, he lowered the step and offered her his hand. The touch zinged all the way through him.

"Thank you," Thea murmured, stepping over the edge of the boat and sitting next to her son. She looked like a goddess sitting there on the seat, the high-altitude sun making her skin glow.

"We're next," Timothy reminded him, approaching the boat with his mom.

"Welcome aboard." Wes lifted him into the boat and then helped Kelly up the step.

"Nice boat," she commented, sitting across from Thea. "I bet it can go really fast." She winked at Timothy and Ryan, who were now wedged together in a seat near the bow of the boat.

"Yes!" Ryan jumped to his feet. "We want to go super-duper fast! Faster than fast!"

"We'll see." Thea peeked at Wes, but it was like she had some shield up in her eyes. "We should probably start slow and let them test it out. Ryan has never been tubing. That isn't something we usually do while we're here."

Wes pushed the boat out deeper and then hopped in over the side. "He's going to love it. They both are." He had no doubt. Riding on the tube while his father drove him around with the boat had been one of his absolute favorite memories. "But I'll start out slow. Promise." Within five minutes, the boys would likely be yelling at him to go faster, but he would let them decide. "All right, everyone. Hold on." He sat down behind the wheel and started the motor up again before putting the boat into gear. "The tube's already hooked up, but we need to get out a little deeper before you can climb on."

He steered the boat to the middle of the lake and then put the motor in neutral again. "So, Ryan and Timothy are up first?"

"Well, I'm sure as heck not getting on that thing," Kelly said, snapping a picture of the boys on her phone.

"Me neither." Thea seemed to have relaxed a little more. Her smile had come back, and she leaned her head against the headrest as though she wanted the sun to kiss her face.

Wes turned his attention to removing the tube off the back shelf of the boat and setting it on the water. "Ready, boys?"

"I am!" Ryan swatted at his mother's hand as she tried to apply more sunscreen to his nose.

"Hold on there, Sport. Gotta protect your skin from the sun." Wes reached for his own hat to shade his face. At this elevation a sunburn could seriously sneak up on you.

"I don't know if I wanna go. It looks kinda scary." Timothy eyed the tube in the water and stayed right where he was.

"It won't be scary," Ryan argued. "It'll be fun! We'll do it together." He walked over to his friend and reached for his hand, but Timothy didn't budge.

"That's okay." Thea slipped the sunscreen back into the pocket of her swimsuit cover-up. "Timothy doesn't have to go if he doesn't want to."

"Maybe if he saw you go first," Wes suggested to Ryan, though he'd rather have someone else on the tube with the boy for more weight. He'd have to make sure to go nice and slow...

"Or you could come with me, Mom. Please?" Ryan clasped his hands together. "It would be soooo fun! I don't wanna go by myself."

Thea shot Wes a look like she was begging for help. But unfortunately he said, "I have to drive the boat." So he couldn't bail her out this time.

"Please, Mom. Please, please, please?" Ryan begged.

"You sure you don't want to go first, Timmy?" Kelly was obviously trying to give Thea an out, but Wes could see the younger boy wasn't about to get on that tube right now.

The kid tipped up his chin and swung his head side to side in a definite no.

"It's okay. I'll go with you, Ryan." To Thea's credit, she didn't groan or even sound the least bit put out. That only made Wes like her more.

She slipped the cover-up off over her head, and Wes found himself unable to move or breathe again. There was nothing remarkable about the hot-pink one-piece swimsuit she wore, but she was striking—her curves and the contours of her body, the softness of her skin.

"You'd better not dump me in that freezing-cold lake." She pointed a finger at Wes in warning.

"I won't dump you." He would never do anything she didn't want him to. Just like last night, when she'd rested her head on his chest, he had this overwhelming desire to stand with her, to protect her, to take away some of her burden.

"Okay then." The woman took a deep breath and straightened up her shoulders while she stared at the tube.

"You're awesome," Kelly told her, slipping her arm around Timothy. "See, if Mrs. Davis can do it, so can you, buddy."

"I haven't done anything yet." Thea slipped on a life jacket, which reminded Wes. "Hey, buddy." He walked over to Ryan. "Let me make sure your life vest is good and tight." He checked the buckles and straps to be sure it wasn't going anywhere.

"Can we go now?" Ryan wriggled like a beached trout.

"You sure can. As long as your mom is ready." If he hadn't been standing so close to Thea, Wes might've missed the hesitation in her eyes. Once again, everyone else faded into the background. How could the woman's eyes tell him so much? He hardly knew her.

"I'm ready." Surprisingly, Thea didn't look away from him either.

"Just tell me what you want." He still didn't break their stare. "Thumbs up to go faster. Thumbs down to go slower. And if you're ready to bail on the whole thing, give a good holler."

"Got it." She took another deep breath.

Wes grabbed the rope attached to the tube and pulled it up next to the boat. Ryan leapt on, nearly spilling himself into the lake in the process, and then Wes held the thing steady so Thea could climb on too.

As she went to step over the side, she lost her balance and swayed. Wes secured his hands to her waist to steady her and helped her ease down onto the tube.

"Whoa." Thea lowered to her knees and lay down on her stomach while Ryan settled in next to her. The kid smiled a lot, but Wes had never seen his smile get quite that big.

"This is gonna be the best thing ever," Ryan declared, grinning up at his mom like she was his hero.

Wes couldn't imagine what it would be like to grieve a spouse while trying to be there for your kids and help them move forward. Not to mention becoming the sole guardian, decision-maker, and provider. And yet anyone who watched her could see Thea lived for her kids. Even with Olivia's acting out, she loved her mom; Wes could see it in the way she responded to her.

"We're ready," Ryan sang.

"Are we?" his mother asked, nudging her elbow gently into his ribs.

The boy giggled. "Yes! Let's go!"

"Aye aye, captain." Wes got behind the wheel again and put the gear into drive. He eased the boat forward, keeping an eye on the tube as the line unraveled. "Timothy, my man…you have a very important job." He gestured for the younger boy to sit in the seat next to him. "I need you to keep your eyes on those two while I focus on driving the boat. If one of them falls off, yell at me to stop. Got it?"

The boy nodded slowly, his eyes wide. "Do ya think they'll fall off?" He cast a wary glance at the tube, which was now slowly dragging behind the boat.

"Nah. But keep an eye on them just in case." Hopefully watching them would show him how much fun the tube could be.

The boy nodded again and rose to his knees like he was taking his job very seriously.

With one hand on the wheel, Wes peered over his shoulder. "Ready?" he called above the motor's rattle.

"Ready!" Ryan screamed.

"Hold on!" Wes pushed the lever and increased the speed, doing his best to ease into it. He steered in a straight line, keeping his eyes ahead minus a few glances in the rearview mirror. From the looks of things, the two of them were holding on. "How're they doing back there, Timothy?"

"They're doin' real good." The boy watched with a wide grin. "It looks kinda fun."

"It does look kind of fun." Kelly was watching Ryan and Thea, too, and snapping some pictures.

"I think they want you to go faster." Timothy moved higher on his knees. "Yep! They're giving a thumbs-up. I see it."

"Faster?" Wes turned to gauge the truth of that statement. Sure enough, both Thea and Ryan were holding on with one hand and giving the thumbs-up sign with the other. And their heads were tipped back while they laughed like they were having the time of their lives. He watched for a second and then found himself laughing too. "All right. Faster it is."

Wes cranked the speed up a few notches, watching in the rearview mirror.

Ryan got onto his knees on the tube and raised a fist in the air, whooping and hollering. "Circles! Wanna go in circles!"

Wes could hardly hear him with the wind whistling all around them.

"They want you to go in circles," Timothy informed him dutifully.

Wes hesitated. It got much harder to hold on when the boat went in circles. Instead of going for it, he slowed the boat and carefully turned into a slow, gentle circle so he could pull up right along the tube. "You sure you want circles?"

"Yes!" Ryan tapped his mom's shoulder until she agreed.

"Yes. Fast circles, apparently," Thea said with a laugh. Her face glistened with the spray of the water.

"Okay." He drew the word out, giving her the chance to change her mind. "Make sure you hold on real tight. That water's cold."

"Oh, don't worry. I'm holding on," Thea assured him.

"Me too!" Ryan secured both hands on the handles and scooted closer to his mom. She planted a kiss on his forehead, and Wes pulled his phone out of his pocket to take a picture. He couldn't resist. They'd created a near-perfect moment.

"Normally I don't allow pictures of me in my swimming suit," Thea said. "But since I'm wearing a life jacket, I'll let it slide."

Wes grinned. "I'll text it to you and then delete it. I promise." He slipped the phone back into his pocket. "All right, you two. Hold on to your hats." He steered the boat away to make the line taut and then gave one last glance back before he accelerated. This time, both Ryan and Thea whooped.

"I can't believe she's doing this." Kelly watched the tube, shaking her head with a smile. "Someone needs to give that woman a mother of the year award."

Wes couldn't agree more.

"They're having fun," Timothy told him. "That looks really fun. I'll go next!"

"All right." Wes gave the boy a high five. "Get ready for our first circle." He cranked the wheel to the right, glancing in the rearview mirror. Both Ryan and Thea had flattened themselves on the tube, still holding on tight, and they were cracking up.

"This is the best!" Ryan's shout sounded faint.

Wes kept the circle going, bouncing his gaze between the rearview mirror and the surface of the lake in front of them.

"Look at those waves!" Kelly stood up slightly, snapping more pictures.

"Yeah, those are from the boat." Things were about to get bumpy for Ryan and Thea. He slowed the speed a little so they wouldn't fly off the tube as the waves thudded against the side of the boat.

"Look at them!" Timothy collapsed into giggles. "They're bouncing!"

They sure were. Wes kept an eye on the rearview mirror and slowed even more.

"Faster," Ryan yelled. "We wanna go faster!"

Making sure the water in front of them was clear, Wes turned fully around to see Thea. She gave him a thumbs-up.

He couldn't help but laugh a little himself. She did seem to be having fun. The woman was definitely a trouper. Wes continued to steer the boat into a donut, hitting more waves. He could hear Thea laughing without even turning around.

"I wanna go!" Timothy watched with wide eyes. "I'm not afraid!"

"You can have a turn next," Kelly told him. She looked at Wes. "But I'd like to stay in the boat."

"It's actually fun." Wes trained his eyes on the rearview mirror again. Ryan and Thea hit some more waves, catching a little bit of air. The tube ricocheted, and Wes slowed, knowing what was coming. One side of the tube touched down to the water and flipped, catapulting both Thea and Ryan into the lake.

"They fell in!" Timothy screeched. "Oh no! Are they okay?"

"They'll be fine." Wes cranked the wheel, his eyes searching the water. There! They were both bobbing on the surface only a few feet away from the tube. He slowed the boat to a crawl and approached them. "You two okay?" They had to be freezing.

"Yes!" Ryan hugged his mom. "That was the best wipeout in the history of wipeouts."

"Can't argue with that." Wes tried to gauge what Thea was thinking, but she was turned away from him. "Let me help you into the boat." He put the motor in neutral and put down the ladder at the back while they swam toward him.

"Whew!" Thea reached the boat, and he could finally see her face. Her smile had never looked brighter. "That was an adventure."

"You two were amazing." He helped Ryan up the ladder and then reached for Thea's hand. "You okay?" he asked, hoping to God she wasn't just pretending to be okay for Ryan's sake.

"Never been better." The smile on her face, the shine in her eyes, the droplets of water glistening on her skin all drew him in, and he knew.

He was a goner.

Chapter Eleven

Thea wrapped another towel around her shoulders, doing her best to stop her teeth from chattering.

"You're cold." Wes eyed her with concern from the driver's seat of the boat.

"Only a little." But she hadn't wanted to end the fun. For the last hour, she and Kelly had been riding around on the boat with Ryan, Timothy, and Wes while they pulled different groups of kids on the tube. Her son had absolutely come alive on the water, with the wind in his hair and the sun beaming on his face. But, yes, with her swimming suit still wet and the increase in the wind, the chill was starting to seep into her bones.

"Tell you what..." Wes slowed the boat's speed. "Lunch should be just about ready, and we're almost out of gas, so we'll call it a day."

"Aw, man." Ryan pouted. "I wanted another ride on the tube."

"How about you drive the boat instead?" Wes asked, vacating the driver's seat.

"Really? You'd let me drive?" Judging from the look on her son's face, Wes had just surpassed idol status and progressed to full-on superhero status.

The worry Thea had managed to suppress with the laughter and fun of the last hour clouded her happiness. She understood that Wes had a job and responsibilities, but Ryan was going to be devastated if the man left early. That had to be the source of the disappointment she felt still lingering since her conversation with August earlier. It wasn't because *she* wanted Wes to stay for the whole time.

"Sure you can drive." The man waved her son to him and sat him in the driver's seat. "It's easy. Just push this lever to go a little faster and pull it back to go slower." Wes showed Ryan the ropes and then stepped back. "And make sure you steer too."

Her son seemed to be too excited to sit down. Instead, he stood in front of the driver's seat with his hands on the wheel. "Wow! Can I go *a little* faster?"

"Only a little." Wes stood right behind him as though he was ready to step in if needed.

Ryan moved the lever forward and the boat picked up speed. The extra blast of wind chilled Thea all over again.

"Doing a great job there, Ryan." Kelly took a picture on her phone. Thank goodness someone was taking pictures. Thea's hands were so cold she wasn't sure she would be able to pry them off of the towels she was holding around her.

"All right, slow her down now," Wes instructed. "Do you want a turn, Timothy?"

The younger boy shook his head.

"Then Ryan can bring us home." Wes rested a hand on her son's shoulder, and while it melted her heart, the gesture also made her as cautious as Timothy. As much as she'd like to forget what August had told her, she couldn't.

"Steer us toward that dock there so you all can climb out." Wes pointed out the wooden platform near the boat shed.

Her son stuck out his tongue slightly the way he always did when he was concentrating. "Like this?" He put the motor back into trolling speed and made a slight turn toward the dock.

"I think you're a better driver than me." Wes laughed.

Ryan laughed too. "No way! You're the best. You're the best at everything."

Thea shared a look with Kelly. Over the last hour, her friend seemed to have been watching her closely. Surely, she could detect the hesitations in Thea's expression, one mom to another.

As the boat drew near the dock, Wes gestured for Ryan to move over. "Let me help you steer us in. It can be a little tricky to pull up right next to the dock." He showed Ryan how to maneuver the boat and parked at the end of the platform, quickly hooking the rope to a pole. "Great job, captain." He shook Ryan's hand and then stepped out of the boat and onto the dock. "Everyone is now free to disembark."

Thea moved slowly, unraveling herself from the towels, her muscles stiff with cold. Kelly and Timothy stepped out of the boat first, Wes offering each of them a hand.

"Come on, buddy." Thea put her arm around Ryan. "Let's go change out of our wet clothes so we can head up to lunch."

"I'm not wet. I'm all dry." He threw on the brakes and showed her his Spider-Man swim trunks. "I want to stay with Wes."

Of course he did. He wouldn't want to leave the man's side for the rest of the retreat. "I'm sure he's busy—"

"He can stay and help me if he wants," Wes interrupted. "I'm just going to pull the boat out of the water and leave it on the trailer."

"Can I, Mom? Pretty please with extra sugar on top?" It wasn't fair when Ryan rounded his eyes like that. "You can go change and be right back and then we can go to lunch."

Wasn't he just the little planner? Thea sighed. He'd be bored while she got herself showered and dressed anyway. "I suppose you can stay." She focused only on her son. Not on Wes with his expressive eyes and tanned muscular forearms and his broad shoulders under that tattered T-shirt he wore. When she looked at him, it was hard to remember that kiss last night had been a mistake. It was hard to remember much of anything. But someone had to keep their wits about them when that man was around, and it sure wasn't going to be her son. "But you'd better listen good and be a big helper."

"I'm the biggest helper," Ryan assured her.

"He is," Wes agreed, taking her hand to help her step out of the boat. Geez, with as much electricity as she felt at that slight touch, you'd think she'd grabbed a firework.

"How about you meet us right back here at the dock when you're done, and we'll walk up to lunch together?"

Together. Had his voice lowered a smidge when he'd said that word?

"Sounds good." She avoided looking into his eyes so she didn't get sucked into the alternate universe Wes tempted her to visit. "Maybe you two will even have time to fish like you talked about." If Ryan got in some good fishing time with Wes now, maybe he wouldn't be devastated when the man left.

"We're not planning to fish in the lake." Her son grinned up at his hero. "Right, Wes? We're going to a supersecret fishing hole to fish all day long."

"All day?" She had no choice but to look into Wes's eyes to get a read on how he felt about that.

"I don't know about all day, but for a few hours for sure." Wes's gaze lowered to her lips. "If you're okay with that. I was thinking we could go after the kids get back from camp."

"Yes! That works. Right, Mom?" Ryan bounced up and down, shaking the dock.

Would it work? If Wes stayed around. She stared directly at him, looking for any hesitation. "It's fine with me, as long as you're sure you can take the time."

"Absolutely." The man gave her son a high five. "It's a plan."

"Can't wait! Bye, Mom!" Ryan hopped back into the boat and situated himself in the driver's seat. Apparently, she wasn't going to get a hug out of him.

"Bye, sweetie." She blew him a kiss instead. "I'll see you in about twenty minutes." Depending on how long it took her to thaw out in the shower.

"See you then," Wes called, climbing back into the boat.

"Mmm-hmm." And at some point, she would have to do more than see him. They had to talk about things alone. About the kiss and about the possibility of him leaving now that August had come.

Releasing a sigh, Thea made her way to the sandy shoreline, where Kelly stood waiting for her with a perceptive smirk. "That was quite the fun morning, huh?"

Timothy ran up ahead of them, kicking a soccer ball he'd found on the beach.

Thea pretended to be enamored with the scenery. "It was fun. But I'll be fine if I never have to get on a tube again." However, she would if her son asked her to. She'd do anything to spend time with him, to bond with him. Thea glanced over her shoulder. Ryan had taken the wheel in the boat again. Wes leaned down next to him, pointing something out. Surely his brother had been wrong about Wes leaving. The man sincerely seemed to enjoy spending time with Ryan. He wouldn't promise a fishing trip the morning after camp if he was planning to leave, would he?

"Ryan sure likes Wes, huh?" Kelly fell in step beside her.

"Yeah." Even to her the word sounded weighted.

Her friend seemed to assess her face. "You don't seem too happy about that."

"It's not that I'm not happy." She paused, trying to figure out how to explain it without telling Kelly about how Wes had ditched her way back when. That had happened years ago, after all. She wanted to believe he'd changed. Still, she couldn't seem to move past her doubts. "Ryan has big expectations, that's all. And he tends to get his heart broken easily." He hadn't learned how to guard himself yet. When he liked someone, he was all in, and that would only set him up for some serious disappointment in life.

Kelly turned to face her. "What makes you think he'll get his heart broken?"

She thought back to her conversation with August again. "Wes isn't exactly a grounded, rooted person." He practically lived on the road. "And we'll have to go home eventually." She could see Ryan's tears about leaving now. It would likely take an hour to get him into the car for the long drive back.

Kelly leaned closer, a glimmer of mischief in her eyes. "You sure it's Ryan's heart you're worried about?"

A defensive heat rushed to her face. "What's that supposed to mean?"

Her friend raised her arms in a surrendering shrug. "Look, I know it's not my place to say much. I haven't been through everything you've been through. I know you loved Dylan."

The words grated against Thea's heart, rehashing old wounds that would never fully heal over. She *should've* loved Dylan, but she'd given up on him. And when he died, she'd given up on love.

"But it's okay to move on if you're ready," Kelly went on. "Wes seems like a great guy. He's funny and seems kind. He's great with the kids." Her smile widened. "And he sure seems to care about you."

Why would he care about her? "He's only watching out for me because I'm Jane's friend." And then she'd gone and complicated her feelings by kissing him . . .

"I'm not so sure." Kelly took out her phone and started to flip through pictures. "If he wasn't watching the water in front of us or the kids on the tube, his eyes were on you." She held out the phone to show Thea a picture. It did appear that Wes was looking at her, but you couldn't see exactly where his eyes were focused with those dark sunglasses on. "He was watching you the whole time. Even when I was talking."

"I was sitting right where he had to look when he wanted to see the tube." And, yes, he'd looked at her a lot. She'd looked at him a lot, too, but it couldn't be helped. They'd shared a few moments. Nice moments. Intense moments. Moments that had eased her loneliness. But a few moments didn't add up to a potential for commitment. A few moments didn't change the fact that she couldn't bear to let the marks of regret on her heart show. They went too deep.

"Whatever you say." Kelly started to walk away. "I'm going to change. We'll see you at lunch."

"See you there." Thea turned in the opposite direction to head to her cabin, waving at Olivia, who was playing another beach volleyball game with some of the older kids.

Not wanting to keep Ryan and Wes waiting, she hurried back to the cabin and showered and dressed, only spending ten minutes debating what to wear in front of her closet. Jean shorts and casual flowered shirt would be the perfect outfit to work on the parade float this afternoon. Maybe she'd be able to catch a moment alone with Wes then so she could come out and ask him if he was leaving. For Ryan's sake, of course. She didn't do well with uncertainty.

After quickly blow-drying her hair and applying light makeup so it wouldn't look like she was trying too hard, she hurried out the door and wandered back to the boathouse. Before she rounded the corner, she heard Ryan talking.

"Sometimes I really miss my dad."

The words stopped Thea cold. She wasn't sure if she should be hurt that he wasn't talking to her or relieved that he was talking to someone. She crept closer to the edge of the building to listen.

"I know what you mean," Wes said. "I miss my dad too."

"Do you think my dad's mad at me?" Ryan's voice grew quieter.

"Mad at you?" Wes sounded as shocked as she had been the first time Ryan asked her that question. She'd talked it over with him so many times, but he obviously still thought about the day Dylan had called shortly before his death.

"I didn't talk to him on the phone," her son told Wes. "Before he died. I was outside playing, and I didn't want to come in to talk to him on the phone."

Her heart starting to crumble, Thea peered around the corner. Wes and Ryan were sitting at the edge of the small dock with their legs dangling over the side.

"He's not mad at you," Wes told her son.

Ryan turned his face to Wes's. "How do you know?"

Thea had to stop herself from interrupting. This was a conversation Ryan should be having with her. Not with someone he'd only met two days ago...

"Because if I know one thing about dads, it's that they want their kids to be happy. That's what my dad always said to me." The words kept Thea where she stood. That's why Ryan was talking to Wes about this. He knew he'd lost his dad too.

"Were you happy playing outside?" the man asked.

"Yeah. I was having fun playing with my friends." The same guilt she'd heard before edged into the words. Even though she'd told him time and again he couldn't hold on to the guilt, he couldn't feel bad for something he didn't know would happen, that was the question Ryan always came back to.

Her son's struggle seemed to mimic her own. She didn't know Dylan would die. If she would've, things might've been different.

"Then I think your dad would be happy too." Wes patted Ryan's shoulder.

"My dad wasn't happy very much. He got mad a lot."

What? Oh, God. Why would he tell Wes that? Thea came fully around the corner but was too late to stop him from continuing.

"My dad fought with my mom a lot."

She stopped again, her face blazing.

The revelation didn't seem to fluster Wes the way it did her. "That's pretty normal," he said calmly. "My mom and dad got mad at each other sometimes, but they still loved each other."

She closed her eyes. She had to stop this conversation before Ryan told him everything. She hadn't even realized he'd heard them fighting...

"It made me sad when they yelled—"

"Hey, you two." That was it. Thea rushed onto the dock. She couldn't stand to listen to any more. "Are we ready for lunch?"

"Hi, Mom." Ryan bounced up to his feet. "I'm ready for lunch. I'm hungry. Me and Wes took the boat out of the water. He let me steer his truck too."

She couldn't even look at Wes right now. He must think she was a terrible person, always fighting with a man who was off serving their country. "Wow. Aren't you lucky?" She ruffled her son's hair, but every muscle around her neck had pulled taut. Wes shouldn't be talking to Ryan about such personal things. He had no right to know their private family history. "Hey, sweetie. Why don't you run on up to the dining room for lunch? I need to talk to Wes. We'll be right behind you."

"Okay. I'm starving, and Louise told me we were having macaroni and cheese today. My favorite!" Without waiting for a reply, he tore off in front of them.

Once he'd made it up the hill, Thea didn't waste another second. "What're you doing?" she demanded, turning to face Wes.

He took a step back. "What'd you mean?"

She swallowed the jagged rock in her throat. It was that guilt again, surging through her, bringing out every emotion she'd buried over the years. "Listen, if Ryan wants to talk about his dad, I'd appreciate it if you would send him to me."

Wes glanced around as though the statement had blindsided him, then his questioning gaze targeted hers. "I didn't bring it up."

"I know." She inhaled deeply, grasping for control over her tone. "But he's still dealing with everything and processing his grief, and I want to be the one to discuss it with him." Why had Ryan never mentioned hearing them fight to her? That was something she should address with him.

Wes seemed to regard her for a minute. Then he nodded. "Understood."

"Thank you." If only she could end the conversation there. She had no script for this next part, so she might as well just put it out there. "I also wanted to apologize for kissing you last night."

Wes tilted his head slightly to the right as he looked at her. "I wish you wouldn't."

Huh. That wasn't exactly the response she'd been expecting. "Excuse me?"

"Apologizing means you regret it," he said, never taking his eyes off hers. "That means you want to take it back. And I don't. Regret it or want to take it back."

She let herself stare into his eyes, let herself imagine kissing him again the way her body begged her to. But where would that leave them in a few days? "This isn't what I came here for. I came here to reconnect with my kids. To lead the other families..." Not to share hot kisses with a man she hardly knew.

Wes lifted one shoulder in a halfhearted shrug. "It's not what I came here for either, but sometimes you find something when you're least expecting it."

And sometimes you had to turn away to protect yourself. "I can't find something right now. I'm too fragile. My kids are too fragile." The reaction she'd had when she heard Ryan talk about his father was all the proof she needed. It had made her feel sick. "And I'm not a fling person." That was how things had started out with Dylan before she ended up pregnant...

"What makes you so sure I'm looking for a fling?" The man reached forward to tuck a lock of hair behind her ear.

The tender gesture caught her off guard, weakening her stance. "I know you need to leave. Your brother told me." When Wes didn't deny it, she went on. "He said you're heading back out to the circuit. And we're going back to Texas soon anyway." It was as simple—or as complicated—as that.

Wes inched closer, a look of disappointment tugging at the corners of his mouth. "I'm not set on leaving this week."

But it was a possibility he hadn't completely ruled out either.

"You have to work. I totally get it. Trust me. And I have to be a responsible mom." That was her role, her safety net, the duty she poured herself into. She knew how to be a mom. A good mom. She knew nothing about loving someone. Nothing about giving her whole heart away. "So...I think it would be best for us to be friends with boundaries."

Wes's eyebrows bounced up. "Friends with *boundaries*?"

"Yes." Boundaries that would protect Ryan. And maybe her

too. Thea bit nervously into her lip while Wes seemed to silently consider his answer.

Finally, he gave her a single, slow nod. "Sure. I can do friends with boundaries. If that's what you want."

"It is." The only question was, could she follow her own advice?

Chapter Twelve

Wes put the finishing touches on the "Silverado Lake or Bust" sign he had made for the back of their covered wagon float.

The parents were assisting their kids with selecting miner costumes from the collection he'd borrowed from the local community theater—old weathered leather and coonskin hats, leather vests, and fake stick-on beards. Ryan and Timothy were having a ball with the props—fake pickaxes and the metal pans used for gold panning. He smiled as he watched the boys engage in a pretend swordfight.

"Love the sign." Those were the first words Thea had spoken to him in the two hours they'd worked on the float. He hadn't said much to her either. After their conversation by the boat shed, he didn't know what the rules were. She'd been upset—he could tell by the way her voice had tightened, and he'd suspected her reaction had more to do with what Ryan revealed about the fighting in her marriage than it did with the boy talking about his dad. But he didn't dare ask her. She'd made it clear that he'd crossed a line, and he had no choice but to back off.

"You want me to hang it on the wagon?" she asked cautiously. Even though this whole boundary thing had been her idea, she seemed awkward around him. Like she wasn't sure how to act or what to say either.

"That's okay. I can handle it." He carted the sign to the back of the horse-drawn carriage. They'd had to get really creative to rig up his dad's old wagon to look like a covered wagon from the early 1900s. He'd used some pool noodles from the beach and a heck of a lot of duct tape to make the arches. Louise had been gracious enough to lend them some white sheets from the housekeeping closet. It wasn't a perfect replica by any means, but they'd done a decent job, if he did say so himself.

"I have to admit, I wasn't sure this would work out." Thea followed along behind him. "But the wagon looks amazing. The kids love it."

Wes secured the sign to the back of the carriage with some rope. "I'm glad." He'd had a blast with them all this afternoon, duct-taping and hanging the sheets, and finding crates they could use for chairs in the back of the wagon. They'd decided that every time the parade came to a stop, they'd all pile out and hand candy to the kids from their gold pans.

"Mom, look at me!" Ryan sprinted to them, wearing a coonskin hat and a long, scraggly gray beard. "I look like a real gold miner."

"You sure do. But I'm not ready for you to have this much facial hair." Thea gave the beard a playful tug.

Wes laughed. He might not know the rules, and he might be all wrong for her and her kids, but man, he loved hanging out with Thea. She had this spark he hadn't seen in many other people. And the way she interacted with her kids . . . it only proved she knew how to love people well. Not that he wanted her to love him.

"You sure you don't need any other adults riding in the parade with you?" she asked, straightening her son's hat as though she was afraid to look at Wes.

He'd never learned how to play games, so he went with a direct question. "Do you want to ride with me?"

"Oh. Uh. Sure." She stumbled over the words. "I mean, if that's what you want. I'm happy to be an extra set of eyes on the kids."

"Are you worried I won't be able to keep an eye on them?" Maybe he shouldn't ask, but he wanted to get to the bottom of her mistrust. Maybe it was based on what she thought of him. Or maybe it was based on what she'd experienced in the past. If he didn't know, he'd never change her perceptions.

"I'm not *worried*," Thea said quickly. "I just know how crazy this bunch gets, and I don't want you to have to deal with that all by yourself."

Or maybe she enjoyed spending time with him too. "I'd love to have you ride with me," he told her. Stepping away, he dug through the costume box until he found an old brown fedora with a feather attached to the side. "In fact, I think you'd make a perfect Calamity Jane." He placed the hat on her head.

Thea smiled her real smile—the one that had been hidden for the last few hours. "And I think you'd make a great Davy Crockett," she said, digging out a coonskin hat and placing it on his head.

He was about to tell her he'd be anything she wanted him to be when the dinner bell rang. Just as well. Telling her that likely wouldn't be following the new rules.

"Okay, everyone." Since the chaos didn't ease up at the sound of Louise's signal, he'd best take charge. "Go ahead and put your costumes in the wagon so they're ready for tomorrow. Then you all can head to dinner, and I'll finish up here."

The kids reluctantly pulled off the hats and vests, clamoring to pick out their seats in the back of the wagon. Thea removed her hat too. "Are you sure you don't want me to stay and help?" she asked.

"Nah. I'm just going to make sure we have everything ready to rig up the horses tomorrow, and then I'll join you all."

She seemed to hesitate, as if it wasn't in her nature to leave the work for someone else, but then she stepped away from him. "Thank you. Really."

"It's nothing." He sent her off with a wave. She seemed so genuinely surprised every time he offered her a break, he had to wonder...how had her husband treated her? They'd had some bad moments, according to Ryan, but had it gone deeper than a few fights? He wanted to know. He wanted to know Thea more than he'd ever wanted to know any woman. Frustration tightened his jaw. He likely wouldn't get the opportunity.

Wes stuffed the extra costumes into the box and stashed it in the barn a few feet away. When he walked back to the wagon, August was making his way down the hill. Wonderful. Just the person he wanted to see. "Why the hell would you tell Thea I'm leaving?" he demanded when his brother still stood ten feet away.

Auggie shot him a confused frown. "Why shouldn't I tell her?"

He didn't have an answer for that without giving himself up. With a grunt of frustration, Wes hauled his box of tools to the barn. When he came back, August confronted him with a knowing glare.

"You really were checking Thea out last night."

"It's not like that." He didn't have to check her out. He already knew she was attractive. That wasn't why he found himself looking for her so often.

"Then what's it like?" His brother narrowed his eyes. "Because I can tell you right now, Jane is going to be pretty pissed off if you go after her friend."

"I'm not going after her. I like spending time with her, that's all. And now she thinks I'm hell-bent on leaving when I was supposed to be the one to stay here and help her." This time his frustration came out in a sigh. Why was he even talking to his brother about this? Back in the day, they'd been close, but now they might as well be strangers. An occasional quick text didn't mean August knew him. He didn't know Wes was always the first one to show up at the arena for an event. He didn't know about the extra hours he'd put in working out and training. He didn't know how many injuries he'd ignored in the pursuit of building a career.

August didn't know how one single day—that day, the worst day of his life—drove him to search for redemption. But if he was being honest, Wes might admit he was looking in the wrong place. Every time he walked out of the arena, the rush faded. But the fire he felt when he looked at Thea . . . it had yet to cool. And the wonder he experienced when Ryan gave him a high five or confided in him about his grief had done more to fill the hole in his heart than anything he'd accomplished in his career. "Forget it," he said to his brother. "You wouldn't understand." Those were feelings August didn't think Wes was capable of.

"Holy. Shit." His brother stared at him with one part amusement and three parts disbelief. "You actually like this woman."

He didn't deny it.

"She has kids," Auggie reminded him, as though he wasn't fully aware.

"Yeah, and they're pretty incredible." Spending time with Ryan had made Wes want to be better, to be there for the kid. They had a bond. Maybe because both of them knew what it was like to lose a father. And he may not spend as much time with Olivia, but he found himself feeling protective over her—watching out for her. "I'm not the same person I was back in high school." Their father's death had changed him. Life had changed him. Experience had changed him. "And I'd hope you're not either."

"No. I've changed too." His brother got a pained look on his face. "Except for maybe my big mouth."

Uh-oh. Wes recognized that expression of regret all too well. "What else did you say to her?"

"I might've mentioned how you don't like to be tied down. How you're always on the go, moving from place to place."

As if his brother knew anything about him these days. "Seriously?" He didn't bull-rush him like he would've when they were younger, but he let his disgust show.

"I didn't know you liked her." August had the balls to sound defensive. "If anything, I thought you wanted to have a fling with her."

Why did everyone—including Thea herself—figure he wasn't capable of more than a fling?

"I didn't assume you were looking for a serious relationship."
The disbelief was still evident in his brother's expression.

"Yeah, well, I've never really wanted one before." But with
Thea...he could see something more. He could see being there for
her. He could see making her smile and laugh like she had earlier.
He could see kissing her every day and never getting tired of that
feeling she gave him...

"Whoa. You've got it bad." August might not know him well
anymore, but he could still read him.

"It's not like it matters. As Thea pointed out to me earlier, they
live in Texas, and I live all over the place."

"Long distance is no problem these days," his brother insisted.
"There are plenty of ways to keep in touch."

"Right. It's pretty easy to keep in touch." He let his smirk speak
for him. Other than the occasional text, Wes never heard from his
brother unless he called.

August seemed to get the message. "Yeah, yeah, yeah. I'm
too busy. I work way too much. Trust me. I've heard it all
from Mom."

"You're not going to hear any lectures from me." Wes
hadn't earned the right to lecture his brother on anything. "But it
would be good to see you around here more." He couldn't claim to
be the perfect son, but over the last year since Jane had moved back
to the ranch, Wes had done his best to spend a couple of weeks
here, and he'd actually enjoyed feeling like their family was back
together again. "We miss you around here." He knew their mom
did anyway.

Instead of getting defensive again, Auggie nodded. "I'm hoping
now that I'm at the top, I can get more time off. And there's a chance
I might move back. If our new business venture opens up."

Now it was Wes's turn to stare in disbelief. "Really?" He'd
thought his brother wanted nothing to do with Silverado Lake.

"A small chance. But yes." August had never been easy to read.
Wes couldn't tell if he thought the move would be a good thing or
a bad thing.

He sure wouldn't mind having his brother be more a part of the family again. Before their dad had died, they'd been opposites in nearly every way, but they'd also been good friends. He missed that.

"So what're you going to do about Thea?" When the conversation turned to him, Auggie had always been a master at changing the subject.

"There's not much I can do." Thea didn't seem willing to budge on giving anything between them a shot.

"Well, you can't give up. Not if you have feelings for her." Something on his brother's face changed. "If you really care about her, don't walk away. Don't make the same mistake I did."

"Wait, what?" Two things about that statement stunned him. First, that August would be willing to admit he'd ever made a mistake. And, two... "You cared about someone?" His brother had never said a word about any woman.

"Just trust me." Auggie turned to leave. "Putting yourself out there is a hell of a lot better than living with regrets."

* * *

This was the closest she would ever get to being a celebrity.

Thea waved to the crowd from her position on the carriage's driver's seat next to Wes, taking it all in. She'd never been to a small-town parade, and she could hardly believe the crowds that had gathered to line either side of the streets. "I had no idea Gold Rush Days was such a big deal," she said to Wes, marveling at the cheers and the music that seemed to be coming from all directions.

"Gold Rush Days in Silverado Lake is bigger than the Fourth of July." He tapped the front of his coonskin hat to move it farther up on his forehead and looked at her. "People come all the way from Denver for the festivities."

"I can see why." Somehow the crowds made this town even more beautiful. All those smiling faces. The kids with their bags of candy collected from the floats. Elderly men and women sitting in their lawn chairs, waving at each homemade float as it slowly rolled past. All along the parade route, people had been chatting and laughing, and it seemed they all knew each other. "I miss having a sense of community," Thea confessed, watching the horses in front of them stumble to a stop. "When Dylan was in the military, we had a pretty incredible support system. But it's been a few years, and a lot of those friendships have faded." She knew she wasn't supposed to be delving any deeper with the man, but he was so easy to talk to, so easy to be with. He didn't seem to expect anything from her, and that gave her the freedom to be more honest with him.

"I miss having community too. I mean, I have friends on the circuit, but we don't keep in touch outside of work." Wes kept a strong hold on the reins while the kids all jumped out of the wagon to take candy to the children waiting in front of the sidewalks. Ryan was in full character, telling everyone who would listen that he'd struck gold.

"It's funny. Sometimes, when I was growing up, this town drove me crazy." Wes waved to an older woman who was sitting in a lawn chair nearby. "People used to rat me out to my parents all the time." He laughed. "But now I realize they were trying to help in their own way. It took a village to keep an eye on me. And after my dad died...well, these people made sure my family got through it."

"Yeah. I could see that." Even being an outsider in their midst, there was a sense that she was part of something bigger right along with them. It made her feel less alone.

"We're almost to the end of the route," Wes said, jiggling the reins to get the horses started again. "Afterward, I thought we'd take the kids to the carnival before they head off on their overnight adventure."

"That's a great plan." While his changes to the schedule had irked her at first, now it was almost a relief to let someone else worry about the logistics. "I have a feeling Ryan and Timothy are going to want to do the whole parade again." Even Liv seemed to relish the attention from the crowd and the praise from the kids when she handed them candy. "This was a great idea." She wanted to make sure he knew that, in case she'd been a little testy with him when he'd announced the change in plans.

"I'm glad everyone's having fun."

It didn't bode well for her boundaries that Wes's smile warmed her through every time she saw it.

"This is it." He looked up ahead. "Our last block. Then we can park the wagon and take a walk to the park."

Thea looked back into the wagon as the kids climbed in, giving them the warning. She'd learned it was best to give her son a heads-up when the fun was coming to an end.

"Aw, can't we keep going?" Ryan held out his gold pan. "I still have a ton of candy to give out."

"Then it's time to be generous," Wes said, halting the carriage again. "This is it. Your last chance to get rid of the candy before we go ride the Ferris wheel. Make it good."

The kids all scrambled out of the wagon again, walking up and down the street, making children of all ages squeal with excitement.

Within a few minutes, Wes gave a whistle, rounding the kids up for the final trek down that last block. Thea had to admit she was a little disappointed too. It had been fun to see the town from this vantage point. They'd all been so welcoming and friendly. They'd made her feel like a guest of honor at their parade.

After parking on the side of an alley, Wes climbed out of the carriage and then helped her down, his hand warm and strong wrapped around hers.

The kids surrounded them, all asking a million questions at once.

"Can we ride the Ferris wheel now?"

"Can we get cotton candy?"

"Can we play that bottle game?"

Thea wasn't sure who to answer first. "Whoa. Hold on." She'd already mentioned to the other parents that they would meet at the park after the parade, so while Wes tied the horses to a parking meter, she waved them all in that direction.

One by one they passed her by, some running, others—like Olivia and Preston—walking quickly. "Everyone look for your parents," she called before she lost them for good. After half a block, most of them were out of sight, and Wes had caught up to her.

"I told you they were a crazy bunch." She scanned the streets ahead. At least they were staying in groups so no one was alone.

"They're crazy all right," Wes said. "But they're a great group of kids too. It's been fun to hang out with them."

"They've had fun hanging out with you." And so had she. Thea couldn't tell him that, though. She couldn't cross that line with him again. No matter how much she wanted to.

The rest of the way to the park, they chatted about the rides. "I've never been to a carnival," she admitted. She hadn't been allowed to do anything like that when she was a kid.

"Never?" Wes gaped at her. "But you haven't lived until you've consumed a whole funnel cake just before getting on the Tilt-A-Whirl."

She laughed. "That sounds like a recipe for disaster."

"Mom!" Ryan ran up to them before they'd even stepped foot on the grass. "Did you see all the stuff here? They have everything! A Ferris wheel and a Tilt-A-Whirl and even bumper cars! We have to do it all!"

"We'll try," she promised, scanning the crowd around them. It appeared all of the children had successfully reunited with their parents. Liv waved at her, but she was too busy talking to Preston and the twins to walk over.

Seeing that her daughter was happy and likely wouldn't want to be hanging out with them, Thea turned to Wes. "So, where should we start?"

"We?" He seemed to search her face.

"Yes, you're coming with us." Ryan grabbed the man's hand

and started to drag him toward the ticket booth. "We should do the Ferris wheel first and then the Tilt-A-Whirl and then the bumper cars and then we can do it all again."

"Sounds like a plan to me." Wes glanced over his shoulder as though looking for her approval.

"That's a great plan." Sure, Wes would likely leave, and they would go back to Texas, but right now she only wanted Ryan to have fun. She only wanted to have fun. For once she didn't want to worry about what would happen tomorrow.

"Woo-hoo!" her son squealed, leading them to the ticket booth.

For the next hour, they went on so many rides, Thea's head was spinning. Her neck ached from the bumper cars, too—thanks to Ryan's repeated fender benders—but she couldn't remember the last time she'd laughed so hard.

"I think it's time for some ice cream," Wes said as they stumbled off their third Tilt-A-Whirl ride.

"That's a great idea." Thea blinked, trying to ease the dizziness. If she had to go in one more circle, she might not walk straight the rest of the day.

They waited in line until each of them held a huge homemade strawberry ice cream cone. Was it possible that ice cream tasted better in the mountains?

"Come on." Ryan nudged them both with his elbows. "Let's sit on that bench right there and eat our ice cream. After that we can go on the Tilt-A-Whirl again."

Thea squeezed her eyes shut. "I don't know about—"

The twang of a country song came from Wes's back pocket and interrupted.

"Sorry. I should've turned that off." He pulled out his phone and glanced at the screen. "It's Toby. I'd better take it."

"Sure. We'll wait over there." Thea put her hand on Ryan's shoulder and directed him to the bench. It was a relief to finally sit down.

"What was your favorite ride so far?" her son asked, licking the ice cream mustache off his top lip.

"Hmmm." She handed him a napkin. "I think it was the nice, slow Ferris wheel."

"Really?" Her son's nose crinkled up as though he'd never understand that choice. "I like the Tilt-A-Whirl best."

"You don't say," Thea teased.

"It's the fastest and the funnest and..."

Ryan continued chatting, but Thea couldn't hear him anymore.

Wes was jogging back to them, his eyes wide and his tanned face looking almost sallow.

She rose from the bench and rushed to meet him, her heart all knotted up. "What? What is it? What's wrong?"

The man looked into her eyes but didn't seem to see her.

"It's Jane." He paused and swallowed hard. "Toby said she's really sick. Her blood pressure's too high and she's throwing up. They have to take the baby now."

Chapter Thirteen

Thea was talking to him, but everything sounded muffled, like he had plunged underwater.

Toby's panicked voice kept playing over and over in his head—louder than the voices around him, louder than the crazy-fast pulse of his own heart.

It's bad, Wes. Her organs are shutting down. They said she might not make it.

"I don't understand." He couldn't understand. Jane was in the hospital. She was supposed to be safe. They were supposed to be able to help her there. He hadn't been worried about her. He hadn't realized anything could go wrong...

"Do they know what's going on?" Thea's question finally broke through his mental chaos.

"Help." He mentally went back through every word Toby had said. "He said it's something called HELLP syndrome." Wes looked at his phone again.

"Oh, God." The gravity in Thea's voice lifted his head.

"What is it? What is HELLP?"

She hesitated. "It's associated with preeclampsia. A friend of a friend got it years ago, but she was much further along in her pregnancy."

His throat constricted, cutting off airflow. "What happened to her?"

"She made it." Thea touched his arm in a comforting gesture. "And the baby was fine..."

But Jane was only thirty weeks along. That wasn't far enough. The baby was too small.

"We got your text." Kelly approached Thea. Cal and Timothy trailed along behind. "What's up?"

While Thea explained to them what was going on, Wes googled "HELLP" on his phone. He shouldn't have. Why did people seem to post only the terrible outcomes online? His eyes skimmed over the articles, the facts.

The mortality rate is 30 percent.

"I have to go." He shoved his phone back into his pocket, adrenaline racing through him. He had to drive down to Denver right now. He had to see Jane and make sure she pulled through this.

"Of course." Thea tossed her ice cream into a trash can. He'd already ditched his when he heard Toby's hoarse voice.

"What's going on?" Ryan wandered into the group, still working on his oversized waffle cone.

"Wes's sister is very sick," Thea told him.

"Oh, no. I'm sorry." The boy threw one arm around his waist, and Wes hugged him back. He wanted to cry, but no tears would come.

"I can take care of getting the horses and the wagon back to the ranch," Cal offered. Everyone else started throwing out offers for other ways they could help—getting all their parade float supplies stored back at the ranch, organizing dinner for him...

"That would be great. Thank you all." A thick black smoke seemed to have filled his lungs.

Thea stepped in closer and he finally found the ability to focus on her eyes. They were calming and warm, stilling his inner chaos. "Do you want me to come with you?"

"Yes." He couldn't face the three-hour drive to Denver alone. Especially if he didn't get there in time...

"We'll take care of the kids," Kelly said. "They're all packed up for the camp tonight anyway. We can get them back to the ranch before the bus comes to pick them up."

"Thank you." Thea hugged her and then dug in her purse. "Here. Give this phone to Liv, since I'll be away."

"I'll say prayers for your sister." Ryan tugged on his shirt, and Wes knelt down to the kid's eye level. "That means a lot, Sport." Fear threatened to strangle him—the same deep, haunting fear he'd felt when he'd learned his dad was missing in the river. He hated how it took over, how it seemed to cloud everything else.

"We can take my car." Thea dug a set of keys out of her purse. "I'll drive."

Somehow, Wes managed to get to his feet again. He followed her across the grassy meadow and down half a block to where she'd parked before the parade.

"What about August?" she asked as they climbed into the SUV. "Will he want to come with us?"

"I tried to call him. But he's in some meeting somewhere." Wes hadn't paid attention to where he'd gone earlier that morning. He clicked his seat belt and stared out the windshield. All the vibrant colors of the mountains seemed to have dimmed.

He couldn't lose his baby sister. When they were little, he'd always watched out for Jane. He'd always wanted to push her stroller when they were walking downtown. He used to take her his stuffed animals when she'd cry in her crib...

"I'm sure she's in the best possible hands." Thea pulled the car out onto the street, and it was a damn good thing she was driving because he'd be tearing through town like a lunatic right now if he was behind the wheel.

"I hope so." He was holding on to hope. Thea helped him hold on to hope with her soothing voice and her steady hands. "I can't lose her. Not now. Not when our family is finally together again." When their father had died, the loss had fractured their connections. August had made himself scarce. Jane had moved away and hid behind her studies and work. And he'd chased one job on the circuit to the next, afraid to go home, afraid to face what he'd done to his family.

Wes turned to the window. Somehow, they were already on the highway, heading up to the top of the pass.

"I'm sure it was hard on all of you losing your father the way you did." The caution in her tone hinted at a deep understanding of a grief that never went away. It made sense she understood. She'd lost someone she loved deeply too.

"He shouldn't have died." Wes turned his face to hers, letting her see all of it—the guilt, the pain he still held on to all these years later. "He wouldn't have died if I would've showed up that day."

She shifted her gaze from the road in front of them to look at him. *Really* look at him. "I'm sure that's not true." Sympathy welled up in her eyes.

He wasn't used to someone believing the best in him. Or even someone looking for the best in him. Would she still see any good in him after he told her the truth? "I was supposed to go with him. On that kayaking trip. He wasn't supposed to go alone. If I would've been there—"

"He still might've passed away," Thea interrupted in a stern voice. "He still might've had the accident. You would've been in a different kayak."

"But I'll never know for sure." He would always have to wonder if he could've saved his father's life out on that river. "He constantly told me to be more responsible. To be a man of my word like he was. And I never listened. I did what I wanted and didn't care who it hurt."

"You were a kid," Thea murmured.

He watched a tear slowly roll down the contour of her cheek. "I was still sleeping when my mom called to tell me they found his kayak upside down in the river." She might as well hear the whole truth. "I was so hung over I couldn't even drive myself down there to help the search party." Jane had come to pick him up, her whole face swollen from crying. He'd never forget that drive. He'd never forget each and every detail. George Strait had been twanging on the car radio. He'd worn his decrepit old Nikes, thinking they'd be good for trying to walk along the riverbank. "We sat on the side of the river for five hours, completely helpless until they found him."

Now the tears streamed freely down Thea's cheeks as she watched the road.

The emotion she showed so freely pried his heart open a crack. He'd never let himself feel anything too deeply. He'd never let himself say any of the words out loud, but now he couldn't seem to hold them in anymore. "My dad was right about me." Everyone had been right about him. He hadn't taken anything seriously enough. He hadn't been reliable. "I was too selfish, and I passed up the last opportunity I had to spend time with my father."

Thea slowed the car and guided it onto the side of the road. She faced him fully, her eyes looking into the deepest part of him, as though she was still searching for the good. "You told Ryan your dad said all he wanted was for his kids to be happy. I heard you say that."

"He told us that all the time." Whenever Wes messed up, his dad would always say, *I want you to be happy, son. And things like this won't help you find long-term happiness.*

"Then maybe the best way to honor his memory is to let go of the questions that burden you so much." Thea reached over and slipped her hand into his, threading their fingers together, flooding him with warmth.

He couldn't remember the last time someone had held his hand. Maybe when he'd dated around in high school, since that was a cool form of PDA back then, but he'd never felt such power come from a single touch.

"Maybe the best thing you can do for your father now is build a life full of happiness."

* * *

Come on, come on, come on. Wes sat taller and tried to see over the long line of cars clogging up the intersection at the stoplight.

They were two miles away from the hospital, and there had been no word from Toby. Whenever he called his brother-in-law, the phone went right to voice mail.

"Almost there," Thea murmured, glaring at the cars in front of them as though willing them to move.

He sat back and tried to relax. "We've gotten this far. We can make it two more miles." He might not have made it if it hadn't been for her calming presence. Thea had made the trip bearable. Somehow, she had made his guilt and regret from the past manageable. After she'd pulled over outside of Silverado Lake, they'd talked for the first two hours—mainly about his father and his memories. But for the last hour, he'd needed to be silent, to focus all of his energy on blocking out the worst-case scenarios that seemed to gain momentum the closer they got to the hospital. Thea had simply let him be, humming along to the music occasionally, which took the edge off his panic.

Maybe the best thing you can do for your father now is build a life of happiness. He'd never thought of that before. Never thought that instead of being disappointed in him, his dad would want him to find peace. Instead of punishing him for his mistakes, his dad would want him to use his mistakes to build a better life. And maybe he'd gotten it all wrong chasing a career that kept him out on the road, that only gave him opportunities for superficial relationships.

Looking back now, he realized his dad hadn't told him how to find happiness. He hadn't given him a formula, but his father had shown him what happiness looked like. He'd shown him that happiness didn't come from what you did, but from how you lived.

His dad had centered his entire life around people. Not around things. Not around a career. Charlie Harding had built a place where he could serve and get to know people. He'd lived to spend time with his family. And his dad had been one of the happiest people Wes had ever known.

His father had never cared much about money. And neither did Wes. He didn't care about success and notoriety. He cared about it even less now that he'd found some of both. He liked his job well enough, but it would never be enough.

Finally, the line of cars in front of them started to move again. Thea switched lanes three times, passing slower cars, and then turned into the hospital's main entrance.

"I'll drop you off at the front and meet you up there," she said, taking the curve fast.

"You sure?" Could he go in there and face this alone?

"Yes." She pulled up in front of the glass doors. "Who knows how long it'll take to get a parking spot. Go find Jane and Toby."

"Thank you." The words were wholly inadequate, but he let his eyes speak his gratitude.

"Everything's going to be okay." When she said that, he believed her.

Wes climbed out of the car and fired off a text to Toby. Where are you? I'm here. Where should I go?

He booked it inside through the automatic doors and jogged to a reception desk. "Labor and delivery?" At least that's where he assumed he should start.

"Fourth floor," the woman said. "Elevators are right over there." She pointed to a hallway on the left.

"Thank you," he called, already running for the elevators. He pressed the button and waited. Just as he stepped inside, his phone dinged with a text from Toby.

I'll meet you in the labor and delivery waiting room.

The elevator seemed to crawl a centimeter at a time all the way up. Finally, the doors rolled open and Wes rushed out, jogging down another hallway before he careened around a corner and nearly ran into Toby.

"Damn, I'm glad to see you." His brother-in-law embraced him.

Was that a good sign or a bad sign? Wes wasn't sure. They'd never actually hugged before. Instead of shooting off his mouth and asking the barrage of questions he had bottled up, he looked

Toby over. "You okay?" He'd never seen his brother-in-law look so haggard. His jeans and T-shirt were wrinkled, and he had at least a week's worth of growth on his normally clean-shaven jaw.

"I don't know how to answer that." Toby sank onto a nearby couch while Wes opted to stand, bracing himself for whatever news was coming.

"Jane's blood pressure is still high." His brother-in-law massaged his temples as though he had a headache. "They had to sedate her and move her to the ICU, but at least she's stable right now."

Wes nodded, unable to speak, hardly managing to breathe, to swallow. He was too choked up. Jane had made it, but she hadn't come out unscathed.

"And baby girl is in the NICU," Toby went on. "That's where I've been. Trying to watch over her and make sure they're taking care of her."

The huge tangle of worry that had tightened his chest suddenly unraveled. "So, they both made it."

"Yes." Toby rose from the couch. "Baby girl is almost three pounds, which is bigger than they thought she would be. She's in an incubator and is on oxygen, but she seems real strong."

"Like her mama," Wes managed to say without breaking down.

"Like her mama," his brother-in-law agreed. "I'll tell you, man...I've never been so scared—"

"Did you find her?" Thea ran toward them, and something deep inside of Wes settled.

"Yes." He walked to meet her. "She's stable but in the ICU, and baby girl is three pounds and so far looking strong."

"Thank God." Thea paused and seemed to catch her breath.

"Thea?" Toby joined them, his shoulders still bent under an unseen weight. "It's good to see you. Thanks for coming."

"I had to come." She squeezed his hand. "I'm sorry you have to deal with this."

"We're getting through. Taking it one step at a time," Toby said. "All Jane has been talking about since we got here is how bummed she is that she couldn't be at the ranch for your retreat."

"We've been in good hands." The smile Thea offered Wes wrapped him in her warmth. "What's going on at the ranch is the last thing she should be worried about. We want to know how we can help support her."

"Glad to hear." Toby seemed to be looking back and forth between Thea and Wes with blatant curiosity. "It was nice of you to come," he said to Thea.

"I didn't want Wes to have to make the drive alone." She squeezed Wes's hand, and he didn't want to let go.

"I'm not sure I would've made it here without her." With his head such a mess on the way down, he could've ended up driving right off a cliff.

"It'll mean a lot to Jane to have you both here." Toby glanced at his watch. "Speaking of . . . I was just headed back up to see her. ICU visiting hours are almost over, but I can try to get you in."

"I want to see her." Wes needed to see her. Once he saw Jane for himself, maybe his heart rate would finally settle.

"I'll wait here." Thea walked to a nearby chair and sat. "I have to call Liv and check in anyway. This will be the perfect opportunity."

He would've rather had her by his side but told her he'd be back soon and followed Toby to the elevators. Now that the worry and adrenaline had started to subside, a bone-weary tiredness set in. "You holding up okay?" he asked his brother-in-law as they stepped into the elevator.

"I've had my moments today." Toby punched the button for the third floor. "But if I had been the one in danger, I know Jane would've kept it together, so I did my best."

The doors opened, and they stepped out into another sterile hallway. "Things are going okay at the ranch?" his brother-in-law asked, walking deliberately down the hall as if he'd followed this path many times.

"Sure. Yeah." Wes fell in stride with him. "I think the whole group is enjoying their retreat." And he was enjoying it far more than he'd thought he would.

They passed through a small waiting room and paused in front of a set of double doors. Toby eyed him, seeming to look for something. "August has been checking in on Jane. With him back, I'd have thought you would head down to Texas for your event."

Texas was the last place he wanted to be right now. "I'm planning to stay, see the retreat out."

Amusement loosened Toby's tense expression. "That have anything to do with Thea?"

"It might." But now...damn, he was glad he'd stayed. So he could be here for Jane, and for Toby too.

"Okay..." His brother-in-law seemed to let his vague answer go. "I'll walk you back to Jane's room, and then I'm going to find the nurse so I can get an update." He opened the door and let Toby go in first. The smell of antiseptic came on strong in here. Wes followed his brother-in-law past partially open doors. It was eerily quiet, just the beeps of machines.

"She's in here." Toby pushed open one of the doors and gestured for Wes to go in. He hesitated.

"She's going to be okay, right?" He had to ask.

"We need to believe she is," Toby said firmly.

That wasn't the answer he'd wanted—he would've much rather heard a definitive yes—but Wes nodded and walked into the room anyway.

He wasn't at all prepared to see his sister lying there, tubes winding from her forearm, oxygen in her nose.

A sudden sense of utter and complete helplessness flooded him— the same way it had back when he'd sat on the riverbank waiting for searchers to find his father. It wasn't so much fear as it was claustrophobia—the feeling of being stuck where he didn't want to be, and he couldn't save himself or anyone else around him.

Looking at Jane now, it struck him that he would change places with her in a heartbeat. *Jane would've held it together.* Toby's words came back to him.

She would've held it together, and so should he. "Hey, sis." He walked to a chair next to the bed and sat.

Her face seemed pale, and she looked small underneath the pile of blankets. Some of her hair had spilled over her cheek, so he gently brushed it away. She hated when her hair got in her face.

"I heard my new niece is tough. A lot like her mama," he murmured. "You need to get better so you can hold her."

There was no indication she could hear him. No twitch of her lips or flutter of her eyelids.

Once again, he wondered how this had happened. How had they gotten here? One day his sister had been completely healthy, and the next she'd had to fight for her life. He'd known how short life was—how quickly the rug could be pulled out from under you. But he'd forgotten. *Life is short, son. That's why you have to make the minutes count.* That had been one of his father's favorite sayings.

Had he made the minutes count?

"Hey." Toby pushed through the door. "The nurse said not much has changed, but she'll keep me posted. They have to kick us out. Visiting hours are over." He strode to the bed and leaned over his wife, kissing her forehead and whispering something Wes couldn't hear.

Wes rose from the chair and backed into the corner of the room to give his brother-in-law a minute. He couldn't imagine what it would be like to see the person he loved most in the world lying there.

After he'd adjusted her blankets and kissed her once more, Toby approached Wes. "I'll be coming in to check on her through the night."

"I can stay." He likely wouldn't get much sleep in the waiting room anyway.

"They won't let you." Toby waved him through the door, and they walked back down the hallway. "I have two hotel rooms nearby. One is mine, but I've only used it to shower and get cleaned up. My parents have been staying in the other room, but they headed back up to Silverado Lake an hour ago to get some things from the ranch for us and won't be back until tomorrow."

He held the door open for Toby, and they walked into the ICU waiting room. "You and Thea are welcome to them." He dug through his wallet and pulled out two card keys, but then paused. "Or maybe you only need one room?"

"Thanks for the offer." Wes took both keys. There was no way he trusted himself to spend the night alone with Thea. Not tonight. Not any night.

Chapter Fourteen

Thea stared through the vending machine's spotted glass, taking her time with her selection. Neither she nor Wes had eaten anything since the ice cream at the carnival, and hunger was starting to settle in.

She hadn't made a vending machine dinner since her college days, but according to the hospital website, the cafeteria was already closed, so it looked like their options were limited.

Let's see... Peanut butter crackers and mixed nuts for protein. Cheetos for salty indulgence. Granola bar for some whole grains. And Oreos, Snickers, and M&M's for good old-fashioned comfort food. Thea managed to stash it all in her purse and then retraced her steps back to the labor and delivery waiting room.

The place happened to be empty at the moment, so she set up camp on a small couch that faced a window overlooking the mountains. Outside, the sun had started to set, casting a vibrant array of colors into the sky, and even with the stress and the worry that had accumulated for her friend, she let herself breathe deeply.

Jane was at least stable and being well cared for. The baby's prognosis sounded very promising. They were here, and Wes was with his sister, where he needed to be.

All the way down from the mountains, she'd seen how heavily the fear weighed on him, she'd seen his internal agony over the past and the future, and she'd wanted to ease his pain. She couldn't describe what drew her to him, but she was finding it harder to fight the pull.

"Great view."

Thea lifted her head and looked behind her. Wes and Toby were crossing the room.

"Hi." She scrambled to stand, nearly knocking over her purse in the process. "How is she?"

"No real change," Toby answered. "Her blood pressure is still elevated, but they're hopeful it'll come back down tonight with rest and the meds." The man's expression looked as tortured as Wes's had during the drive.

"I'm sure. Her body's been through a lot of trauma. It'll probably take a while." It had been hard enough to recover after having two normal deliveries. She couldn't imagine what her friend would have to go through after enduring such physical trauma.

"I'm gonna head back to baby girl." Toby checked his watch. "It's time for another feeding, and I want to be there to see how it goes."

Wes placed a hand on his brother-in-law's shoulder. "You sure you don't want me to stay tonight? I can camp out on the couch, and then I'll be right here if you need anything."

"Nah. They're not letting anyone else into baby girl's room yet, and you can't get into the ICU until morning anyway." Toby pulled out his phone. "I'll text you the hotel address and room numbers. Don't worry about me. I'll catch some z's here and there, but you might as well get a good night's sleep before you have to head back up the mountain tomorrow. Jane would be worried about you driving if you didn't."

Wes nodded, but he didn't look too happy about the decision. "I'll check with you first thing in the morning. And I'd like to hang out a little longer here. Just in case she wakes up or something."

"Thanks." Toby gave Wes a hug and shook Thea's hand again. "It means a lot to have you two here. Really."

"I'm glad we could be here." Her eyes got all teary. Seeing the emotion in these two tough cowboys made it hard to keep her composure.

"Keep us posted," Wes called as his brother-in-law hurried away.

"You'll be the first to know anything," Toby promised before he disappeared around a corner.

"It looks like you've got quite the setup here." Wes came around to the other side of the couch and sat, his shoulders slumping.

"Watching the sunset always make things seem a little bit better." She sat next to him. "It's a good reminder that even though terrible things happen sometimes, there is still beauty, something bigger out there to put your hope in." At least that's what she always thought when she happened to be sitting on the back deck at dusk.

"Yes. Thank goodness for that." Wes focused his gaze out the window.

Thea let a few seconds of silence sit between them before she asked, "How does Jane look?"

"Not so great." He turned his face to hers, and she could see a tic work through his jaw.

"I'm sure." It wouldn't be easy to see anyone you loved in the ICU. "But I bet she knew you were there."

"I hope so." He stared at the floor. "Jane and I . . . we used to be close, but after Dad died, everything fell apart. I used to watch out for her when we were kids, but then we hardly talked for years."

Thea said nothing. She simply moved her hand to cover his. The feel of his skin against hers sparked a fierce desire to be closer to him. To take away some of his burden. To make him happy. Her heart startled at how strongly she wanted to abandon herself to those feelings.

"If she doesn't wake up . . ." He shook his head. "I don't know.

I should've helped her through that time after the accident. But I was too consumed with my own guilt."

Yes, guilt had a way of haunting a person. She knew that first-hand. "But you're here for her now," Thea reminded him. "And that's what she'll always remember."

Wes leaned back against the cushions, his eyes on her. "How do you always know the perfect thing to say?"

"Oh, I assure you . . . I rarely know the perfect thing to say." Like when she told him the kiss was a mistake, for instance. Sitting here with him, away from everything else, away from responsibilities and reminders of her past, she didn't want the kiss to be a mistake. She didn't want to pretend she wasn't dying to kiss him again. Thea held her breath and searched his eyes.

Wes's posture changed. He sat a little taller as though hyper-aware of her feelings. "You always seem to know the perfect thing to say to me," he murmured in that deep vibrato that resounded all through her.

Because her heart responded to him. She wasn't even sure why. On paper, she and Wes made no sense, but the man had a hold on her heart.

"Thea . . ." Wes turned his body fully to hers, but in the process his elbow knocked over her purse and an avalanche of food spilled out onto the floor.

Wes started to gather up the snacks and their moment passed. He wasn't going to kiss her again now.

"What's all this?" he asked, holding up a candy bar.

Thea shot him a sheepish smile, hoping he mistook her red face for embarrassment instead of passion. "I thought maybe you could use some dinner."

The man laughed. "Cheetos and granola bars and chocolate. Talk about gourmet."

"Don't forget about the nuts." Right as the words came out of her mouth, she realized how that sounded. "The mixed nuts I mean. For protein." See? She never knew the right thing to say.

But Wes only laughed harder. "I never forget about the nuts."

Thea giggled too. Maybe it was the exhaustion from the long drive and the stress of worrying about Jane and the pressure of her feelings for him building in her chest, but it felt good to laugh. "Well, I'm starting with the M&M's," she informed him. In situations like this one, it was chocolate first, nutrition later.

"Then I'll go with the Snickers." He raised his eyebrows at her. "Chocolate and nuts."

She found it easy to laugh with him. Easy to sit next to him as they both unwrapped the goodies and shared a sunset picnic of assorted junk food in front of a hospital window while they went back to talking about easy topics like his life out on the road and her kids.

"Ryan is the coolest kid." Wes finished off the Cheetos. "He's hilarious. But he's also...thoughtful."

"Yeah. He's changed since his dad died." It was funny, she'd only seen the bigger changes in her son during the last couple of months. "He's a bit more serious than he used to be."

"He's pretty wise for a ten-year-old." Wes offered her a bit of the granola bar.

She supposed she should take a bite to keep up appearances that she cared about nutrition instead of eating all the chocolate. "He is wise," she agreed. "It was hard for him to lose Dylan. But I think it also gave him more empathy for other people who are going through difficult times." Empathy in her kids had always been more important to her than perfect grades and academic smarts. She wanted them to care about people.

Wes set down the granola bar and faced her. "I'm sure it was hard on you too." His eyes seemed to search, but Thea focused on digging another M&M out of the wrapper. Wes had let her see so much of him, but she couldn't do this. She couldn't go into the details of her past, of her marriage. It was easier to focus on him.

"Of course. Yes. It was very hard." The words weren't a lie. Dylan's death had blindsided her. But not because of how much she'd loved him or the fact that he was her second half, like everyone assumed. It killed her to pretend, to live with the secret that their marriage had been in shambles, but it felt like a betrayal to tell anyone the truth. Instead of saying more, Thea collected some of the wrappers and walked them to the trash can.

"How did you get through it?" Wes asked when she sat back down.

The question made her throat burn. Was she through it? How could she ever be through the aftermath of his death when she knew the truth? *I abandoned him right before he left.*

Thankfully, Wes's phone rang, so she didn't have to answer.

"It's Toby." He rose and walked a few steps away. "Uh-huh. Yes. Okay. Yeah, we'll check in with you first thing." Wes pocketed the phone. "He said Jane's blood pressure is coming down a little more. But they're going to keep her sedated overnight. Hopefully we can see her first thing tomorrow. I guess we should go try to get some sleep."

"Right. Definitely." Sleep would be good. Sleep would protect her from having to answer any more questions.

"I saw a hotel a few blocks away. We could get our own rooms," she said quickly. At this point, that would be best. Wes was too easy to talk to. He made her want to let down her guard.

"Toby has two rooms." Wes reached out a hand to help her up. "He offered them to us for tonight since his parents are back in Silverado Lake."

"Perfect." He would go to sleep in his room, and she would go to sleep in her room, and these feelings the man tilled up in her could stay stuffed deep inside, where they belonged. "I'm ready when you are." Ready to retreat back to her own space.

"Lead the way." Wes gestured for her to go first.

Right. Now she had to remember where she parked the car. Thea looked for the landmarks she'd seen on the way in and eventually— after only one wrong turn—they made it to her SUV. Wes read directions to navigate to the hotel, and within minutes they'd pulled up in front of a large brick structure. "Looks like a nice place." It had a boutique look to it, with the bricks and columns. Definitely not your run-of-the-mill average hotel.

"Toby's parents have always had expensive taste." Wes pointed to a driveway off to the left. "I think we have to do valet."

"Swanky." Thea pulled up to the valet stand. They climbed out of the car, and Wes held the doors open for her. The hotel's interior was modern and clean but somehow still homey.

"We're on the third floor." Wes waved back to the friendly clerk at the reception counter. They stepped inside the elevator and zipped up to the third floor. "I guess I should've thought to go back to the ranch before we left so you could pack a bag."

Thea stepped out onto the third floor. "It's fine." Given the shock of hearing about Jane, a change of clothes had been the last thing on her mind. "It'll be like camping."

"Do you like camping?" He led her down the left hallway, and they passed door after door.

"Not at all," Thea admitted. "I never sleep well in a tent." Granted, she'd only attempted it twice in her life, but both times she'd woken to every little sound nearby, sure it was some dangerous animal ready to attack the tent.

"I probably won't sleep much tonight." Wes paused in front of a door near the end of the hallway and held out one of the keys. "This is you. I'm next door." He pointed to the last door at the end of the hall.

Thea's heart started to pound a little harder. "Okay." She made the mistake of peering up into his eyes. She saw so much in them. Strength, but also the burdens he carried. The familiar pressure built in her chest again, the same way it had in the waiting room. Every time this happened—every time she got caught in this crazy pull between them—it got harder to push him away.

"Thank you for coming with me." The tone of his voice had dropped lower, quieter. "I'm glad you're here."

"Me too," she whispered, unable to look away. Being with Wes, looking into his eyes, knowing he saw her made her feel a little less lonely. She thought back to the moment she'd kissed him in front of the boat shed, how it had opened a part of her back up, how passion had flooded her, taking her away from everything else, and that craving overtook her again.

It had been too long since she'd felt something. But she could feel something now. She could kiss him and she could open that door and invite him into her room. She could give herself over to the feelings just for one night.

"When you said kissing me was a mistake...?" Wes inched closer, but she didn't want to talk. Talking would be too practical. Talking would make her think too much. Instead, she pressed her lips to his to show him she didn't regret anything.

This time, Wes didn't hesitate, didn't pull back. He wrapped his arms around her, shifting her back up against the hotel room door, and kissing her with a tenderness she'd never experienced before.

"The key." Thea gasped, feeling for the card in his hand. She found it and managed to focus enough to slide the key into the slot, letting them into the room. They stumbled inside, still kissing, arms tangled, and Wes nudged the door shut with his foot.

Thea savored the warmth of his mouth, the strength of his arms secured around her. Had kissing always been this good? She couldn't remember. And no one had ever kissed her like Wes.

Letting go of everything else, she let her desires drive her hands to the hem of Wes's shirt. She pulled it up and over his head, dropping it on the floor next to them. For a second, she stared at the muscle, that taut skin, then she lifted her finger to trace a jagged scar that ran along the edge of his left lower rib.

"Caught a horn there," he murmured, out of breath.

"Ouch." She lowered her lips to the mark of brutality, kissing his skin.

A sharp intake of breath tightened Wes's abs, accompanied by a deep resounding groan. He cupped the back of her head, gently drawing her face back to his. "What do you want?"

She knew why he was asking. Because she'd told him she wanted to be friends. With boundaries. But what were boundaries when they kept you locked inside yourself? What were boundaries when they isolated you?

Wes made her want to be free.

"I want this. I want you." Her body ached with want. "I need to feel close to someone. I need to know I'm not alone." For tonight, she needed to know someone was there.

Wes gazed into her eyes for a few seconds, smoothing his hand over her hair. "Me too." He lowered his lips to her neck, slowing down the moment, breathing tenderness against her skin.

Thea tipped back her head, drowning in the heat he generated inside of her.

Wes kissed his way across her jawline and up to her ear. "I can't just be your friend," he murmured. "I want you too much, Thea Davis."

She smiled at him, projecting a sass she didn't even know she was capable of. "Just you wait, Wes Harding," she said with an extra twang. Backing up a step, she pulled her shirt over her head, thankful she'd actually used those Victoria's Secret coupons she'd gotten in the mail.

Wes moved his heated gaze over her. "I could stand here and look at you all day." He stepped closer and eased a hand onto her hip. "Do you know how beautiful you are?"

She almost laughed or deflected like she usually did when someone paid her a compliment, but the intensity in the man's eyes stopped her. He meant it. He wasn't giving her some line or being flippant. He really saw her that way.

Thea kissed him again, not sure how to explain to him that no one had ever told her she was beautiful. Not her dead husband, not her parents, not any man who'd ever bothered to look at her. Instead of telling him that, she kissed him again, urgently unbuckling his belt, pulling open the button fly of his jeans, and then shoving the pants and his boxer briefs down his hips.

Wes pushed down her shorts and underwear just as greedily, then brought his lips back to hers, kissing her with passion and tenderness and a need that mimicked her own.

Thea stepped out of her shorts and backed to the bed, pulling him with her. They fell to the mattress, and Wes reached around her, undoing her bra strap with one hand. She shifted onto her side, wriggling out of the straps, ready to be free of any barriers between them. She only wanted to feel his skin against hers, his heat, his passion.

Wes turned on his side to face her, tracing his finger over her breast, up to the peak of her nipple. "I want to feel every inch of you." He lowered his mouth to where his finger had touched, kissing and licking and stealing the breath from her lungs. His hand moved from the contour of her waist down lower, and she hitched her leg up over his hip to give him access.

With his mouth still on her breast, Wes skimmed his fingers between her thighs, and Thea's head fell back with a moan. He seemed to know her, to know what she needed, where she needed to be touched, how to make her gasp and beg.

Fighting the pull of a powerful climax, she let her hands wander too. Down his hard abs, past his hips. When she stroked his erection, he stopped moving. "You do crazy things to me," he growled, lifting his face to hers. The desire she saw in his eyes only urged her on. She'd never lost herself this way with anyone else. Before Wes, there had always been this underlying insecurity...that she wasn't enough.

But when he looked at her like this, like she held him in the palm of her hand, every doubt slipped away.

Unable to wait any longer, Thea pressed against him, guiding him into her, shuddering with ecstasy at the power of the moment. Wes held her tightly against him, murmuring that he cared about her, that he wanted to make her feel good.

"I've never felt this good," she whispered, nibbling on his ear.

He answered with a moan, and their bodies found a rhythm together. Wes's eyes locked on hers, bringing a connection that transcended anything physical. He wanted to see her, wanted to know her. She moved with him, while a knot of pleasure wound tighter and tighter. Pleas rose from her lips. She had no idea what she was saying. She only knew she couldn't hold on. So she let go, sighing his name, quaking with the release of ecstasy that broke her apart. Wes held her together in his arms, pushing deeper into her. His whole body tensed with a long, sexy moan as he came apart right along with her.

When the rush started to subside, Thea opened her eyes to find Wes staring into them. He kissed her softly, and she had never felt so cherished.

Chapter Fifteen

Wes never thought this day would come.

He wasn't the type to lounge around in bed—well, not since the day his father had died anyway. That morning he'd slept in, and the day had turned into the worst one of his life.

These days his internal clock woke him at six a.m. sharp, and he typically tore out of bed. But for once, he wasn't in a hurry to get the day started. Not with Thea next to him. She lay on her side, facing him, her eyes still closed, her breathing rhythmic and peaceful. Some of her tawny hair had spilled over her bare shoulder, and no woman had ever looked sexier to him than she did right this minute.

He leaned over to kiss that bare shoulder, reveling in the silkiness of her skin.

"Mmm." Thea smiled but didn't open her eyes or move one muscle.

"Good morning," he murmured, nudging her lips with his.

"Morning already?" She still wouldn't open her eyes.

"I'm afraid so." He pulled her into his arms.

She opened one eye and smirked. "For *some* reason it feels like we just went to sleep."

Could he help it if he'd wanted to explore her body all night? "You made it very difficult for me to want to go to sleep."

Both eyes opened and her smile deepened. "Oh, I'm not complaining. You made it very difficult for me to want to go to sleep too." She reached her hands around to the back of his neck and drew his face closer. "I'd pull an all-nighter with you any night."

He kissed her. "I'm free ton—"

The phone rang and brought reality slamming back into him. He looked at the clock. Not even six thirty. This couldn't be good news.

Thea must've seen the panic in his eyes. She reached for his hand, and once again the woman settled him as he grabbed the phone. "Hello?"

"Hey, sorry to call so early," Toby said. "I tried your cell and the other room, but no one answered. Wasn't sure which room you were in. Hopefully I didn't wake Thea."

He let out a breath. His brother-in-law didn't sound upset. In fact, Toby almost sounded...chipper. "Oh. Uh. Yeah. Actually...she's with me." Might as well be honest. He didn't have the mental presence right now to fabricate a lie.

"Ah." To his credit, Toby didn't react to the news. "Well, Jane is awake and bossing everyone around in the NICU from her wheelchair, and she'd love to see you both."

"She's awake?" Wes jolted out of bed. "And bossy?" That meant she was practically back to her old self already.

"Yes to both." Toby sounded like he was back to his old self too. "We're down at the NICU. You can text me when you get here."

"We'll be there as soon as we can." Wes cradled the phone and jumped back into the bed, capturing Thea in a bear hug.

"Good news, I take it?" she asked, laughing.

"Jane's awake and she's bossing everyone around. She's in the NICU with the baby."

"Then we'd best get over there." Thea started to slip away from him, but he wasn't ready to let her go yet. "Hold on." He pulled her back into his embrace. So much had happened between them last night. Not just the sex. It went deeper. He wasn't sure what it was, he only knew he'd never experienced something like that with anyone else.

They'd lain in bed talking until only a few hours ago. Thea talked about her kids a lot. She talked about her job. But she didn't talk about the man she'd lost. And he didn't want her to feel like she couldn't talk to him about her past. He didn't want her love for her late husband to be something that could come between them. "I just want to tell you I would never try to take Dylan's place in your heart. I know how much you must've loved him."

That had been the wrong thing to say. He knew it immediately. Her eyes shied away from his, and she pushed back. "I'd rather not talk about my marriage. We really should get to the hospital." Thea rolled out of bed and started to get dressed. "I hope we get to see the baby. I can't imagine how tiny a three-pound baby will be. Ryan was my little peanut, and he was still over six pounds."

Wes said nothing. He sat up and watched her hastily pull on her shorts.

"Liv was closer to eight pounds," Thea went on. "She hardly fit into any of the newborn clothes." She bent over to put on her sandals. "A three-pound baby is going to be so tiny." She quickly stood and then disappeared into the bathroom.

What had just happened? It took Wes a second to get going. But at the rate Thea was moving, she'd likely be out the door before he could even get his boxers on. He found his clothes, listening to the sink run in the bathroom. So, she hadn't been avoiding talk about her late husband on Wes's account. She simply didn't want to talk about her marriage.

My parents yell at each other a lot. He hadn't thought too much of it when Ryan brought that up. Hell, his parents had gotten into some good shouting matches occasionally, if memory served. But maybe there was more to the boy's statement than he'd originally thought.

Wes pulled on his boxers and jeans, doing up the buckle before putting on his shirt. Whatever the reason she wanted to avoid that conversation, he wouldn't push her.

"Ready?" Thea rushed out of the bathroom. She'd pulled her hair back into a loose ponytail, exposing those same spots where he'd kissed her neck last night. But Wes didn't dare approach her now. The vibe had changed between them. She seemed determined to look everywhere but at his face.

"I'll get the keys." Thea snatched them off the dresser, and Wes stooped to put on his boots before she could run out of the room and leave him behind.

On the way out of the hotel, Thea maintained a good five-step distance between them. She handed her valet ticket to the attendant, and the kid hurried off.

Seeing as how they had a minute, Wes faced her directly. "Are you okay?"

"Yep. I'm great." Her smile was a little too bright to be believable. "I'm excited to see the baby. Aren't you?"

"Sure. I can't wait to meet my niece." But he also wanted to know why it suddenly felt like Thea was running away from him.

The kid drove up in the Volvo, giving the woman another good excuse to avoid him.

Wes slipped the attendant a tip before Thea could, and they both climbed into the car. He quickly fired off a text to Toby to let him know they were on their way.

"I hope the kids did okay," Thea said, turning up the radio.

"I'm sure they did." The camp they'd stayed at was one of the best in the state. He'd grown up going there with his family, and those adventures were still some of his best memories. "Hey, maybe I can take Ryan on that fishing trip today. You could come too if you want." Then they could spend more time together...

"I'm not sure that's a great idea." Thea slammed on the brakes hard at a red light.

He braced his hands against the dashboard. This whole morning was turning out to be a wild ride. "The fishing isn't a good idea? Or you coming with?" He had a feeling he already knew the answer.

"Me coming with." Her fingers tapped the steering wheel impatiently. "I don't want Ryan to get the wrong idea about us."

After last night, Ryan might not be the only one in danger of getting the wrong idea. "What would the wrong idea be?" he asked, trying to read her expression.

"You know..." She pressed the gas pedal and peeled out into the intersection the second the light turned green. "That there's something between us. A future. I don't want him to get his hopes up."

"Right." He couldn't blame her for being protective of her kid. "That's probably best." But he couldn't imagine not seeing Thea anymore. Not spending time with her. Not hearing her laugh. As impractical as that was, given their two very different lives. "I'm pretty sure we stepped past being friends with boundaries last night." And it wouldn't be easy to go back now. Not now that he knew how it felt to hold her in his arms.

"I guess we did." Thea pulled the SUV into a parking spot near the hospital's main entrance and cut the engine. "So maybe we'll have to be friends with benefits then."

"Friends." After last night, she was still trying to friendzone him?

"What other option is there?" She tossed her keys into her purse and got out of the car, clearly avoiding his gaze. "Anything more than that wouldn't be practical. Serious relationships aren't your speed anyway."

The words scraped a nerve. Wes climbed out of the car too. "Right. Because I'm too unreliable. Irresponsible. Too wild." He'd been hearing that mantra his whole life.

"That's not what I meant." She finally stopped moving long enough to look at him. Really look at him. "You travel half the year. I live in Texas. You're free to go wherever you want—to do whatever you want. And I have two children who've already been through too much. I won't risk their hearts."

What about her? She'd been through too much too. But she wouldn't want to talk about Dylan with him. He'd already learned that. "I'll do whatever you want. Be whatever you want me to be, Thea." He made sure to wait until her eyes were fully connected with his. "But being friends won't change the fact that I care about you, that I want to know you more. Like I told you last night, you do crazy things to me. I may have never been in a serious relationship before, but that doesn't mean I can't be." Having said his piece, he turned and walked into the building.

After a few steps, Thea fell in stride with him, but she didn't speak, so he didn't either. They rode the elevator in silence, and when the doors finally opened, Thea rushed out ahead of him.

Toby was waiting for them in a small waiting room outside the NICU. "That was faster than I thought," he commented with a good-natured smile.

Wes didn't smile back. He noticed Thea wasn't smiling either. "How's baby girl this morning?"

"Uh." Toby seemed to glance back and forth between the two of them. "She's great. Jane got to hold her for a while, but they're warming her again in the incubator. I can take you back one at a time if you'd like to see her."

"You go first." Thea stepped back, a sad expression tingeing her eyes and mouth. "I need to check in with the kids anyway."

Wes nodded, sensing her urgency to get away from him. Why was she so intent on putting distance between them? That wasn't a question he'd be able to get an answer to now. "Sounds great." He faced Toby. "Lead the way."

His brother-in-law waited until they'd checked in at the nurses' station before making any comments. "You want to talk about why neither one of you are smiling this morning?"

"Nope." They cruised through a pair of double doors. Machines seemed to be beeping everywhere, and colorful curtains separated incubators and rocking chairs. The place seemed empty at the moment. Only one nurse was tending to a baby on the other side of the room.

"Roger that." Toby waved him on. "We're down at the end here. They made sure we got a mountain view."

They passed a few more curtains and found Jane in the last station. She was sitting in a rocking chair next to an incubator.

"Hey, sis." Wes hugged her quickly and then looked her over. The color had come back to her face, and while her eyes looked tired, she was smiling as big and brightly as she had on her wedding day.

"Thanks for coming." She stayed seated but peered into the incubator. "Meet your new little goddaughter and niece, Charlee Sue."

"Charlee." That bittersweet ache lodged itself into his windpipe again. She had named her after their father.

"We wanted her to know her grandpop's legacy," Toby said, joining him next to the incubator.

"It's perfect." Their dad would've been the best grandpa. Wes gazed down at the doll-like figure nestled snugly in a blanket, and he couldn't be sure, but tears may have clouded his vision. A knitted cap was pulled down almost to the baby's eyes, but he could see a miniature nose and bowed lips. "She's *tiny*." She could probably fit in the palm of his hand.

"Tiny but mighty," his sister said proudly. "So far she's a champ. She's doing everything the doctors want her to do and shocking them all, of course."

"She's beautiful." He pulled out his phone and took a picture he could text to August. When his brother had finally called back last night—interrupting him and Thea—Auggie had said he would stay at the ranch until Wes came back, and then he'd go down for his turn to visit. "What about you?" He turned his attention back to Jane. "How are you feeling?"

"Perfect, minus the huge scar across my belly." She rolled her eyes. "They're hardly letting me stand up at all yet."

"Well, considering you were in the ICU last night, I'm okay with that." Toby leaned over and kissed his wife's forehead.

Wes watched the two of them while he fought off a trace of jealousy. They'd never looked happier. Both of them were beaming in the light of their new daughter. "You look great, sis."

"Don't you 'look great' me." Her eyebrows rose, a sure sign the niceties were over. "You spent the night with Thea last night?"

He should've been ready for that. Wes shot his brother-in-law a look. *Traitor.*

Toby shrugged. "You know how persuasive she can be. She dragged it out of me."

Sure she did.

"Listen, buster." His sister pointed at him—another bad sign. "Thea is my friend. She's not some hottie from out on the road. She's got two kids."

As if he wasn't aware of that fact. "First of all...hottie?" Who even used that word anymore? "And second, I know Ryan and Olivia. I know how amazing Thea is. I know she's smart and dedicated and hardworking." He could keep listing off the woman's attributes, but he decided to stop there. "You don't have to worry about her getting too attached to me. She only wants to be friends. She told me herself this morning."

Jane's eyes narrowed as she studied him. "But you want more? Oh my God! You really like her. Like...*like* her, like her."

He didn't argue, but it didn't matter how much he like-liked Thea. "I'm not what she wants." For herself. For her kids. "I'm not grounded enough for her. I'm not dependable enough. She probably would rather have some guy with a desk job who works nine to five and will be home on the weekends." And maybe that's what she deserved. Maybe that would be better for her family.

"A desk job?" Toby looked disgusted. "I can't imagine anything worse."

That's because Toby was like him. He liked to be out on the road. He liked the adventure of it, the challenges. The rodeo circuit had been Wes's life since he was eighteen years old. He hadn't known anything else. But for the first time, he wanted to.

"Three months ago, I would've agreed with you." Jane was no longer scowling at him. "But that's not true anymore. You *are* dependable."

Now it was his turn to raise his eyebrows at her. She'd always acted like he couldn't handle any responsibility.

"I'm not kidding." His sister put on her serious face. "Look at you. You gave up the chance at a promotion to help us out. And you're here now. You could've left when August got to the ranch, but you didn't."

"You know I'd do anything for you guys." He peered at little Charlee again. "I'll do anything for her." He'd always be there for his niece, no matter what.

"That's the thing about you, Wes." Jane shifted as though she wanted to stand up, but then seemed to think better of it. "You'd do anything for anyone. Underneath all that wild and impulsive energy, you've always had the biggest heart. You got it from our father."

Her words put him in a choke hold. All he'd ever wanted was to be like their father. But Charlie Harding was organized and deliberate. He'd always been a planner. Wes had never been any of those things. "You think I'm like Dad?" he asked, beating back emotion.

"You're more like him than you think," his sister said quietly. "I know you would love Thea well. Just like Dad loved Mom. And that matters more than your travel schedule."

"I'm not sure loving her would be enough." If he thought it would make a difference, he would learn how. He would make that his true calling...

Jane took her husband's hand. "Trust me, bro. Love is always enough."

Chapter Sixteen

Thea stood at the window, staring out at the empty streets. At only a few minutes after seven o'clock the world still seemed to be asleep.

There wasn't much to see, but she couldn't seem to make herself sit down across the room. After hardly sleeping all night, she should be exhausted, but instead a nervous energy made her restless. She couldn't stop picturing Wes's face before he'd walked away with Toby. She hadn't meant to hurt him, but when he'd said he knew how much she must've loved her husband something in her had iced over.

If he only knew the truth. Instead of sending her husband off with a kiss to fight overseas, she'd told him she wanted a divorce. Dylan hadn't even reacted when she'd told him. His eyes had been empty. Would it have been different if she'd held on to hope and sent him off with a kiss and a heartfelt *I love you*? Would he have fought harder to save himself? Would he have died more peacefully knowing she held him in her heart?

Her phone rang, and she quickly rifled through her purse, searching for it. The kids must finally be awake. She'd texted Liv a half hour ago but hadn't heard back. They'd probably been sleeping still, but that hadn't stopped her from worrying. She couldn't wait to talk to them.

"Hey, Liv," she said, turning on the speaker since no one was around. "How was your night?"

"Hi, Mom!" Ryan shouted into the phone. "Our night was amazing! Wasn't it, Liv?"

"It was pretty cool," her daughter agreed with a yawn.

Wow, coming from Liv, that meant it had to be spectacular. "What'd you do?"

"We went rock climbing, and I made it to the top!" Ryan sure didn't sound like he'd just woken up. "And Liv made it too! Preston was super nice and helped her a lot."

I'll bet he did. Despite her own messy love life right now, she had to smile. "That's great, honey. Sounds like fun."

Liv mumbled a response she couldn't quite make out. Yep, her daughter must've just woken up. It always took Liv at least an hour to really find her voice in the morning.

"How's your friend?" Ryan asked.

"She's doing much better. Thanks for asking, buddy." Thea checked the doors where Toby and Wes had disappeared. Still no sign of them. But as worried as Wes had been yesterday, the man likely wouldn't want to leave his sister's side.

"How's Wes?" Ryan asked. "I really miss him. Do you think maybe he'll take me fishing today?"

Thea's face warmed. Thank God her son asked a million questions at once. That meant she didn't have to answer how Wes was doing. "I think a fishing trip can be arranged."

"Yes! Yes! Yes!" Ryan squealed.

"Stop being so loud," Olivia snapped. "Some of us are still trying to sleep."

"We're supposed to be getting ready for breakfast," Ryan retorted. "We have to eat so we can do the ropes course later."

"Oh, that sounds fun." Thea switched the phone to her other ear. "Make sure you take some pictures for me, okay, Liv?"

"Mmm-hmm," her daughter mumbled.

"Make sure you talk to Wes about fishing," her son instructed. "We have to go, but we'll see you later."

"Okay. Bye. Love you both."

After a quick *love you* back, her kids disconnected the call.

Thea stuffed the phone back into her purse, trying not to think about how little they seemed to miss her. There'd been a time not all that long ago when they would've begged her to come pick them up because they hated being away from her.

When Liv had been in kindergarten, Thea had to run over to the school during her lunch hour because her daughter kept having meltdowns, she missed her so much. Oh, how things had changed. Things needed to change—she got that. Her kids needed to grow and have new experiences and develop their confidence, but that didn't make it any easier to let them go. What would her life be like in another five years when Ryan was fifteen and Liv was getting ready to go to college? She didn't even want to think about it.

"How are the kids?" Wes's voice startled her.

She turned around, both regret and want swelling in her chest. "They're good." Seeing Toby standing nearby, she put on a smile she didn't feel. "They're having a great time at the camp, so thank you for that."

"I'm glad," Wes said in a formal voice that sounded completely different from the one he'd used in bed last night.

That was her fault. She'd pushed him away. An unexpressed sigh made her lungs pound. She'd never in her life experienced such conflicting emotions. She wanted to throw her arms around the man, and yet she also wanted to keep her secrets and failures safely hidden behind her walls.

Realizing both men were looking at her, she found a new topic of conversation. "How's Jane this morning?"

"She looks a hell of a lot better than she did last night." Wes glanced at his brother-in-law as if waiting for confirmation.

"She looks better than ever," Toby agreed. "Wait until you see her with the baby. I didn't think she could get more beautiful, but I was wrong."

"I'd love to see her." Thea snuck a quick glance at Wes's face again. There were many things she should tell him, but they were things she'd never told anyone, and she didn't know how to stop pretending.

"Toby'll show you back," Wes informed her in that neutral tone she didn't like. "And then I'm taking him to get some breakfast while you and Jane visit. I'm on strict orders from my sister to make sure he eats a healthy meal."

"Don't gotta tell me twice." Toby waved Thea to follow him. He checked them in with a nurse, who buzzed them through some double doors, and then he led her back to a corner of the NICU.

"Thea!" Jane threw out her arms as if she wanted a hug, but she didn't stand. Good. She was being careful.

"Hey." She bent to hug her friend, the tears already burning in the corners of her eyes. "You gave us a scare," she said, pulling back.

"It wasn't the way I'd pictured everything going, that's for sure." For having been through so much in the last several days, Jane still looked as beautiful as ever. Her eyes seemed to shine brighter than they ever had. That was the magic baby dust. Thea remembered it well. Even years later, her babies still made her light up.

"But everything turned out okay." Her friend seemed as relieved as everyone else. "And now you get to meet Charlee Sue." She laid a hand on the incubator, where a miniature angel lay swaddled in a soft white blanket.

An awed sigh slipped out as Thea pressed in as close as she could. "Look at that nose! And her sweet tiny lips." Seriously. Little Charlee already had the most beautiful face. "She is absolutely perfect."

"I know." Jane moved her face right next to Thea's. "I can't seem to stop staring at her. I pictured her for so long, but I never realized how beautiful she would really be."

A few tears escaped down Thea's cheeks. "It's truly miraculous when you see them after all those months of dreaming." Those were some of the only moments she'd felt close to Dylan. He'd been able to be there for both Liv's and Ryan's births, and the miracle of the new lives they'd created had brought them together. The magic never seemed to last long, though. Shortly after they'd arrived home from the hospital each time, Dylan had been shipped back overseas.

"Could you see yourself having another one?"

Jane's question forced her upright. "Oh. Wow. Uh." She peered at the baby again, overcome by the flashes of memories from those early days with her children. The sleepless nights and the stressful midnight feedings and the times they'd been sick. More tears broke apart her vision. "Yeah." That was her heart's most honest answer. "I miss having a baby. There's no better feeling in the world." She quickly dried her tears with her sleeve before she lost her grip on reality. "But it's not like that will be an option for me." She'd already proved she couldn't make a relationship work once. "I'm pretty sure that ship has sailed. And I'm happy with Liv and Ryan. They're my whole world."

Jane's smile softened into a look of understanding. "Before they're born, it's impossible to imagine how much you'll love them. And then after they're born, it just...seems to spill out from every part of you."

"That never goes away." Even with the heartbreak they'd endured. Even with the different stages her children went through. Thea sat in a hard-backed chair across from Jane's rocker. "I still walk into their rooms every night after they're asleep, and I'm in awe that they belong to me."

"I can understand that." Jane gazed lovingly at her new daughter. "How are Ryan and Liv anyway?"

"They're great." The answer came out automatically. That was the answer she always gave. Everything was great. The kids were great, she was great. She'd learned over the years that her life all had to be great. But this was Jane. And things weren't great at the moment. Things were hard. "I mean...Liv is going through some of that teen stuff. It's a whole new world. She actually brought a vape pen on this trip, and Wes caught her using it by the boathouse."

Jane laughed so loud that Charlee seemed to startle. "Wes ratted *her* out? Now that's ironic."

"I could tell he didn't want her to get into trouble." She smiled, too, remembering how uncomfortable Wes had seemed when he'd come to find her by the fire. "But yeah. He came and got me." And then she'd kissed him. Probably best if she didn't mention that part. "He said he'd made some mistakes back in high school."

"Oh, for sure." Jane shook her head, but amusement colored her expression. "In some ways I always envied him, though," she said thoughtfully. "He really knew how to connect with people. Like my dad did." She shrugged. "August and I didn't get that gene, but Wes...he always seemed to know what someone needed to hear, or how to approach someone in just the right way. He didn't have a lot of focus, and all of us dismissed him as irresponsible, but looking back on our growing-up years, he always put people first."

"I'm not surprised." Somehow, Wes had managed to get closer to reaching past her walls than anyone in the last three years. But the second he'd mentioned Dylan, the second she thought she might have to tell him something about herself, she'd shut down.

Jane shifted in the chair, wincing slightly. "I'm impressed that Wes didn't wimp out and let Olivia off the hook. But maybe I shouldn't be surprised. He gave up a lot to stay at the ranch for the retreat. He really stepped up."

Thea held back a grin. This was starting to sound like quite the sales pitch.

"He can still be a goofball," her friend went on. "But he's also been around the ranch more over the last year. Visiting us. Helping my mom and us with everything."

Jane didn't have to worry about selling Wes's positive qualities to her. She'd seen them firsthand. "Ryan loves him," Thea admitted. "He latched onto him the second day we were here when Wes happened to see him out on the lake alone." The memory still made his heart shudder. Thank God Wes had been there...

Jane's eyes widened. "He was on the lake alone?"

"I'd slept in way past my usual six o'clock wake-up time," Thea explained. "And he snuck out to do some fishing all by himself. So, Wes has already busted both of my kids this week."

"Again, it's ironic that my brother told on him." Amusement danced in her friend's eyes. "That's totally something Wes would've done back in the day."

Maybe that's why Wes and Ryan got along so well. They did seem to be cut from a similar cloth. Both a bit spontaneous and determined to enjoy life. "Ever since then, Wes is all Ryan talks about."

Jane studied her for a few seconds. "You don't seem to think that's a good thing."

Her friend had always been able to read her. Even back in college Thea had been great at pretending. "I'm very protective of both my kids." It was easy to revert back to her signature excuse. In a way, her kids had become her wall. They'd given her an excuse to hide. "They've already had a lot taken away from them. I don't want them to have to go through anything like that again."

"What about *you*?" Jane asked as though she saw right through the justification. "How do you feel about Wes?"

It was clear Jane knew something had happened between them, so there was no use lying. "He makes me wish things were different. That *I* was different." But she already knew she couldn't be what he needed. She'd tried, but she hadn't been what Dylan needed either. "Wes is a good man." Over the last few days, she'd seen deeply into his heart. "But things are complicated for me." Her heart kept pulling her in one direction and then her head would butt in and remind her of every reason she had failed.

Jane reached for her hand, squeezing it tightly. "Thea, no one would blame you for being afraid to love someone again. Not after losing Dylan."

If only that were her problem—that she'd loved Dylan so much, her heart had yet to heal. The truth was much uglier than that. She couldn't heal. Because she would never know what those last moments were like for him. For the most part Dylan's first lieutenant had spared her the horrible details of his death. After his platoon had been ambushed, her husband was shot. They had done everything they could for him. That's all she knew. She hadn't done everything she could for him, though. Had he felt alone in the world? Had he given up instead of fighting to live?

Those were the questions she would take into every other relationship. Those were the questions that would haunt her forever.

Chapter Seventeen

Wes had never liked to wake up a beautiful woman. Especially when said woman hadn't looked at him—really looked at him—since he'd brought up her dead husband earlier that morning in the hotel room they'd shared.

With Thea asleep in the passenger's seat next to him, he could pretend things weren't awkward between them. He could pretend she hadn't let him get close only to force him back out. The problem was, he had to wake her up. They would arrive back at the ranch in fifteen minutes, and then these last moments alone with her would be gone.

When they'd left the hospital, he hoped the drive back would give them a chance to talk through what had happened between them. Knowing how exhausted Thea was, he had offered to drive, and when she'd reclined her seat and told him she was going to take a short nap, he didn't stop her. Over two and a half hours later, their window to talk through things was closing.

He took his eyes off the road to glance at her again. She seemed peaceful with her head tilted slightly to the right and her breathing deep and rhythmic. He remembered when she'd woken up in bed next to him earlier that morning, how she'd smiled without opening her eyes. He'd give anything to see that smile right about now. Instead, he prepared himself for the distanced caution she'd displayed all morning.

"Hey." Wes gently reached for her shoulder, giving it a squeeze. "Time to wake up."

Thea stretched and shifted before opening her eyes. "Where are we?" she asked in a groggy voice.

"We'll be coming up to Silverado Lake in a few minutes." And whatever notion he'd had about the two of them resolving anything would go up in smoke.

"Wow." Thea sat up straight and brought the seat back in line with his. "I can't believe I slept that long."

"You needed the rest." They hadn't gotten more than a few hours of sleep, and yet Wes didn't feel tired.

For a second he swore her mask slipped, and he caught a glimpse of the same vulnerability he'd seen in her last night. But then Thea sighed and looked out the window as if getting herself together.

When she turned back to him, her expression was formal. "I'm sorry about last night." She said it as though last night had been nothing more than a minor mistake. "Being at the hospital was pretty intense. I think I got caught up in the emotion."

"Please don't apologize again." Wes didn't plan on pretending their night together had meant nothing. "I didn't regret kissing you. And I don't regret making love to you." But it was clear she had plenty of regrets.

It took a few seconds for her to answer. "I don't regret it either," she finally murmured. "But I can't give you more."

"I understand." He knew how it felt to live with a hole in your life, to feel like you would never be a complete person again because of what you'd lost. He didn't like it, but he understood. "If you'd rather I not take Ryan fishing, I can tell him it won't work out this trip."

"No." Thea's smile seemed to cover up a pain he couldn't soothe. "I think it would be great for you to take him. He'll love it.

We didn't have any big plans with the rest of the group until later this afternoon anyway."

Right. Later that afternoon, they were supposed to go on a trail ride. And then tomorrow they were having the boat race across the lake. And more breakfasts and lunches and dinners. He wasn't sure exactly how he would be able to get through the rest of the retreat treating Thea like nothing more than a guest at the ranch. "Maybe I'll check with the other dads and see if they want to come too." Wes looked up ahead to where the turnoff for the ranch loomed.

"I'm sure they would all love it." Thea pulled down the visor and started to mess with her hair as she looked in the small mirror.

"You're perfect exactly like you are," he told her. She couldn't look more beautiful if she tried.

"Thank you." There was her real smile. The one he'd been missing.

Silence fell over them, and he let it sit as he navigated the ranch's driveway. It seemed there was nothing left to say. Once they got out of the car, they would go back to acting like nothing more than acquaintances.

He slowed the SUV as they came up over the hill. The wilderness camp bus was parked farther down, in front of the main lodge, and the kids were getting off, being reunited with their parents.

As Wes guided the car to park next to the bus, Thea rested her hand on his arm. "Last night was one of the best nights of my life," she said quietly. "I want you to know that."

"I'm glad." But knowing that didn't make it any easier for him to walk away from her.

He parked the car and they both got out just as Ryan stepped off the bus.

"Wes!" Instead of greeting his mom first, the boy came charging at him. "Hey, Sport." He returned the kid's hug. "I think you'd best give one of those to your mom. She missed you."

"Mom!" The boy turned and nearly plowed Thea over with a bear hug around the waist.

Thea shot Wes a grateful look over her son's head. "Hey, buddy. How was the ropes course?"

"It was amazing! I walked a tightrope!" He demonstrated by walking a straight line, carefully putting one foot in front of the other.

"We got to do a zip line too," Timothy added, leaving his parents behind to join Ryan on the pretend ropes course. "Olivia screamed really really really loud." Both boys giggled.

"It wasn't that loud," the girl called from a few feet away.

The boys ignored her and continued zipping around as though imagining they were back on the zip line.

"I have to admit, I wasn't sure about the wilderness camp," Thea said to Wes. "But clearly it was one of the highlights of this trip for them."

"And what's been your highlight of the trip?" he asked so no one else could hear. He knew what his answer would be.

"I think it's pretty obvious." She shot him a smile over her shoulder and walked over to talk to her daughter.

While the families continued to catch up, Wes helped the bus driver unload their bags. When Wes walked back to the group, Cal met him. "Thanks for setting that up. The kids had a blast."

"No problem." Coordinating fun things for these families was the absolute least he could do. "Glad they had a great time."

"We're going fishing today, right, Wes? You're taking me to your favorite fishing spot!" Ryan ran to join them. "Hey, Mr. Cal, maybe you and Timothy could come!"

"Yes." Wes had to grin at the kid. He'd never seen so much enthusiasm in such a small package. "I was thinking we'd invite whoever wanted to come with us to my secret fishing spot." By now everyone had gathered around.

"That's a great idea," Luciana said. "Carlos would love to go. I wanted to take the girls shopping in town this afternoon anyway."

"Gabe could use a little guy time too," Abby added. "Piper and I are planning to paint our nails." She put an arm around her young daughter.

"And I foresee a lengthy beach nap in my future." Kelly seemed just as enthusiastic about that prospect as Ryan had about the fishing.

"Do you want to come, Mom?" Ryan zipped over to Thea. "I could teach you how to cast..."

Thea seemed to hesitate.

Wes couldn't help but wonder if Ryan was feeling left out because he couldn't go with his dad.

"Do you *want* me to come?" she asked her son.

Wes almost said yes, he'd love for her to come, but Ryan's nose scrunched. "Well, it's kind of a boy trip, and Wes is gonna help me fish, so you might get bored."

"Maybe another time." Thea smiled. "I thought I would take Liv out for lunch at that cute café I saw in town."

"Good, because I definitely don't want to go fishing." Olivia turned up her nose.

"That's settled then." At least Wes wouldn't have to keep pretending he wasn't head over heels for Thea all afternoon. "Why don't you all go put your stuff away and get some hiking boots on? I'll organize the gear and meet you down by the boathouse."

Everyone started to disperse, except for Ryan. "Can I come with you?" His eyes grew rounder. "I'm real good at setting up fishing stuff. Right, Mom?"

"You are," Thea agreed.

Wes met her gaze and she gave a slight nod. "It's fine with me if it's fine with Wes. I can take your bag back to the cabin for you."

"Yes! Thanks, Mom!" Give the boy a couple more years, and he really would be able to knock her over with those hugs.

"Sure." Thea wrapped her arms around him and kissed the top of his head. "I hope you catch a great big fish."

"I will," Ryan promised. "Don't worry. Won't I, Wes?"

"I know you will." That spot had never left him disappointed before. "I'll take pictures," he told Thea. "And don't worry." He rested his hand on Ryan's shoulder. "I know all the best angles to make the fish look even bigger."

Thea laughed as she picked up Ryan's backpack. "Thank you." There was a gravity in her tone that hinted she was grateful for more than the fishing trip.

"You're welcome." Hopefully the look he gave her let her know he would do anything for her, for her kids.

"I guess we'll see you a little bit later then." She gave Ryan one more kiss.

"Aw, Mom." He wiped his cheek.

They walked to the edge of the parking lot, where they would have to go their separate ways.

"It's a good half-hour hike, so I'm assuming we'll be back around two," he said to Thea. That would give them an hour to rest before the big trail ride.

"No way!" Ryan looked at him like he was crazy. "We want to fish all night."

"You listen to Wes." Thea sent a stern expression in her son's direction. "When he says it's time to leave, it's time to leave."

"I will listen," Ryan promised with an angelic smile. "Promise."

"Just keep an eye on him," she whispered. "He has a tendency to get overexcited and wander off."

"I'll take good care of him." He'd take good care of her, too, if she'd let him.

"Bye, Mom!" Ryan practically pushed her toward the path to the cabins. "Have fun at lunch."

"You have fun too," she called, following Olivia down the hill.

Wes and Ryan headed off in the opposite direction, following the worn path to the boathouse.

"At least she didn't call me Ry-ry." The kid looked up at him with a deadpan expression. "That's even more embarrassing than the kisses."

Wes laughed. "I don't know about that. My mom used to blow me kisses from the car when she'd drop me off at school. Now that was embarrassing."

The boy gaped up at him. "In front of *everyone*?"

"Pretty much." Wes pulled his keys out of his pocket and

unlocked the boathouse's door, opening it for Ryan. "But I appreci-ate it now. Having a mom who loved me that much. That's nothing to be embarrassed about." It had taken him years to appreciate his mother too. After his father had died, he'd gained a new respect for his mom. She'd put aside her own grief to do her best to get them through theirs.

Ryan didn't answer. He was already distracted with the collec-tion of fishing gear hanging on the wall. But someday he would appreciate how much Thea had done for him too.

"Wow! Look at all these poles!" Amazingly, he didn't grab one.

"You want to hold one?" Wes asked, reaching for one of his favorites—a red spin/fly combo rod his dad had used often.

"Really? I can touch it?" Ryan seemed almost afraid to take the pole in his hands.

"Sure." Wes held it out to him.

"I wasn't allowed to touch my dad's fishing stuff." The boy held the rod as though he was afraid he'd drop it. "It all costed too much money."

"Well, you don't have to worry about that here. These aren't too fancy." Wes started taking down poles and lining them up against the wall so the others could have their pick. Then he pulled down a few of the backpacks he used for tackle boxes.

"What's the biggest fish you ever caught?" Ryan asked, watch-ing him sort through the lures.

"Hmmm." There'd been quite a few fish that had been a chal-lenge to bring in, but one stood out in his memories. "I caught an eighteen-inch rainbow trout once. Right in the spot we're headed to now, in fact."

"Wow!" The boy picked up a small minnow lure and inspected it. "How much did it weigh?"

"It was about nine pounds, which is pretty good for a trout." If he did say so himself. "I was only a few years older than you. And my dad had to help me reel that fish in. The thing nearly broke my line, it was so heavy." He remembered how he and his dad had worked together, and then how his father had handed the rod back to him at one point. *You've got this, son. I'll be here to talk you through it, but you don't need me to do this for you.*

In that moment, Wes had been sure his dad was wrong. He hadn't thought there was any way he could bring that fish in. But his dad had refused to take the rod back, instead talking him through landing the fish, and eventually he'd held it up for a picture before throwing it back into the water.

Even though his dad wasn't here anymore, he still managed to talk Wes through things. To speak from his memories...

"I wish you were my dad." The boy's words seemed to come out of nowhere.

He didn't know what to say, how to respond. Wasn't this what Thea had been concerned about? That Ryan would get too attached to him?

"I mean, I still love my dad and everything," Ryan explained quickly. "But he's gone now. And it would be kind of nice to have a new dad to go fishing with sometimes."

Wes let out the breath still trapped in his lungs. The kid hadn't said that because he wanted Wes to marry his mom, or because he even thought that was within the realm of possibility. He was simply saying he felt lonely.

"I wish I had a dad to go fishing with too." He took a knee in front of Ryan. "But fishing with a friend can be pretty great."

Ryan's grin resumed its position, stretching from one ear to the other. "I'm really glad we're friends."

"So am I, Sport." Somehow, being around Ryan made his dad's presence in his life feel even more real.

Chapter Eighteen

Thea parked the SUV in front of the library. Across the street in the park, the carnival was still going on.

God, it felt like years ago that she and Ryan and Wes had been walking around the park, riding all the rides, eating ice cream like a little family. That had been one of the best days she'd had all year. And then last night...

Desire clutched her heart, but she led Liv down the sidewalk as if she could outrun it. "What do you want to do?" she asked Olivia, tearing her mind off Wes.

"I don't know." Liv looked around." What's that?" She pointed to the green space next to the park where a bunch of blue-and-white tents stood.

"That, my dear, is a good old-fashioned craft fair." It had been ages since she'd walked around a little pop-up market where artisans sold their handmade goods. "They usually have all kinds of unique things for sale. We can go look around if you want."

"Sure." Her daughter unclicked her seat belt, and they climbed out of the car. "This is actually a pretty cool town," Liv said as they walked across the street.

"I'm sorry, what?" Thea pretended to be shocked by the

statement. "I seem to remember you telling me how boring this trip would be a few weeks before we left." That was before her daughter had met Preston, however.

"I'm not saying I'd want to live here or anything." Olivia rolled her eyes, but it was in a good-natured way. "I'm just saying... it's kind of nice to be in a small town where everyone's friendly and they all hang out together at festivals like this."

They entered the park, and Thea knew exactly what Liv was talking about. People stood around the tents chatting like they had all day to be friendly. There seemed to be no rushing and hurrying. Just simple enjoyment that made her want to join in. "Oh, look over there." She pointed to a small red canopy tent selling home-made soaps.

They wandered over, and she picked up a lavender bath bar, breathing in the calming scent. "Doesn't that smell amazing?"

"I like this one better." Her daughter selected a birthday-cake-shaped soap. "It smells like vanilla."

"They're all natural," the girl sitting at the counter told them. "Made with only the best essential oils."

"We'll take the birthday cake." Thea pulled out her purse, delighted with the girl's happy smile.

"Wonderful! You'll love it." She took the money and packaged up the soap for them.

Liv eyed her as they walked away. "Who are you and what have you done with my mother?"

Thea had to laugh. Olivia was obliviously referring to the fact that Thea never ever under any circumstances made spontaneous purchases that weren't included in her budget. As a single mom she was usually extra careful, but today... well, it wouldn't hurt to buy her daughter a few treats. "It's been forever since we've had a girls' bonding day." That was mainly her fault. She kept them on a busy schedule back home. Between school and sports and Liv's dance classes, they didn't make a lot of time for activities like this. "If you see a few things you like, maybe I'll get them for you."

Liv stopped walking. "I'm kind of worried about you."

"Oh, shush." Thea linked her daughter's arm through hers and nudged her along. "I love it here in this small town too. It's not going to hurt to support the local economy." Shopping felt different when you could tell how much the seller appreciated the money.

"Let's look over there." Her daughter pointed to a white tent with handmade jewelry strewn out on a table.

"Lead the way."

They tried on rings while they chatted with the woman who'd spent the last year making the jewelry and then traveling around the country in her RV to sell it at fairs.

"Look at this necklace, Mom." Liv held a dainty sterling silver pendant of a mountain with the word *faith* spelled out underneath.

"Faith moves mountains," the woman said, somehow making the old adage sound believable.

Thea had to admit she was a little jealous of the woman's free spirit. She looked to be maybe a few years older than her—in her forties possibly, but she wore a white peasant shirt and had tied back her hair with a colorful bandanna.

"Try it on if you'd like," the woman offered. "If you buy it, I'll give you twenty-five percent off."

It was as if the woman knew Thea was a bargain shopper. She helped Liv get the necklace clasped, and even she gasped when she saw the pendant lying against her daughter's collarbone. "It's so pretty. We'll take it."

"We don't have to, Mom." Olivia hurriedly unclasped the necklace. "It's kind of expensive—"

"We'll take it," Thea said again, handing over the money.

"It looks lovely on you." The woman smiled at Liv. "And now you'll always remember there's no obstacle that can ever stand in your way."

Yes, please let her remember that. Thea hoped her daughter had more faith than she did.

After Thea put the necklace back on Liv, they walked away. "What'd you say we head to that café and get something to eat?"

"Sounds good. I'm starving." Her daughter touched the pendant. "Thanks for the necklace. You didn't have to buy it."

"I know I didn't have to. I wanted to." What good was having a daughter if she couldn't spoil her once in a while?

They made their way down the block, window-shopping at the fun boutiques and greeting people with smiles and hellos. By the time they finally got a seat in the café, Thea was ready to order the whole menu.

"Hey!" A familiar face rushed over to greet them at their table.

"Beth, right?" Thea hoped she had remembered Jane's friend's name correctly. "We met at the wedding."

"Yes!" The woman's soft brown eyes were warm. "And you're Thea. We didn't get to chat long, but I knew I recognized you when you walked in. I heard you got to see the baby. And Jane, of course. She's important too. How are they?"

"I did. Just this morning." Wow, had that really only been a few hours ago? "She looked great. And the baby is beautiful."

"I'm so glad." Beth let out a deep sigh. "I was terrified for them both. But it sounds like everything's going to be okay?"

"Yes," Thea assured her. "Given the circumstances, they're both doing wonderfully." She gestured to Liv, who was perusing the menu. "This is *my* baby girl. Olivia."

"Nice to meet you." Beth shook Liv's hand. "What can I get you two? Order anything you'd like. It's on the house."

"Oh, no," Thea said automatically. "We couldn't—"

"Jane's friends don't pay here," Beth informed her sternly.

Getting freebies had always made Thea uncomfortable. She'd been taught to pay her own way, but it seemed like she wouldn't get a choice. "How about two burgers, fries, and chocolate milk shakes?"

For about the hundredth time that afternoon, Liv gaped at her.

"Coming right up." Beth scurried away and Thea shrugged at her daughter. She didn't usually order fried food either, but ... "This is a special occasion." Before her daughter could question her further, Thea folded her hands on the table and asked innocently,

"It sounds like you had a good time with Preston at the wilderness camp, huh?"

A smile plumped her daughter's cheeks, bringing out a hidden dimple Thea hadn't seen in a while. *Uh-oh.* She recognized that look. Liv was smitten.

"He's the nicest guy I've ever met," her daughter declared. "I mean, he's pretty shy so he doesn't talk a lot, but he's thoughtful, you know?"

Thea nodded. She was starting to know what thoughtfulness looked like.

"He's not like the stupid boys from my school who are always trying to get attention."

Liv had had crushes on some of those boys before, but Thea didn't bring that up. She was glad her daughter was starting to see the difference.

"Do you think maybe Preston and I could go to a movie sometime or something?" her daughter asked hopefully.

"Well…" Thea tried to tread carefully. Liv was opening up to her, and that hadn't happened in a while. "You're still too young to date, but if you and some friends wanted to go to a movie with Preston and some of his friends, I think we could make that happen." With Thea and Kelly hiding in the back of the theater keeping watch, of course. They hadn't known the family long, but she already knew they would stay in touch after this trip.

Right then, a server swooped in and delivered two enormous chocolate milk shakes topped with a tower of whipped cream and chocolate sprinkles.

Whoa boy, that was going to take her all day to finish.

Olivia didn't seem intimidated at all. She used her spoon to eat the whipped cream first. "Was going to the hospital with Wes like a date?"

"No. Oh, no." Thea sat up straighter. Liv could never know what had happened between her and Wes last night. She had never discussed dating with them. She'd never had to. Her heart had been too weighted down to respond to any of the men she knew or had met since Dylan's death. Until Wes. "We were both concerned about Jane, that's all." She stopped talking so no lies would come out of her mouth. She couldn't tell her daughter nothing had happened between them because that wasn't true. So much had happened...

"Oh." Was that disappointment flickering in her daughter's eyes? Olivia stirred her chocolate shake with the spoon, her gaze fixed on the whipped cream. "You know it would be okay, right? If you, like, did want to go on a date sometime?" Her daughter peeked up at her as though afraid to see her reaction. "Ryan and I would be fine with it."

Thea's heart leapt up into her throat. "Oh, honey. I don't need to date." She'd been fine alone before she'd met Wes. After they went back to Texas, she would find it easier to move on and forget about the way he'd made her feel. At least that's what she was counting on. "You and Ryan are all I need."

Her daughter ate a spoonful of whipped cream and carefully wiped her mouth. "You know I'm going to be eighteen in less than five years, right?"

Thea preferred not to think about that. "I know." And she would start looking for a time-freeze machine first thing tomorrow.

Liv set down her spoon, her face serious. "Ryan and I are both going to grow up. And we want you to be happy, Mom. I know things were hard with you and Dad—"

"What?" Thea nearly choked on the word. "What do you mean, things were hard?" Her daughter didn't know they were headed for a divorce, did she? She couldn't know...

Liv studied her. "Do you remember the time you made a really nice dinner for all of us after Dad got home from his longest deployment? I think I was in fifth grade..."

"Yes. I remember." She remembered every dinner she'd made for Dylan after he'd come home. Even the ones he hadn't eaten.

"You spent all day cooking in the kitchen." Her daughter's tone gentled. "You made his favorite steak." Liv wrinkled her nose with disgust. She'd never been that into red meat. "We were all sitting at the dining room table, waiting for him, and then he came down the stairs and walked out the door saying he had to meet the guys."

That night, Thea had laughed it off, doing her best to hide her hurt from her children. She'd never wanted them to know about the problems in her marriage. She'd wanted so desperately to give them a happy family.

"And there was that time you got us all tickets to go see the *Lion King* play because it was Ryan's favorite movie?" Liv sipped on her shake.

Thea winced at another failed attempt to get Dylan to engage with the kids. She had no idea Olivia would remember all of these things.

"Right before we left, Dad said he had to stay home and fix a sprinkler."

"It was the sprinkler box." As if that made his refusal to go any better. There were brown patches in the yard, and he couldn't stand the look of them. He had always obsessed over those details— wanting everything on the outside to look perfect. Maybe because the inside of their relationship was such a mess.

"There were other things like that," her daughter said quietly. "Too many to remember. Too many to count. I was there, Mom. You tried. You tried to make him spend time with us. You tried to make him happy. But he wasn't. He never seemed happy. No matter what you did. No matter what I did. No matter what Ryan did."

Thea closed her eyes. She couldn't stand to see the pain in Liv's eyes. She thought she'd shielded her kids from feeling Dylan's indifference, but obviously his emotional absence had impacted her daughter far more than Thea had realized.

"Maybe he was depressed or something," her daughter went on. "I don't know. But he didn't try to fix anything. Preston said his dad goes to a counselor sometimes. Dad could've done that, too, but he didn't. He didn't want to change."

"Maybe he was afraid of change," Thea said quietly. For a long time it had angered her that Dylan refused to seek help for his issues. And on some level she knew she couldn't subject her kids to his mood swings and withdrawals forever. But she had to believe he didn't know what to do. "Sometimes the fear of the unknown is harder to tackle than living with the same patterns and defense mechanisms you've hidden behind your whole life." She should know. But she didn't want to be stuck anymore. And she certainly didn't want to take the guilt or any anger with her into the next chapter of her story. "Honey...your dad loved you kids." He never knew how to show it, but she believed with all her heart he'd loved their children. After he died, she'd tried to protect their memories of him, casting him in a different light so they could remember only the happier times. "I could've tried harder. I could've done more." Instead, she'd sent him off to battle with horrible, hateful words.

"You always tell me it's not my job to make other people happy," Liv reminded her. "You tell me happiness is a choice everyone has to make for themselves."

"I'm glad to know you listen to me." Even if it meant she had to hear her own lectures delivered back to her. "You're right, honey. I did try." She forgotten about most of those memories her daughter had brought up. Living in the shadows of Dylan's death, it was easier to remember her failures.

"Dad didn't choose to be happy. He could've. But he didn't. He wasn't nice to you." Her daughter slid Thea's shake back in front of her. "You deserve to have someone who is nice to you. You deserve to be happy. Ryan and I really want that for you. So if you do ever find someone who makes you happy, please don't feel bad about going on a date."

"Oh, Liv." Her sweet little Olivia. Tears gathered in her eyes. "You have the most tender heart." She hadn't given her daughter enough credit. Somewhere in there, mixed in with the teen drama, maturity and love had started to bloom too. "Thank you." For reminding her she had tried with Dylan. Those last words to him had been a mistake, but they didn't represent all of their years together. They didn't represent how hard she had tried, how deeply she'd wanted him to be happy too. "Maybe I can try to keep an open mind." Maybe spending last night with Wes had changed something in her—maybe it made her want to tell the truth for the first time in years.

"Well, you may want to at least *consider* going on a date with Wes." Her daughter smiled at her with a swift raise of her eyebrows. "He's funny and goofy, but he's also thoughtful. Especially with Ryan. And, I guess, even when he busted me. But he's also super nice to you. And that's what matters most."

"Thanks for the advice." Thea laughed, a lightness of heart raising her up. "You're right." She took a drink of her shake through the straw, savoring the rich chocolate taste, feeling younger and freer. "Maybe I can choose to be happy."

It would take work, and some serious therapy focused on her, but for the first time, she felt maybe it was possible to climb out from underneath the guilt and regret to build the kind of love she'd always dreamed of finding.

Chapter Nineteen

There was a reason Wes hadn't been back to this spot since his father had died.

Even when he'd been younger, he knew places evoked emotion, and he'd never been prepared to confront the memories that lived here. But it was time. Long past time, in fact. By not coming back to a place both he and his father had loved, he'd denied a part of his father's legacy, his significance, and he refused to keep avoiding the emotions.

"Wow, this is quite the hidden spot." Cal came up from behind him and slipped off his backpack.

"It's pretty awesome." Preston already had his pole out. "Can I fish over there?" He pointed to where the pond narrowed into the mouth of the creek.

"That's a great spot." Wes took in the view while he watched Ryan and Timothy splash each other as they waded in the small pond. "There's really no bad spot here." Off to the left, a waterfall tumbled down the wall of rock he'd loved to climb as a kid, opening up into a deep pool before the banks widened into the fishing pond. The whole scene was hemmed in by jagged, snow-covered mountain peaks.

"Look at that waterfall!" Ryan and Timothy splashed their way to the edge of the deeper pool.

Wes met them there. "I used to climb up all those rocks and jump into the pool. With my dad's help, of course." He didn't want the kids getting any fancy ideas. The rock wall had to be at least twenty feet tall, and it had always been slippery because of the spray.

"That's so cool!" Ryan looked up at him in awe.

"I think it's kinda scary," Timothy said, moving in his dad's direction.

"We can just admire it from a distance." Wes unlatched the fishing pole from the outside of his backpack. They hadn't really come equipped to swim anyway. "The best part about this place is the fishing. I can promise you that."

"Yes!" Ryan sprinted over to where he'd dropped his backpack. "I can't wait to use this fishing pole. It's the coolest."

Wes turned to the rest of the group scattered behind him. "We can spread out. Let me know if you need help rigging up any of the gear."

Everyone dispersed, with Timothy and Cal walking the path to the south side of the pond and Carlos and Gabe meandering farther north. Wes joined Ryan on a large flat rock where the pool and the pond met. "This is actually one of the best spots on the lake," he whispered to the kid.

Ryan paused from tying on a fly beneath the bobber Wes had rigged up earlier. "Really?"

"Really. The fish like the deeper water." He pointed to the pool. "But then they come to the shallower water to feed on bugs."

"I hope they feed on my bug." Ryan went back to work on the fly, his tongue sticking out slightly while he focused.

Wes pulled out his cell phone and snapped a picture. "I'm sure the fish will love that fly." It had never let him down before. He handed Ryan the small scissors from his tackle box so the boy could cut off the extra line. "It looks exactly like the ones they're feeding on."

"That's what I thought." Ryan stood up and shuffled to the edge of the rock, where he brought the pole back and then cast the fly onto the pond's surface.

"Wow, sweet cast." Wes sat on the other side of him where he wouldn't interfere.

"Thanks." The boy shot him a toothy grin. "I've been practicing real hard at home."

"I can tell." Wes took another picture of him reeling in the line.

"I'll try again. I bet I can get it even farther this time." Ryan wound up again and then sent the fly hurtling through the air. It landed with a delicate splash a good foot away from where he'd put it the first time.

"This is the hard part." The kid sat next to Wes, never taking his eyes off the bobber. "Catching a fish sure seems to take a long time."

"Yeah, it takes a lot of patience," Wes agreed, remembering how hard it had been at Ryan's age for him to sit still. "My dad used to pass the time by telling stories about the miners who'd settled in these hills back in the 1800s."

"Did they find gold?" Ryan seemed to have forgotten all about the bobber. Instead, he focused on Wes.

"Some did." He pointed to the top of the waterfall. "According to my dad, some prospectors found gold right up in that creek there." He realized suddenly, as he looked into Ryan's excited face, that his father had likely made up the whole story, but Wes went on to tell it anyway. "There was one miner in particular who came all the way from Canada to settle right here on this land. They called him Wild Bill, and most people thought he was an outlaw on the run."

"Like the police were chasing him?" Ryan turned to face Wes fully.

"Exactly. But they could never find him, because he was a true mountain man." He glanced at the bobber to make sure they hadn't missed a fish. "Legend has it that Wild Bill built his house somewhere inside the mountain. Some people think he still lives there today."

"You mean like a ghost?" Ryan rose to his knees as though the excitement was too much for him. "I love ghost stories!"

"Yes, a ghost. But he's a good ghost. My dad told me—"

The fishing pole jerked out of Ryan's hand and Wes snatched it right before they lost it in the lake. "Looks like you've got one, Sport."

"Ohmygosh ohmygosh ohmygosh." Ryan scrambled to his feet, and Wes handed him the pole.

"Hold it tight," he instructed, stepping in for support. "Reel it in a little bit at a time."

"It feels like a whopper!" Ryan turned the reel a few times. "It's *so* heavy!"

"Must be a decent-sized fish." Wes hurried over to where he'd left his pack and dug out his foldable net. "Good job. Just like that. Nice and easy."

Ryan continued to tug and then reel, tug and reel. Finally, Wes got a glimpse of the fish. "It's a rainbow trout." He could see the almost iridescent scales beneath the surface.

"Good job!" Timothy yelled across the lake. "Go, Ryan!"

The boy beamed. "He's putting up a fight, but I'm gonna get him in!"

"You've got him." Wes readied the net. "Just a few more turns on that reel and he's all yours." Well, for a few minutes before they released him, anyway.

"There's his head!" Ryan pulled on the reel. "I see him! Wow! He's huge!"

"He's a nice one." Wes knelt and dipped the net into the water, capturing the fish. "Take a good look. We have to hurry to get the hook out." He grabbed the line and lifted the fish out of the net. "Wow, he's at least fifteen inches."

"He's so pretty." The boy pushed his face close to the fish.

"Hold him up." Wes handed him the line and backed up to take a quick picture before removing the hook from the fish's mouth while Ryan held it steady in his hands. "All right. We need to throw him back into the pond so he can breathe."

Ryan nodded solemnly. "Bye, Mr. Fish. Thanks for getting caught." The boy knelt down and gently placed the fish back into the water, watching it swim away.

For a second, Wes thought he might be sad, but when he stood back up, Ryan started to jump up and down. "I caught a fish! I caught a fish!"

The others in the group applauded from their spots around the pond.

"I can't wait to tell my mom." Ryan was still bouncing.

"I can text her the picture right now," Wes offered. "We should have decent cell reception here." He showed Ryan the text and then fired it off to Thea. She responded right away with about fifteen smiley emojis and What a catch!

"I'll bet you can get another one." Wes inspected the pole to make sure the fly and sinkers were still securely attached.

"I hope so!"

"Hey, Wes." Cal waved to get his attention. "I think we've got a tangle here or something. The pole won't cast."

"Be right there." He handed Ryan his fishing pole back. "I'm going to help Cal and Timothy. Why don't you see if you can bring in another whopper?"

"I will," Ryan promised. "I bet he went back and told all his fishy friends that I was super nice to him."

Wes chuckled as he followed the shoreline around to where Cal and Timothy stood.

"Let's see what we've got." He opened the reel, and, sure enough, the line had tangled good.

"Sorry," little Timothy murmured. "I don't think I was doing it right."

"Not a problem at all." Wes took a knee and started to pull out the line so he could find the tangle and cut it off. "You can try again as soon as we sort this out," he told the boy.

"It's been a while since we've been fishing, hasn't it, bud?" Cal patted his son's shoulder and then directed his attention to Wes. "Do you guys ever rent out cabins to vacationers? I'm thinking we ought to come back sometime."

Wes pulled out his pocketknife and snipped the line on the other side of a serious knot. "We mainly do weddings at the ranch these days. But yeah, if we have openings, especially during the week, we'll rent cabins out to families we know."

While they chatted about potential dates that fall, Timothy wandered away.

"Looks like we're almost back in business." Wes started to restring the pole. "Maybe we should switch out the fly—"

"Do you know where Ryan went?" Timothy had come back holding a stick.

"He's right—" Wes went to point out their fishing spot on the rock, but the boy was gone. "He was just there. I swear." It couldn't have been more than ten minutes since he'd walked over here . . . He turned in a slow circle, his heart flipping inside out. Where could he have—

"Up there." Cal pointed to the rocks above the waterfall. Ryan had climbed about three-quarters of the way up and was still moving.

"Jesus." Wes bolted to the pool, dodging rocks and tree stumps. "Ryan!" The shout scorched his throat. "Ryan! Stop! Stay right there!" Panic and dread and adrenaline spilled through him, shrinking his vision to where the boy had suddenly frozen even higher up on the rock wall.

"I'm stuck!" Ryan yelled, starting to cry. "It's slippery!"

"Hold on!" Wes lunged at the wall and started to scale it, his feet and hands slipping on the crevices. "Don't let go, Sport." He tried to calm his voice so he wouldn't scare the kid. "Everything's gonna be all right." Wes ran his hands along the wall, searching for the best holds. Underneath one of his boots, the rocks gave out, and he slipped down a good foot, tearing a gash into his thigh. Gritting his teeth, he scrambled back up, thrashing his hands on the granite.

"What should I do?" Ryan cried above him. "I don't know what to do."

"Hold on." Wes tried to catch his breath. He couldn't let him fall. "All you have to do is hold on and I'll get you." He was close. Only about three more feet and he'd have him . . .

"My hands hurt!" Ryan turned his head to look down at Wes

and the movement seemed to knock him off balance. He fell away from the rocks with a deafening scream.

"No!" Wes let go of the wall and let himself fall, too, splashing into the pool just after Ryan. Within seconds, he had the boy in his arms, and he swam him to the edge, lifting him out of the water.

Blood trickled down the boy's face from a gash on his forehead, and Ryan wouldn't open his eyes. He must've hit his head on the way down. He'd been up so high. What about his neck? His spine?

"No." Wes leaned his head onto the boy's chest, detecting both breaths and a pulse. "Call nine-one-one," he sputtered to Cal, who had knelt next to him. "Tell them we need a medevac chopper. Now."

The man stood, already on the phone.

Preston ran over, out of breath. "Is he going to be okay?"

He didn't know. Wes didn't know what to do, how to help him. "Ryan." He pulled the boy's eyelids open. "Ryan, wake up. You have to wake up."

Carlos knelt next to Wes. "It sounds like the sheriff is en route. They're dispatching a chopper too."

"We need to keep him warm." Wes tore off his wet shirt and used it to stop the bleeding. "I have an emergency blanket in my backpack."

"I'm on it." Carlos disappeared.

"You'll be okay, Ryan," Wes said over and over. His hands shook.

"Here's the blanket." Carlos unfolded the mylar solar material and they worked together to wrap it gently around Ryan.

"His breathing and pulse sound good," Carlos said, as though trying to reassure Wes.

But nothing could reassure him. Nothing could stop the devastating pain in his chest. How could he have let this happen?

"They were able to pinpoint our location." Cal ran back over, holding his crying son in his arms. "They're hoping the chopper will be here in ten minutes."

Wes pushed back and sat, still watching Ryan's chest rise and fall. Wait… he hovered closer. Ryan's eyelids fluttered.

"Ryan?" Wes stroked his hair. "Hey, Sport. Wake up. You have to wake up."

A groan uttered from the boy's mouth and his eyes opened wider. "Wes?" He blinked and squinted. "My head hurts." He moved like he wanted to sit up, but Wes gently held him down. "You have to stay right here for now." He couldn't let him move. Not until they ruled out neck and spinal injuries. "It's okay," he said, trying to soothe the tears that started to leak from the boy's eyes. "You had a fall, and we had to call some people to come and help you. They'll be here any minute."

"Where's my mom?" Ryan sputtered. "I want my mom."

"I know." He held the boy's hand, trying to steady his own so Ryan couldn't feel the fear trembling through him. "You'll see her soon. I promise. But right now, we need to be still."

"I'm tired." Ryan closed his eyes again.

"Do you want me to try to get hold of Thea?" Gabe asked, standing a few feet away.

"Yes." It tore him apart to think about what this would do to her, but she had to know. "Tell her to meet us at the Yampa Valley Medical Center." He had no doubt that's where they would be going. "Ryan?" He gently nudged the boy again. "Wake up."

"Don't want to," the boy muttered.

"I'll tell you more about Wild Bill," Wes said desperately.

"Who's Wild Bill?" The kid opened his eyes halfway.

He didn't remember the story Wes had told him only twenty minutes ago. That wasn't a good sign.

"Wild Bill is the outlaw who lives in the mountain." He told him the whole story this time—the same story his dad had told him to keep him calm when they were fishing. He talked until he heard the chopper blades whapping above them.

Ryan didn't say much, but at least he kept his eyes open.

"What's that noise?" Ryan tried to sit up again.

"It's a helicopter," Wes told him, gently keeping his shoulders on the ground. "You get to go for a ride."

"I do?" The boy peered up at him with a hint of his old spark. "Can you come with me?"

"Yes." Wes squeezed his hand. "Of course I'll come."

The noise grew louder and louder, nearly drowning out Wes's pulse in his ears. He held Ryan's hand until the medics ran over and directed him out of the way. Carlos told them what happened while Wes stepped back, feeling like he might collapse.

"You can't beat yourself up about this," Cal said, laying a hand on his shoulder. "None of us were paying attention. Any one of us could've stopped him."

"I was responsible for him." Thea had even warned him the boy had a tendency to get excited and wander off. "I should've been watching. I should've been paying attention." He was the one who told Ryan he used to climb up that wall.

"This was my fault." He had no business being in charge of a kid.

Chapter Twenty

I'm stuffed." Thea slumped back against the booth and set down her spoon.

The apple pie Beth had brought them proved to be too much for either one of them to finish.

"Me too." Liv held her arm around her stomach and groaned, but Thea wanted to take a picture of her daughter's happy smile so she would always remember it. "That was the best unhealthy lunch I've ever had."

"The best," she echoed. How long had it been since she'd let herself indulge in diner food and dessert? Way too long. "It was the best company too," she told her daughter, almost getting emotional. "I think we need to do an indulgent girls' lunch at least once a month." She'd missed this more than she realized. When Liv was younger, they used to do mommy-daughter dates all the time, but the older her kids got, the more out of control their schedules felt.

"Maybe we should hold off on the apple pie, though." Her daughter shoved the plate as far away from them as she could. "I don't know if I'll be able to walk out of here."

"Yeah, but that cinnamon ice cream on top was worth it." Thea didn't regret one bite of this lunch, no matter how full her stomach felt. She dug into her purse to pull out her wallet, even though Beth had insisted they wouldn't pay. The woman hadn't specifically told her she wasn't allowed to leave a generous tip.

Carefully, she hid two twenty-dollar bills under the plate and then pulled out her phone to check the time. Huh. That was weird. "I have two missed calls from Gabe."

"Ryan probably wanted to tell you all about the biggest fish in the world." Liv slid out of the booth. "I'm sure we'll be hearing about it for the next year."

"Maybe." But why wouldn't he have called on Wes's phone? Unease settled in her stomach, along with the heavy food. "We should find Beth to thank her, and then I'll call him back." Liv had to be right.

"He'll probably say it was five feet long," her daughter said with a laugh.

"And fifty pounds," Thea added. Ryan had always excelled in the art of exaggeration.

"But I'm so glad he got to go." With Wes. Her heart seemed to skip and stutter just thinking about the man. She couldn't wait to see him, to catch a few minutes alone with him to tell him she wanted to try, to explore the bond that had started to form between them. "Oh, there's Beth." Thea wandered along the café's long counter to where Beth stood behind the espresso machine.

The woman saw them coming. "Are you two ladies done already? I have a decadent chocolate torte in the back I could bring out..."

"We couldn't eat one more bite." Even the thought of putting a spoonful of chocolate cake into her mouth made Thea a little nauseous. "But that was the best lunch we've had in forever."

"So good," Liv confirmed.

"Glad you enjoyed it." Beth stepped around the counter and gave them both hugs. "It was fun to see you. I'm hoping to drive down to see Jane and the baby tomorrow."

"I know she'd love it." Toby and Jane would be down in Denver for at least a month with little Charlee in the NICU. "I'm hoping to stop and see her on our way home too."

They chatted for a few more minutes about the trip and their time at the ranch, but then a waiter called Beth away.

Thea and Liv said their goodbyes and stepped out into the bright sunshine. "I'd better call Gabe back. Just in case."

Liv linked her arm through Thea's. "Put it on speaker so I can tease Ryan about catching a whale."

"No teasing," she said, hitting the callback button and putting the phone on speaker. "You know how seriously Ryan takes his fish stories." And she didn't want to ruin this one for him.

The phone rang a few times before the line clicked. "Thea?" Gabe sounded out of breath. That meant they were likely on their hike back to the ranch.

"Hi, Gabe. Did Ryan want to talk to me?"

"No..."

The hoarseness in his voice sent her heart into a free fall. She didn't have time to brace herself before Gabe said, "Ryan had an accident."

"What?" She pulled away from Olivia and took the phone off speaker, bringing it to her ear instead.

"Ryan fell." The man's voice was garbled. Or maybe that was her brain. She couldn't seem to hear clearly. Or see.

"He was climbing some rock and he fell. Hit his head."

The world started to spin around her. "He's okay." She wasn't sure if she was telling herself or Gabe.

"What happened, Mom?" Liv's face had gone white.

Thea turned away so she could hear. Focus on what Gabe was telling her.

"He lost consciousness for a few minutes, but then he woke up. We called in a search and rescue helicopter, and they're taking him to Yampa Valley Medical Center."

"Where is that?" Thea could hardly get the words out. Her lungs squeezed, making her gasp.

"It's about a half hour away," Gabe said. "Wes is with him."

"I don't understand." Holding the phone too tightly against her ear, she grabbed Liv's hand and started to run down the block. Where was the car? Where was her damn car? "How could he have fallen?" How could they have let her son get hurt?

"He slipped away when none of us were watching. We're not sure how. Listen to me, Thea." In the midst of her panic, Gabe's voice sounded farther away. "You have to stay calm to drive. If you don't think you can, I can pick you up, but we're still hiking down."

"No." She spotted her Volvo half a block down. "I'm not waiting." She and Liv sprinted across the street. "Is he going to be okay?" That's what she needed to know.

"I know they're taking every precaution, but he was awake and talking to Wes when they loaded him into the helicopter."

That wasn't an answer, damn it! Thea let go of Liv and tore through her purse looking for her keys. She somehow managed to hit the unlock button. "We're going now," she told Gabe before hanging up the phone. Her hands felt clumsy as she opened the door and slid into the car.

Liv got in next to her. Tears streamed down her daughter's face. "Is he gonna be okay?"

"Yes." Thea refused to accept any other answer. The three of them had already suffered enough. "Ryan is going to be okay." Her baby was going to be okay. She started the car and peeled out while they clicked in their seat belts. "I need you to look up Yampa Valley Medical Center." She didn't dare touch her phone while she was driving, especially with her heart racing this way.

Her daughter started to tap on her phone. "What happened to him, Mom?" Liv's voice wobbled as though she was afraid to know.

Thea was afraid too. She reached over and held Liv's hand in hers. "He was climbing on some rocks and he fell. They think he hit his head. That's all I know, honey."

Her daughter touched the pendant lying against her collarbone.

Yes, if ever they needed faith, now was the time. "He'll be okay." Seeing her daughter's fear made Thea's less overpowering. She'd been strong before. She could do this. She could get both of her children through this. "They said he was awake." She didn't mention that he'd lost consciousness.

"Why'd they have to call a helicopter then?" Her daughter suddenly sounded ten years younger.

"They're taking every precaution," she said, even though she knew they wouldn't have called in a helicopter if they hadn't suspected serious injuries. "We're going to have faith."

She squeezed Liv's hand again, feeling less shaky.

Following the phone's instructions, they made it to the hospital ten minutes faster than their predicted arrival time. Thea pulled into a parking spot outside the ER, and she and Liv raced in through the glass doors.

"My son was flown here," she told the man behind the desk before he could greet them. "Ryan Davis. He fell and hit his head."

"I know right where he is." The man left his chair and waved her to follow him through a secured door. He jogged down a hallway with her and Liv on his heels and then gestured to a door. "That's his room."

Thea felt her legs giving out as she stepped through the door.

Ryan wasn't there. Only Wes sat in a chair.

"Thea, I'm so sorry." He jolted to his feet.

The tears she'd managed to hold back flooded her eyes. "Where is he?"

"They took him down for a CT scan." Wes reached for her, but then his arm fell back to his side. "He should be back any minute. They think he has a concussion but want to make sure they're not missing anything." A hollowness seemed to appear in his eyes.

"I don't understand how this happened." Now the tears wouldn't stop. She sat herself in the chair next to a small desk. They were supposed to be fishing. They were going on a fishing trip. "How did he fall?"

Liv hovered next to her, resting a hand on her shoulder.

"He climbed up some rocks." Wes kept his distance and stared at the floor. "I was helping Cal with a fishing pole." The man closed his eyes and shook his head. "I should've been watching—"

"Mom!" A nurse wheeled Ryan's gurney into the room. "You're here! I got to ride in a helicopter!"

"I know, buddy." As soon as the nurse had positioned the gurney in place, Thea fell over him, hugging him against her.

Liv hurried to the other side of the bed, completing their little hug circle. "Oh my God, Ry-ry. I've never been so happy to see you."

"I'm *fine*," her son insisted impatiently.

"He's had some ibuprofen," the nurse added.

Thea lifted her head, inspecting her son's face and then his head. Other than a white bandage, he really did look fine. Relief started the tears again. "I love you." What if she hadn't been able to tell him that? What if she hadn't been able to hold him again? "You and your sister are the most important things in my life."

"I know, I know." He patted her like he wanted her to stop making a scene. "I love you too," her son said with a sense of duty.

"The doctor will be right in to talk with you." The nurse jotted a few things on a chart and then faced Wes. "If you'll come with me, Mr. Harding, we can get that leg stitched up for you. It'll only take ten minutes."

Thea straightened and turned around. She hadn't even noticed the white gauze tied around Wes's right thigh. And he was wearing one of those scrub tops nurses wore. "You're hurt."

"He's got a big owie," Ryan confirmed. "It was bleeding all over the place."

"It's nothing." Wes's expression stayed blank, and Thea couldn't tell what he was thinking.

"It's a laceration all the way to the bone, and we need to clean it out and stitch it up." The nurse waved him out of the room.

"Will you come back as soon as you're done?" her son pleaded. "I wanna see my fish picture again!" Ryan looked at Thea. "I don't even remember catching it, can you believe that? I caught a whopper, and I don't even remember!"

There had to be a head injury then . . .

"I texted the picture to your mom." Wes's smile was forced.

"Glad you're feeling better, Sport." He walked out of the room without a goodbye or a promise to return.

"The helicopter was so cool!" Ryan sat up in the bed, shoving off the white sheet. "It was really loud, and when we lifted off, my stomach felt like I was on a roller coaster. I even puked!"

"That's gross." Liv edged onto the bed next to her brother, affectionately smoothing his hair down.

"We could see everything up high." Her son pouted. "But they only let me sit up for a sec and then I had to lay down the whole time." He continued to detail every second of the helicopter ride, and Thea let him. She dragged over a chair and let him chatter and exaggerate while she breathed deeply, watching her son, watching her daughter, overcome with a heart-wrenching love for them both.

When Ryan finally got to the part where they arrived at the hospital, she had to interrupt. This conversation couldn't wait. "It all sounds very exciting, but why were you climbing on the rocks in the first place, buddy?"

Her son darted his gaze around, obviously not wanting to answer the question.

That's what she thought.

"Didn't I tell you to listen to Wes?" The mix of relief and joy made it difficult to sound too stern. "Did Wes give you permission to climb on the rocks?"

"Not *really*. But he told me he used to climb on the rocks with his dad." Lately, her son had been really into technicalities, always trying to tweak the details in his favor.

Not gonna work today. "But you didn't ask him before you went climbing?"

Ryan's shoulders slumped. "No. I didn't ask."

"Ryan..." Thea took her son's hand in hers. "You could have been very badly injured. Do you understand that?" Just like when he'd snuck out onto the lake by himself that morning. Her son didn't have a gift for thinking through potential consequences ahead of time.

"I'm overjoyed that you're okay." She couldn't even imagine the alternative. "But you can never ever do risky things like that without making sure it's safe. Without making sure an adult says it's safe."

Her son's eyes filled with tears, and she could see the genuine regret. "Wes seems really sad, Mom. I didn't mean to make him sad."

"I know. You scared us, honey." She couldn't imagine what it must've been like for Wes to see him fall, to see him unconscious. He already put too much on himself. This wasn't going to help.

"Can you go talk to him for me?" Her son scrubbed his fists into his eyes like he wanted to get rid of the tears. "Can you tell him I'm real sorry and I'll never do anything like that again?"

"Sure I can." Thea pushed out of the chair, but as she went to walk through the door, the doctor appeared.

"Mrs. Davis?" The woman stretched out her hand. "I'm Dr. Grady."

"Nice to meet you." She swallowed hard, preparing for the worst. It was possible something had shown up on the CT scan...

"Why don't we step out into the hall?" The doctor directed her out the door.

"Keep an eye on him," Thea told Liv. She couldn't have him wandering off in the hospital.

Once they'd made it into the hall, the doctor smiled. "The CT scan was clear. We didn't see any evidence of swelling in the brain or any internal injuries we might've missed, so that's great news."

"Thank God." Her emotions seemed to be riding on a swing. One minute she felt joy; the next, raw fear.

"We do believe he hit his head pretty hard on the way down," the doctor went on. "I feel he has a moderate, grade two concussion, and we'd like to keep him here overnight under observation."

"Yes. Of course." That was nothing compared to what she'd thought they'd be dealing with when she'd first gotten the call. She pushed out a sigh. "Thank you for everything."

The doctor nodded. "I'm sure I don't have to tell you it could've been much worse. If Mr. Harding hadn't pulled him out of the water so fast—"

"Water?" Ryan had fallen into the water unconscious? Nausea swirled in her stomach. She was glad she hadn't known that on the way to the hospital . . .

"Yes. From the sound of things, Ryan fell into a pool of water at the base of a waterfall. Mr. Harding was able to get him out within seconds."

It occurred to her right then that she hadn't thanked Wes. She hadn't even acknowledged his apology. She'd been too focused on Ryan—on her fears—to ask for the whole story.

"We'll put in for a transfer and get Ryan up to the general care floor for the night." The doctor reached out her hand once more. "Nice to meet you. I'm glad he's going to be okay."

Thea managed another weak "Thank you" and then quickly walked away in search of Wes.

"Mrs. Davis?" the man from the reception desk called from a doorway. "You have some visitors out in the waiting room."

"Oh." She hurried through the door he held open for her. Wes must've gone out there to wait for her.

Instead of finding Wes in the reception area, the rest of the families from the ranch had gathered near the windows, some of them pacing, some of them sitting.

"Thea!" Kelly raced to hug her. "Oh my God. How's Ryan? Is he going to be okay?"

"Yes." She held on to her friend for an extra second. "He has a concussion, but otherwise, they think he'll be fine."

"See?" Cal knelt in front of Timothy. "I told you he'd be okay."

"It's a good thing Wes moved so fast," Gabe said. "Before I even knew what was happening, Wes was already halfway up that wall."

"It would've been a lot worse if he hadn't been there," Carlos added.

So she'd heard. Thea glanced around the waiting room, but besides her friends it was empty. "Has anyone seen Wes?" She had to thank him. She had to wrap her arms around him and tell him what happened to Ryan wasn't his fault.

"He left." Abby peered out the window. "Only a few minutes ago. I ran into him in the parking lot. August picked him up."

"I can call him if you want," Cal offered. "Tell him to come back if you need him for something."

"No. That's okay. I can talk to him tomorrow when we get back to the ranch."

But she feared she'd already missed her chance.

Chapter Twenty-One

Wes stared out the windshield of his brother's posh rental truck as though he was taking in the scenery, but he saw only one thing—Ryan falling again and again and again.

And he felt that same visceral reaction every time—the burning in his lungs, the sharp, sickening drop of his heart. He'd seen the boy falling, he'd known Ryan would get hurt, and he couldn't do anything to stop it from happening. He'd been helpless. Like that day he'd sat on the riverbank waiting for them to find his father, knowing something bad was coming and not being able to change it.

Wes closed his eyes, willing the trembling in his hands to stop. Maybe he should've gone to tell Ryan and Thea goodbye, but he'd wanted to get out of there. Get away. Since August had been on his way to see them anyway, Wes asked his brother to take him back.

"So..." August turned to glance at him.

He had to give his brother credit. For most of the drive, he'd kept his mouth shut, but now that they were almost back to the ranch, his brother turned off the radio.

"You want to talk about what happened out there?"

He didn't want to talk about it. He didn't want to keep reliving it. He didn't want to remember the moment he'd pulled Ryan out of the water and the boy wouldn't open his eyes. "Talk about what? How everyone was right about me?" He was no good for Ryan. He was no good for Thea. He didn't know the first thing about the responsibilities attached to being a father figure.

"What the hell is that supposed to mean?" August took his eyes off the road to give him the same stern look their dad used to give him—mouth set, eyes drawn.

"I know you blame me for what happened to Dad." Wes couldn't look at him while he said the words. "It was my fault. I should've been there."

"Whatever." August shook his head. "You have no idea what you're talking about, Wes."

"You've never looked at me the same. Neither has Jane." He knew because Wes had never looked at himself the same either.

"It was an *accident*." August seemed impatient as he navigated the route through town. "It could've happened to anyone. Just like Ryan falling. Kids get hurt right under their parents' noses all the time."

"It never happened to our father. We never got hurt when he was there." Their dad had made sure to always take every safety precaution. He never would've turned his back on either of them even for a second out there when they were ten years old.

"It sounds like Ryan will be fine," August said, taking a quick right onto the ranch's driveway as though he couldn't wait to escape this conversation. "That's all that matters."

"He could've been killed." If it had taken Wes any longer to find him in the water. Or if he'd fallen wrong and broken his neck. He shuddered. If it had been any worse, he wouldn't be able to live with himself.

The image of Ryan falling flashed again.

"He wasn't killed." August pulled the truck up in front of the lodge and cut the engine. "And even if he had been, it wouldn't be your fault."

Easy for him to say. August hadn't been there. He hadn't heard Thea specifically warn him about Ryan's tendency to wander. Wes got out of the truck and slammed the door.

His brother marched around the bumper to stand across from him. "You have to stop taking stuff like this on. I don't give a shit what you think. I've never blamed you for what happened on the river all those years ago. And neither has Jane." August raised his voice. "I know you want to take the blame on your own shoulders like some martyr, but you were not responsible for Dad's death."

Wes stared down his brother. He'd always had more brawn than August, but he hadn't used it against him more than a handful of times. Now, though, he was really tempted. "I was supposed to be with him." And his brother knew it. Everyone knew it. Nothing could change that fact. Not time or excuses.

"Yeah, and he knew he shouldn't go out alone, Wes." August had never gotten angry easily, but now his jaw tightened and his eyes narrowed the way they used to when Wes would steal his favorite hat back when they were kids. "He knew the dangers. He always told us never to go out on the river alone. And then he went and did it."

Anger shook through his brother's tone, but for the first time, Wes realized it wasn't directed at him. August was angry with their father. He could see the sharpness of his brother's eyes.

"Getting in the kayak that day was *his* choice. Not yours." His brother seemed to regain control over his tone. "He could've waited, or he could've gone and dragged your hungover ass out of bed. He was an adult, Wes. And he's responsible for his choices."

That hadn't been their dad's style, though. He hadn't been forceful. He'd let them make their own mistakes. And now Wes had to live with his.

"I'm going to Texas." That was where he belonged—on the road doing a job that didn't require anything past his physical skills. He didn't have to think too much out there. He didn't have to give anything. He didn't have to feel anything. "I should've left when you got here. I'm gonna pack up my truck and leave tonight."

"You're just going to leave the kid without saying goodbye? And what about Thea? Jane told me you care about her." His brother stepped up toe-to-toe with him. In the years he'd been away, August had gained more muscle mass, but Wes could still take him, especially now with the fury pumping through him.

"Leaving says more about you than an accident that happened on your watch." August stood his ground as if he was ready for whatever punch Wes would throw.

But Wes wasn't eighteen anymore, and he'd learned when to walk away. Without responding, he turned and headed for his cabin. His brother could think whatever he wanted. He could say whatever he wanted. August didn't have to live with the images in Wes's head.

He jogged the path to his cabin tucked into the woods behind the lodge. When he reached the porch, he pulled out his phone and called Craig. The man answered after two rings. "You change your mind yet, Harding?"

"Yeah. I did. I'll be there late tonight." It'd likely take him a good ten hours to drive down to Amarillo, but he could be out of here within the hour.

"Smart man," Craig said. "I had a feeling you'd come around. Didn't even find a replacement for you yet."

"Good. Perfect." Wes plowed through the cabin door and went right to the bedroom to pull his duffel bags out of the closet. "I'll text you when I get to the hotel."

"Don't worry about it. Just meet me for breakfast tomorrow morning. We have a lot to discuss. Including your raise."

"Looking forward to it." Wes ended the call and pocketed his phone. He spent the next half hour ripping clothes out of the drawers and packing up his few belongings. He'd never had much—he liked to travel light. That made it easier to pick up and move on to the next place. Everything easily fit into two bags. He hauled them both out to his truck and threw them into the bed.

Leaving says more about you than an accident that happened on your watch.

August was right. He couldn't leave without saying goodbye. Not that Thea would want to see him. The panic and fear on her face at the hospital had been enough to break him. He'd done that to her. He'd given her a reason to worry. No, he couldn't talk to her. He couldn't see them, but he could do something else.

Leaving the keys in the ignition of his truck, he tromped down to the boathouse. Cal and Gabe and Carlos had brought back the fishing gear and had stacked it right where he told them to.

Wes looked through the backpacks until he found the red fishing pole Ryan had loved so much. After rifling through some of the old cabinets, he managed to find a pen and notepad. Only problem was, he didn't know what to say. He couldn't put what he felt for Thea into words. And he wasn't sure how to tell the kid what spending time with him this week had meant to him.

"Hey, Sport," he finally scrawled. "This pole belongs to you. You earned it. Keep catching the big ones. Keep in touch."

He didn't count on that last part happening, but Ryan could always email him, or even text him if his mom would allow it.

Wes folded up the paper and grabbed the fishing pole. He stepped outside and was immediately struck with a memory of kissing Thea in this spot right here. He remembered how she'd wrapped her arms around him, how good it had felt to hold her, how he hadn't wanted to let her go.

And then at the hospital, she hadn't wanted to go near him. He didn't blame her. She couldn't blame him any more than he blamed himself.

Wes walked away, leaving the memory behind. He would forget, eventually. He would force himself to forget. His life was much simpler when he didn't open himself up to feeling anything.

He carried the fishing pole and note to Thea's cabin and carefully positioned them against the door so they'd see them right away. Without looking back, he walked the path along the lake, taking in the view once more.

He didn't know when he'd be back this time. Hopefully within a few months, when the season wound down. Or maybe he'd make a quick visit home to see Charlee when they got released from the hospital. He would figure something out. Right now, he needed to escape.

Blocking out everything, he jogged to his truck and jumped in. Then he drove away without looking back.

Chapter Twenty-Two

I'm bored, Moooom." Ryan nudged the back of the driver's seat with his sweet little foot.

Lord, help her. She'd heard that same phrase at least fifteen times that morning while they were waiting to be discharged from the hospital. Ryan had not taken to being still like the doctor had ordered.

"You can play a game on my phone," Liv offered, handing it to him from the passenger's seat.

"Absolutely not." She gave Ryan her toughest gaze in the rear-view mirror. His sister may be a pushover right now, but Thea wasn't going to let him puppy-dog-eye her into disobeying the doctor. "No screen time for at least two weeks. And then it's only okay if *our* doctor clears you."

The list of concussion protocols was at least three pages long.

"Aw, man. That means I don't get to play *Minecraft*." Her son kicked the back of her seat again.

"Well, at least we're almost back to the ranch. You'll probably be too busy fishing for the next few days to think much about *Minecraft* anyway." She would have to keep a close eye on him to make sure he didn't overdo it. That would be quite the challenge.

"Do you think maybe Wes would take me back to the fishing spot?"

The hope in Ryan's tone cut into her. "No, honey. I don't think so. The hike is too much, and the doctor said you need to take it easy." Besides that, she wasn't sure Wes would want to spend more time with him after what Ryan had put him through. She'd tried to call him three times last night, but he hadn't picked up any of her calls.

"Maybe he'll take me in the canoe to fish then." Her son strained against his seat belt to lean forward. "You don't think he's mad at me, do you?"

"No. I don't think he's mad." It wasn't anger she'd read in his expression and mannerisms at the hospital. Thea fought the urge to delve into another lecture. They had already talked at length about his poor choice to sneak off and climb the rocks unsupervised. They'd talked about how it had affected her and Liv and Wes and all of their friends at the ranch. And no screen time for the next two weeks would be quite an effective natural consequence.

"I'll take you fishing, buddy." Liv turned around in her seat and smiled at her brother. "As long as you take them off the hook. I'm not touching a slimy fish."

"Deal." Ryan reached his hand forward and they shook on it.

Thea tempered a smile. If anything good had come out of this whole nightmare, it was that her children were best buddies again. They hadn't bickered for a whole day now, which had to be some kind of record.

"I see the ranch!" Ryan buzzed down his window. "We need to find Wes right away. It's almost nighttime, and that's a good time to fish."

Thea glanced at her clock. It felt like ten years had passed since she'd driven to the hospital yesterday, but it hadn't even been twenty-four hours. "We still have quite a while until evening. And I think we'll head back to our cabin and get settled first." She hadn't slept the last two nights. Last night the nurses kept coming in to check on them, and then the night before...

Her cheeks flamed with the memory of being in Wes's arms. She had no doubt she would find herself there again if he would open them to her. Sitting at the hospital had given her more time to process her conversation with Liv. Maybe she could start to acknowledge that she'd done her best. She hadn't been perfect when it came to Dylan, but she'd tried and she'd learned, and now maybe she did have something to offer. Maybe she did want to step out in courage so her children wouldn't learn to hide from relationships and deep connections with people who cared for them.

Thea guided the SUV past the lodge and down the small hill to park in front of their cabin, anticipation beating through her heart. She was just as eager to see Wes as Ryan was.

"What's that?" Ryan undid his seat belt and ejected himself from the car the second she put the gear into park.

Yeah, it was going to be impossible to keep him still.

Thea collected her purse and the paperwork from the hospital before climbing out and joining her kids on the porch. The second she laid eyes on that fishing pole and the note, her heart spiraled downward. She didn't have to read the note to know.

Wes was gone.

"He gave me a fishing pole, Mom!" Ryan waved the note at her. "He said it's mine! He said to keep catching the big ones!"

A wave of sorrow crashed over her, but she held on to her smile and took the note from Ryan's hand. It was a goodbye letter. Short and simple, but also concrete. After telling her he would stay, he'd gone and left for that event in Texas August had told her about.

Liv read the note over her shoulder. "Where did he go?" she whispered under Ryan's chatter about what an amazing fishing pole he'd gotten. He was oblivious that the man he'd idolized had walked away without so much as a proper goodbye.

"He had an event in Texas. He wasn't going to go, but I guess he changed his mind." She kept her voice low so Ryan wouldn't overhear and so Liv couldn't detect the notes of heartache she was trying to hide. It was one thing for Wes to walk away from her. But what was she supposed to tell her son?

"Oh, no." Her daughter leaned her head onto Thea's shoulder. "I'm sorry, Mom."

"So am I." Sorry, sad, angry. She'd believed him when he told her he would stay earlier that week. "Why don't you go inside, Liv?" She had to tell Ryan now. He'd likely find out when they went up to dinner anyway, and he'd need a little time to calm down first.

"Okay." Her daughter trudged into the cabin, shoulders slumped in an obvious show of solidarity for her brother.

"Hey, Ry-ry, can you come sit by me for a minute?" Thea lowered to the first step on the porch and checked her emotion. She had to be careful how she handled this.

Her son hurried to sit next to her. "Look, Mom. This reel is a spin reel and a fly reel. Now I just need Wes to teach me how to fly-fish."

Don't cry. Whatever she did, she could not cry. No matter how acutely she felt Wes's sudden desertion, Ryan would feel it ten times more. "Honey, you know how Wes is really busy with work and has to travel a lot?"

"Yeah. Because he's in the rodeos." Ryan continued to tinker with the pole. "He's pretty much famous, and he's one of my best friends too."

"He is a good friend." At least he had been. "But he had to travel to a really important event down in Texas this week. So, he's not going to be here anymore."

Her son stopped messing with the line and glared up at her. "Yes, he is. He told me in the helicopter we could go fishing again. Since we didn't get to be there very long."

"I'm sure he *wants* to fish." Wes had likely said whatever he thought would make Ryan feel better. "But he's gone, honey. He left for Texas." She had no doubt they wouldn't find him if they walked to his cabin right now.

"No he's not." Ryan jumped to his feet. "He wouldn't leave without saying goodbye. He wouldn't leave without taking me fishing again."

Thea squeezed her eyes shut, but tears gathered the second she opened them. "I'm sure he didn't want to leave. But he had to work. That's why he left the note. That's why he told you to keep in touch."

Ryan looked down at the fishing pole. "He's not coming back?"

"I don't think so." She stood and gathered him under her arm, pulling him into a hug. "At least not right away. But you can text him if you want." Though she didn't know if he would respond. With the man suddenly leaving like this, she didn't know a lot of things.

"So I'm never gonna see him again?" The words ended with a high-pitched squeak that warned of impending tears.

"I don't know about that." The poor boy. He had such a hard time letting people go. She couldn't understand what was going through Wes's mind. He knew how much Ryan looked up to him. And what about her? Wes was the one who had asked her for more. And then, just when she was ready to offer more, he was the one to turn his back.

A few tears slipped down Ryan's cheeks.

Thea wanted to cry too. "He wanted you to keep in touch, though." She squeezed her son's shoulder, but Ryan wriggled out of her grasp.

"I don't want to keep in touch with him. And I don't want this stupid fishing pole." He threw it off the porch and stomped inside.

Thea let him go. He was tired, and he hadn't gotten much sleep at the hospital either. It wouldn't hurt him to have a little space to process the news. It wouldn't hurt her to have some space to let herself feel the loss. She rested her arms on her knees and put her head down, the exhaustion and disappointment setting in.

"I'd ask how you're doing, but I think I already know the answer."

The sound of August's voice startled her. Thea lifted her head but couldn't quite find the energy to greet Wes's brother with a smile. "Fair warning. I'm running on very little sleep." He might as well know that now. She couldn't be sure exactly what her emotions were going to do at the moment, and she didn't want to scare him off.

August accepted her caution with a nod and sat next to her. "I came by to check on you and Ryan. On behalf of all of us at the ranch, we want you to know how sorry we are about his accident, and it's important you know we'll do everything we can to support you."

Thea would've laughed if her heart wasn't so heavy. "I'm not going to sue you because my son snuck off and climbed up some rocks." The thought had never even occurred to her. "I love this place too much." She loved the people here too much. Even the one who'd scarred her heart.

"I know. I still have to say it, though." August pushed off the stairs to grab the fishing pole and then sat back down. "I take it Ryan wasn't thrilled to hear that my brother took off?"

"That's putting it mildly." She took the fishing pole from August and set it on the porch behind them. "He's going to want it eventually. When he's had some time to get used to the idea that Wes is gone." Her son's heart simply hurt, and anger was easier to manage. She knew that to be true.

"I know this probably won't help, but Wes didn't want to leave," August said. "It was a reaction. He's always been impulsive. Sometimes he acts on those impulses without thinking things through."

"So I've heard." She'd known what people had said about Wes—Jane included. But she'd seen something else in the man. His deep concern for other people. The way he related to Ryan. She hadn't expected to feel such a connection with him. "I didn't think he'd leave," she admitted. "Not after he told me he would stay." Since Dylan had rarely kept his word, it surprised her that she'd trusted Wes so easily.

August plucked a piece of long grass next to the stairs and rolled it between his fingers. "When our father died, Wes didn't just take it hard." He seemed to choose his words carefully. "My brother suffered a lot of trauma that day. The only way he could deal with it was to escape. That's how he's lived his life ever since. And I think what happened with Ryan triggered that same trauma again."

"I know." She'd seen the trauma from his past when they'd driven down to see Jane in the hospital. He still lived it. "But I don't know what to do for him." Maybe it was better this way. Wes had made the decision for her. She wouldn't have to worry about letting him all the way into her heart and risking failing again. She wouldn't have to put her kids through a potential breakup down the road. There might be fewer complications without Wes in her life.

And yet...those few moments she'd let her guard down, the time she'd spent in his arms...What she felt for him might've been worth the complications.

"I'm not exactly qualified to give advice when it comes to relationships," August said after a thoughtful silence. "But maybe all he needs is for you to not give up on him. Not yet."

Give up. That's what she'd done with Dylan. And maybe it was okay to give up sometimes. Like her daughter had so eloquently reminded her, she couldn't change someone else's heart. But things had been different with Dylan. *She'd* been different. She was stronger now. She knew more of what she wanted from life. She knew how it felt to start opening her heart, and she didn't want to turn back now.

"He'll figure it out," August said. "I know he will. It might take him some time, but he'll come to his senses eventually. I have a lot of faith in him."

"So do I." How could she not? He'd been there when she'd needed to cry. He'd been there to tell her she was a good mom when she needed to hear it the most. He'd respected her when she'd needed space. The moments they shared flickered in her mind, reminders that Wes was good. He was safe. He was loyal. And he was wounded too. "I won't give up on him." She'd already wasted too much time hiding. Now it was time for her to learn how to fight for what she really wanted.

Chapter Twenty-Three

Thea had never been nervous about moderating a group discussion before—that had always been part of her job. But now she was half tempted to hide behind the fireplace in the lodge's great room so she wouldn't have to face the rest of the adults who would file in any minute for their support group discussion.

It had become a tradition on these trips to sit down about halfway through the retreat and share what the participants were learning, what challenges they were facing, and what they wanted to work through before the week was over.

In the past, Thea had always moderated—focusing on other people's responses and not on herself as the leader, but that would change today. It had to change. In order to be honest with herself, she had to be honest with everyone else first. And living out a tough truth had never been easy for her.

Maybe it was because Dylan had been so focused on appearances. Or maybe it was because her parents never let her make mistakes. Whatever had kept her living behind a façade, she had to step out in front of it now and be real with the people who would understand.

Thankfully, at breakfast, August had volunteered to supervise the kids down at the lake while the parents had their meeting. He'd made her a promise that there would be no rock climbing—only fishing, swimming, and paddleboarding with life vests securely fastened.

Ryan was still moping around and claimed he didn't want to fish, but she had a feeling that would change when he got down to the water.

The diversion for the kids had given her time to prepare for the group session—maybe not mentally, but at least she'd set up the muffins and coffee Louise had made for them.

She poured herself a cup and gazed out the windows overlooking the lake. There was her son standing on the dock casting his line again. She knew it. Ryan couldn't resist the red fishing pole. He couldn't resist the call of the lake.

"Looks like Ryan has bounced back fast." Kelly came to stand alongside her.

"He's pretty resilient." Thankfully. She'd taken time to explain more about Wes's quick departure to him. How it had scared him to see Ryan fall and how sometimes adults needed a little space when something bad happened. They'd talked about Wes's feelings instead of simply focusing on Ryan's feelings, and after that her son had sent a text message apologizing for sneaking off. Wes had quickly responded, telling Wes that he forgave him and didn't want him to feel bad. But he still hadn't made a promise to come back to the ranch.

"Coffee! Yes!" Abby hurried to join them, filling herself a mug. "I love Louise's coffee. I have no idea how I'm going to make my own when I go back home. It won't be the same."

"The view won't be the same either." Luciana came around the fireplace and gazed out the window with a sigh. "Coming here has made me wonder why I live in Texas."

"Those mountains do have a certain appeal," Kelly agreed. "But I don't think I could handle the winters." She shuddered. "All that snow half the year? I'd freeze."

"I think it would be magical." Thea had only seen snow a

handful of times in her life. "Think about it...Snuggling up by the cozy fire and drinking hot chocolate? It would be perfect."

"You do mean snuggling up with Wes in front of the fire, don't you?" Kelly nudged her shoulder into Thea's playfully, and she was grateful the men had congregated over by the bookshelf so they couldn't hear the teasing.

"Oh, she's definitely interested." Abby shared a look with Luciana. "We all have seen that look before."

Instead of denying it, Thea smiled, letting herself picture her and Wes curled up on that couch together while soft snowflakes fell against the windows. There would be a Christmas tree with twinkling lights right there in that corner and garlands on the fireplace, where their stockings would be hanging from the mantel.

She couldn't imagine anything better, though they would both have some work in front of them to get there.

"Tell me why the man left again?" Luciana crossed her arms. "He could've at least said goodbye so we would've had the chance to play matchmaker for the two of you."

"I don't think they needed any help in that department," Kelly murmured with a wink at Thea.

"What happened with Ryan really freaked him out." Thea moved around the chair so she could sit on the couch. "And I think he needed some space."

"Ah." Abby sat next to her. "That makes sense. I remember the first time Piper fell off her bike. I lost it. There was all this blood, and her cry absolutely broke my heart. I felt like the worst mother in the world for taking off her training wheels."

"It's a terrible feeling when something like that happens, even when it's your own kid," Luciana added, moving to the chair across from them. "I can't imagine how you'd feel if it happened to someone else's kid on your watch."

"But you two are going to keep in touch, right?" Kelly sat on the fireplace's stone hearth. "I mean, you seem to have some pretty good chemistry. That doesn't happen with just anyone."

"I'm hoping we keep in touch." She was hoping for a lot more than that, but Thea decided not to expand on the answer with the men joining their circle. She really had to get this meeting started before she lost her nerve.

"So, as you all know, this is our check-in time during the retreat to talk about how things are going in our families. But before we get started on that, there are some things I need to say."

She paused to gather her composure. How had she practiced this again? She couldn't quite remember her script.

"What is it?" Abby slipped her arm around Thea's shoulders. "Is everything okay?"

"Everything hasn't been okay for a long time." That was the best place to start. She turned off her inner editor so she could keep going. "I know you all think I lead these trips because I have wisdom gained from experience living the military life. And that's true to an extent." She took a second to glance at each person sitting there. "But when I see you all interacting as husband and wife—how you care for each other and how you seem to know what the other person needs—I realize my marriage to Dylan was nothing like that."

"Oh, honey." Kelly set her mug down on the coffee table. "None of us have perfect marriages."

"Far from it," Cal threw in.

"I know that." She laughed a little. "I didn't mean you had perfect marriages. But I see a bond between you all that Dylan and I never had." Without analyzing her thoughts, she simply plowed forward. "The truth is, we didn't have much of a relationship, and before he left for his last deployment, I told him I wanted a divorce." Crying hadn't been part of the plan, but it seemed she had no choice. Instead of fighting it, she let the tears come. Maybe that was part of healing too.

"We understand." Luciana handed her a box of tissues from the coffee table. "You haven't said anything that all of us haven't felt at one time or another."

Everyone seemed to agree with a nod.

The thing that was the hardest for her to accept, though, was that she'd meant those words when she said them. The timing had been a mistake, but she'd meant what she said to Dylan. She hadn't wanted herself or her children to have to walk on eggshells around their father forever. It hadn't been healthy for any of them. "People assumed we had this great marriage, this great life together, and then when he died, my sole purpose became protecting our secret." But as she'd learned, secrets usually brought more harm than good.

"I didn't feel like I could be honest about what our life together was truly like, and in hiding from other people, I shut them out." That was why she'd turned on Wes after they'd kissed in front of the boathouse and again after they'd made love. He'd seen too much, and it scared her. But if she was going to find her way back to him, she couldn't keep up that pattern. She had to break it starting today.

"This week, I've realized a lot of things about myself. The biggest one being that I won't be able to find the kind of love I so badly wanted with Dylan with anyone else until I can be open and authentic. So, thank you for giving me a space to start."

"Thank you for giving us *all* a space to start," Kelly said. "I struggle with the same thing. I want everything to be perfect, so that's the image I project, but mostly I'm a mess."

"Amen." Luciana sighed into her coffee.

"It's not a perfect and easy life we've chosen." Cal looked to Gabe and Carlos for confirmation.

They both nodded.

"But I think it's that imperfectness that makes us need each other even more. As spouses and as friends who can relate."

Murmurs of agreement went around, and maybe for the first time in her whole life, Thea knew she wasn't alone. She had a group of friends who understood, who'd seen her worst and still believed the best of her. "Thank you all." She dabbed her eyes with a tissue.

She didn't know what she'd feared before they'd sat down together—judgment, maybe? But she only felt their love and concern for her. "That's really all I wanted you to know." She hadn't meant to make the group session all about her. "We can open it up for more sharing about how your week has gone, how your families are doing." She'd rather let someone else have a turn to cry.

"Hold on." Kelly raised her hand. "What about Wes? You're not just going to let him run away, are you?"

"Oh boy. Here we go," Cal muttered, shaking his head.

"You *can't* let him run away." Abby grabbed Thea's arm like the very idea of her and Wes not being together made her frantic. "You should call him!"

"Call him?" Carlos shook his head. "No, no. You don't want to *call* him."

Thea gaped at them. If she didn't know better, she'd think the whole group had been discussing her and Wes's love life behind their backs.

Kelly gasped and stood. "You have to go after him!"

"Yes." Gabe pointed at her. "Exactly. You have to make the grand gesture. Just like in that movie." He turned to Abby. "What was that movie again?"

"You mean *Sweet Home Alabama*?" His wife laughed. "You hated that movie."

"I pretended to hate it, but I really thought, man, that lady loves that guy."

Thea cracked up. "You guys are crazy." But she had to admit, the idea had a certain appeal...

"You could leave tonight." Gabe pulled out his phone. "And then show up at his event tomorrow. I think he said he usually has to be at the arena by ten o'clock. Looks like Amarillo is about a nine-hour drive from here."

Thea did the math. If they hurried, they could be there by eleven o'clock and find a hotel. "But we're supposed to have four more days here with you all." Her kids wouldn't want to cut the trip short. They were having way too much fun to leave now.

"You can come back!" Luciana jumped up and joined Kelly in front of the fireplace. "And then you can bring Wes back with you!"

"In that case, you should fly down there," Carlos insisted. "Then you can drive back with him." He shrugged as if that settled that.

"There's an airport in Amarillo." Gabe was tapping on his phone. "Looks like there's a flight from Denver leaving tonight at six."

"Tonight?" She—the most planned and scheduled person—was supposed to zoom down to the airport and hop on a plane *tonight*? She couldn't tell if it was nerves or excitement buzzing through her. She would definitely have to clear it with a phone call to Ryan's doctor. And..."What if he doesn't want to see us?" Maybe August was wrong. Maybe Wes ran because he didn't want to put up with a mom and her kids...

"Are you serious right now?" Kelly looked at Cal, who finished her sentence for her. "Trust me, Thea. I know what it looks like when a man is falling in love with someone, and Wes is a goner."

"Oh!" Now Abby flew off the couch, obviously driven by yet another great idea. "I'm sure August can help you get tickets to surprise Wes. He's his brother, after all. You could show up with the kids at the rodeo and watch him."

"Great idea." Luciana pulled Thea to her feet. "Let's go talk to August. And you need to tell Ryan and Liv right away. If you're going to do this, you have to be at the airport in four hours."

Thea somehow managed to stand, even with her head spinning. She let them sweep her toward the door with their plans and their excited chatter, but once they'd stepped outside, Kelly stopped abruptly. She faced Thea. "Wait. I think we're getting a little carried away here. You need to decide if this is what *you* want to do."

"Yes." It seemed her heart had already decided for her. "I mean, this is not something I would've come up with on my own in a million years without all of you, but I want him in my life. I want him in our lives." And he might say no. Or he might not be ready for that, but she would never know if she didn't go after him and try. For a split second, she thought about leaving the kids at the ranch. Would her son be even more heartbroken if Wes wasn't glad to see them?

That conversation with Liv made courage bloom in her heart again. No. It didn't matter what Wes said. This was her chance to fight for what she wanted. This was her chance to stand strong, and she wanted her kids to be part of this.

Kelly squealed and did a little dance. "Then let's make this happen." She pointed at her husband. "Your mission is to go talk to August. I'm sure he knows who Wes works for. Tell him they need front-row tickets to that rodeo. He's great at talking his way into things."

"On it." Cal and Gabe and Carlos jogged down the hill.

"And you." Kelly spun back to her. "You need to talk to your kids. Tell them the plan. Make sure they're on board."

"Right." She wasn't worried about Liv. Her daughter had already made it clear how much she liked Wes. Ryan, on the other hand, could be mighty stubborn when he wanted to be.

"Go, go, go." Abby patted her back, sending her off. "While you discuss with them, we'll pack you and the kids some food for the trip to Denver."

Her three friends scurried back into the great room, leaving Thea to walk down to the beach alone.

The men had already cornered August near the boathouse, and Wes's brother had a big grin on his face, so all seemed to be well there. Now to approach Ryan.

Her son stood on the dock with his fishing pole, his eyes trained on the bobber hovering on the surface of the lake. Liv sat behind him, still relishing her protective sister role, apparently.

"You're fishing again," Thea said as she made her way to the end of the dock.

"I had to." Ryan kept his eyes on the water. "You shoulda seen August earlier. He has no idea how to cast, Mom. He's a *terrible* fisherman. I had to show him how it's done."

Huh. It seemed August had more insight into children than she'd given him credit for. "That's great, honey. I'm sure he appreciated you teaching him how to fish."

"Well, someone had to," he muttered.

Smiling, Thea sat down next to Liv. "I have something I want to run by you two." And she didn't have time to beat around the bush. "What would you think about taking a quick trip down to Texas?"

"No." Ryan whirled, the lure on his fishing line zipping over their heads. "I'm not leaving. We're supposed to be here for ten days! It's only been a few days."

It had been a little more than a few days, but Thea didn't correct him.

Liv had narrowed her eyes and was studying Thea's face. "A quick trip? Why?"

"To go watch Wes in a rodeo." Thea said the words as indifferently as she could manage with her heart racing this way.

"Wait." Her son set the fishing pole down and came over. "We would only go watch Wes, and then we would come back to the ranch?"

"We would go watch Wes, and then we'd ask him to come back with us." She held her breath until her son's entire face broke into a smile.

"Yes!" Her son nearly lost hold of his fishing pole. "We have to bring Wes back! We have to go get him!"

"I'm in." Her daughter was grinning too. "Does this mean you might actually go on a date with him?"

"A date?" Ryan jumped up and down, nearly landing himself in the lake. "You're going on a date with him? You *like* him?"

"I really like him," Thea confirmed.

"And I'm pretty sure he likes her too," Liv informed her brother.

Her son gasped. "Are you going to get married? That would be a dream come true! I could fish all the time!"

"I don't know, honey." She stood and pulled her boy in for a hug. "If we did, that would be a long way off. We would have to spend some time together. Really get to know each other."

"But we might come up to the ranch more then? Right?" her son pressed.

"We *might*." She knelt to his level, ignoring the possibility that

Wes would tell her he wasn't interested. She had to have faith in what her heart was saying to her. "So we're doing this? We're going to Texas?"

"Yes!" Ryan grabbed Thea's hand and dragged her off the dock. "Come on! Let's go get Wes."

Chapter Twenty-Four

Wes pulled on his protective vest and secured the straps tightly around his rib cage. He reached into his locker and found his jersey, pulling it over his head.

"Dude, what's up with you today?" Colin, Wes's least favorite colleague, stood alongside him, suiting up too. "You should be walking around here with a strut in your step, being the head honcho and all. Instead, you're moping around."

"I'm not moping." He sat on the bench to put on his boots and walk himself out of there before Colin really got to him. Most days he had patience with the younger guys—he was typically able to hold his tongue when they were shooting off their mouths about women and the stupid shit they did.

But today there were no guarantees. He was in a mood. He'd been in a mood since he'd driven away from the ranch, and it wasn't looking like he'd snap out of it anytime soon.

"You're real hard to please." Colin sat next to him. The man had zero ability to read body language. "I mean, now you're where all of us want to be, and you still look like someone shit in your coffee this morning."

"I'm taking the job seriously. That's all it is." The words held a certain degree of truth. He had seriously started to wonder if this was all he would ever have. The traveling and the suiting up before competitions. The anonymous crowd praising his performance, but not really knowing him or seeing past the backflip he could land.

After what had happened to Ryan, all Wes could think about was getting back to work. And now that he was here, all he could think about was what he'd walked away from. About *who* he'd walked away from.

"All I'm saying is, if you don't kick up the energy a notch, this event is gonna be a bust." Colin crammed his enormous feet into his boots. "Those people out there feed off you, man. Whatever's got you all bummed out, you'd better let it go. Don't ruin this for the rest of us."

He was about to tell the man to mind his own damn business when a text chimed on his phone. Wes pulled it out of his back pocket and stared at the screen, taking a punch in the gut.

I miss you. I hope you do real good at your competition today. I'll be cheering for you! Love, Ryan

The hard resolve he'd built to walk away and move on crumbled with one simple text. He didn't deserve to be missed. Especially after he'd left without bothering to say goodbye. And yet the kid didn't hold it against him. What about Ryan's mom, though? He sighed, thinking of how he'd let Thea down.

"Who's Ryan?"

Wes hadn't even noticed that Colin had moved to stand behind him, reading the text over his shoulder. He was about to tell him to leave him the hell alone, but he stopped himself. "He's a kid I met at the ranch. Lost his dad three years ago. I took him fishing."

It sounded simple, but being with the kid had impacted him big-time. Funny how he'd felt more like himself when he was with Ryan—and when he was with Thea—than he did out here.

That was what had him in a mood. He knew now how little fulfillment a job brought. Especially a job where he had no connections. He got along with the guys okay—and with Craig—

but they weren't a family, and that's what he'd been missing since his dad died.

In some ways, over the last year he and Jane had made strides on rebuilding the family they'd lost, but what would it be like to have his own family?

One of his father's old adages came back to him: *You can have whatever job you want, son, but it'll never mean as much to you as the people you care about.* He hadn't understood those words until he'd had a few heart-to-hearts with a kid who amazed him. Until he'd held Thea in his arms all night. Until he'd seen a little bit of Olivia's resilience after he'd held her accountable for a bad choice. He cared about all three of them. He might suck at being a role model sometimes, like when Ryan was able to sneak off and nearly get himself killed, but he wanted to someday be the man those kids relied on. The man Thea relied on.

"Is this Ryan kid coming today?" Colin asked, stretching out his shoulders and getting loose.

"No." Wes swiped on his phone screen until he found the picture he'd taken of Ryan holding the fish. That moment had turned so fast. But he supposed that was the truth of life. Just when things were good—just when you thought it was easy, you got hit with a challenge. And instead of walking away, he had to learn to stick it out.

"Probably better he's not here," Colin said. "You need to get your head in the game. We gotta get out there. It's almost time for this thing to start."

"Be right there." Wes let the man go ahead without him. He opened up his texts again.

I miss you too, Ryan, he typed. And I wish you were all here. If he ever had the privilege of seeing them again—if Thea hadn't written him off for good yet—he would get on his knees and tell them that he was sorry, that he was messed up and completely lacking, and would likely never be good enough for them, but none of that would stop him from trying to be a better man.

He stood and secured his phone in his locker, then slipped on his cowboy hat and followed the hallway that led to the arena. The MC was already announcing the lineup for the bull riding event. Wes's crew stood along the fence waiting for the introductions.

"There he is." Craig strode to meet him. "You ready for this, Harding? Word is you're distracted today."

"I'm ready." He shot Colin a glare. The man was likely gunning for his spot at the top. "I always come through, don't I?" He'd been devoting himself to this job for the last several years. He knew how to get the job done, even when he wasn't feeling it.

"All right then." His boss backed off. "We've got a full crowd today. Make sure they get their money's worth."

"We're on it." Wes gathered Colin and Darrell around him and gave them the rundown of the setup. He'd be center today, and they'd run the flanks. "Anytime the bull comes for you, feel free to add in some theatrics, but remember, rider safety is the number one priority. If he gets hurt, it's on us."

Both men gave him a nod. As much as he didn't like Colin, at least the kid had some serious talent. He wasn't worried about either of these men messing up.

The announcer called their names, introducing them to the crowd. Wes ducked the fence, leading the way out for a quick lap around the arena where they did their typical wave. Might as well get this party started right. As they approached their holding area, he jumped up on the fence and did his backflip, landing his boots in a cloud of dust. The crowd went nuts for it, jumping to their feet and cheering. Wes waved one more time and then took his post by the south fence.

"First rider up, Scot Kline riding Ripper!" The announcer drew out the syllables, getting the crowd all riled up.

Game time. Wes gave the thumbs-up signal to Colin and then to Darrell. They were both ready. He kept his eyes trained on the bull in the chute and crouched so he could be on his toes. Doing his best to block out everything else, he tried to get in his zone.

The rider climbed up the fence and slid onto the bull's back, and then the gate swung wide open.

Ripper tore into the center of the arena, bucking his hind legs, but Scot had experience. He moved with the bull, and Wes followed on the outskirts, ready to jump in the second Scot dismounted. The seconds slowed. *Five, six, seven, eight.* The rider let go and used one last buck to jump off to the left, landing on his knees in the dirt.

Wes was right there with him, waving his arms to turn Ripper's fury on him. The bull snorted and lunged at him, his hooves skidding in the dirt.

That's it. Follow me. Wes jogged backward, dodging his feet left and right, making the bull guess. Finally, Ripper got tired of the act and charged straight for him, driving Wes up onto the fence. The crowd noise turned thunderous as Wes balanced his boots on the top rung and waved. It seemed the long pause bored the bull, and Ripper trotted away, following the fence back to the chute.

Wes prepared to do his signature backflip off the rails when he heard his name. He knew that voice. He swung his head left and then right, searching.

There was Ryan. Right in the front row behind the fence. And Liv. And Thea. His eyes met hers, and a sense of relief he'd never known flooded him. Without thinking, he jumped off the fence and into the stands and found himself on his knees in front of her.

The crowd hushed, and he could only imagine what Craig must be thinking, but he didn't care. He didn't care that a thousand cellphone cameras were pointed in his direction. He didn't care that the next rider would be climbing the fence in only a few minutes. She had come all this way. And that mattered more than any of this.

"I'm sorry," he told her, taking her hands in his. "You can walk away from me if you want, but I swear I will never walk away from you again."

Tears streamed down her cheeks. She leaned forward, her lips forming that soft smile he loved so much. "You have no idea how glad I am to hear you say that." Thea moved closer, touching her lips to his, and the kiss told him everything would be okay.

The crowd seemed to think so too. The cheering started again, and even the announcer got in on the scene.

"It appears we have a slight delay, folks. Our very own Hallmark movie unfolding right before our eyes."

"It's disgusting," Ryan said with a giggle.

Wes pried himself away from Thea and hugged the kid.

"That bull chasing you was the coolest thing I've ever seen in my whole entire life." Ryan pushed Wes back. "Can you teach me how to do that?"

"We'll see," Wes and Thea said at the same time.

"I didn't think it was cool." Liv's eyes were wide. "I thought that thing was going to run you over!"

"Nah. I'm always faster." Wes gave her a quick hug too.

"All right, folks, we have to keep things moving here." The announcer's voice boomed through the speakers. "Next rider up is..."

Wes shuffled back to Thea. "I have to go back to work."

"Yes, you do." She kissed him once more. "But we'll be waiting for you right here when you're done."

Wes held her gaze as long as he could before he had to turn around and hop the fence back into the arena.

For the next two hours, the seconds dragged by like years. Somehow, he kept his focus, even with his gaze constantly drifting back to Thea and Ryan and Liv. Knowing they were there filled him with a new energy, and it seemed to pay off. After the last rider had tested his luck, Craig came to find him in the locker room. "You killed it out there today. And that stunt with the woman? Brilliant."

"That wasn't a stunt." Wes rushed to pull off his jersey and protective vest, shoving them into his gear bag.

"Well, whatever it was, the crowd loved it." His boss clapped him on the back. "The job is yours this season. Lead at every event I've got contracted."

"I'll let you know." He had to talk it over with Thea. He slipped into his T-shirt and threw the rest of his stuff into his bag.

"But you'll be in Oklahoma next week, right?" The man looked panicked. "That's one of our biggest events."

"I'll be there." He'd already committed, and he wouldn't break his word. But for the long term...well, he'd have to see how things worked out. "See you then." Wes hurried out of the locker room and jogged down the hall to the arena. Thea and her kids were waiting for him in their seats like she said they would be. He tossed his bag onto the ground and made his way down the aisle.

Thea met him halfway, but Ryan squeezed in between them before he could say anything to her.

"Wes! Wasn't this the best surprise ever?"

"The absolute best." He still couldn't believe they were standing here with him. All three of them. It was the best sight he'd ever seen. "How did you get here?"

"We flew on an airplane," the kid informed him.

"Everyone helped us plan the surprise," Liv added. "August even talked to your boss and got us the tickets."

"Wow." He'd have to call his brother right away. He owed him a thank-you. And an apology.

"But we were kind of hoping you could drive us back to the ranch." Thea cleared her throat. She smiled, but there was also a cautious distance in her eyes. He'd put it there by walking away without a goodbye. It didn't matter that he regretted it. He'd hurt her.

Wes patted Ryan's shoulder. "Hey, I've got a few bandannas in my bag." He reached in and pulled them out, handing one to Ryan and one to Liv. "The bull riders are signing autographs right down there." He pointed in the direction of the chute. "Why don't you go meet them?"

"Awesome!" Ryan bounded away with his sister not far behind, reminding him to take it easy.

Thea watched her kids go, her smile fading.

"You have every right to be upset." Wes slipped off his hat

and threw it onto his bag. He inched closer to her. "I messed up, but I hope you can forgive me. I didn't know how to deal with everything, and—"

"Stop." The woman's eyes held him captive. They were bright and beautiful—projecting her strength. "No excuses. I forgive you. But that can't happen again. If you want to walk away, next time you will talk to me first."

"I will." Though he didn't plan to walk away from her again. He would make the most of this second chance. "I swear to you, Thea...you will never have to wonder how much I care about you."

The distance between them melted away. She wrapped her arms around his waist and brought him close, her smile-softened lips drawing him in. He kissed her like it was the last time he would have the chance, savoring the taste of her, the feel of her body close to his.

Thea pulled back so their lips were barely separated. "I don't know how I ever could've thought this was a mistake." Her smile turned playful. "You do crazy things to me, Wes Harding."

"You haven't seen anything yet," he breathed against her neck.

"We got the autographs!" Ryan wedged himself between them again. "Now let's hit the road so we can get back to the ranch and fish in the canoe!"

"I don't think that's what they had in mind," Liv said with a smirk.

It looked like he and Thea would have to take a rain check. "It doesn't matter what we do." Wes gathered them all in for a group hug. "As long as we do it together."

Chapter Twenty-Five

Hello?" Kelly nudged Thea in the ribs. "Are you listening to a word I'm saying?"

"Uh-huh." She was half listening anyway. There happened to be a major distraction in the form of Wes walking around the dining room, refilling everyone's water glasses, and try as she might, Thea couldn't seem to pry her gaze away from the man.

"Oh my gravy, would you two just sneak off together already?" her friend implored her with wide eyes. "The simmering chemistry between you two is killing me."

Thankfully the kids had taken to eating dinner at their own table near the windows so they couldn't hear the conversation. Though Thea might not mind listening in on what Preston and Liv were talking about. The two of them were laughing and chatting as though they were the only ones in the room. They were adorable.

"The simmering chemistry is killing all of us," Abby whined.

Luciana agreed with a laugh.

"You think it's killing *you guys*?" Thea tortured herself with another long glance at Wes. "We haven't been able to find more than ten minutes alone since we got back to the ranch." For the last three days, Wes had been amazing with Ryan and Liv—swimming and fishing and paddleboarding and playing volleyball. But that hadn't exactly given them time to focus on each other or have any important conversations about the future. "Now it's our last night here, and I don't know if we'll be able to talk or...well..." She let her raised eyebrows speak for her. One night with Wes had simply not been enough.

"I don't think you need to worry about not getting any alone time together tonight." Abby shared a mysterious smile with the other two.

Before Thea could ask what that was all about, Wes carried the water pitcher to their table.

"You can sit down with us, you know." Kelly pulled out the empty chair on the other side of her.

"Nope." Wes set down his pitcher. "When I'm here, I'm on the clock, taking care of things so you all don't have to."

"And you've done a great job," Luciana said. "In fact, I think you've been working a little too hard these last couple of days."

"Definitely," Abby agreed.

Okay, these three were obviously up to something.

"You might be right." Wes set down the pitcher. "Actually, I might need to take tonight off." His smile was as cryptic as her friends'. "Are you busy tonight?" he asked Thea.

Oh, her heart when he grinned at her like that. "I don't know. Am I?"

"Can I have your attention, everyone." August walked in between the kids' table and the grown-ups' table. "Since it's your last night at the ranch, we wanted to invite the kids to camp out on the back lawn."

The kids' table erupted into excited chatter.

"We'll watch outdoor movies and play games and sleep under the stars one more time before you head home."

The parents cheered, too, but Thea's heart sank a little. Did that mean Wes would be keeping an eye on the kids all night?

"August is going to take this one," Wes murmured as if he could sense her concern. "And I was hoping you'd go on a little adventure with me."

"Of course she will," Kelly answered for her.

Thea swatted her friend. "I will." She would go anywhere with this man, especially knowing their time together was short.

"I'll pick you up at your cabin at seven thirty." He caressed her shoulder, and the touch made her shiver with longing. "Wear something comfortable. And make sure you have sturdy shoes."

She grabbed his hand and held on. "Where are we going?"

"You'll see." He brushed a kiss onto her hand and then walked away and disappeared into the kitchen.

"All right." Thea leaned in Kelly's direction. "Spill it. What are we doing tonight? You're obviously in on it."

Her friend shrugged. "We only knew about the campout. Wes kept everything else a secret. But I bet it will be good." She stood up and slipped on her sweatshirt. "And now if you'll excuse me, I'm going to go get ready for my own romantic date with that man right there." She pointed out Cal, who was over joking around with the kids.

"I should get ready too." Abby pushed back from the table. "After this, who knows when we'll get another date night."

"Hey, maybe we should do date night swaps with the kids when we get back home." As had become her custom, Luciana stacked the plates. "We could each take turn to host all the kids once a month, giving us the chance to have a date night."

"Love it!" Kelly glanced at Thea. "And you know you could leave your kids with us for a weekend, if you needed to make a trip to Colorado. Or East Texas. Or Oklahoma."

"Us too," her other friends agreed.

A week ago, Thea would've told them no, thank you. She would've wanted to keep her world small. But right now life seemed to be expanding in the best way possible. "That would be amazing." She'd never had close enough friends to watch her kids before.

"Mom!" Ryan waved his arms from across the room. "We have to go! We have to get ready for the sleepover!"

The kids started to disperse in a chaotic flurry of activity, imploring their parents to hurry. Thea joined up with her kids near the doors. "Are you sure you want to sleep outside?" She was mainly asking Liv.

"Are you kidding?" Ryan answered for both of them. "It's going to be awesome! August even told us he'd make us popcorn and we could have some candy."

"It'll be cool." Her daughter was the epitome of cool. "The twins and Preston and I are going to be next to each other so we can play games on our phones too."

"Sounds like fun." She tried not to appear too overeager to have a night off of her own.

"What're you gonna do, Mom?" Ryan suddenly looked concerned. "You want to sleep out with us?"

"Oh, no. I think I'll stick to my nice soft bed, thank you very much." Or Wes's nice soft bed? "You need to listen to August, though." She couldn't believe the man was taking on all the kids.

"We will," Ryan assured her before bounding down the hill to talk to Timothy.

Thea slipped her arm around her daughter. "You can keep an eye on your brother too?"

"After what he pulled on the fishing trip?" Liv shook her head. "Don't worry. I'll watch him like a hawk."

"Thanks, honey." She wasn't sure how she'd been blessed to get such amazing children, but she was grateful.

For the next hour, she and the kids spent time packing up most of their things so they'd be ready to head back to Texas in the morning. Ryan grumbled about leaving the whole time, and Thea let him. She didn't want to go either.

Just before seven thirty, she walked them to the lawn behind the lodge, where August had set up an outdoor movie screen and seven sleeping bags. She told her kids good night and stopped by the table where August was setting out pop and snacks. "You're sure you're up for this?" She eyed the copious amounts of sugar.

"How hard can it be?"

She decided not to answer that. "I'll have my cell phone on if you need anything."

"I won't need anything." Wes's brother held up a bag of M&M's. "I have all the leverage I need to get them to behave."

She couldn't argue with that. "Thanks for doing this."

"I'm glad I can help." Like Wes, August had a genuineness about him, and she got the sense that he always said what he meant. "I couldn't be happier for you two."

She couldn't be happier either. After taking a picture of all the kids settled in the sleeping bags, she hurried back to the cabin to change into a pair of yoga pants and a sweatshirt. *Real sexy*, she thought, lacing up her hiking boots. At least she'd taken some time earlier that day to fix up her hair. It had been a long time since she'd had anyone to impress.

After a glance in the mirror, she added some tinted ChapStick to keep her lips soft. She almost laughed when Wes knocked on the front door all formal, like he was really picking her up for a date.

Thea's heart seemed to pick up a new rhythm as she rushed through the small living room and opened the door. Instead of saying hello, she simply walked into Wes's arms and kissed him the way she'd been aching to kiss him all day. "Do we have to go out?" she whispered against his lips. "We could always stay in." This was exactly where she wanted to stay, in his arms, pressed against him...only with fewer clothes on.

Wes laughed as he kissed her again. "You'll like where we're going. I promise."

"I like this." She moved her lips along his jawline and down to his neck. How had she ever thought she could keep any boundaries with this man?

"Me too." He guided her lips back to his. "But hold that thought. We have a short walk, and then we can pick up right where we left off. I promise." The man had the nerve to pull back and offer her his hand.

"Fine," she huffed. "I guess a little walk would be okay."

They stepped outside, and she was glad she'd put on her sweat-shirt. The air had chilled with dusk, but it felt perfect as they walked along the lake, her hand tucked under Wes's arm. Even though they were heading away from the lodge, she could hear the movie. "What are they watching?"

"*The Princess Bride*." Wes guided her in front of him when the path narrowed and kept his hand at the small of her back.

"A true classic." She used to have a huge crush on Westley.

"As you wish." Wes took her hand again, walking alongside her.

"I haven't wished for anything yet." Warmth seemed to fill her with that tingly anticipation she was beginning to love.

"Doesn't matter what you wish for," he told her, pausing in the thick of the trees. "I would give it all." Wes leaned in as though he was about to kiss her but brought his lips to her ear at the last second. "Close your eyes."

"Okay…" Not that it would matter much. With the dark closing in all around them, she couldn't see a lot anyway.

Wes threaded his fingers through hers and led her a few yards forward before he paused again. "Open them."

She saw the lights first. Beautiful white string lights stretched from the surrounding trees to the top of a white teepee. Two flaps were open, showing off what looked like a soft mattress covered with blankets and pillows inside. In front of the teepee, a small campfire flickered. On both sides of the teepee, the evergreen trees hemmed them in, sheltering the space and turning it into a private cozy refuge.

"This is incredible." She'd never liked camping, but she might never want to sleep indoors again.

"I thought this would give us a chance to be alone. With no interruptions." Wes tugged on her hand, leading her to the teepee, and they both crouched and ducked inside. Thea sat on the edge of the mattress to remove her boots and then lay back into the soft comfort with a luxurious sigh. Millions of stars were visible through the gaps in the top of the teepee. "This might be more comfortable than my bed at home."

Wes kicked off his boots and eased onto his side next to her. "I know things have been crazy since we got back."

Thea turned on her side to face him. "I'm not sure life will ever stop being crazy." Not with kids and jobs and the constant surprises.

"It won't," he agreed. "But I wanted to take tonight for you and me. I wanted everything else to pause so I could tell you I'm falling in love with you. I'm falling in love with your kids. I don't know if you have any room in your heart for me—"

Thea stopped him right there. "I have room in my heart again for the first time in a long time." She'd never felt as complete as she did right then in that moment. "I know I pushed you away before, but you have to understand...Dylan and I had a very rocky marriage." She gazed steadily into Wes's eyes. It felt like she'd been looking into them forever. "We got married too young. I was pregnant, and I didn't think I had any other choices." There were so many other parts of her story she would tell him in time, but now she wanted him to know one thing. "I didn't have the kind of marriage I wanted to have. We fought and ignored each other and never found a way to deal with our issues." Sharing the next part didn't shake her like it had before. "Before he left for that last deployment, I told him I wanted a divorce."

Wes nodded as if he understood where her pain came from. He said nothing, but his hand found hers again.

"That was the last time I saw him, and I will always regret those words." They might've been true. She didn't know if she and Dylan would have ever been able to work through the problems individually or as a couple, but she wanted the words back. "That won't happen again. I want things to be different next time. I won't take anyone for granted."

"I feel the same way." Wes smoothed her hair away from her cheek. "We both know how quickly someone can be taken away. I won't take anyone for granted, and I won't live with regrets. Not anymore."

"Then let's make the most of this night." Thea started to unbutton his shirt. "And tomorrow we'll figure out the rest."

Chapter Twenty-Six

If she had to stare at this computer for one more minute, Thea was going to go cross-eyed.

She closed her laptop with a sigh and looked at the clock on her office wall. She really should've been out of here a half hour ago, but with the school year starting back up, she'd done double the number of evaluations this week and had to finish inputting all of her reports.

But seriously. She was starting to get a headache from all the screen time.

Unfortunately, her phone couldn't seem to take a hint. It buzzed and vibrated across the surface of her desk. All it took was one wary look at Kelly's picture glowing on her phone screen to erase her bad mood and bring out her smile. It was nice to have a best friend.

When she realized she'd have to stay at work a little later, she'd called on Kelly for school pickup duty.

"Happy birthday!" her friend sang into the receiver. "Just wanted to let you know I got the kiddos settled at your house."

"Thank you." She tried to make the words sound less mopey than she'd felt all day. It wasn't that she didn't appreciate the texts and the phone calls and social media greetings she'd received—especially the message from Wes—but all she really wanted for her birthday was to be with him. They'd both made an effort to see each other as often as they could since July, but now that the kids were back in school and her job was in full swing, it had gotten harder. She appreciated the lengthy phone calls they had and the text conversations and the video calls, but more and more she ached to feel his arms around her.

"So, do you have big plans for tonight?" Kelly's voice echoed like she was on her Bluetooth in the car.

"No." After the day she'd had, she'd likely pick up a pizza and eat it on the floor in front of a movie with the kids. Wes would call her later, and she'd probably be on the phone with him for a good two hours, which would help cheer her up. But a kiss...oh, a kiss would mean everything to her today.

"You don't sound as happy as you should on your birthday," her friend said, not letting her off the hook. "What's up?"

Thea didn't make it a habit to whine, but this was Kelly. She'd get it. "I'm missing him." It had only been two weeks since Wes had come to visit for the weekend, but it seemed to get harder every time they parted. "We probably won't get up to the ranch again until fall break." Another whole month and a half. "And he's busy with a few more events before the season is up." She might as well add a *woe is me* onto the end of that sentence.

"That *sucks*."

She appreciated her friend commiserating with her instead of reminding her she'd seen the man two weeks ago. True friends sometimes just let things suck.

"You have every right to go home and mope," Kelly said. "Take a bubble bath, drink some wine, and binge-watch some rom-coms."

"You give the best advice, you know that?" It helped to laugh.

"You're right. I totally do." Her friend laughed with her. "We're still on for our girls' night out with Abby and Luciana on Sunday, right? We want to celebrate you."

"I wouldn't miss it." Especially since Cal, Gabe, and Carlos had volunteered to take all the kids to a movie. Over the last two months, these families had become her family.

"Perfect! Hey, I gotta run." Kelly suddenly sounded rushed. "Don't forget about that bubble bath."

"I won't." Though she might be too tired to make it happen by the time she got home. Thea said goodbye to her friend and shoved the phone into her purse. Leaving the pile of work for Monday, she collected her things and shuffled down the hall, waving to a few coworkers before she stepped outside. She did, indeed, pick up a pizza—pepperoni, mushroom, and olive, since the deal was that she and each one of her kids got to choose a topping.

Too tired to rearrange the bikes and yard toys in the garage, she parked in the driveway and lumbered to the front door, somehow carrying her shoulder bag, the shoes Ryan had left in the car, and the pizza.

"I'm home!" Thea let her son's shoes fall to the floor and shrugged the strap of her bag off her shoulder. Huh. It looked strangely clean in her front entry. No sweatshirts lying on the ground, and what had happened to the ten pairs of shoes Liv usually kept near the front door?

"We're in here!" her kids shouted in unison.

From the dining room? What were they doing in the dining room? "I hope you're hungry—" Thea rounded the corner and dropped the pizza box right onto the carpet.

Wes stood on the other side of the table, dressed in black jeans and a denim button-up, but best of all he was wearing the smile she swore belonged to her alone. Ryan stood on one side of him, wearing the bow tie she'd gotten him for his choir concert. Liv stood on Wes's other side in one of her long dresses.

"You're here." Thea tried to take it all in, but the tears were building. The table had been set with her grandmother's china. There were balloons and flowers and presents.

"Surprise!" Ryan squealed.

"Happy birthday, Mom." Liv hurried to hug her.

Happy didn't begin to describe it. "Thank you." She kissed the top of her daughter's head. "This is amazing." Her teary gaze drifted back to the cowboy across the table. "When did you come?"

"He got here this morning," Ryan reported. "And he cleaned the house while we were at school, and then we went shopping right after, and then we came home and helped him make your favorite dinner."

So Kelly hadn't picked up the kids after all. And all that bubble bath talk...Thea shook her head. Her friend had known she'd be very busy tonight all along.

"You made eggplant parmigiana?" She hadn't meant to gasp, but *she* didn't even make that at home.

Wes edged his way around the table. "Louise walked us through it on FaceTime." He kissed Thea's cheek—always too well behaved in front of the children—and pulled out her chair. "And then we made a chocolate cake for dessert."

A timer dinged from the kitchen. "I'll be right back," Wes said slyly.

Thea watched his backside until he disappeared into the kitchen. Oh, those jeans. She would have to make sure to tell him how much she liked them later.

"You two are awfully good at keeping surprises." She squeezed Ryan's and Liv's hands. "How long have you been planning this?"

"We talked about it when he was here a few weeks ago." Liv seemed quite pleased with herself. "The eggplant parmigiana was my idea."

"And I said we had to have chocolate cake." Ryan sat in his usual chair next to her, but Liv walked over and picked up the pizza box off the floor. Thea had forgotten all about it.

Her daughter set the box aside on the buffet and served Thea a helping of a yummy-looking salad with feta and cranberries.

"This is the sweetest thing you two have ever done."

"And Wes too," Liv reminded her.

"Yes, and Wes too." She would definitely thank him properly when she had the first opportunity.

"Well, at least it *smells* good." The man carted in the casserole dish, wearing her oven mitts, and she'd never seen anything hotter.

"It smells delicious." Thea smoothed her cloth napkin over her lap and caught Wes's eye. "This is the best birthday I've ever had."

"And you haven't even opened your presents yet." Ryan pointed out the two small packages sitting next to a huge bouquet of flowers in the center of the table.

"My best present is having you three here." Right now she had everything that mattered.

"You might want to wait to say that until after you've tried dinner." Wes eyed the casserole dish with an exaggerated frown. "Cooking isn't my specialty, but I would try anything for you."

He'd proven that with all of the traveling and the FaceTiming and the visits into her and the kids' chaotic worlds.

"Well, I'm starving." Liv dished up a piece of the eggplant parmigiana and then passed it to Thea.

"It looks perfect." Nothing could ruin this night.

It tasted perfect too—the melted cheese, the garlic, the herbs Ryan informed her they'd clipped from the garden. While they ate, Wes told them about his last event, entertaining the kids with details about each of the bulls he'd faced.

"I'm gonna be in the rodeos someday too." Ryan wiped a smear of sauce off his chin.

Wes shot Thea a repentant look, as though he wasn't sure that's what she wanted for her son.

"I think you'd be great in the rodeos." She brightened her smile first at Ryan and then at Wes. She couldn't have chosen a better role model for Ryan. Over the last two months, the man had made sure to spend time with both Ryan and Liv, going to their baseball and volleyball games when he was in town and taking them out for ice cream. He hadn't only focused on building a relationship with her; he been intentional with them, too, and the three of them had formed a strong bond.

Thea pushed away her plate. "I can't eat another bite. But that was the best eggplant parmigiana I have ever had." The dish never came with that much love in a restaurant.

"I'll make sure to tell Louise." Wes stacked her plate on his and then collected Ryan's and Liv's. "Ready to open some presents?" he asked, setting the plates aside.

"Open ours first!" Ryan got on his knees so he could reach one of the packages sitting in the center of the table.

Thea took her time, soaking in the anticipation on her kids' faces. She wasn't sure she'd ever seen them so excited about giving her a gift. "What's this?" She pulled the paper away and opened the small box, revealing a beautiful white-gold mountain pendant.

"Oh, it's gorgeous, you two." She carefully lifted out the necklace and handed it to Liv. "Help me put it on."

"Ryan and I picked it out together." Her daughter clasped the dainty chain around her neck. "We've been saving our money since the summer."

"I love it." Thea touched the small charm, which lay right against her collarbone. "It reminds me of the ranch." Where she'd opened her heart. When she'd found love . . .

"Okay. I'm next," Wes said as though he couldn't wait anymore either. He shared a secretive smile with the kids and handed her the second package.

It was light, beautifully wrapped in silver paper. "You didn't have to get me anything. You being here is so much. It's everything."

"Think of it as a gift for all of us." Wes watched her remove the paper, his face almost as eager as her son's.

What did that mean? Thea ripped the rest of the paper away and opened the box to find a key.

"Wes moved here!" her son blurted. He slapped a hand over his mouth. "Oops. Sorry."

"It's okay, Sport." Wes leaned over the table and took her hand. "That's a key to my new condo."

"It's five minutes away," Liv said excitedly.

"A condo." Thea carefully lifted the key out with her free hand and held it tightly in her fist. "You moved here?" She raised her eyes to his, feeling the love and wonder rise up again. They'd talked about him finding a place closer the last time he was here, but she hadn't wanted to push it. She never dreamed he would surprise her with something so big.

"I want to be close to you," he murmured. "And to you." He looked at Ryan. "And to you." He looked at Liv. "You three mean the world to me, and I hate being far away. So this is going to be my home base."

"Isn't that the best, Mom?" Ryan clapped his hands. "We can go fishing all the time, and we can go see movies, and we can play games all together!"

"It's the best." Thea dabbed at the tears in her eyes. Just when she thought her birthday couldn't possibly get any better.

"Come on, Ryan." As if sensing the adults could use a minute alone, Liv stood and pulled her brother out of his chair, leading him in the direction of the kitchen. "We're on dish duty. And we'll put candles on the cake too."

"Yes!" Ryan cheered. "Lots and lots and *lots* of candles."

"Hey now," Thea scolded, laughing. "It's not *that* many candles."

Both of her kids disappeared from the room, giggling.

"I thought about making sure you were okay with it before I signed the lease." Wes rose from his chair and hurried around the table. "But I wanted to surprise you."

Thea stood and wrapped her arms around him. "This is the best surprise anyone has ever given me." She nudged his lips with hers. "It's torture saying goodbye to you all the time."

"Tell me about it." Wes moved his hands down her back, settling them on her waist as he urged her closer. He kissed her deeply, pulling her into the rhythm their lips had perfected together, settling her heart and making her dizzy all at once. "I love you, Thea. I love your kids. And I want to be here for you whenever you need me."

He had been there for her. And she'd been there for him too. Since they'd started dating, her heart had grown bigger and she'd become braver. She'd given her heart away to this man, holding nothing back, and had learned more about love in these last few months than she'd learned in her lifetime before. "We love you too." And that was enough. She would still make mistakes. There would be difficult moments and hard-fought battles, but she wouldn't squander this second chance to love deeply and fully, because love was worth all it cost.

Epilogue

"Wes. Hey, Wes." Something shook his shoulder. He turned onto his side and found himself staring straight into Ryan's excited eyes.

"Do you think we could go fishing now?" The boy whispered so hopefully, he couldn't simply groan and turn over like he wanted to.

Trying to get his bearings, Wes squinted at the clock. Not surprisingly, it wasn't even seven yet, but the kid had already geared up in his trapper's hat, bulky winter jacket, and ski mittens.

"Remember how you told me the fish are the most active in the morning?" Ryan started to peel the covers away from Wes. "I think we have the best chance of catching our lunch right now."

Even at the crack of dawn, Ryan never failed to make him laugh. "You're right. I'm coming." He whispered, too, doing his best to not wake Thea, who still lay sleeping soundly next to him. Easing his way off the bed, Wes pulled on his sweatpants and a sweatshirt, and then tiptoed his way into the hall.

Damn, it was early. Maybe he shouldn't have introduced the kid to ice fishing. Then again, fishing was where they had their best talks, and they were only here for a few days of their Christmas break, so they had to take advantage of every minute.

When he met Ryan in the kitchen, the kid had added ski goggles, snow pants, and boots to his ensemble.

"All suited up, huh?" he asked, casting a longing glance at the empty coffeepot.

"The sun's coming up soon, and we have to get to breakfast by eight sharp," the boy reminded him.

"Let's head out then." As much as he'd like to have stayed in bed with Thea, he didn't want to miss this time with Ryan. There'd been something he'd been meaning to ask the kid, and now would likely be his last chance.

After Wes had pulled on all his gear, they followed their typical path to the lake—Ryan bouncing with each step. Overnight, they'd gained another few inches of snow, but now the sky was pink and clear. Their boots crunched through the snow as they tromped through knee-deep drifts to the hole they'd carved in the iced-over lake yesterday.

"I'm feeling lucky today," Ryan told him, leaning over to peer into the water as if he could spot the fish.

"Me too." A surge of energy seemed to fill Wes, and he couldn't keep the secret to himself anymore. Wes started to ready their poles, pulling off his gloves to tie on the lures. "Hey, Sport...there's something important I've been wanting to talk to you about."

"Okay." The boy didn't take his eyes off the water, but that was typical. Wes had never seen a kid so serious about fishing, except for maybe himself at that age. Ryan didn't mind the low temperatures or the chilly wind. He was just as enthusiastic about fishing in the winter as he was in the summer.

"You know how much I love your mom. And you. And Liv." After he'd moved to Texas, he saw them a lot, but he'd wanted to give them some space too. He hadn't wanted the kids to have to adjust to too much too soon. But even living in a condo five minutes away from them, the time they'd spent together still hadn't been enough for him. A lifetime wouldn't be enough. He was ready for more, and he hoped they were too.

"We love you too." Ryan finally looked up at him. "My mom smiles a lot more now than she used to."

Wes pulled his gloves back on and set the poles aside. That only confirmed he was making the right decision. He knew Thea was the only woman for him, and he knew he would love her and her kids for the rest of his life. "I smile a lot more too. But I don't like going home to my own house."

"I know. It really stinks we can't be together all the time." Ryan went back to staring into the hole.

"What if we could be together all the time?" Wes held his breath, waiting for the boy's reaction.

Ryan's gaze slowly climbed to Wes's face, his eyes wide behind the tinted ski goggles.

"I was thinking I'd like to marry your mom," he said when Ryan stayed quiet. "I'd like us to be a family so we can be together more. So we can do everything together." So he could sleep with the woman he loved every night and not just when they were visiting the ranch.

The boy started to nod, his mouth hanging open, and then suddenly he ripped off the ski goggles to reveal tears streaming down his cheeks. "I can't believe how lucky I am. I'm going to have another great dad!"

Seeing the boy's emotion choked him up too. "It would be the greatest honor in my life to be your and Olivia's dad. If that's what you both want." He wouldn't push to adopt them, but if they were open to it, he would move hell and high water to make it happen.

"I've wanted you to be my dad since I met you," Ryan sobbed. "I've missed my dad so much. I'll always miss him, but now I have you." He plowed into Wes with a hug so fierce they both almost fell into their fishing hole.

"And I have you. And your mom. And Liv." So much more than he'd ever thought he would have. He held the boy close against his chest, feeling a different sort of beat in his heart. Something stronger and more powerful.

Ryan pulled away, wiping away the tears with his sleeves of his coat. "When are you gonna ask her? Today? It has to be today! We're supposed to leave in a few days, and I have to go back to school soon."

"I know." Wes didn't want to wait any more than Ryan wanted him to. That ring was burning a hole in his coat pocket. "I will definitely ask her today. I want you to be there. And Liv. And Jane and Toby and Charlee."

"What about Miss Mara?" the boy questioned. He'd really taken to Wes's mom over the last several months.

"Yes, Miss Mara too." Wes picked up his fishing pole again. "But I think you're going to have to start calling her Grandma."

Ryan gasped. "Yes! Grandma! And I'll get to call you Dad."

Wes strained his jaw against the tears, though he figured he'd better get used to them. This whole "Dad" business had done something to his heart. "I'd love nothing more."

For the next hour, he and Ryan fished the way they usually did, trading ghost stories and making up new ones together. They caught three nice-sized rainbows between the two of them. One by one, they let them go and watched them swim away.

By the time they tromped off the lake, Thea and Liv were on their way up to the lodge for breakfast.

Wes held Ryan back for a second before they met up. "You can't say a word until I'm ready, Sport. Got that?"

"Got it." The kid zipped his fingers across his lips as though he was sworn to secrecy.

Wes greeted Thea with a kiss, and they held hands all the way up to the lodge. Ryan told them all about their three fish, and somehow the rainbow trout grew into monsters.

When they walked into the dining room, Toby and Jane were already seated at the table with little Charlee nestled into her dad's arms.

After shedding his winter gear, Wes stole his niece, snuggling her up against his chest. At just over thirteen pounds, she was putting on weight fast.

"She's adorable." Thea leaned in to give Charlee a kiss on the nose, and Wes kissed his future fiancée's forehead.

The baby stirred and then stretched her arms up over her head with a yawn.

"Guess what, Uncle Toby and Aunt Jane?" Ryan sat with them at the table.

For a second Wes feared he was going to give up their secret, but instead the boy told them about his rainbow trout.

"I think you've caught more fish than me this year," Toby said with an exaggerated pout.

"Not a fair comparison when you spent a good portion of the summer at the hospital," Wes reminded him. They'd been in the NICU for four weeks and had been careful about keeping little Charlee safe and healthy while she grew. "But I'm happy to babysit anytime."

"Me too." Thea held out her arms with a pleading look, and Wes let her take his niece. Not for long, though. He'd need her left hand free in a few minutes.

"There's my family." His mother came hurrying into the dining room as though she was afraid to miss out on anything. "You kids should eat first. I'll take the baby."

Wes watched his mom beam with pride as she stole the baby from Thea's arms. She found every excuse in the book to hog her granddaughter. But that was perfect for his purposes today.

"Before we eat, I wanted to ask Thea something." Wes didn't do anything fancy. He simply lowered himself to one knee before the woman who had changed his life and took her hand.

The whole room seemed to offer a collective gasp, except for Ryan, who slapped his hands over his mouth.

"Thea Davis, I have been waiting for you my whole life. And I can't wait anymore." That was the plain truth of it. He wanted to make their commitment to each other official. He wanted to be there in the middle of the night when one of the kids was sick and needed him. He wanted to hold Thea into the morning hours. "I want to be a family. Whatever that looks like for us. Whatever that means."

He reached into his pocket and pulled out the ring he'd found at a jewelry shop in Tulsa during his last event. It was a simple solitaire diamond as bright and shining as the woman he loved. "Will you marry me?"

"Yes." Thea laughed through her tears. "Oh my God, I was hoping you'd ask me here, because I can't wait either."

All around them people were crying. Jane and Toby hugged. His mother somehow managed to snap a picture on her phone while still holding the baby.

Wes slipped the ring onto Thea's finger and stood, pulling Liv and Ryan into their embrace.

This was it. His life. Everything he needed.

The journey he'd taken to find this woman and her children had involved years of searching. But now he could finally lay it all down and live the kind of life that would make his father proud.

About the Author

Sara Richardson grew up chasing adventure in Colorado's rugged mountains. She's climbed to the top of a fourteen-thousand-foot peak at midnight, swum through class IV rapids, completed her wilderness first-aid certification, and spent seven days at a time tromping through the wilderness with a thirty-pound backpack strapped to her shoulders.

Eventually Sara did the responsible thing and got an education in writing and journalism. After a brief stint in the corporate writing world, she stopped ignoring the voices in her head and started writing fiction. Now she uses her experience as a mountain adventure guide to write stories that incorporate adventure with romance. Sara lives and plays in Colorado, where she still indulges her adventurous spirit, with her saint of a husband and two young sons.

You can learn more at:
SaraRichardson.net
Twitter @SaraR_Books
Facebook.com/SaraRichardsonBooks
Instagram @SaraRichardsonBooks

Sara Richardson returns to Silverado Lake with a heartwarming romance for August Harding. Look for his story in *Last Dance with a Cowboy*!

Available Fall 2021

For a bonus story from another author that you'll love, please turn the page to read *It's All about That Cowboy* by Carly Bloom.

When Jessica Acosta left Big Verde, Texas, she swore to never look back. But when an unexpected homecoming brings her face-to-face with her high school sweetheart, Jessica is shocked to find the chemistry between them is as strong as ever. Only Jess can't forget how Casey Long broke her heart...even if he *has* traded in his bad boy rep for a sheriff's badge. Casey's never gotten over Jess leaving, and having her back in town feels like a second chance. But can Casey and Jess move beyond the pain of the past...to have the future they both deserve?

FOREVER

Acknowledgments

This was my first novella, and I admit to having been a bit nervous about it. I'm not really known for being a short-winded girl, and conversations with me almost always require pulling up a chair. I honestly wasn't sure I could write a complete story in under thirty thousand words, but with the help of a few of my usual suspects (and some new unsuspecting innocents), I was able to pull it off.

You might think there'd be fewer people to thank with a shorter book, but you'd be wrong.

As usual, thank you to Alison Bliss for always believing in me and telling me I could do it, and to Sam Tschida for telling me *Quit yer bitchin', Sylvia Plath.* Y'all don't realize it, but you're Good Cop and Bad Cop, and I need you both desperately. And thank you to Jessica Snyder for being the voice of reason, and to Amy Bearce (hugely!!) for reading every single scene on Facebook Messenger. That had to be a special kind of hell.

Thank you to SARA members Molly Mirren, Jolene Navarro, Frances Trilone, Makenna Lee, and Sasha Summers for helping me plot this puppy (with cocktails).

And thank you to my agent, Paige Wheeler, for always having my back; and to my editor, Madeleine Colavita, whose feedback gave me confidence and brought out the best in Casey and Jessica.

Last but not least, thank you to my readers for always being ready to pull up a chair.

Now let me tell you a story.

Chapter One

Jessica Acosta sat alone at Big Verde's single stoplight, fingers gripping the steering wheel of the bright red Porsche, feeling conspicuous as hell. Her sensible crossover SUV was in the shop for scheduled maintenance, so yesterday she; her eleven-year-old sister, Hope; and her boss, Carmen, had driven all the way from Houston in Carmen's tiny red attention whore of a car. *As if Carmen, with her bright blue hair and multiple piercings and tattoos, needed it.*

It had been cramped but fun. They'd jammed to *all* the girl jams, talked *all* the girl talk, and squealed *all* the girl squeals when they'd hit the 130 toll road outside of Seguin with its eighty-five-miles-per-hour speed limit.

Hope had loved it. Like Carmen, she was an adrenaline junkie. Jessica was more of a white-knuckled party pooper. But somebody had to be the grown-up of the trio, and it was usually her.

They'd checked into the Big Verde Motor Inn last night, only to check right back out. Carmen hadn't liked the way the room smelled. Or the way it looked. She said the duvets had probably never been washed. She looked at a speck of something and insisted it was a bedbug.

Jessica hadn't been able to detect the smell—or bedbugs—and she knew Carmen's criticisms were only meant to land them in the nearby Village Château, a fancy hotel with a really great restaurant Carmen was dying to try.

Since Hope had asthma, allergies, and was getting over a cold, Jessica couldn't risk the chance that Carmen's delicate nose really had detected mold. So now they had a suite at the Village Château, where Hope and Carmen were probably living it up in luxury this very moment.

It was just as well. It would be easier for Carmen to entertain Hope there while Jessica was at the funeral.

Jessica looked up and down Main Street. Big Verde was her hometown, but she might as well be a stranger here. She and her mom had left the morning after high school graduation, and she'd never been back.

Until now.

She was here for Mavis Long's funeral and what she assumed to be a reading of her will. The lawyer hadn't called it that, but what else could it be? *If you could be at my office on Monday at 9:00, we have some items to discuss at the request of Miss Mavis.*

It was no surprise to Jessica that Hope would be mentioned in the will. Mavis had promised, and she kept her promises. But if word of it got out—and it would—the folks in Big Verde would be extremely surprised. Perplexed. Titillated. Other words that indicated excitement over gossip fodder.

Whispers.

Scandal.

Drama.

Welcome home!

Jessica shuddered and drummed her fingers on the steering wheel.

Her goal had been to get in and out of the funeral like a ninja, not to roll in like a drag queen firing a glitter bomb. Not that drag queens necessarily drove red Porsches, but both would draw about the same amount of attention in downtown Big Verde, Texas.

She slunk down in her seat. *Change, light. Change.*

The town hadn't even *had* a stoplight when she'd grown up here. And since nobody had driven through the intersection during the approximately eleven billion hours she'd been sitting at it, Big Verde *still* shouldn't have one.

It had to be broken. And if it was, everybody in town knew it, and they were probably watching through their storefront windows to see how long it would take the stranger—*her!*—to figure it out.

She tapped the gas pedal in frustration, which resulted in inadvertent engine-revving. A sideways glance at the boutique called Cathy's Closet confirmed she had drawn some attention. A face peeked through the green shoe polish letters on the window—FE FI FO FUM . . . KEEP THOSE BADGERS ON THE RUN!—to stare at her.

It was Friday, and the Big Verde Giants would apparently be battling the Smithtown Badgers at the football field later tonight. The band would play, the cheerleaders would cheer, and unless they'd hired a new coach since Jessica's cheerleading days, the Giants would lose.

Cathy's Closet was new. Cute clothes in the window. It had been a hardware store back in the day. A woman who was probably Cathy came out to sweep the pristine sidewalk and covertly stare at Jessica.

Jessica squinted back from behind her big sunglasses. *Was that Cathy Schneider?* Holy cow! It was! Cathy had hardly changed at all. Not only was she still rocking her seventh-grade hairdo, but she wore enough accessory items to sink a ship. Thankfully, Jessica's dark sunglasses shielded her eyes from the glare of Cathy's bangle bracelets.

Jessica nearly waved. She and Cathy had been friends once. But Cathy didn't seem to recognize her now, and anyway, Jessica wasn't here for reunions. She was here to pay her respects to Mavis Long quickly, quietly, and without fanfare.

In a bright red Porsche.

Jessica swallowed a lump the size of Texas. Cathy wasn't going to be the only person from her past she'd see this weekend. In a town the size of Big Verde, literally everyone was someone from her past, but it was Casey Long who had her concerned. She'd prepared a little speech—*Hey, Casey. How have you been? Remember how you took my virginity and tossed me aside like yesterday's garbage?*—but hoped she wouldn't have to use it. Who knew? Maybe Casey wasn't even in Big Verde anymore. Maybe he'd hit it big in the rodeo world, just like he'd always dreamed, and was halfway across the country trying not to fall off a bull.

She imagined him being tossed across an arena by an angry black bull with flaring nostrils and cartoon smoke coming out of its ears. And then she realized she'd accidentally revved the Porsche's engine again. *Getting ready to charge.*

She sighed. Even if Casey didn't live in Big Verde anymore, he'd come home for his great-aunt's funeral. He was a Long, so there would be no getting out of it.

This was ridiculous. How long could a woman sit at an intersection? There was nothing coming as far as the eye could see, so when Cathy turned her back, Jessica eased into the intersection, and then hurried across. The tires squealed just a little, because she wasn't used to so much power.

And that's when she heard the siren.

Her body broke out in a sweat. Her skin felt like it was being poked by a million needles. A rush of adrenaline and pure, white-hot panic overtook her.

Breathe. At worst, it's a traffic ticket. Just breathe.

* * *

Dammit. Dammit. Dammit.

Casey was going to be late for his great-aunt's funeral. Some dumbass in a red Porsche had run the light just as he'd turned onto Main Street.

He'd have been happy to ignore it—pretend he hadn't seen it—except he couldn't because (a) you couldn't pretend not to see a red Porsche in Big Verde and (b) there was an audience. He had no choice but to pull the guy over and provide some much-needed excitement for Big Verde's downtown business district.

Cathy Schneider held up a...*broom?* as he drove by, and Danny Moreno, the pharmacist at the Rite Aid, waved and smiled in approval when Casey turned the cruiser's lights on.

The idiot pulled over in front of the Pump 'n' Go, so at least Casey wouldn't have to chase him. Four old ranchers, who'd probably been talking shit at the coffee bar, came out to the sidewalk, ready to watch the show.

Casey pulled up behind the Porsche. Big Verde was a small town of locals, but the pretty Texas Hill Country views and green, clear waters of the Rio Verde attracted tourists and city folks looking for country homes. Most of them were nice families who pumped much-needed revenue into the town during the summer. But a few of them were assholes.

He squinted at the Porsche and ran the plates.

It was registered to Carmen Foraccio. The name sounded vaguely familiar, but he couldn't place it. He got out of his cruiser and waved at the sidewalk gawkers before adopting his most menacing scowl.

"Go get 'em, tiger!" one of the ranchers yelled.

Casey couldn't let a grin ruin the scowl he'd perfected, so he ignored the fan club. He'd give the lady a warning and be done with it.

The car's window was rolled halfway down, but he couldn't see inside. At six feet four inches tall, he towered over the car, which seemed like a damn toy next to him. The top of it barely passed his belt buckle. "Good morning," he said in the general direction of the window beneath him. "You just blew through a red light."

"I'm sorry, Officer. I think that light must be broken."

It wasn't broken. But it did tend to have a mind of its own. Casey had sneaked through it a few times himself, although never while on duty.

"License and proof of insurance, please," Casey responded. He didn't have time to stand here socializing.

"Okay, hold on a sec."

Casey sighed and tapped his foot.

The voice, like the name, sounded familiar. It stirred up a feeling of nostalgia, which was weird, because when he tried to locate Carmen Foraccio in his memory banks, he came up blank.

He backed up a bit and peeked through the window. And what he saw was a very nice, round ass in a tight black skirt as the woman dug around in the glove compartment. The skirt crawled up her thighs as she struggled, and Casey straightened quickly, feeling as if he'd sneaked a peek on purpose, which he absolutely had not.

"I'm trying to find the insurance card," the woman said with a muffled voice.

Casey shifted from foot to foot as he experienced... *Irritation? Excitement?*

He'd definitely heard that voice before.

"Still looking!" she called.

Casey looked at his watch. "Ma'am, that's fine. Just your license please. I'll look up the insurance."

"Um, okay. Hold on…"

He glanced in the window again. Got an eyeful of curvy thigh as Ms. Foraccio switched course to dig behind the passenger seat.

"It's in my purse."

Casey stared up at the blue sky. Whistled. Tried not to look back into the car or at the sidewalk Pump 'n' Go gawkers who were by now hoping to witness a pat down.

"Oh…," the woman said with a shaky voice that made Casey wonder what was coming next.

"My…"

He glanced back inside the car to see the woman frantically patting herself down and squirming in the seat.

"God."

She looked up at him. Big movie star glasses concealed nearly the entire upper half of her heart-shaped face. Below the glasses were pouty lips, pink and shiny from something that probably tasted like bubble gum, not that he was thinking about what her lips tasted like.

A part of him was definitely thinking about what her lips tasted like. And another part of him, for some stupid reason, felt like it already knew.

"Is there a problem, ma'am?"

He hoped his voice sounded firmer than he felt, because for some damn reason his legs were shaky.

"I think I left my purse at the hotel."

Casey stood up straight and pinched the bridge of his nose.

"Ms. Foraccio, I'm afraid I'm going to need you to step out of the vehicle."

He sighed and cracked his knuckles.

Shit.

Chapter Two

Jessica couldn't believe she'd left her purse at the hotel. The car was registered to Carmen, so this should be interesting.

She lowered the window the rest of the way. She couldn't see his badge. Just his waist, which was bedazzled by a huge silver belt buckle. HILL COUNTRY TRI-COUNTY RODEO CHAMP.

Not surprising in Big Verde. And she didn't doubt his cop status, since in addition to the belt buckle, he also had a nightstick and a holstered gun.

"Please step out of the vehicle," the officer repeated.

"Am I going to be arrested?"

"Not if you do what I ask and exit the vehicle. Unless you're wanted for murder or have a shit ton of parking tickets."

Jesus. Would this guy back up or bend down? She really didn't want to continue talking to the belt buckle. She was nervous, and that made her want to do things like lean out the window, put her lips right up to that ridiculous chunk of rodeo metal, and yell, "I'll take a burger and fries! And supersize it!"

She swallowed those words right down and instead said, "I need to make a phone call." Dang! Her phone was in her purse.

"We're not at the part where you get to make a phone call yet," the smart-ass said. "Now I need you to get out of the car, nice and slow."

The man took a couple of steps back and bent down to peer in the window. It was a relief to put some distance between her and the belt buckle.

Aviator cop glasses rested on a long Roman nose, over lips drawn into a tight, straight line. And below those lips, which were full and promising despite being pursed like they'd just sucked on a lemon, was a very familiar chin. With a cleft.

Jessica gripped the steering wheel as her body went into fight-or-flight mode.

Fight: *Hey, Casey. How have you been? Remember how you took my virginity and tossed me aside like yesterday's garbage?*

Or

Flight: *This Porsche could outrun a cop, right?*

Also: *Casey was a cop? What the hell?*

Without thinking—because thoughts were impossible once your lizard brain took over—she revved the engine.

"Ma'am—"

That voice! It was lower than she remembered, but it was definitely the voice of Casey Long.

What was he doing in law enforcement? She never would have seen that coming. In high school, Casey had been the town's rebel teen, and they'd been such a dumb cliché—Good Girl falls for Bad Boy—before Casey had gotten what he'd wanted and then forgotten her.

She'd never forgotten him, though. And even in her terrified rage, something softened inside her. Dang it. That was what made him dangerous.

The engine raced again. She must have depressed the pedal without realizing it.

"Don't even think about it," he said.

She was totally thinking about it.

"Ma'am, I'm late for a funeral. And I hate funerals almost as much as I hate weddings. I do, however, love a good car chase. So, you can damn well bet I'll catch you. And then I'll spend the rest of the morning doing the paperwork associated with your arrest, which will get me out of having to go to the funeral. If I'm lucky, I can drag it out and escape the reception as well." He cracked his knuckles. "Your call."

Jessica bit her bottom lip so she wouldn't fuss at him for wanting to miss his own aunt's funeral. Heartless. The bastard was still completely heartless.

His jaw jutted out stubbornly. She knew a pair of icy blue eyes glared at her from behind the shades. Eyes you could fall into. Eyes that were so hypnotic they could make you do just about anything.

She turned off the ignition. Unbuckled her seat belt.

"Nice and slow now," Casey said, hand hovering near his gun.

She opened the door and stepped out, shrinking beneath the scrutiny of the growing crowd at the Pump 'n' Go.

"Remove your sunglasses, please."

The sound of his voice sent vibrations through her body; vibrations that were not entirely unpleasant. Some things might have changed, like Casey being a freaking cop, but the effect of his voice on her body hadn't. She suspected her pupils were dilated.

She pursed her lips in annoyance, and glanced at the nightstick and holstered gun on his belt. Slowly, she took off her sunglasses and looked up. Way up, because Casey had added a couple of inches to his height since the last time she'd seen him. He was at least a foot taller than she was.

His stubborn jaw went slack with recognition.

She gave a little wave. "Hi, Casey."

So much for the prepared speech.

Casey yanked his aviators off, and she had to blink *once, twice, three times* at those baby blues.

"Jess? Jessica Acosta?"

She sighed. At least he remembered her name.

"The one and only. Sorry I'm not the fabulous Carmen Follacio—"

"Pardon?"

Jesus! She'd said *Follacio*, which sounded dang close to *fellatio*.

"I'm not Carmen *Foraccio*," Jessica tried again. "She's loaned me her car."

Casey, still looking stunned, ran a hand through his dark wavy hair. His face indicated he was drawing a blank. Was it possible he hadn't heard of Carmen Foraccio, famous celebrity chef and star of the Food Channel's hit show *Funky Fusions*?

But that hair. He still wore it longer than he should. It curled past his collar and showed no signs of thinning. It took everything Jessica had to keep her hands to herself. As usual, she ran her mouth as a distraction. "Are you really a cop, or did you steal that car?"

"Darlin', I'm the sheriff of Verde County. If one of us is driving a stolen car, my bet is on you."

Did he really just call her *darlin'*?

She crossed her arms over her chest, but then Casey grinned at her, and she felt it all the way to her angrily tapping toes. She couldn't tell if he was grinning in a teasing way, or in an *I can't wait to put you in handcuffs* way.

Both options made her tingle all over, so maybe she shouldn't be thinking about handcuffs. But there they were. Hanging on Casey's belt.

The grin finally reached his eyes, as if he found the idea of himself as a sheriff every bit as amusing as she did, and it set a herd of butterflies loose in her stomach.

Casey Long had been the town's teenage hooligan. Only he hadn't ridden a motorcycle. He'd ridden bulls. And if the gigantic rodeo belt buckle was any indication, he still did.

Casey started writing in his little book. He ripped out a page and handed it to her. "This is for the stoplight."

He ripped out another. "And this is for having no proof of insurance."

And another. "And this is for not having a driver's license on you."

She looked at the three pieces of paper. Warnings. He'd given her warnings.

"Thank you, Casey. Seriously, I'm just trying—"

"Jess," he said, cutting her off. "Why are you back?"

Suddenly, the fuller face and lower voice and broader shoulders disappeared, and she was looking into the emotional blue eyes of eighteen-year-old Casey Long. It made eighteen-year-old Jess pop to the surface of her consciousness like a cork.

And eighteen-year-old Jess had not been very smart.

* * *

What the hell was Jessica Acosta doing back in Big Verde? God. His hands were shaking.

Unacceptable.

She looked 100 percent the same. And that meant 100 percent hot. But lots of women were hot. They didn't do to him whatever the hell it was that Jess was doing to him. He wanted to laugh. He wanted to vomit. He wanted to handcuff her and throw her in the back of his cruiser and never let her out of his sight, because the last time he'd let her out of his sight, she'd run off and he'd never seen her again.

Until now.

He struggled to maintain control over his facial features. But it was hard. He'd fantasized about this encounter for years, and it typically played out in one of two scenarios.

Scenario One: He reads her the riot act. *You think you can just waltz out of somebody's life without so much as a good-bye and then just show up out of the blue like nothing happened?* Then they attack each other and have sex.

Scenario Two: He falls to the ground in a heap and cries like a baby because he's so damn glad to see her again. Then they attack each other and have sex.

She stood there with her arms crossed, her toes tapping, and her eyes flitting back and forth from him to her car, no doubt ready to jump right in and leave him standing in her dust. Maybe he should have thought of a third scenario involving a car chase.

He cleared his throat. "Coming home for a visit?"

"Funeral," she stammered.

There was only one funeral in Big Verde today. "Aunt Mavis's?"

Jess nodded.

Why on earth would she be going to Aunt Mavis's funeral? Of all the reasons to come home, why would it be for that? A million questions were piling up in his throat. He swallowed so they wouldn't fly out of his mouth, but they got stuck halfway down.

"Jess…"

Why did you leave? Where did you go? Didn't you know it would crush me?

She'd left the day after high school graduation. They'd shared their hopes and dreams for the future—he'd wanted to be a professional bull rider and Jess wanted to open a restaurant—and promised to be together forever, just the night before.

Forever hadn't even lasted twenty-four hours. She and her mom had skipped town without a trace.

Jess stared at the ground. Offered no explanation.

Casey found his voice. "Well, we're both going to be late if we don't get a move on. We might have to use the lights."

"What? Wait, no—"

"Let's go, Ms. Acosta." A horrible thought smacked him in the face. "It is still Ms. Acosta, isn't it?"

"Yes, but—"

"Let's go then."

She wasn't married. He tried not to feel giddy about it and failed.

Jessica got back in her car, and Casey jogged to his cruiser. Then he pulled out onto the road and passed Jess, turned on the lights, and waited for her to follow.

He didn't know why he'd turned the damn lights on. The funeral home was two blocks up. But Jessica Acosta was back in town, and that made him feel excited and happy and uncomfortable all at the same time. The occasion seemed to call for lights and sirens.

Chapter Three

Jessica's stomach clenched at the sight of so many cars lining the street. Small-town funerals were big deals, and everyone in Big Verde would be at this one. People often sat around looking for who *hadn't* come instead of who had.

For a town matriarch like Mavis Long, the place would be packed. In fact, people had gathered on the lawn, where chairs were set up and speakers were mounted on tripods. The little chapel was probably out of seating already.

Jessica drove slowly past all the pickups, SUVs, and cars, trying to ignore the flashing lights in front of her.

What had possessed Casey to turn on the dang lights? Was he out of his mind?

A few folks were still getting out of their vehicles, chatting with each other and attempting to tame unruly cowlicks on little boys. Most were in their Sunday best. This meant western leisure suits for the older men, and clean jeans with shirts tucked in for the younger men and boys. Most ladies and girls wore conservative dresses. *Very* conservative dresses.

Jessica's sweaty palms stuck to the steering wheel as she looked for a place to park. She wiped them, one at a time, on her black skirt. Her *short* black skirt. When she'd picked it out, she hadn't been thinking about Big Verde's fashion trends or how appropriate it might be for a small-town funeral.

There was literally no place to park. Good grief. She was not going to drag out this freak show by circling the block.

Two piercing blasts from a siren cut through the air, causing her to jump and bite her lip, which she'd apparently been chewing in nervous angst. What had she done wrong now?

Casey had pulled into a spot farther up the block. He got out and started waving his arms. *At her.*

Everyone watched as she slowly drove toward Casey, who was now making motions one might use when guiding a jetliner to a terminal or signaling marine mammals to do tricks. Was he afraid there might be one lone holdout who wasn't already looking at her? What was next? People gathered in the splash zone to watch her park?

Sweat dripped down her back as Casey proceeded to direct her, inch by inch, into the parking space directly behind him.

Once parked, she sat back with a sigh. She just needed a moment to—

The door magically opened and a big hand extended inside.

So much for taking a moment.

"The funeral's about to start," Casey said.

She took his hand. It was warm. Strong. Both foreign and famil-iar. How many times had she held it at the movies or while walking down the halls of Big Verde High? She blushed, remembering how Casey's fingers had roamed her body like curious explorers of unknown lands.

He'd been the first to trace her lips with his thumb. The first to brush her nipples with his fingers. The first to cup her ass while pulling her close...

"You okay, Jess?"

She swallowed. Collected herself. And stood up on shaky legs.

He offered his arm, which would seem dramatic in Houston, but in Big Verde it just meant he was a gentleman.

Casey Long. A gentleman.

They started down the sidewalk. People smiled politely, but most were older, and she didn't see any recognition in their faces. Just interest.

Maybe she'd survive this day after all.

* * *

Casey nodded at everybody who said *Howdy, Sheriff,* as he and Jessica headed for the door. It would be nice if they'd stop their gawking. Jessica would stop traffic in any town, but in Big Verde, she was damn near paralyzing.

She was nervous. The little things she did with her hair, the fluffing and tossing. She'd been doing it since high school. It was still cute as hell.

"I'm really sorry about your great-aunt, Casey," she said.

Lots of people had said that to him over the past few days. Some of them had meant it casually. Some had meant it deeply. Some hadn't meant it at all. What he heard in Jess's voice was heart-wrenching sincerity. As if she were not only sorry, but also somehow deeply saddened.

Mavis had been well known in the small town. But as far as he knew—and he knew damn near everything—Jessica hadn't kept up with anyone in Big Verde. How did she even know Mavis had died?

He cleared his throat. "So where are you living now?"

"Houston," she said.

She didn't follow it up with what she did or who she lived with or how long she'd been there. Just *Houston.*

Why had she driven all the way here for the funeral? Other folks in Big Verde had died since Jess had left. Folks she'd probably known better. There'd been no trips home for their funerals. There had to be more to this story.

"Aunt Mavis's death is a terrible loss for our family," he said. "But it wasn't exactly unexpected."

Jessica stopped walking and looked at him. "She wasn't even sick. It was totally unexpected."

How would she know if his great-aunt had been sick?

"Well, she was ninety years old, Jess. That's what I meant by it not being unexpected. Nobody lives forever."

Jessica shook her head, as if his response disappointed her, and started walking again.

"Howdy, Sheriff!" Casey looked up to see Matt Hurley loping cheerfully their way. "Beautiful day!"

The only thing about Matt that said "undertaker" was his dark suit. Other than that, he was all smiles and grins.

"Hey, pretty lady. I don't think I've seen you around here before."

And inappropriate comments.

Matt had started going bald in junior high, but the process had stunted somewhere around eleventh grade, leaving him with a few stragglers he grew out and combed across his forehead. The back of his head was left completely unattended, probably because Matt couldn't see it in the mirror and therefore assumed it didn't exist.

He didn't let his appearance dampen his enthusiasm for the ladies, though.

Jessica removed her sunglasses. "Hi, Matt."

Matt's skinny face suddenly became animated. His Adam's apple bobbed as he searched for words. What he finally came up with—loudly and right outside the building where Casey's aunt lay in a coffin—was, "Goddamn, girl! Look at you! Jess is back in town!"

Jess seemed to melt, as if willing herself to disappear.

Matt threw the door open. The small chapel was filled to capacity, and Jessica shrank back against Casey. His entire body lit up like someone had poked him with a cattle prod. He wanted to wrap his arms around her, pull her even closer, but he couldn't. He needed to get control of himself. This wasn't the same girl who'd left him twelve years before. She was a grown woman, and he hardly knew her.

He couldn't quite accept the truth of that.

She was probably nervous, and Matt wasn't doing anything to help matters, so Casey put his hand at the small of her back. He hoped it would reassure her that she was among friends.

Miss Mills, the organist for the First Baptist Church, sat at the front of the chapel playing "How Great Thou Art" on the funeral home's electric keyboard. The fact that she did this at a Methodist funeral said something about the importance and station of Aunt Mavis in the community.

Matt hollered, "Look, everybody! It's Big Verde High's homecoming queen of the class of..." He looked at Casey. "What year was it, Casey? Let's see, you were two years ahead of me—"

Miss Mills stopped playing.

Everyone looked at them.

"Matt, I think I'll have a seat up there with my family. I was running a little late due to increased criminal activity in the town." He winked at Jess.

Miss Mills picked up where she left off, and slowly everybody went back to looking mournful. They were accustomed to Matt's outbursts.

Matt, as if suddenly remembering where they were, made a rousing attempt at appearing solemn.

"The Hurley family is honored to be here for you during your time of need. Please accept our sincere condolences."

"Why, thank you—"

Matt turned back to Jess. "Where did you get that kick-ass car?"

Casey patted Matt on the back, a little harder than necessary, because that's what it typically took to shut him up, and then led Jessica by her elbow to the pews set off to the side of the casket where the family was seated.

Jessica trembled. Was she really that nervous? His own knees were a bit shaky, but it was because being around Jess again rocked him to his core.

"Casey, no. I'm not family. I'll sit somewhere else."

"There is nowhere else," he said. "And you came all this way. Everyone will be pleased to see you."

That might be a stretch. They would be surprised, though. Because Jess being here for Aunt Mavis's funeral made absolutely zero sense. To lessen the tension, he decided to do the polite thing and inquire about her mother.

"How's your mama? Doing okay, I hope."

Jessica stiffened even more. "She passed away two years ago. Heart attack."

Jesus. He had shit timing. "I'm very sorry to hear it."

And he was too. Even though Jessica's mom had hated his guts. In all fairness, most girls' moms had hated his guts.

Gerome Kowalski, owner of the infamous Rancho Cañada Verde and a man Casey had known his entire life, came forward with his hand extended. He'd be delivering the eulogy. "Casey, Mavis will be very much missed by this community."

"Thank you, Gerome. This is such a nice turnout for her. In fact, Jessica came all the way—"

Jessica was headed to the coffin. And she appeared to be sniffing and weeping.

"Is that little Jessica Acosta?" Gerome asked.

"Yes, sir. She's come back for Aunt Mavis's funeral."

Gerome nodded. "That's right nice of her. I'd expect as much."

So, there *was* a reason Jessica was back. But what was it?

There were currents that flowed beneath Main Street in every small town, and the secrets they carried were hidden from most.

Gerome was one of the few who always knew. And like Aunt Mavis, he kept those secrets to himself.

It was infuriating.

Chapter Four

God. She felt like such an idiot. She hadn't intended to bawl her eyes out at Mavis's funeral. But dang it, Gerome Kowalski knew Mavis. He got Mavis. And the eulogy had captured her perfectly. Hard and unyielding. Demanding and critical. Almost impossible to please. And yet, also kind and loyal. Generous and sympathetic. Even fun.

Jessica smiled. Hope could make Mavis act silly. A person hadn't lived until they'd seen Mavis jump out from behind a chair in a power pantsuit, wielding a light-up laser gun.

And she could be fierce. Like when she'd stood between an angry landlord and Jessica's mom, who'd already paid the rent, no matter what the landlord said.

Their little family had mattered to Mavis Long, and she had mattered to them.

Dang it. The tears started up again.

The service was over, and people were lining up to pay their respects to the family, so Jessica went to the back of the alcove to wait it out. She'd leave as soon as she thought she could get away without having to talk to anybody.

Mavis's only son, Senator Wade Long, who'd once been the

sheriff of Verde County, stood on the front row accepting condolences. Jessica shivered and ran her hands up and down her arms. She'd known he would be here, but she was nothing to him. He wouldn't recognize her, and even if he did, what could he do?

Wade Long was the reason she and her mom had been forced to leave Big Verde. Her mom had been pregnant with Wade's baby. *Pregnant with Hope.*

Back then, Wade had his sights on the Texas legislature, and although he and his wife were well on their way to divorce, he couldn't have his constituents knowing he'd fathered a child with an undocumented immigrant.

To this day, as far as Jessica knew, nobody had ever found out. Well, almost nobody. Mavis Long had discovered the secret.

Jessica sniffed and willed a new tide of tears away. She'd never forget opening the door of their sparse little apartment in Houston to see Mavis Long standing there, hair perfectly coifed, demanding to see her only grandchild. She'd only wanted to know if Hope's financial needs were being met. She hadn't intended to have a relationship with her...*to be a grandma.*

But one look at chubby little two-year-old Hope had melted Mavis's resolve. She'd lost a bit of her stiff-spined composure at the sight of Hope's sweet almond-shaped eyes, and she'd lost 100 percent of her heart.

Jessica hadn't known her hardworking mom was undocumented. Not until Wade Long threatened to have her deported if she ever told a soul. He ordered her to leave Big Verde and never come back.

Nothing had ever been the same again. Ever since that day, Jessica had lived her life with the fear that her world could dissolve at any minute. And she'd never dared to dream of coming home to Big Verde. Not if there was even the slightest chance that Wade would make good on his threat and her mom would be deported.

But now her mom was dead. And Mavis was too. Wade Long couldn't do anything to her family. But Jessica's hands wouldn't stop trembling.

A short blond woman came zigzagging through the crowd. She was heading Jessica's way, face lit up by a smile.

"Jessica! Hi!"

It was Maggie Mackey. Jessica had always liked her. She'd been a tomboy who didn't care what people thought. Jessica had cared what *everybody* thought, so she had admired Maggie's attitude.

There was a ring on her finger. Who had she married?

Dang it. She was already falling into the small-town pattern of wondering about other people's business.

"What are you doing here?" Maggie had always gotten straight to the point. No polite chitchat for her. "How long are you staying?"

"Not long. I'm just here for Mavis's funeral."

Maggie cocked an eyebrow but didn't question her further. "I hope you're coming to the reception. It's at the Methodist Church Fellowship Hall. Everyone would love to see you."

"Oh, I don't know—"

Leaving Big Verde had been traumatic. It had taken years to get over it. Why rekindle old relationships? She was heading back to Houston—where nobody knew or cared about your business— on Monday. Houston had never been much of a home, but the anonymity it allowed was good for keeping secrets.

"Well?" Maggie asked, hands on hips. "Are you coming or not?"

"Of course she's coming," Casey said.

Where had he come from? And why wasn't he up at the line with the rest of the family? Casey was acting as if he was afraid to let her out of his sight. Strange behavior for a man who'd never once tried to find her after she'd left Big Verde.

"Look who's hovering about," Maggie said with a grin.

Was Casey *blushing*? Her own cheeks felt a bit warm. Holy crap, was *she* blushing? She thought she'd prepared for the inevitable reunion with Casey. She'd spent the last four days fortifying her emotional shields, but all it took to decimate them was a smile and a slight blush from Sheriff Long.

Heck, her shields had disintegrated as soon as she'd heard his voice when he pulled her over.

"There's a little too much schmoozing going on over there with my uncle," Casey said, nodding at the Good Senator. Jessica could barely contain a shiver of disgust, and Casey's slight sneer indicated he didn't exactly have warm, fuzzy feelings for the man either.

"He's not your uncle," Maggie said.

Casey shrugged. "He's older than me. He's a relative. He's not my grandfather. That makes him an uncle."

"He's your great-aunt's son," Maggie argued. "And that makes him your second cousin once removed. Or maybe it's your first cousin twice removed..." She furrowed her brow. "You know what? Why don't you just refer to him as your uncle."

Or they could all just refer to him as the anti-Christ and be done with it.

Casey put his hand at the small of Jessica's back and gave a gentle nudge. It sent thrills up and down her spine, but as they exited the funeral home, she still had every intention of heading down the sidewalk to her car.

So why was she crossing the street toward the Methodist Church Fellowship Hall?

Ten minutes later she sat at a folding table, picking at macaroni salad and trying to look small so nobody would talk to her. She kept an eye on Casey while he worked the room. It was so weird to see him patting backs, shaking hands, asking about cattle and crops. She'd seen Wade Long do the very same thing. But unlike Wade, Casey seemed genuinely interested in the folks he talked to.

He was keeping an eye on her too. As if he was afraid to look away for too long. Why? He'd seduced her. And then tossed her aside. *Just like a Long,* her mom had said.

Jessica hadn't wanted to believe that Casey was like that. But then he'd ignored her letters. Never tried to find her. She thought she'd worked through it and didn't care anymore.

She was wrong, though. She cared.

Casey finished chatting with an older gentleman and then came and sat down beside her. "Sorry," he said. "It's an election year."

Jessica nodded. The last year she'd spent in Big Verde had been an election year, too, and Wade Long had been in full politician mode. Unlike previous elections, he'd had a challenger. He'd left no hand unshaken and no funeral unattended. There hadn't been any room for even a hint of a scandal, much less a pregnant undocumented immigrant.

Casey poked at a blob of what looked like Jell-O with fruit and nuts in it. It jiggled obscenely. "I prefer the funerals on your side of town," he said. "Food's better."

Jessica stiffened. "What do you mean *on my side of town*?"

Casey put a paper napkin in his lap and glanced at her, shooting a spark of electricity right through her body with those blue eyes. "The Catholic side."

Okay. Well, it was true that Jessica had grown up in the neighborhood adjacent to the Catholic church. And that most of the people in that neighborhood were Catholic.

Casey curled his lip at the Jell-O on his plate. "As far as funeral foods go, the Catholics win hands down."

Jessica looked at the blob of mayonnaise and macaroni dangling on her fork. He had a point. A funeral in her neighborhood had meant barbacoa tacos, trays of enchiladas, Spanish rice, and big, steaming pots of beans made by the Catholic Daughters.

"With the Lutherans and the Baptists, you might get some sausage and whatnot," Casey continued. "But Methodists are going to torture you to death with tiny little sandwiches filled with vegetables and things they call salads that are mostly Jell-O. Also, they put marshmallows where they don't belong, and they have a weird thing for mayonnaise."

Jessica grinned. She and Casey had always gotten a kick out of observing and commenting on the habits of Big Verde's social circles. It was so easy to fall into those habits. "And what's with that punch?" she asked. "Why is Methodist punch always green?"

"This is fancy punch," Casey said. "It's got sherbet in it."

He brought the tiny crystal cup up to his lips, holding up his pinky as he did so, and took a dainty sip. And then he suddenly jerked forward, spilling the rest all over his tie.

A little boy had grabbed his arm. "Casey!"

Casey remained completely calm. "Hey there, Dalton."

A woman was right behind the child, apologizing. "I'm so sorry. Dalton, get down."

Jessica smiled at Dalton, and when he smiled back, she realized she was looking into a little face that shone just as bright as Hope's. Like Hope, the child had Down syndrome.

"I hate this tie," Casey said. "He did me a favor."

Then he picked Dalton up and set him on his lap. "Marissa, do you remember Jessica?"

"Marissa Mayes?" Jessica asked. "Oh my goodness! Hi!"

"Of course I remember!" Marissa squealed. "I recognized you as soon as you walked into the chapel. And I'm Marissa Reed now. I married Bobby."

Bobby Reed had been the high school quarterback, and Marissa had been a cheerleader with Jessica. It warmed her heart to know they'd gotten married and were still together. "How is Bobby?"

"He's doing great. Wait until he hears you're back in town!"

Jessica wasn't going to be around long enough to socialize, but she didn't bother saying so. It would be nice, though, to catch up with old friends.

"Is Dalton yours?"

"Sure is," Marissa said proudly.

"He's a handsome young man," Jessica said, and Marissa beamed even more.

"What brings you to Big V?" Marissa asked. "Surely not Miss Mavis's funeral?"

Casey looked at Jessica intently, as if that was the burning question of the day.

"I'm here for the funeral," Jessica said simply, knowing that her answer only added to the confusion.

As she looked at Marissa's curious face, ten million different stories suddenly crashed into her brain—fun stories—and surprisingly, she wanted to rehash them all. *Remember that time we toilet-papered Coach Reiner's house? Remember when I helped you sneak into Bobby's bedroom window but we picked the wrong one and you ended up staring at his mom in her nightgown?*

"JD!" Marissa shouted, earning glares from a nearby table of elderlies. "JD, come see who's here!"

Marissa's older brother, JD Mayes, strolled through the crowd with his plate of jiggly food. And even though they were indoors, he wore his signature white Stetson. Some things never changed.

JD's eyes widened at the sight of her. "Jess!"

He rushed over and gave her a warm hug.

Hubba-hubba. The cowboy still had it. He'd taken Jessica for many spins around the dance floor back in the day. They'd even held hands once in the movie theater. But that was as far as it had gone, because Jessica had only had eyes for one cowboy: Casey Long.

* * *

It felt like a high school reunion, watching JD, Marissa, and Jessica talk about old times. Casey couldn't help but grin. Jessica had been a good student—class valedictorian—and a cheerleader. Casey had been more of a troublemaker. Only two things had mattered to him: Jess and bull riding. Other than that, it had been all speeding tickets, underage drinking, disrespect for authority (he still had that issue if the authority hadn't earned it), and a chip on his shoulder the size of Texas. His crooked uncle had taken care of the speeding tickets and the underage drinking—all fixed with a wave of the magic Long wand. But the only thing that could get him to say *yes, sir* or *no, ma'am* to assholes was the threat of not being able to rodeo.

Jess had seen something in him that no one else had. She'd gotten him to pay more attention to his grades, even though he hadn't planned on going to college. He'd wanted to make her proud; to be the kind of boy she wouldn't be ashamed of. She'd been an angel, and as he listened to her chat with Dalton about his toy tractors, he figured she probably still was.

"Hey, Earth to Casey," JD said, giving him an elbow.

He'd been daydreaming. "Sorry. What was that?"

"I just told Jess about the charity rodeo tomorrow. She says she can't make it, but I think all she needs is a little encouragement. Dalton, here, is doing his part..."

Dalton put his hands together like he was praying, and with his tongue poking out from where his two front teeth should be, he said, "*Pwease.*"

Jess laughed, and it flowed through Casey's chest like a bubbling brook.

Anything that would keep Jess in Big Verde longer was a good thing. He was dying to question her, to find out why she and her mom had left Big Verde in such haste. Had her mother hated him that much? "Yeah, you should come to the rodeo, Jess. JD and I are competing in the team roping—"

"Wait," Jess interrupted. "On the same team?"

JD laughed. "Yeah, we're the current Tri-County champs, believe it or not."

"I don't believe it," Jess said.

Casey was pretty sure that the last time Jess had seen him and JD together, JD had him in a headlock while Mr. Preston, the principal, was shouting at them to break it up.

"We kick ass," Casey said. JD gave him a fist bump, and then Dalton insisted on fist-bumping everyone within his immediate reach while muttering *kick ass.*

"Thanks so much," Marissa said with an eye roll.

JD gave a small salute with a wink.

"You don't ride bulls anymore?" Jessica asked.

Casey flinched. Painful subject. "I suffered an injury a while back."

Exactly twelve years ago when I got on a bull not caring whether I lived or died because the girl I loved left without saying a word.

"Damn near died," JD said.

Jessica's eyes widened, and she reached out with her hand to...touch his face? He wouldn't know, because she yanked it back just as quickly. His skin yearned for the feel of her fingertips, and he fought the urge to lean toward her.

"But you're okay now, right?"

His brain struggled to make out what she'd said. JD lifted the brim of his hat and raised an eyebrow in question. *Are you going to answer her?*

Casey cleared his throat. "Yeah. My back kinks up occasionally. I just don't care to be thrown and rolled by a fifteen-hundred-pound asshole bull again. Broke a few bones."

Seven, to be exact.

"Asshole bull!" Dalton shouted with glee.

"Dalton, that's football talk. We don't say *asshole* unless there's a game on," Marissa chided.

"Hey, Dalton, why don't you tell Jess about Hope House? Maybe she'll want to come to the rodeo if you do."

Jessica's head snapped up, eyes wide as saucers. "Hope House? What's that?"

Why did Jess look so curious? Or was it sad? Or maybe it was happy. Her mercurial eyes seemed to display every single emotion on the spectrum.

"Hope House is fun," Dalton said.

"It's a place where special kids and adults get to hang out," Casey said. "They do all sorts of stuff. They train for the Special Olympics, and we even teach a few of them how to rodeo."

"Dalton is a mutton buster," Marissa said, referring to the children's rodeo activity of clinging to the back of a running sheep like your life depended on it.

"Who started Hope House?" Jess asked.

"Aunt Mavis," Casey said. "It's one of the reasons so many folks have turned out to honor her. She was a great woman. Gruff on the outside, maybe, but a heart of gold."

Chapter Five

The lobby of the Village Château was cool and calm. The heavy dark furniture Jessica remembered from the last time she'd been here—the graduation party thrown for Casey by the Longs—was gone. Now it was muted neutral tones and local Hill Country art.

She took the stairs to the second floor where their suite was. With the exception of the grand ballroom, which still sported thick brocade carpeting, sparkling chandeliers, and a gigantic, ornate fireplace, the general air of the establishment was way less formal. It was really nice. Comfortable. And the aromas wafting up from the Château's restaurant were divine. Her stomach growled. Gelatin salads could carry a girl only so far.

She walked down the hall to room 204 and started to insert her key. But the door jerked open before she had a chance.

"I got my head under the water," Hope squealed. Then she threw her arms around Jessica.

"Good for you! See? I told you it was no big deal."

With Hope attached, Jessica entered the room to find Carmen lying on the bed, blue hair still wet, looking utterly exhausted. "Oh, it was a big deal, all right," Carmen said.

"And I went down the slide!" Hope said. "I went all the way under."

Hope had an irrational fear of getting her face wet. Ride a roller coaster? No problem. Trampoline? You bet. Blow bubbles in the water? Not so much. So this was big news.

"Maybe I should let Carmen take you swimming more often."

Carmen lifted her head. "Maybe Carmen wouldn't survive that."

Ha! Carmen could look as pitiful as she wanted, but she and Hope were thick as thieves. They both loved to cook. They both loved to eat. And neither one cared what anybody thought.

"Hey," Jessica said, sitting on the bed. "Thanks. You know there aren't many people I trust to watch Hope. In fact, I think there might just be, you know, the *one* people."

Carmen grinned slightly and narrowed her eyes. "Yeah. You owe me."

There was no way to get a smooshy *you're welcome* out of Carmen. Her real-life persona was pretty much the same as her television one. In your face. Loud. Colorful. And though she minced garlic at vision-blurring speed, she did not mince words.

Hope faked a sigh and rolled her eyes. "Carmen's tired and cranky."

"I'm not the only one," Carmen replied. "Why don't you go watch some more television and relax?"

"You're trying to get rid of me," Hope said.

Jessica laughed. Woe to the person who underestimated Hope because of her Down syndrome.

"You're right. I am. Your sister and I need to talk."

"But you've *been* talking," Hope whined.

"Retreat to the dungeon," Carmen ordered. "We'll get dinner in an hour."

Hope clapped her hands and smacked her lips. "Yum. Can we eat in the room?"

"You bet."

Hope happily went into the other room and closed the door.

"You were gone longer than expected," Carmen said.

"I went to the reception after the funeral."

Carmen sat up. "You did?"

"Yeah. It was kind of fun."

"That's what they say about funerals. Fun times."

"It's just that I saw some old friends. It was nice."

"That's a little more normal."

Normal. What was that supposed to feel like? She hadn't felt "normal" since learning her mom was undocumented. It had turned her world upside down. There'd been no stability or security after that. Of course, there'd *never* been any, but she hadn't known it. After learning the truth, she'd lived in fear of a traffic ticket or auto accident. Of literally anything and everything that could end up separating their family. And that included sharing their secret with anyone. So, they hadn't.

Except for Mavis.

Now that her mom was dead, there was no longer anything to fear. But living without a noose around your neck was hard to get used to. The noose felt…*loosened.* Not gone. That was why she hadn't been able to leave Hope back in Houston, even though Carmen could have taken just as good care of her there.

If at all possible, Hope went where Jessica went.

"I saw Casey," she whispered.

Carmen's eyes widened. She smirked like a blue-haired elf. "Did you talk to him?"

"Yes. Quite a bit, actually. He's the sheriff now."

"You're kidding!"

"No, he really is. He pulled me over for running a red light. Did you know you don't have proof of insurance in your car?"

Carmen rolled her eyes. "How long has it been since you've been laid?"

"Carmen!"

"Well?"

Jessica went to the window. The lagoon-shaped pool, complete with slide and waterfall, brought back the memory of Casey's graduation party. It had been a luau theme, and the pool hadn't been so fancy. Just a plain rectangular lap pool. But to Jessica, a kid who'd grown up swimming in the Rio Verde, it had seemed magical and romantic. There had been floating candles and little paper boats, and then afterward, she and Casey had...

It had been too long since she'd been laid.

Carmen joined her at the window. "So that's where the magic happened, huh? By the pool?"

"Well, not right by the pool," Jessica said. She pointed to the right, where a fire pit blazed. "There used to be a thick clump of palm trees. Casey had laid out a blanket." The blush crept in. "We had a bottle of champagne he'd lifted from the Château's restaurant."

She'd never tasted champagne before. The bubbles had made her sneeze.

"That's so romantic." Carmen sighed. Then she grinned. "But was the sex awful? The first time is usually nothing to write home about."

A couple sat down on the lounge in front of the fire pit and snuggled.

"No, it was actually nice. I mean, I didn't have a mind-blowing orgasm. Or any orgasm. I doubt I even knew what one was. But Casey was sweet and took his time..."

Her voice faded as the memory took over. Casey had more than taken his time. He'd explored her body with intense curiosity and a blush-rendering thoroughness. All of the things that had been only hinted at during make-out sessions on the couch or in the back row of the movie theater had come to fruition.

Later, as they'd lain in the shadows of the palms in the moonlight, he'd confessed it had been his first time. And that he loved her.

Jess, you're my first. And I want you to be my last. Promise we'll be together forever.

She'd promised.

She turned away from the window. It was time to let it go. She'd paid her respects to Mavis. She'd seen a few friends, and it had been pleasant. Now she just had to lie low at the Château—

harder than if they'd stayed at the Big Verde Motor Inn—and visit the lawyer on Monday.

"Are you going to see him again?" Carmen asked.

"I don't think so. I went into the ladies' room, and when I came out, people said he'd taken off. Something about cattle being loose on the highway."

"Lame," Carmen said.

"Well, not really," Jessica said, feeling suddenly defensive. "That's actually a dangerous situation."

Carmen snorted. "If you say so."

Jessica had been bitterly disappointed by Casey's hasty departure. There was so much she'd wanted to ask him, but what would be the point? It was probably best to hide out the rest of the weekend.

As if reading her mind, Carmen said, "So are we allowed to leave the premises of the hotel this weekend? Or are we trapped here while you hide from Sheriff Long?"

"Which Sheriff Long would you be referring to?" Jessica asked. "The Sheriff Long who pulled me over this morning? Or the former Sheriff Long who happens to be Hope's daddy? Because I'm hiding from them both."

"Sheriff Long is my daddy?"

Carmen gasped. Jessica's throat closed up. They both turned to face Hope, who stood in the doorway. How long had she been there?

* * *

Casey sat on a fancy chair that was too small for his large frame and stared into his beer. He was dazed. The clinking plates, laughter, and conversations around him were muted, as if he wore earmuffs.

One funeral reception should have been enough. But now he had to suffer through a private family gathering at the Village Château. Mavis would have hated all the fuss.

Someone poked him in the arm. "You all right, pardner?"

JD gazed at him with concern.

"I'm just sad about Aunt Mavis," Casey said, but really, he was completely distracted with thoughts of Jessica. He'd had to leave the fellowship hall without even saying good-bye, much less getting any answers.

"Liar," JD said.

"Pardon?"

"It's not Mavis you're missing."

"Why are you even here? This is a private gathering for family only," Casey said. "And I *am* sad about Mavis."

"I know you are. But that's not why you're moping around. And I think we're related in some way or other."

He was *not* moping. Although seeing as how he was crammed into this chair in a corner, staring out the window with a warm beer in one hand and a plate of untouched food in the other, he could see how a fella might think he was.

Dammit. It had been twelve years. He should be over this teen-age shit by now. But seeing Jess had brought on a rush of emotions he couldn't quite sort out. They'd talked about getting married, for Christ's sake. She'd just needed to get her mama to come around. Then they were going to live happily ever after. Stupid teenage stuff.

But it had seemed real.

He took a sip of beer but had trouble getting it to go down.

"Unless there are two red Porsches in Big Verde, she's right here at the Village Château," JD said.

Casey's heart sped up. "Are you sure? I figured she'd gone back to Houston right after the funeral."

"I didn't hear her say she was going to do that," JD said. "I heard you ask her if she was sticking around long, and she said she wasn't. That's pretty vague. Maybe she's heading back tomorrow."

Casey's heart started pounding again. Like nearly out of his chest.

"I think I'll head to the bar for a drink," he said.

You could see the lobby of the hotel from the restaurant's bar.

She'd have to come down eventually, even if it was tomorrow morning...

"There's an open bar right here," JD said with a grin, nodding at the bartender doling out booze in the corner of the room. "But you go do whatever it is you've got to do."

Chapter Six

Jessica sat at the bar, sipping a margarita and trying to catch a buzz. After settling Hope down, she'd asked Carmen what the hell she was supposed to do now. And Carmen had said, "Get drunk."

Normally, she'd have blown that off and set herself about fixing everything. But these were not normal times.

So here she sat.

It had been a huge mistake to bring Hope to Big Verde. Carmen was right. Nobody was coming to take anybody away. She should have let her stay with Carmen in Houston. But the last thing her mom had said was *Take care of Hope.*

Her mom. She'd die all over again if she knew Jessica had blabbed about Wade Long being Hope's father right in front of Hope! Maybe Hope would forget about it.

She caught the bartender's eye and raised her empty glass. He nodded and began measuring ingredients into the blender.

Hope wouldn't forget about it.

She'd been so excited and confused by what she'd heard that she couldn't even eat her dinner. And Hope *lived* for food.

Carmen had gone on and on about how good it was—which

meant it was *really* good—while Hope had asked a million questions.

Carmen: This fried Brie is to die for!

Hope: But where is my daddy?

Jessica: He's not really your dad—

Carmen: Did you taste the sauerbraten?

Hope: Will he buy me a doll?

Jessica had felt too sick to eat. How could she explain to an eleven-year-old that her "daddy" had used his power and privilege to coerce a woman into a sexual relationship? And that when the relationship resulted in a pregnancy, he'd threatened to have her deported.

Her mom had sworn her to secrecy. And Jessica had understood the importance of cooperation. It didn't need to be spelled out for her. If Wade Long alerted the authorities, her pregnant mom would have been forced to leave the country.

While sobbing, she'd written a letter to Casey.

Dear Casey,

Something horrible has happened and my mom and I have to move to Houston. I will write you when I get there, so you can come find me. I'm having to sneak this in the mail. THIS IS TOP SECRET. Do not tell a soul!

I love you. We'll be together again soon.

Jessica

She'd put a stamp on it and dropped it in a box in a strip mall when they'd stopped for fast food.

Two weeks later, she'd dropped another letter in the mail. Begging him to call. *Hang up if my mom answers! I love you, Casey. Come find me.*

Three more letters. *Come find me! Casey, why aren't you answering?*

He never did. Her mom said all Long men were horrible. They took what they wanted and discarded you. Jessica hadn't believed it at first.

With time, though...

She sighed, worrying about Hope. How could she explain this? Hope's tendency to fixate on things meant she repeated herself endlessly. And this was one thing nobody wanted to hear. Carmen had taken her swimming again in the hopes of distracting her. *She'll forget all about it after some ice cream and a swim.*

Only she wouldn't. And Jessica knew it.

The bartender set her second margarita in front of her. She decided to go for the guzzle. She sucked up about a third of the frosty beverage through the straw, and then grimaced and grabbed her head because (a) brain freeze and (b) Casey had just walked into the bar.

What the hell was he doing here? She grabbed her glass—she wasn't abandoning her margarita—and slunk off the barstool. But she couldn't escape with him standing in the doorway. A large potted tree caught her eye. Maybe she'd hide behind that until Casey moved and she could make a run for it.

Their eyes met. She probably looked like a deer caught in headlights.

The tension Casey had carried in his shoulders since he'd first walked into the bar seemed to seep away. And then he smiled.

It made her gasp. Seeing a smile spread across Casey Long's otherwise stern and stoic face was like seeing a vibrant flower in the middle of the desert (and thinking it had bloomed just for you). It warmed every single inch of her body except for the fingers wrapped around the frozen margarita. Actually, they felt warm too. And she became even warmer—and a bit tingly—as Casey made a beeline for her.

Why hadn't she put on any lipstick? She looked down at her feet. Flip-flops! Although she'd have looked silly wearing anything else with her cutoff shorts and Hello Kitty T-shirt. What had she been thinking when she came down here like this? Her mother would have been mortified.

It's important to look our best. People judge.

Boy, did they ever. Especially in small towns.

"Tell me you weren't about to dodge behind a potted plant," Casey said with a grin.

* * *

Shit, she was cute. Would she deny that she'd been making a run for the plant? Or would she own it?

"There goes my life as a supersecret agent," she said with a shrug. She owned it.

"You don't have to hide from me, you know," he said. It hurt that she wanted to, but he understood. It was awkward. So much time had passed...

Yet, as he looked into her big brown eyes, it hardly felt like it. Hair in a ponytail, shorts, and a T-shirt; he recognized this girl. Hell, if she put on a cheerleading outfit and went out onto the field tonight, nobody would even question it.

He swallowed. Thinking about Jess in a cheerleading outfit was making it difficult to form words into a sentence, and he had enough difficulty with that as it was.

"I wasn't hiding *from you,* per se. I just figured all the locals would be at the football game tonight and it would be safe to come down dressed like..." She looked down at her gorgeous tanned legs. "This."

She held out a foot and a flip-flop with ribbons tied all over it dangled from her toes.

"That's high fashion for Big Verde. And tonight's an away game. Folks don't necessarily want to drive all the way to Smithville to cheer the Giants on to their eighty-seventh straight loss."

"Fair-weather fans," Jessica said.

She'd cheered her little heart out for those Giants once, all while stealing sideways glances at Casey while he stood along the fence with his ragtag group of rodeo pals. He remembered trying to act cool when his friends wanted to leave, pretending to care about the pathetic football game when all he really cared about was seeing Jessica do one of her famous split jumps.

Those legs. Could she still do the splits?

"I lost interest in football when a certain cheerleader moved away," he said. "But I'm here tonight for a family celebration of Aunt Mavis. It's in the hospitality suite."

"Oh, I'm sorry! Don't you need to be getting back?"

"She would have hated the fuss," he said.

Jessica nodded in agreement.

Casey was missing something. He just knew it. But he didn't have a clue as to what. "Want to go for a walk?" he blurted.

He was desperate to not let her out of his sight. When he thought she'd left earlier, dammit, he was eighteen again. Eighteen and heartbroken. Ready to put out an APB to track her ass down.

She wouldn't stay forever. But right now, he could barely think beyond the current moment. And in the current moment, he needed to touch her. A strand of hair had conveniently escaped her ponytail, and he gently tucked it behind her ear.

Jessica licked her bottom lip and trailed her eyes down the front of his dress shirt. She looked very much as if she was imagining what might be underneath it, and the odds of her finding out were increasing, since he suddenly felt warm. Every damn inch of him might as well be on fire, just from the heat of her eyes.

He tried not to look as if he might be doing the same to her, but it was hard. He'd already noted all the things about her that were familiar, but he was dying to discover the ways in which she'd changed. And not just physically (although she did still look cute enough for a cheerleading outfit). The way her eyes continued to roam his body indicated the years had given her confidence. And he liked the way it looked on her.

"Well?" he asked, raising an eyebrow and holding out his hand. "How about that walk? You can keep your drink; we won't leave the property."

Jessica nodded, as if she'd made her decision. Then she took the straw between her lips, and while never taking her eyes off his, she sucked down the rest of her margarita.

"Hold on there. You're going to get a—"

She winced and shut her eyes. "Brain freeze," she said. "I know."

With a satisfied sigh, she set her empty glass on a nearby table and took his hand. When her fingers touched his, every hair on his body stood up, as if lightning were about to strike him dead.

Chapter Seven

Was she really holding Casey Long's hand?

She wanted to pinch herself to see if she was dreaming. Or slap herself in order to wake up. Or maybe just slap herself because holy cow they were heading out the French doors toward the pool, where Hope and Carmen were swimming.

Dang!

"Pardon?"

She'd said it out loud.

Casey looked at her quizzically.

Jessica could see Hope paddling around under the waterfall. She turned, forcing Casey to look away from the pool. Luckily, they were in the shadow of the corner of the building, where Hope and Carmen probably wouldn't spot them.

Being spotted would be disastrous. Not only would Carmen embarrass Jessica by making hubba-hubba eyes and giving thumbs-ups and God only knows what else, but there was a good chance Hope would accost him with *Hi! Are you my daddy?*

And wouldn't that be a kicker?

Plus, she just didn't want anybody in Big Verde, not even

Casey, knowing about Hope. There was no real threat from Wade anymore, but fear was strong glue for making habits stick.

She steered Casey toward the fire pit. They could sit on one of the outdoor couches with their backs to the pool. In the moonlight, they'd just look like any two people.

"I just meant *wow.* I hardly recognize the Château."

"It's changed quite a bit since you and I—" Casey paused. Cleared his throat. "Since the last time we were here."

The last time they were here they'd made love. Made plans. Promised to be together forever.

"They've got a fancy German chef now," Casey continued. "Rumor has it, he's trying to buy the restaurant from the hotel."

"Frederick Mueller," Jessica said.

Casey raised an eyebrow. "Somebody's been keeping up with the news in Big Verde."

"You realize I work for Carmen Foraccio, right?"

Casey gave her a blank look.

"You've never heard of Carmen?"

"The name sounds a bit familiar. Is she famous?"

"Do you watch the Food Channel?"

"Is that like a TV show?"

"Oh my God. Um, well, it's a network that features shows about food. And Carmen's show is at the top. She's a celebrity chef. Have you heard of La Casa Bleu? Or *Funky Fusions*?"

"JD and I ate at La Casa Bleu when we were roping in Vegas. Italian food."

"Well, it's Italian and French. It's a fusion place. There's one in Houston too. It's the original location."

"Oh really? Do you eat there often?"

"I manage it," Jessica said proudly.

"Wow, Jess. That's pretty amazing." A huge smile lit up Casey's face.

"What are you so happy about?"

"It's just that, well, you said that's what you wanted to do, right?

Run a fancy restaurant like the Village Château? And look at you. You're doing it. And a famous one, at that."

As a kid, Jessica had been practically obsessed with the Village Château restaurant. It represented high society to her—Big Verde style—and she'd longed to be the kind of person who ate there regularly.

"They had pretty good spaghetti," Casey added with a wink.

"You got *spaghetti*?"

"The most expensive spaghetti I've ever eaten in my life. Although I think it had a special French sauce on it, so maybe that was why. Is Carmen the chef?"

"She used to be. And she still oversees the menu and all the recipes. Everything is made according to her specifications. But she doesn't spend much time in the kitchen anymore. Her show takes up most of her time."

"*Funky Fusions*," Casey said. "I think I've seen it. She goes around eating all kinds of crazy shit, right?"

Jessica laughed. "That's the show."

They arrived at the fire pit. From here, they could still hear occasional giggles and shrieks from Hope, but they were muffled by breezes and distance.

Jessica sat and patted the seat next to her, hoping Casey would hurry up and join her. The lighting was dim—ground sconces and the glow of the fire—but she didn't trust that someone couldn't make them out if they looked really hard. And Carmen was nosy.

"Somebody's having fun over there," Casey said with a grin, looking over his shoulder at the pool.

Jessica grabbed his hand and yanked. "Sit."

It wasn't very effective, as far as yanks went. Casey was over six feet of solid muscle, and he glanced down at her like she was a tiny kitten yanking his chain.

"Hold your horses," he said, and then he sat down next to her and stretched out his long legs, crossing his ankles and revealing some really nice cowboy boots. His slacks were gray, and there was no gun or badge on his belt. His shirt was white, and Jessica watched as his fingers nimbly loosened his tie.

She swallowed as those same fingers then trailed down his shirt to settle on his thigh, which was hard and muscular and straining the fabric of his slacks. When she succeeded in wrenching her eyes away from that lovely vision and directing them back to Casey's face, she was met by a very sexy smirk.

Followed by a wink.

"That margarita getting to you?"

Maybe just a little. The brain freeze had melted into a warm glow.

"How did you end up in law enforcement?"

"Surprised?"

"Understatement."

Casey laughed. "Well, believe it or not, I got in some trouble after the bull riding didn't work out. Nothing awful. Just fighting and drinking. I think I was embarrassing the family."

She'd worried that Casey might fall back into his wild ways after she'd left. And it seemed he had.

"And?"

Casey stared at the fire, appearing relaxed. "Aunt Mavis made me volunteer my time to help some truly troubled youth. Kids with real problems, way bigger than mine. And I discovered I was pretty good at it. So, I decided to get a degree in criminal justice."

A warm swell of pride spread throughout her chest. "I knew you could do it, Casey," she whispered.

He looked up, the reflection of the flames dancing in his blue eyes. "It was hard," he said. "Without you."

Then why didn't he come after her? Why did he ignore her letters?

The words were on the tip of her tongue. *Just ask him.*

She took a deep breath, but Casey started talking again. "I was a cop in San Antonio for a couple of years. I didn't much care for city life, so I came home. Decided to run for sheriff."

"Family tradition," Jessica said, hoping the bitterness didn't show in her voice.

"I know what Wade did, Jess."

Jessica's head snapped up. Her pulse pounded in her head. "You do?"

"He's a crook. Hell, he fixed *my* record. He threw his weight around. God only knows what all shit he was ... *is* ... wrapped up in. Aunt Mavis was ashamed of him. She actually told me so once."

So he didn't know. Not specifically.

He uncrossed his legs and turned to face her. They were suddenly mighty close. She could smell his aftershave. His eyes locked on hers, and she clenched the cushion of the seat to keep from falling right into those baby blues.

Casey didn't blink. "I'm not like Wade. This is my county. My town. My people. And I take care of them."

If she'd thought Casey Long the bad boy had turned her on, it was only because she'd never met Casey Long the good guy. She wanted to grab that stern face and kiss it senseless.

"Do you remember what happened here?" she blurted.

Casey furrowed his brow, as if she'd said something offensive. "How could I ever forget it, Jess?" Then his expression softened, and he gently touched her cheek with his thumb. "It was my first time."

The touch of his thumb on her cheek sent shivers all the way to her toes. "Oh, you're sticking to that story?" she asked, feeling a little breathless.

Casey smiled. "I am totally sticking to that story. Because it's the truth. And I'm pretty sure you know it, based on my performance. I don't think I made it to the eight-second buzzer."

Jessica laughed at the bull riding reference. But sincerity shone in Casey's eyes. She'd been his first. And if he hadn't been lying about that, was he telling the truth about everything else? Had he truly been in love with her?

His eyes had darkened, and he leaned in even closer. She stared at his lips and brushed his chin with her fingers.

"I'm better now," he said. "I can go well past eight seconds."

"Had lots of practice?" Jessica asked with an embarrassingly shaky voice.

"I wouldn't say lots. But I know where all the important spots are." The lips she couldn't take her eyes off of curled up in an adorable smirk. "And I know just what to do to them."

She believed him. He was practically doing it with his eyes. And all of her important spots were responding appropriately. She squeezed her thighs together as Casey's eyes settled on her lips.

Was it the margarita making her feel this way? No. There wasn't enough alcohol in it to lead to wherever this was going. The only thing leading her now was her heart.

And her important spots. Which were pretty much on fire.

The look in Casey's eyes promised he could put out fires, no problem.

As if on cue, the fire in the pit suddenly went out, making Jessica gasp.

"Must be ten o'clock," Casey said. "That means the pool is closed."

Oh dear. Jessica looked back at the pool. Carmen and Hope were both out, wrapping themselves in towels. There was nobody else around.

"The lights and pit are on a timer," Casey added. "That's why the fire went out."

"Not out entirely," she muttered. Then she put her hand to her mouth, because she hadn't meant to say it out loud.

Casey gently pulled her hand away. "Let's see what we can do about that," he said, bringing his lips to hers.

Chapter Eight

Her lips. God, even better than he remembered. In some ways, he was reliving the past—this was Jess, *his Jess*—but he was also navigating new territory. New delicious territory.

This was grown-up Jess. And grown-up Jess knew how to kiss.

She pressed her breasts into his chest, and he ran his hand down her back, mapping all the womanly curves and planes of her body. When he got to her hip, she twisted to give him better access, and he slipped his hand beneath to cup her nice, round ass.

She responded with a moan that nearly made him come undone.

He was impossibly hard. What he had going on couldn't be referred to as *wood*. It was more like granite. And speaking of *undone,* she had his tie off. He didn't even know when that had happened. Her fingers traveled the trail of his shirt's buttons.

She sighed against his lips. "We're in public."

Did she mean *We're in public so we need to stop* or *We're in public and I'm seriously turned on*?

She pulled away and gazed at him. There was just a sliver of a moon, but it lit up her eyes.

"We're probably doing a little more than we should out here. Somebody might see us," she said.

They hadn't done nearly enough.

Casey glanced around. "It's pretty dark out. They'd have to walk right up on us."

Jess licked her plump lips, already swollen from kissing. Her chest rose and fell quickly, but she wasn't quite breathless. And Casey wanted her breathless.

"But someone might do that," Jess said. "Walk right up on us."

Casey shifted nervously. He *was* the sheriff. Having sex in a public place probably wasn't the smartest idea he'd ever had. Jessica definitely brought out something wild in him, but his days of living on the wild side were over.

"Let's go to your room," he suggested. "That seems like a better plan."

Jessica had his shirt unbuttoned and was staring at his chest. It was probably a bit broader and more muscled than when he was a skinny kid in high school, and it definitely had more hair.

"Jess, did you hear me? Your room?"

She looked back to his eyes with a sheepish little grin on her face. He couldn't know for sure in the dim lighting, but he suspected she was blushing. She sighed deeply. "Actually, that won't work. I'm not traveling alone."

Ah. He should have guessed that with the Porsche. "Carmen?"

"Yes," Jess said. Casey followed her gaze to the second floor of the hotel, where a balcony light was on. The other rooms were dark. While the restaurant did a booming business with travelers and locals alike, the hotel didn't see much activity during the off-season.

He wasn't going to let this opportunity get away. But they couldn't keep making out by the fire pit. It had been a blissfully long time since a Long family scandal, and Casey would like to continue that streak.

His place was up in the hills, only about fifteen minutes away, but he suspected if Jess had time to think about things, she'd cool off. Hell, if *he* had time to think about things . . .

Nah. He wasn't going to cool off. If anything, he was heating up even more.

He scanned the area. There was a patch of cedar trees, but they wouldn't provide enough cover. And besides, he and Jess weren't going to bang on the ground like animals.

He glanced at Jess. She was biting her bottom lip and eyeing his chest and looking every bit as if she was all in for banging on the ground like animals.

A loud humming sound started up as the pool pump kicked in. The pump and other equipment were concealed behind a wooden fence surrounded by shrubbery. You had to go through a little gate to get in there; Casey knew this because he'd once been called out to investigate a violent racoon. Such was life as a small-town county sheriff.

The enclosed area was roomy enough to hold a chaise lounge, of which there were plenty by the pool.

Jess saw where he was looking.

"What's behind the fence?"

"Pool equipment."

"We couldn't—"

Oh yes, they could. Casey jumped up and walked to the pool. He picked out a sturdy chaise lounge, hoisted it up, and carried it past the fire pit to the gate that led inside the small fenced-in area.

Jessica hurried over. "What do you think we're going to do on that?"

"I don't know. Maybe we'll lounge? Look at the stars? Make out like fiends?"

"What if somebody is watching us right now?"

There wasn't a soul around. "Even if someone were looking from one of the windows, they couldn't possibly see anything other than shadows, and besides, we're about to be hidden by this nifty fence."

"You sound pretty sure about that."

He extended a hand. "Come on, Jess. Let's do something wild."

* * *

Casey Long stood in the shadows with his shirt open, looking dangerous as hell and holding out a hand. How many times had Jessica dreamed of feeling his touch again? She couldn't shake the feeling that she was dreaming.

Nothing could come of a hookup with Casey. Jessica would be back at her crazy life in Houston on Monday, and she and Casey would probably never talk to each other again. But for now...

"Okay," she blurted.

It had been a long time since she'd done anything that could be considered even remotely wild or risky.

Casey gently pulled her in and closed the gate behind them. She went straight into his arms and pressed against him. God, she loved the feel of him. So tall—he'd always been tall—but now he was also *big*. She rose on her toes and kissed him, eliciting a sexy groan that was louder than the hum of the pool equipment.

"Shit, Jess," he said against her lips. "You taste so good."

He abandoned her lips and went down her jaw to her neck, licking the sensitive skin behind her ear. "I want to taste all of you," he whispered. "Every inch."

Jessica's breath hitched. Was he talking about what she thought he was? The one time they'd been together had been sweet, but they'd both been inexperienced. She hadn't even *known* about that particular activity, much less experienced it.

Casey's hands roamed beneath her T-shirt as he kissed her neck. Her knees were so weak they probably wouldn't hold her up much longer.

As if sensing her imminent collapse, Casey steered her toward the chaise lounge. "Sit," he ordered in a low and raspy voice.

Jessica followed instructions, and Casey pressed the back of the chair all the way down. Then he stood over her, running his hands through his hair and gazing down as if she were a feast and he couldn't decide where to start.

"You've filled out a little," she said, staring at his chest.

"So have you," he replied, staring at hers.

His eyes shone with lust, which Jessica greatly appreciated. But she'd done a little more than fill out. She was thirty and although she was in good shape, her body reflected the years. She didn't have saggy old-lady boobs, but they weren't exactly perky anymore either. She wanted to tell Casey he'd missed her best years, but her best years had been spent working, going to school, and taking care of her mom and Hope.

Everybody had missed her best years, including her.

Casey took his shirt off, dropping it to the ground. Ho. Lee. Cow.

The man looked like a Greek god. Broad, chiseled chest with *way* more hair than she remembered. Hard, sculpted abs. Her fingers itched to explore.

"Your turn," he said, sitting on the chaise next to her. The chair creaked and sank into the grass.

Insecurity crept in. "I don't know that I want to take anything all the way off. We might need to make a run for it."

"I'll accept that for now," he said, running his hand beneath her shirt, up her belly, and between her breasts, dragging her T-shirt with it. "But next time, everything is coming off."

Next time? Was he really thinking there would be a—

Her thought was interrupted by Casey lifting her bra up over her breasts, not even bothering to unclasp it. He let out a shuddering sigh as he stared. "God, woman. You're gorgeous."

Before Jessica could say a word, Casey bent over and covered a nipple with his warm mouth.

That was it. She was gone. Run for it? Ha! If anyone walked up on them now, Jessica wouldn't even know it.

Casey's hand trailed up her leg to the inside of her thigh. *When had she opened her legs?* Probably as soon as she'd felt his lips on her breast. She panted embarrassingly as his fingers traced ticklish patterns on her skin.

The jean cutoffs were pretty short. Shorter than a woman Jessica's age should wear them, but right now they were coming in handy, as Casey had no trouble slipping his fingers inside the denim. He brushed her panties, and she moaned and arched her back. The combination of what his fingers were doing and what his lips were doing was almost too much.

Casey lifted his head and watched her while still working magic with his fingers. "Can I—"

He was talking to her. She'd seen his mouth move, but it was so freaking hard to hold her focus. "Can you what?" she gasped.

"Can I…"

"Hmm?"

"Jess, I want inside you."

"Yes," she whispered. "Please."

His finger slipped inside. Followed quickly by another. And then his mouth was on hers, forceful, but not crushing, and he was exploring—with tongue and fingers—slowly and intentionally, as if he had all the time in the world.

Jessica thought she might lose her mind. She wasn't in the mood for a Sunday drive. She was excited. Starved. Impatient. And he was torturing her. It was delicious torture, but still torture.

She ran her hands down Casey's back and gripped his very firm butt in an encouraging way. He responded and ground against her, harder and faster, as if he'd picked up on her sense of urgency. One of his legs was over hers; the other one was— *Where was the other one?* Probably on the ground. The chaise simply wasn't big enough for the both of them.

Casey kissed her neck. Sucked on it. When was the last time Jessica had petted and made out with someone? She reached between them and felt the hard length of him. He whimpered into her neck and rubbed himself frantically against her as the chaise lounge squeaked and squawked.

They were both hot and sweaty and panting like animals, and this was…*fun.*

She hadn't felt this excited, crazy, and *free* since the last time she'd made out with Casey Long.

Casey stopped moving and slowly pulled his hand away. The

only sound was the humming of the pool pump and their haggard breathing.

"What's wrong?" she asked.

"I told you I wanted to taste you. All of you."

She watched as he brought his fingers to his mouth, licked them, and then closed his eyes as if he'd just tasted heaven.

Oh boy. That was hot. And she knew what was coming next. Or at least she hoped she did. She unbuttoned her shorts and slid down the zipper. Then she raised her hips, and Casey pulled off the shorts, along with her panties, in one fell swoop. No time for modesty now. Jessica's hormones were in the pilot's seat, and they were going full throttle.

Without even a hint of hesitancy, Casey hoisted her legs up and over the armrests of the chaise. "Still pretty flexible, I see," he said with a grin.

Jessica gasped as the cool night air kissed her sensitive flesh, and then Casey kissed it too.

Goose bumps. Tingling. *Humming.*

Was it the pool pump? Or was it her?

"Oh, Casey…"

It was definitely her.

Casey moaned in answer and continued what he was doing. Plus a few other things with his fingers. Like pinching her nipples.

"So good," he mumbled against her. The vibration of his voice almost did her in. "So." He licked her lightly. "Damn." He licked her again. "Good." He thrust his tongue inside her, and that was all it took.

Fireworks exploded behind Jessica's eyes as her body spasmed. Her toes curled. Her fingers tingled. She'd thought women who described their orgasms in that way were exaggerating. But it turned out, she'd been having inferior orgasms.

Casey held her in a gentle suction until she couldn't take it anymore. She gently pushed his face away, and he rose above her, gazing into her eyes.

"Was that okay?"

She nearly laughed. "Better than okay. You've learned some new tricks."

"Would you like to see some more?"

"What else have you got up your sleeve?"

Casey rose to his knees and unbuckled his belt. "Actually, it's in my pants."

Chapter Nine

Casey couldn't believe this was happening. What had started off as him heading to his great-aunt's funeral had ended with him crouched behind a fence and shrubbery having sex with the literal woman of his dreams. One who happened to be an ex-cheerleader. And judging by the position her legs were currently in, she could still do the splits.

He was doing several things he could be arrested for, including destruction of property, because there wasn't any way the chaise lounge would survive the night.

It was by far the best day he'd had in a long time. Possibly in forever.

"Do you have a condom?" Jessica asked.

Shit. The question had the effect of a dart piercing a balloon. He patted his pockets even though he knew he didn't have one. "I don't think—"

Jessica snapped her legs shut.

"Jesus. Hold on. Don't do anything hasty."

He looked around helplessly, dick out like a flagpole, as if a condom would materialize out of thin air.

"Do you have one or not?" Jess asked.

"Nope."

"Oh no! Are you serious?"

"I didn't think to grab one on my way to my great-aunt's funeral."

Jess sat up. Pulled her bra back down over her delicious, bouncy breasts. She was shutting down the party, and Casey didn't blame her one bit. How could he? But he was still mighty frustrated and damn near ready to explode.

His hands shook as he leaned over and snagged her shorts with the panties inside and tossed them to her.

"Thanks," she said, standing up and slipping them on. "I'm sorry—"

"Don't apologize, Jess. I'm glad you had the wherewithal to think about protection. I was, well, you know. Out of my ever-loving mind." And he still was. It was pretty obvious, too, since he was standing there with his dick out, although it had definitely lost some of its enthusiasm. He started to zip up.

"Don't do that," Jess said, licking her lips. "There are other ways to have fun."

Casey raised an eyebrow and stopped zipping.

Jessica sat on the chaise, and its legs gave out. She grunted as she bounced on her butt.

Casey snorted. And then Jess started to giggle. It rolled through him and tickled his ribs as he fought off the urge to join in.

"Come here," she said, rising to her knees and still smiling.

"Jess, you don't have to do this," Casey said. "I'm fine. I've had a great time. Really."

Getting her off had been way more than a great time. He really didn't need to do anything more.

Jessica smirked at his hardening dick, which begged to disagree. She crooked a finger. "You're giving yourself away."

Casey took a step toward her—the lady had given him an order and he wasn't about to disappoint her—but over the humming of the pump and the pounding of his pulse in his head, he thought he heard footsteps.

Dammit. He put a finger to his lips while shoving his dick in his pants.

Sure enough, someone was coming. Casey looked over his shoulder to see Tyler Murphy peering over the top of the fence.

"Hey, Sheriff Long, is everything okay?"

Tyler was a busboy for the restaurant. He was also Casey's neighbor's kid. "Yeah, Tyler. Everything's fine."

He glanced back at Jess. She was wild-eyed and putting herself back together while trying to back into the shadows.

"Be careful, Jess—"

Too late. Jessica stepped back and tripped on the broken chaise lounge. Casey lunged and caught her, and when their eyes met, she started to giggle again.

Casey got an idea.

"This young lady has had a bit too much to drink. I heard her wandering around back here." He looked intently at Jess. "Feeling better now, ma'am?"

Jessica crossed her arms and faked a hiccup. "Yes, Sheriff," she slurred. "Much better."

None of that explained why Casey wasn't wearing a shirt, and Tyler didn't look 100 percent convinced. But what the hell was the kid doing back here anyway? Casey sniffed in the boy's direction and picked up the faint, skunky odor of marijuana. "Did you come out here to check on the pump?" he asked. "Because that's a weird chore for a busboy."

Even in the dark, Casey could see the whites of Tyler's eyes as he caught on to the position he was in. The kid probably came out here regularly to toke up. If Casey felt like looking, he was pretty sure he'd be able to find telltale signs of previous activity. He wouldn't be surprised if there were stems and papers scattered about.

Tyler seemed to come to the same conclusion. "Uh, I was just out here collecting cups and shit—uh, sorry—from around the pool and I thought I heard—"

Casey raised an eyebrow, crossed his arms over his bare chest.

"Thought I heard this lady being sick or something."

Jessica fake-hiccupped again, and Casey nearly busted out laughing. Everybody understood one another then.

He nodded at Tyler. "I've got it under control."

"Yes, sir," Tyler said with a smirk. "It sure looks like it."

"Get on back to work," Casey said.

Tyler saluted, turned, and loped back off in the direction of the hotel.

Casey picked up his shirt and slipped it on. Jess still had her hand over her mouth, but it wasn't containing her giggles very well.

"Get some control over yourself, woman," Casey said with a wink. "Or I'll throw you in the drunk tank."

"We don't have to call it quits, you know," she said. "We can go somewhere else."

"Nah. I think we should quit while we're ahead. I had a really good time." He looked at her little T-shirt, her shorts with the top button still undone, and her mussed-up hair. "A *really* good time."

"So, let's keep going. Swing by the Rite Aid and pick up a pack of condoms, head to your place, and get busy." She wiggled her hips.

God. It sounded so easy. And he loved how eager she was. But it was late, and there were other things to consider. "As much as I'd love to, I can't just waltz into the Rite Aid with you to buy condoms. For one thing, I'm the sheriff."

"Sheriffs don't have sex?"

"They do it discreetly."

"Oh, is that what we were doing?" One corner of her mouth curled up. "Being discreet here in the shrubs behind the pool pump?"

Damn. That crooked little grin. He'd love to wipe it off her face with a kiss.

"And the Rite Aid is closed anyway," he added. "They roll up the sidewalks around here pretty early."

He picked up the broken chaise. "I'm going to toss this in the dumpster behind the restaurant," he said. "And then I'm going to help a poor drunk lady get back into the hotel safely."

Jess pouted.

Those lips. He wanted to drop the chaise and tackle her to the ground. But he couldn't. For one thing, no condom. For another, he had an early day tomorrow.

"Are you going to come watch me and JD rope at the rodeo? It's for a good cause, and I'm really hoping you'll stick around awhile."

Jessica twisted a strand of hair around her finger, a habit that took him straight back to high school. But then she looked at him and smiled.

"I'll think about it."

"You think about it real hard."

"Will you be wearing chaps?"

"I'd get laughed out of the arena."

Jess looked bitterly disappointed. "That's too bad. I like chaps."

"I'll wear chaps," he blurted. "If it means you'll come."

He swallowed.

"To the rodeo," he added. "Not just, you know, come."

They both busted out laughing again. Silly, uncontrollable, insane laughter. They stopped when they literally couldn't breathe anymore.

"I really, really like chaps," Jess said.

She licked her lips. *Licked her damn lips like she was thinking about him in a pair of chaps and nothing else.*

"And I'll also have a handy dandy rope, if that turns you on."

She squeezed her thighs together, realized she'd done it, and unclenched them with a sly little grin that said she knew he'd noticed.

"What time does the Rite Aid open tomorrow?"

"Now, darlin', tomorrow is Sunday. It's closed. You can't buy condoms on the Lord's Day. It's bad enough that you're even thinking about it."

"Oh, I'm thinking about it, Casey Long. We might have to drive to the nearest town to hit up a Walmart."

"That could be arranged," Casey said. "After the rodeo."

Jessica bit her lip, and Casey got up right close. "I might have to tie you up so you don't leave again."

The blush that lit up Jess's cheeks said she wasn't entirely opposed to the idea. Casey was going to be in for a long, sleepless night.

* * *

Jessica lathered up in the shower. The smile on her face was starting to make her cheeks sore, but she couldn't get rid of it, no matter how hard she tried. Not that she was trying very hard.

Hard. Holy cow, Casey had been hard. She felt awful that she hadn't been able to return any favors and do something about it. But they'd been caught!

Her smile got even wider.

She'd been like a teen again. A dumb, horny, risk-taking teen.

She hadn't risked anything in twelve years. Not for her own happiness, and not for love.

Love. She did *not* love Casey. But dang it, she definitely had a major crush going on. It felt just like old times.

Yep. She was definitely a kid again. Although a kid would have insisted this crush was something more. Because it felt like her world was going to end on Monday when she had to go back to Houston. And because the thought of not seeing Casey again hurt just as much this time as it had the last.

Only this time, she wasn't going to leave with any secrets. Wade Long couldn't hurt her. People could talk if they wanted, but she was taking Hope to the rodeo tomorrow. It had been wonderful to see old friends today. It would be even better to see them tomorrow.

* * *

Casey sat at the bar. He'd wandered around the pool after dropping Jess off in the lobby—she'd refused to let him walk her to the room—picking up the cups and napkins and trash that Tyler had missed.

The bar was empty and they were closing up shop, but Casey was a Long *and* the sheriff. He could stay as long as he wanted. He wouldn't do that, though. He didn't believe in tossing his weight around with the family name. He'd just shoot the shit with the bartender until the kid was done drying glasses.

"Hey, Zeke, who does the purchasing for the pool furniture and whatnot around here? I accidentally broke a chaise lounge and I'd like to replace it."

Zeke picked up a glass from the washer and began drying it off. "Stella will know what to do about the chaise. Although she'll just tell you to forget about it."

Stella was the general manager, and Zeke was probably right. It would be best for Casey to just replace it himself.

Casey sucked down the last of his beer and pulled out his wallet.

"On the house, Sheriff. You know that," Zeke said.

"Bullshit," Casey said, slapping some cash on the counter. "I'd better get home. Early day tomorrow for the rodeo."

"You and JD roping?"

"Yeah. We don't stand a chance, though. I heard a lot of the Rancho Cañada Verde cowboys are entering."

Zeke laughed. "You're going to get your asses kicked."

"I know. But it's for Hope House. I'm happy to have my ass kicked for little Dalton Reed and his friends." He stood up and stuffed his wallet back in his pocket.

"Hold on, Sheriff," Zeke said, digging beneath the counter. "You know that lady you were with earlier? The one who was here at the bar?"

Casey crossed his arms. "Jessica Acosta. What about her?"

Zeke held up a slim leather wallet. "She left this when she followed you out the door."

Wow. Good thing Zeke found it. Although in Big Verde, most people would turn it in. It was just one of the things he loved about the people of his town. "Thanks, Zeke—"

Zeke's face broke out in a grin. "I guess she forgot all about it while y'all were busting the chaise by the pool pump."

"Damn Tyler Murphy," Casey muttered.

Zeke laughed and handed over the wallet. "She's in room 204."

Casey's pulse sped up. He'd get to see Jessica again, even if only for a few minutes. "Thanks."

He left the bar and climbed the ornate staircase in the lobby. When he got to room 204, he stopped and took a deep breath. He was still riding the high that came from messing around, and he had a partial boner to prove it. But what was making him sweat was something much deeper. It had been so satisfying to tell Jess about his life, how he'd pulled himself together and gone to college, become a cop, and then finally been elected sheriff. It was as if he'd worked all this time just to be able to someday look her in the eye and tell her he'd done it. He'd become the man she'd always known he could be.

I knew you could do it, Casey.

Of everything they'd said and done tonight, those words had been the sweetest. He was a better man because of Jessica Acosta. No doubt about it. He'd been a hellion who gave his family fits. Drove his teachers insane. Irritated the hell out of the fine folks in town who saw him as an entitled, spoiled brat.

But Jessica had seen something else in him. He'd thought she was crazy. Believed she just had a good-girl crush on a bad boy. But at some point, he'd decided to become the guy she thought he was. Even after she left, or maybe *because* she'd left, he kept trying. And he'd done it.

He squared his shoulders. Made sure his shirt was tucked in. And then he knocked.

The door opened. And it wasn't Jess who answered. Or her friend, Carmen.

It was a little girl. "Hi!" she said.

"Hi yourself. Is your, uh..." He tried looking over her shoulder into the room, but she'd only opened the door about six inches.

"Who are you?" the child asked.

He wanted to ask her the same question. "I'm Casey."

That seemed to be all she needed to hear. She opened the door wide, and Casey peered in, but still didn't see Jessica.

The little girl put her hands on her hips. "I'm Hope."

Casey finally got a good look at her. She was probably ten or eleven years old and cute as a button. And she had the same infectious grin as Dalton Reed. She had Down syndrome.

Casey smiled back.

"My grandma used to live here," Hope said.

Casey rubbed his chin. Was she somehow local? Did he have the wrong room?

He looked at the number on the door. It was 204. That was the room Zeke had sent him to. And besides, if this little cutie was local, he'd know it.

"My, my, my," a sultry voice said.

Finally. An adult. Casey looked up to see a gorgeous woman with big blue eyes and hair to match staring over Hope's head. He realized he'd seen her on television at least once or twice. "You must be Carmen," he said.

"Mmm-hmm," Carmen said, looking him up and down with a little smirk that suggested he might need to have a talk with Miss Acosta about kissing and telling.

He hoped she hadn't left out the part where he'd made her toes curl.

"And you must be Sheriff Long," Carmen said.

"You're Sheriff Long?" Hope asked.

"Uh-oh," Carmen muttered. "Listen, Hope, he's not—"

"Sheriff Long is my daddy!"

What the hell? Casey took a step back. The room began to spin a little.

My grandma used to live here.

Shit.

"Uh, hold on a minute, cowboy," Carmen said. Then she shouted, "Jessica!"

Hope ran into the hall and wrapped her arms around Casey. Jess came to the door with her hair wrapped in a towel, her eyes wide, and her mouth hanging open.

"Hope, come here," she said, unwrapping the child from his legs.

"No, no! Let me go!" Hope wailed. "He's my daddy!"

All the color had drained from Jess's face as she held on to Hope. A man across the hall poked his head out the door. "Is everything okay?"

"It's fine," Jessica said.

The man looked to Casey, but Casey couldn't talk.

Nothing was fine.

Hope's little face was streaked with tears. This was his child? And he hadn't even known about her?

"Jess," he said. His voice didn't sound right. He felt like he was choking. "How could you?"

He turned and stumbled down the hall, ran down the stairs, and didn't stop running until he got to his truck. People shouted his name, asked if he was all right.

But he barely heard them.

He had to get somewhere to sort this all out. Somewhere private. A place where his own damn child wouldn't see him freak out.

Chapter Ten

Jessica scanned the arena from the stands. The rodeo had officially begun over an hour ago. They'd gotten there early, in the hopes that Casey would too. But nobody had seen him. They'd already sat through the opening ceremony, the mutton bustin'—Dalton had placed third—and the women's barrel racing event. The youth calf scramble was next, and then it was team roping.

That was Casey's event.

Jessica twisted the hem of her T-shirt into a knot. Surely, Casey wouldn't have gone and done something stupid? What if he'd drunk himself into a stupor? He'd been terribly upset, and Jessica had wanted to run after him. But he was an adult, and Hope was not.

Hope had needed her more.

And Casey shouldn't have run away.

Even so, her heart ached for him.

She spotted JD's white hat and stood up. "Stay here," she said to Carmen and Hope.

She worked her way down the bleachers, stopping every two seconds to say hi to someone because that's how it was in Big Verde. She finally made her way to where JD stood by the fence, phone to his ear. Their eyes met and he shook his head.

"Still not answering?" she asked.

JD shoved his phone back in his pocket. "You want to tell me what got him so upset that he just took off the night before the rodeo?"

Jessica scowled at him. "That's what you're worried about? The rodeo?"

"Well, I'm sure as hell not worried he's been kidnapped. He's pissed or something is all."

He yanked on his white Stetson with a pointed look that said, *At you.*

"We didn't fight," she said. "It was a misunderstanding, and he took off before I could explain everything to him."

"I don't need to know the details. But Jess, that man has never stopped pining for you. He's lonely, but he functions. Sometimes he even manages to be happy. You can't just come barging back into town and mess with people's lives."

Is that what she'd done? She closed her eyes at the memory of the look on his face when Hope had blurted out that he was her father.

She swallowed down a bit of bile, but then she said, "He's never stopped pining for me? Really?"

JD looked at the arena where the calf scramble had started. The crowd was cheering and going nuts for the kids participating, and Hope was probably having a blast. "Really," he said. "So be careful with him."

Obviously, she had to tell Casey that Hope wasn't his. But she wasn't sure what would come after that. It wasn't like she could make a life with a man who—

She gasped, earning a quizzical look from JD beneath the brim of his hat. *When had she started thinking about making a life with Casey?*

Exactly twelve years ago. And she'd never stopped.

She was lonely, but she functioned. Sometimes she even managed to be happy. But she'd never stopped pining for Casey Long.

Yes, they'd been kids. But there were plenty of old happy couples who'd started off as high school sweethearts. Maybe not many. But sometimes when you know, you just know.

"Team roping is next," JD said through a clenched jaw. "That asshole better show up."

Slowly, and with her eyes on the entrance gate, Jessica made her way back to Carmen and Hope.

"Still not here?" Carmen asked.

Jessica shook her head.

"My fault?" Hope asked.

She didn't fully grasp what had happened. And even though they'd talked and talked and talked last night, Jessica wasn't positive that Hope understood Casey wasn't her dad.

"None of this is your fault."

Hope smiled. "Can I ride a sheep?"

Jessica sat down. "No, you're too big."

"Can I ride a horse?"

That could probably be arranged.

* * *

Casey pulled through the gate of the fairgrounds. He sure hoped he hadn't missed his and JD's event. JD would never forgive him.

Well, he would, but it would be a miserable two weeks waiting for him to get around to it.

He parked his pickup next to JD's and looked at his face in the rearview mirror. He hadn't shaved and there were bags beneath his eyes. Staying up all night will do that.

A daughter. He had a daughter.

It all made sense now. The Acostas had left because Jess had been pregnant. Eighteen years old with her whole life ahead of her, and he'd knocked her up. No wonder she'd called it *game over* last night when he hadn't had a condom. She'd had her life ruined once already.

He remembered the child's sweet, perfect face.

Not ruined. But definitely altered. Things had not gone the way Jessica and her mom had painstakingly planned.

Hope. It was a beautiful name.

There was an abandoned stone chapel on Harper's Hill. It was technically private property; part of the twelve-thousand-acre Rancho Cañada Verde owned by the Kowalski family. But Gerome Kowalski didn't mind that Casey went there from time to time, and that's where he'd spent the night, trying to wrap his mind around this new reality.

At first, he'd been angry. Angry at Jess for keeping his own child a secret from him. But then he'd tried to put himself in her shoes. She'd been a teenager, and her mom had been in control. Had she really had a choice?

What would he have done at eighteen? He liked to think he'd have stepped up to the plate. But the truth was, he didn't know. Not for sure. This was why adults told teens they needed to be old enough to handle the consequences of sex. As a grown man, Casey knew this. He'd had that particular talk with more than one kid. But at eighteen...

None of that mattered now. Jessica had come home, and she'd probably been trying to work up the nerve to tell him about Hope. She must have felt terrified, not knowing how he'd react.

And he'd reacted horribly.

But Hope had been so happy and thrilled to meet him. He'd seen nothing but joy in her face, and although he couldn't see himself, he had a pretty good idea of what he'd looked like. And she didn't need to see that.

He'd collected himself at the stone chapel. Regained his composure. And he was ready to face Hope with a smile and open arms. He was her daddy, goddammit. And if the way his heart ached at the thought of Jess ever escaping his sight again was any indication, he still loved her mama.

Yesterday he'd been Big Verde's most available sheriff. Today, he had a family.

They'd make this work. *If* Jess could even stand the sight of him after last night.

He grabbed his hat off the seat and stuck it on his head just as his door was yanked open. JD grabbed him by the arm. "Jesus Christ, Casey! I don't know where you've been or why you haven't answered your phone, but we're on in a few minutes. I got us pushed back as far as I could. Get your ass out of the truck."

JD gave a hard yank and Casey stumbled out of the truck, slamming the door behind him.

"Why the hell are you wearing *chaps*?" JD asked.

"What's wrong with chaps?"

"You look like an idiot."

The two of them started walking.

"Are we saddled up?" Casey asked.

"Of course we're saddled up. And I warmed up Genevieve for you, but you need to get on that pony and ride around a bit. *If* we've even got time for that."

Casey glanced at the stands when they walked through the gate. He didn't see Jessica, and that worried him. But surely she hadn't gone back to Houston. Not after everything that had happened. Unless she was so disgusted by his behavior that she never wanted to see him again.

"Get your mind off of that woman," JD said. "I know you think team roping is a breeze compared to bull riding, but you can still get hurt."

JD was right. Casey had to get his head on straight.

Fifteen minutes later he and Genevieve were in the box, looking at JD sitting atop Brazen on the other side of the chute. There was a young steer in the chute between them, raring to go. Casey's adrenaline was pumping. This was practically the best part.

He and JD had been partners for six years and friends and/or foes for damn near a lifetime. He wasn't exactly sure what it was he did with his eyes to say *ready,* but JD saw it and gave a small, tight nod of his head.

The gates opened, and they were off.

JD was the header, and Casey rode heeler. They thundered across the arena with JD in the lead. He was on fire. He tossed the rope and it flew through the air, hooking the steer's horns. Now it was Casey's turn, as heeler, to go for the legs. The arena seemed to shrink as he homed in on the steer, rope held high in the air, and then it was gone. Flying.

The steer kicked up, and the rope ensnared its legs with perfect timing. Effortlessly, Casey got the rope around the saddle horn in a perfect dally before he looked up. The arena came back into focus and there was Jessica, hanging on the fence, with Hope next to her.

They waved, grinned, and shouted just as the rope went taut, jerking the horse. Distracted, Casey wasn't ready, and in what seemed like slow motion, he fell off the horse.

Fell. Off. The. Damn. Horse.

He landed with a thud and saw stars. Got the breath knocked out of him too.

JD rode up next to him. Concern shone in his eyes, but only for a brief second. Then he started laughing. "I told you to get your mind off that woman. Are you sure you used to ride bulls?"

"Ha-ha," Casey wheezed. "Very funny."

It didn't feel funny, though. A sharp pain nearly gutted him when he inhaled. And when he went to stand up, he discovered he couldn't. *Goddammit.*

JD jumped down from his horse, concern back in his eyes. "Hey, bud. You okay?"

No. He was not okay. But he would be. "It's just my back."

Soon he was surrounded by people saying things like *Don't move* and *How many fingers am I holding up?* Someone also mentioned *ambulance.*

An EMT who looked maybe twelve years old called for a long backboard and a neck brace.

Jesus. He just needed a few minutes to come out of this spasm…

Suddenly Jessica was there. She dropped to her knees next to him and leaned over. "Casey, are you okay?"

Her dark hair brushed his cheek. She smelled like sunshine and sounded like an angel and her eyes were wide with fright.

"I'm fine," he said, although for some reason, he was having trouble getting air in his lungs. "Where's my daughter?"

Jessica put a finger to his lips. "Shh..."

"Where is—"

"Casey, Hope's not your daughter. Everything is fine."

Everything was fine?

Everything was definitely *not* fine. Because that meant—

He couldn't finish the thought. "Jess, if she's not my child, then whose is she?"

Before he could get an answer, someone stuck a stupid oxygen mask over his face.

Chapter Eleven

Jess watched the ambulance leave. She hadn't been able to answer Casey's question because the EMTs needed her out of the way. But Casey's reaction to her thoughtless response, which she'd meant to be reassuring, answered any questions she'd had about him.

When informed that he wasn't the daddy of an eleven-year-old girl with Down syndrome whom he'd never met before, the emotion that had shown on his face was disappointment. Maybe even grief.

Casey Long was a special kind of man.

JD had heard everything but was busy acting like he hadn't. "He'll be fine," he said.

"How do you know that? He could have a broken back or a punctured lung or a concussion or—"

"He's embarrassed is all. And he should be. The idiot fell off his damn horse."

Carmen and Hope joined them as the dust settled and everybody started going back about their business. "Is he okay?" Hope asked.

JD took off his hat and held out his hand. "Howdy. I'm JD. And don't you worry your pretty little head. He'll be just fine. Sheriff Long probably needs some horseback riding lessons."

Oh no! Jessica held her breath. He'd said *Sheriff Long.*

She looked at Hope, praying she wasn't about to blurt out something that would no doubt end up on the front page of the *Big Verde News* the next day, but what she saw was a blushing eleven-year-old. *Blushing!*

"I'm Hope," she said, taking JD's hand.

Well, JD *was* very handsome. The two of them shook hands and simultaneously charmed the heck out of each other while Carmen touched up her lipstick.

"You know," JD said, "we have a place here in Big Verde called Hope House. Since it practically has your name on it, I think you should stop by and check it out before you leave. My sister teaches cooking classes there, and she has a little boy named Dalton."

"Cooking!" Hope said, clapping her hands.

"She loves to cook," Carmen said. "In fact, she's one of the best chefs at La Casa Bleu."

That wasn't quite true. Hope loved to be in the kitchen, but in a place like La Casa Bleu, the pace was frantic. She could never be in there during the chaotic dinner rush. However, she loved repetitive tasks and was a stickler for details. The pastry chef adored her, and nobody could *put a cherry on top* like Hope.

"I knew it!" JD said. "You're Carmen Foraccio, aren't you?"

"Guilty as charged," Carmen said. "And I assume you went to school with Jessica?"

"High school heartthrob," Jessica said.

Carmen fluttered her eyelashes. "No doubt."

"Man, I love your show," JD sputtered, taking off his hat as a sign of respect. "Gosh, I watch it all the time."

It was weird to think of JD watching cooking shows, and even weirder to see him acting starstruck. Although, if the blush on Carmen's cheeks was any indication, she was equally dazzled.

"Should we go to the hospital?" Jessica asked. Because *hello! Casey was hurt!*

"It would really embarrass him," JD said. "So sure, let's go."

Jessica hated to drag Hope away from the rodeo. She'd been having so much fun up until the time Casey fell off his horse. "Carmen, do you guys want to stay here? I'm sure I can catch a ride with JD."

Two cowboys walked up. The pockets on their shirts said RANCHO CAÑADA VERDE. These were real working cowboys, as Rancho Cañada Verde was one of the few cattle ranches in Texas that still managed cattle on horseback. Its cowboys had been sweeping the rodeo without even trying.

"JD, we feel honored to have been here to witness Casey riding a horse for the very first time," one of them said.

Both cowboys laughed and then followed it up with a high five. They looked nearly identical. They had to be twins.

"Shut up, guys. He just had some kind of—"

"Spasm? Conniption fit?" the other cowboy said, with a smirk that bordered on full-out grin.

"Ladies," JD said, "these irreverent jerks are Beau and Bryce Montgomery."

Both cowboys removed their hats. "Ah," one of them said, gazing at the three of them with his blue eyes.

"We get it now," said the other.

"Pardon?" JD asked.

"It was a woman."

"Yep."

One brother looked at the other. "The question is…"

"Which woman?"

Jessica's cheeks grew warm, no matter how hard she willed them not to. Beau or Bryce—she had no idea which one—winked at her. "Bingo."

* * *

Casey looked at Dr. Martin. "Happy now?"

The X-rays had shown nothing was broken. Casey's back was in a damn spasm and his ribs were bruised, but that was it. And he'd been carried out of the arena on a stretcher while every cowboy within a ten-mile radius had laughed his ass off.

They'd never have laughed over a serious injury. During his bull riding days, Casey had seen guys get their necks broken. He'd seen ropers lose their thumbs. He'd seen a man tossed into the air by a bull who seemed to think he was a rag doll.

But he'd never seen a man just fall off his horse for no good reason.

Except there *had* been a reason. He'd seen his whole damn world watching him from the fence and the realization had momentarily tilted the universe.

"I'm happy that you're not mortally wounded," Dr. Martin said. "Unless you're planning to die of embarrassment, that is."

Casey gave him the side-eye. Partly because he deserved it, but mostly because he couldn't turn his head.

"You'll need to take it easy for the next few days. I'll give you some muscle relaxants—"

Casey waved his hand dismissively, but the movement made him wince.

"And you should stick to the bed or recliner."

Like that was gonna happen.

"And avoid reading. You might have a slight concussion."

"Thanks, Doc."

Casey got down from the exam table gingerly. He'd been through this before and knew what to do. Warm compresses. Cold compresses. He'd try to avoid the muscle relaxants, since they made him wonky and he needed his mind clear.

There was much thinking to be done.

Last night he'd been in a downright state of shock and panic when Hope had called him Daddy. She'd seemed pretty damn sure about it, after all. But he believed Jess when she said he wasn't the child's father.

Then who was?

Wondering made his jaw and head hurt even more than his

back. Jessica had been gone for almost twelve years. If she hadn't been pregnant when she and her mom had stolen out of Big Verde in the middle of the night without leaving so much as a note, then she'd become pregnant very shortly thereafter.

But somehow, he knew it was the reason they'd left. Jess had been pregnant. In high school. But it didn't make sense, unless she'd slept with someone besides him. And while he knew folks made mistakes, particularly young folks, he just didn't buy it. Not Jessica. She'd been levelheaded and practical, even at eighteen. The most foolish thing she'd ever done was *him,* and nothing in her behavior during their time together had indicated she was anything other than head over heels in love with him.

And he'd felt the same.

Jessica had come back to Big Verde for a reason, and he thought he'd figured out what it was. But he'd been way off.

He walked down the hospital's short hallway and out the back door where the ambulance had deposited him earlier. The bright sunlight hurt his head, and Doc might be right about that slight concussion. He reached in his pocket for his keys and looked around for his truck.

Shit.

The truck was at the arena. How the holy hell was he supposed to get home?

A silver Lexus pulled up.

Jesus Christ, not now.

The tinted window rolled down slowly, and there sat Annabelle Vasquez. She wasn't the only woman in Big Verde who regularly pursued him, but she was no doubt the most aggressive. And she was wearing a goddamn candy striper uniform.

Blue Jays. That's what the hospital volunteer ladies called themselves.

Now would be a good time to make a dash for his truck, only he couldn't dash if his life depended on it, and there was no truck.

"I heard about your little accident," Anna said with a smirk. Her eyes roamed the full length of his body. "You didn't hurt anything on your way down, did you?"

Why did everything she say sound so dirty?

"No, ma'am. It wasn't until I hit the dirt that everything started to hurt."

"Hmm. Well, I'm early for my shift. Do you need a ride home?"

"That's mighty nice of you to offer, but—" He looked around. It wasn't like he had many options.

Anna raised an eyebrow, then leaned over and opened the door.

And Casey got an eyeful. He could see clear down to her belly button in that getup. Surely the old ladies like Mrs. Dunbar and Miss Mills didn't wear the same outfit?

"Is that the official hospital volunteer uniform?"

"It's the same general idea," Anna said. "I had mine altered a bit."

Casey got in the car, feeling like this was the beginning of a very bad slasher film where you just knew it wasn't going to end well. Or, as Anna reached across him to help grab the seat belt, "accidentally" touching his arm, shoulder, thigh, chest, and *lap,* the beginning of a low-budget porno.

"Okay, Sheriff," she purred. "Get ready to ride."

He gulped and stared out the window.

As they pulled out of the parking lot she added, "Nice chaps."

* * *

Jessica followed a winding road to the top of Lookout Hill and stopped in front of a private lane. The number on the fence post matched the address JD had given her.

They'd gone by the hospital only to discover that Casey had been released nearly as soon as he got there. The doctor had told them he had some bruised ribs and was perfectly fine—HIPAA laws apparently hadn't reached Big Verde—but Jessica wanted to see for herself.

She peered down the lane at the white rock house. For some

reason, her hands were sweaty. Casey was going to have some questions, and she wasn't sure she was up to answering them. Hope was a Long, but Jessica had never intended on anyone knowing. Mavis had loved her only grandchild, but she had never suggested bringing Hope home to Big Verde.

Maybe Mavis was ashamed. Just like Jessica had been ashamed over her mom's citizenship status. Jessica had felt like she'd done something wrong, even though she hadn't. It didn't make sense, but shame and embarrassment weren't necessarily reasonable emotions.

But Mavis had started Hope House.

Surely that meant something.

Jessica bit her lip and slowly turned the steering wheel to start down the lane. She wasn't sure how much she wanted to tell Casey, but she needed to see him. To know he really was okay. When he'd fallen, her heart had nearly stopped. She hadn't been that terrified since the hospital called to say her mom had a heart attack. It was that same horrible, helpless feeling. The *I might really lose someone* feeling.

Movement caught her eye. Someone was getting out of a silver car on the driveway. And even from a distance, Jessica could see that it was Annabelle Vasquez, who hadn't changed a bit. What the heck was she doing at Casey's house?

Annabelle and Jessica had been co-head cheerleaders. Jessica had been chosen first, and then Anna had thrown such a fit that her parents had gone to the school board. Next thing Jessica knew, she was sharing the highly coveted position with Big Verde's version of Nellie Oleson.

Not that she was still mad about such a trivial thing. Much.

Anna wore a supertight blue-striped pinafore. Was she actually in a *costume*? She carried a doughnut box in one hand and a Rite Aid bag in the other.

Maybe there were condoms in that bag, and she and Casey were about to play "nurse and patient."

Casey had definitely picked up some skills in the sex department.

Maybe Annabelle was a practice buddy. What did Jessica really know about Casey's life here in Big Verde?

She must have been thinking too hard, because Anna suddenly turned around and looked at her. Jessica slunk down in the seat, which was stupid, and Anna stared through squinted eyes. Then she smiled.

Dang it!

But she didn't wave at Jessica or indicate she should come on up. She just turned on her heel, flipped her hair, and then sashayed her way to the front door, where she went inside without knocking.

Jessica put the car in reverse and backed down the lane to the road.

Casey had a life. And she'd done nothing but make it more difficult since the moment she'd got here. First, she'd made him late for his great-aunt's funeral. Then they nearly got caught behind the pool pump, which would have been embarrassing for her but could have been career-ending for Casey. And finally, he'd been thoroughly traumatized by Hope calling him Daddy, before finally being sweetly disappointed to learn that he wasn't.

And there was the falling-off-the-horse thing. She couldn't forget about that.

Casey seemed to be doing really well in Big Verde. He was happy, content, successful... and maybe he had a thing going with Anna. Who was she to waltz in and ruin it?

Tomorrow, after the reading of the will at the lawyer's office, she and Hope and Carmen would go back to Houston. Casey would remain in Big Verde. They were meant to be high school sweethearts and nothing more.

Maybe you really couldn't go home again.

Chapter Twelve

Casey drifted to the surface of consciousness and then promptly sank back into the warm, fluffy depths of dreamland. He'd been prancing around the arena on his horse while a nice set of pom-poms pressed into his back...

Pom-poms.

Jessica!

His eyes flew open. He kicked off the covers and grimaced, remembering his back.

Gingerly, he shifted his hips. Not too bad. He tried rolling over on his side, and that went okay too. He swung his legs over the side of the bed and sat up, keeping his back straight.

Hot damn. The muscle relaxant Anna had forced down his throat had done the trick. But just how long had he been out?

The lighting in the room indicated it was early evening. Only the hue didn't look quite right. Surely he hadn't slept all night.

He looked at the clock on the nightstand: 8:30 a.m.

Shit! He absolutely had slept all night.

He'd wanted to get to the Village Château at the crack of dawn. Had Jessica already left? No matter. If she had, he'd call into the office and tell them he wasn't coming in. He was driving to Houston. He'd storm into that fancy spaghetti place she worked at, and, well, he didn't know what would come after that. But he wasn't sitting around here wondering why the love of his life walked out. He'd done that once. He wasn't going to do it again.

He stood up, grabbed a clean shirt, looked at his dirty jeans—he'd slept in them to avoid having Anna take his pants off—and decided to just brush them off. Bending over to step into a clean pair might be pushing his luck. He was stiff as hell.

Ten minutes later he headed for the door. He looked out the window and saw his truck parked in the driveway. JD must have driven it over.

With relief, Casey reached for the doorknob. There was a sticky note staring him in the face, just below the peephole.

Gabriel Castro called. Said for you to be at his office at 9:00. Very important. He says he has something of yours. Don't be late. XOXOXO Anna

Casey sighed in frustration. It's like the entire world was conspiring to keep him and Jessica apart. He yanked the door open and walked to his truck. What the hell did Gabriel want? He was a lawyer, so nothing good.

There was barely enough time to make it to Gabriel's office, but Casey wanted to swing by the Château first. The damn lawyer could wait.

His mood improved as he drove down the hill toward town. It was a gorgeous day, and he had a good feeling. He and Jessica had both felt the connection; he just knew it. She wouldn't leave Big Verde for Houston without at least saying good-bye, especially since he'd fallen off his horse yesterday.

His face heated up over that.

But what could he say? That was the effect she had on him.

She'd looked pretty worried.

Casey grinned. A little.

The Château was just on the outskirts of town. He looked around as he pulled into the parking lot. There was no red Porsche. His heart sank. Well, it was more like it took a dive straight to the pit of his stomach.

He swung around the back of the hotel, drove around to the side. No Porsche.

He pulled into a spot and parked. Then he just sat there.

The weekend seemed like a dream. In the course of forty-eight hours, he'd rediscovered and fanned an old flame, thought he was a father, learned he wasn't, decided he was in love, and then...

Well, hell.

She'd left him without so much as a good-bye.

Again.

* * *

Jessica sat nervously in Gabriel Castro's office, flanked by Carmen and Hope. As hard as she tried, she didn't recognize the name. There was a large Castro family in Big Verde, but she didn't remember a Gabriel.

"I just can't place him," she said out loud, chewing her lip.

Carmen snorted. "Would you stop? It's so funny to watch you go all *small town* on me. I'm absolutely positive there were people in Big Verde who floated under your radar."

"But there weren't," Jessica said. "You don't understand Big Verde."

"I understand it has cowboys. Real ones. Like those twins. So it's all good in my book."

The Montgomery twins had come by the Château last night, and Carmen had joined them for a couple of drinks before they'd dragged her to Tony's, a local honky-tonk. It was Carmen's first time in a honky-tonk, and she'd had all kinds of fun. The kind of fun that involved twin cowboys.

"The bar food at Tony's was surprisingly good," Carmen said. "Nothing fancy, but really good. Tony gave me his mom's recipe for buttermilk-battered mushrooms. Did you know she still works in the kitchen? She's ninety-one!"

Jessica tried not to be irritated by Carmen's enthusiasm for All Things Big Verde. She'd been a great help this weekend, looking after Hope and providing emotional support. She was entitled to a little fun.

"I wonder how much money Mavis left Hope," Carmen said in a loud stage whisper.

"How much what?" Hope asked.

"Nothing," Jessica and Carmen answered together. Because there was no point in explaining wills and inheritances to an eleven-year-old.

Hope was Mavis's only grandchild, and Jessica knew she'd be taken care of. If Jessica ever became ill, or too old to care for Hope... Well, it was an overwhelming relief to know Hope would have a nest egg.

She looked at her watch. Lawyers. Why did they always keep you waiting?

The door opened and a tall, handsome man in a crisp gray suit walked in.

"Good morning, ladies," he said. His smile radiated a warmth that lit up his eyes. He had a full head of thick, luscious hair, sparkling white teeth, and dimples that took the edge off of his nearly overwhelming sex appeal. "I'm Gabriel Castro."

He went straight for Hope. "I presume you are Ms. Hope Acosta?" Hope grinned.

He looked at Carmen next. "Ms. Foraccio, I'm a huge fan. It is a pleasure to meet you. I hope you're enjoying your time in Big Verde."

Carmen pumped his hand with enthusiasm. "I'm enjoying it very much."

Finally, he turned his brown eyes on Jessica. "And you must be Jessica, the most enthusiastic cheerleader the Big Verde Giants have ever had. At least that's what I hear."

"I'm sorry. I know you're a Castro, but I just can't place you—"

Gabriel laughed. "No relation. I married into the Big Verde community. I'm originally from Austin."

That explained it. "Oh? Who did you—"

The door opened and Jessica turned. *Casey!*

He looked just as surprised to see her.

"I thought you'd left," he said.

Jessica stood, and Casey crossed the room in three quick steps. The next thing Jessica knew, she was in his arms. The world shrank to just the two of them, Casey's heart beating frantically beneath her cheek while her own pulse pounded in her head. Hope giggled. Carmen sighed. Gabriel cleared his throat.

It was quite possibly a full minute before Casey loosened his grip and took a small step back.

"I wasn't going to leave without saying good-bye," she said. "I came by your house yesterday, but you were busy."

"Busy? I was probably asleep," he said. "Anna made me take a muscle relaxant. It knocked me out."

"Yeah, I saw her."

Casey laughed. "Really? How did that go? Did y'all try to out-high-kick each other?"

Jessica couldn't help it. The idea of that made her snort.

Whatever there was between Casey and Anna—if there was anything at all—it was obviously not romantic. And every cell in her body breathed a sigh of relief. Even though she was leaving for Houston today, and Casey was staying here.

"We didn't speak," Jessica said. "I saw her and I just, you know, left. I didn't want to disturb you."

"You could never disturb me."

They sat down, and Casey leaned over with a slight wince. His breath tickled her ear as he whispered, "Never with Anna. You know me better than that, Jess."

Anna had been her rival. And Casey was loyal beyond a fault.

She shivered from the feel of his breath against her ear.

Gabriel sat in his chair. "I hear you took a tumble yesterday, Sheriff Long."

Casey rolled his eyes. "I'll never live it down."

Hope sat up straight in her seat. "Sheriff Long is my daddy!"

Oh God. They were back to that.

* * *

Casey broke out in a light sweat. Why did Hope keep saying he was her daddy? It was jarring, to say the least. He looked at Jessica, and she merely rolled her eyes. She was irritated, but not surprised, so Casey relaxed.

A little.

"I know Sheriff Long is your daddy," Gabriel said to Hope.

What?

Now Jess's face went white.

"Uh, Jess..."

"And we're here because your grandma Mavis asked us to come together," Gabriel said.

"Her grandma?" Casey blurted. Then he looked at Jess.

"Yes, Casey. That's what I tried to tell you at the arena—"

"Her *grandma*?" Casey repeated. "You're saying Aunt Mavis is her grandma—"

Aunt Mavis had one son. And it was his ass-wipe cousin or uncle or whatever he was, Wade.

The room felt like it flipped sideways as things clicked into place. Casey jumped to his feet in a blinding fit of white rage. That goddamn *asshole*. He started to shake. He needed to punch something, but instead he pulled Jess to her feet, and through clenched teeth, he said, "He...*touched you*? How? When?"

The room went totally still. She'd been eighteen. *Eighteen!* He wrapped his arms around her. No wonder they'd left town that way. Her mom had to protect her.

"Casey, not me."

Jessica was saying something. He let go and stared into her eyes. Her sweet, sweet eyes. Swallowed down another lump.

"My mom," she said. "Hope is my sister."

Gabriel came around his desk. "Have a seat, Casey. I'm so sorry. I misspoke."

"I'm her sister," Hope said, smiling proudly.

Casey sat down. He had no choice, since his knees had basically given out.

Jessica sat, too, and her small hand took hold of his.

He tried to wrap his mind around what he'd just learned. Wade had been having an affair—or something—with Jessica's mom. He'd gotten her pregnant. And she had taken Jessica and left Big Verde without telling a soul where they were going.

"Did you not read the letters, Casey?"

Jessica's face. He focused on that. Why were her eyes tearing up?

"What letters?"

"I suspect these are the letters right here," Gabriel said, holding up five envelopes, all covered in hand-drawn hearts and stamped and addressed to Casey Long.

All were still sealed.

"Where did you get those?" Jessica asked.

"From Mavis," Gabriel said. He handed them to Casey.

Eighteen-year-old Jessica's swirly-girlie handwriting stared up at him. Casey took a deep breath, and with shaking fingers, he popped a kissy-lips seal that would have made him laugh on any other occasion.

"Is it okay for me to read these?" he suddenly asked Jessica.

"Yes, of course," Jessica said. But then she looked at the envelopes with their hearts and flowers and kissy-lips and added, "But maybe not this very minute."

Casey wanted to rip into them as if they contained the secret to immortality or the cure for cancer, but Jessica's cheeks were pink and getting pinker. So, he casually tucked them into his shirt pocket and gave them a gentle pat.

"I don't understand," Jessica said. "How did Mavis end up with those letters?"

Casey explored his memories from twelve years ago, the summer of his graduation. Everything was a blur of pain and panic, because Jessica had disappeared, but he remembered that his parents had gone to Europe. It was supposed to have been a graduation trip for Casey, but he'd been too crushed and depressed to go. He'd stayed home, and Aunt Mavis had come by every day to check on him and other things.

Like the mail.

Gabriel pulled another envelope out of his desk. "I suspect this will explain everything."

There was another letter?

"I had assumed we were here for a reading of Mavis's will," Jess said. And then she quickly added, "Because of Hope."

Gabriel laughed softly. "That only happens in the movies. I mean, I have your copy of the will right here. And I'm happy to go over it with you, if you need me to. Mavis left Hope very well cared for. But you were both called here today because Mavis wanted you and Casey in the same room while I read you this."

Gabriel cleared his throat dramatically. "Dear Jessica and Casey, this is an apology for a terrible thing I have done..."

* * *

Five minutes later, everyone sat quietly, digesting what they'd just heard. Jessica anxiously bit her lip and tried to remain in her seat. Because what she wanted to do was jump up and down and stomp her feet, and that wasn't appropriate at all.

Mavis had intercepted the letters. She'd known about Wade's misdeed and had been afraid Jessica would tell Casey, and then he'd tell someone, and they'd tell someone...

Honestly, Mavis might have been right. They'd been teenagers, and there had been too much at stake. Way more than simply the Long family's reputation.

Casey sighed and leaned forward to rest his elbows on his knees, shaking his head. "I just don't know how my family could have done yours any more wrong."

"In her confession, Mavis asked for our forgiveness. I loved her way too much not to give it to her," Jessica said.

Casey looked at her as if she had two heads. "You really did love her, didn't you?"

"I really did."

And Mavis wasn't the only person she'd loved in Big Verde. What she'd felt for Casey had not been a teenage crush. And what she felt for him now was even stronger. From the moment he'd walked into the room and enveloped her in his arms, she'd felt safe. And for her, that was a strong and rare emotion.

She'd been adrift for twelve years, and Casey was an anchor. She couldn't stand the thought of leaving him again, but she couldn't conceive of a way around it.

"Man," Carmen said. "You folks certainly know how to dish out the drama in this town."

Upon hearing the word *drama*, Hope put a hand to her forehead, as if she were about to swoon. Carmen had taught her to do that whenever someone was being overly dramatic. It made Gabriel laugh and relieved at least some of the tension in the room. And when Hope's stomach chose that moment to growl loudly, that relieved the rest.

"Somebody's hungry," Jessica said. "Should we head to Corner Café for a late breakfast?" She wanted to spend as much time as possible with Casey before heading back to Houston.

A little spark of panic fluttered in her chest. She clutched his hand tightly, and it went away.

"Can we make it brunch?" Carmen asked. "I have a bit of business with Mr. Castro here."

Jessica looked at Gabriel. Was Carmen kidding?

"She's my ten o'clock appointment," he said.

What possible business could Carmen need to conduct in Big Verde that involved a lawyer? Whatever it was, Jessica recognized her friend's stubborn impish grin. There was no point in asking. She wouldn't get it out of her. Not right now anyway.

Chapter Thirteen

Jessica looked out the front window of the Corner Café. A girl who looked about sixteen was busy scrubbing off green shoe polish that spelled out BEAT THE BADGERS!

"Well," she asked Casey. "Did they?"

"Did who what?"

"Did the Big Verde Giants beat the Badgers on Friday?"

Sally Larson, owner of the diner, refilled their coffee cups. "You're kidding, right?" she asked, not even bothering to pretend she wasn't listening to their conversation. "Darlin', the last time the Big Verde Giants beat the Badgers was 1979."

"Oh. Well, there's always next year."

"That's the cheerleader spirit," Sally said, pretending to wipe crumbs off the table. She'd been hovering around their booth like a bee bothering a honeysuckle vine since the moment they sat down. Big Verde had a weekly newspaper, but Sally Larson was the Official Town Gossip, a role she took seriously.

"Homecoming is next week," Casey said. "We're playing the Sweet Home Beavers."

"Do they still write LICK THE BEAVERS! on all the windows?"

"Now, Jess, why wouldn't they?" Casey asked, feigning innocence. When they were in school, everyone had pretended not to know what it meant, and Jessica was pleased the tradition of playing dumb lived on.

"Lick the Beavers!" Hope cheered.

"Oh, dear," Jessica said.

Sally snorted and headed for the kitchen, where Rusty, the cook, had just hit the bell. "Order up!"

Homecoming. There was just something about the Friday night lights of the field, the announcer's voice echoing through the big speakers, the sharp drum cadence of the school fight song…

"It sure would be fun to take Hope to a game," she said.

"Why don't you come down?" Casey asked.

"I don't know. It's typically pretty hard to get away from work on a weekend."

"I'll get you a mum," Casey said, blue eyes twinkling.

"What about me?" Hope asked.

"You too. The biggest mum I can find."

Hope clapped her hands. "Yay! What's a mum?"

Sally came back to the table, balancing a huge tray. She set a short stack of pancakes in front of Hope, huevos rancheros in front of Casey, and scrambled eggs, sausage, and buttered grits in front of Jessica. It all smelled delicious, and for the next few minutes they ate in silence, except for the occasional groan of delight.

"Are you going to eat that last piece of bacon?" Jessica asked, pointing at Casey's plate with her fork.

"Damn, woman. You always could pack it away."

Jessica looked at her plate, which was practically licked clean. "Don't judge," she said. "I'm an emotional eater."

Casey put his hands up. "No judgment," he said. "And you're welcome to eat my bacon."

Jessica's fork stopped midway to his plate. Why had that sounded so dirty? She glanced up and was met by a cocked eyebrow and sexy smirk. *Because he'd meant it to sound dirty.*

Suddenly, Hope snatched the bacon with her chubby little hand and hightailed it to the other side of the diner.

"Sheriff," Sally said. "We have a bacon bandit!"

* * *

Casey watched Hope settle into a corner booth with her stolen goods.

"It's not even her first offense," Jess said, standing up.

"Sit back down," Sally said. She held up a handful of crayons and a piece of paper. "She can stay in her own booth and give y'all some privacy."

Jess sat, but she bit her lip, glancing nervously at Hope in the corner.

"She'll be fine over there," Casey said. "I've got my eye on her."

The tension across Jessica's brow disappeared, and she stopped gnawing on her lip. "It's such a relief to not have to watch her like a hawk everywhere I go," she said. "Believe me. In Houston, she would not be sitting in a restaurant at her very own table. I can't let her out of my sight."

Casey couldn't imagine the stress Jessica had been under all these years, particularly the last two, where she'd been responsible for Hope by herself. "It must be hard," he said.

Carmen seemed like a good friend, but Casey couldn't help but feel that Jessica's life would be easier in a small community like Big Verde, where everyone looked out for each other. At the idea of Jessica and Hope living in Big Verde, Casey's heart thudded around his chest like a battering ram. Would the thought occur to Jessica, as well?

"You have no idea how hard," Jessica said. "The school bus used to drop her off at our apartment. But since Mom died, she goes to an after-school program. She hates it. But she can't always be at work with me, and I can't always be at home."

"You don't have any place like Hope House in Houston? A teacher walks Dalton and some other kids over after school. It's right across the street."

"Oh, there are lots of great places. But they're not near La Casa Bleu or Hope's school, and Houston traffic is horrendous. It's not like I can just get her somewhere in ten minutes."

Casey wanted to point out that you could get from one end of

Big Verde to the other in under ten minutes, but he didn't want to sound as desperate as he felt.

He reached across the table and took both of Jess's hands in his. Now that they'd finished eating, and they had a modicum of privacy—Sally pretended to adjust the blinds in the booth behind them—it was time to take on the elephant in the room.

"Your mom was undocumented?"

Jessica stared at the cup of coffee in front of her. "Yes," she whispered.

"It must be hard to talk about something you'd been forbidden to speak of for so long. But there's nothing to be ashamed of, Jess."

"I didn't know her status when we lived in Big V. And I'm glad I didn't. Because at least for my childhood, I didn't live in fear. In Houston, every day was filled with dread and anxiety. I was terrified of coming home to find Mom gone and Hope all alone in the apartment."

"I wish you'd told me. Maybe my family could have helped. There's something called asylum—"

"She did ask someone from your family for help. That's how she met Wade. She naively assumed the county sheriff would know how to get her on a path to citizenship."

Wade. Casey was going to have a hard time not punching the guy the next time he saw him.

He wanted to soothe Jess with words like *what's passed is past* and *you're safe now.* But he knew from trauma training that those words were hollow. Jessica needed time. And someone to talk to.

And that led to the one burning question tumbling around inside his mouth, waiting for an opportunity to spill out. "When are you heading back to Houston?"

"We have a two o'clock checkout," Jess said. "That is, if Carmen makes it back in time."

"What the hell kind of business could she be stirring up with Gabe?"

"Oh, it could be anything, really. Somebody texted or e-mailed or called about an emergency involving rights or insurance or contracts and voilà! She's sitting in front of a lawyer. It happens all the time. Her life is crazy."

"I bet that means your life in Houston is also crazy."

Jess took a sip of coffee, and Sally topped it off again. "Let's just say I've enjoyed this weekend in Big Verde. I mean, we've definitely had some excitement—"

Casey laughed at the understatement.

"But it's a different kind," Jessica said. "I've missed this place."

Casey swallowed. How could this work out? "Jess, I don't want to lose you again," he whispered.

Sally, who was now pretending to clean a spotless table nearby, sniffled loudly.

"And I don't want to lose you again either," Jess said, squeezing his hand.

"You say you missed Big Verde. That you had never wanted to leave."

"And that's all true. But there's also reality to consider."

"The reality is that you and I were torn apart by our families. We had plans, Jess. Plans to be together. And as far as I know, neither one of us intentionally changed them."

Jess took a deep breath.

Dammit. She was going to say something reasonable.

"I'm raising a Down syndrome child by myself. Thanks to Carmen, I'm able to do it on a good salary. I *do* love Big Verde. But what would I do here? Where would I work? And, Casey—"

Sally stopped wiping the table, and Jessica lowered her voice to a whisper. "We don't really know each other anymore. We're not eighteen."

Casey shook his head and took a couple of seconds to gather his thoughts. She still had feelings for him, that was obvious. And he'd never stopped loving her. Letting her walk out of his life again, without even trying to pick up where they'd left off, seemed like a catastrophic mistake. "I know damn well how old we are. But we *do* know each other. Shit, you made me who I am today. How can you say you don't know me?"

Sally approached with her goddamn coffeepot.

Casey held up his hand. "Not now, Sally."

"Hope!" Jessica stood swiftly, and Casey did the same, without even knowing why.

"I got it, sweetheart," Sally said.

Hope had somehow ended up behind the counter. She was straightening the napkin holders and condiments. Putting them all in a row. Sally praised her for tidying up. "Do you like to put things in nice, neat rows?"

"Sally volunteers at Hope House," Casey assured Jess.

"These are crooked," Hope said. Then she went to work making sure everything lined up, poking her tongue out one corner of her mouth from the effort.

Jess sat back down with a sigh, and so did Casey.

"Listen," Casey said. "We'll work it out. There are five-star restaurants in Austin where you could work. That's not too far away. We just have to iron out some details is all."

Jess began frantically twisting a strand of her hair. "I'm not sure Carmen can live without me."

Casey leaned across the table. Kissed her on the nose and watched her blush. "I'm the one who can't live without you. I'll cancel my reelection campaign. At the end of this term, I can move to Houston, if you want me to."

Boom. He hadn't meant to say it. Hadn't even *thought* about it. But as he watched the tears build up in Jessica's sweet brown eyes, he realized that's what made it honest. Every word had come straight from the heart.

He'd follow her anywhere, because dammit, they deserved to be together.

Forever.

* * *

Jessica couldn't believe her ears. And yet, Casey gazed at her with a fierce intensity that said he meant business.

The man was serious. He was willing to leave his career and home to be with her.

Sally stood wide-eyed, clutching the coffeepot like it was a life preserver and the Corner Café was the *Titanic*. Rusty stared openly from the other side of the counter, spatula suspended in midair.

These were Casey's people. How could she live with herself if she took him away from Big Verde? But how could *she* live if she had to do it without Casey?

The little bell above the door jingled. Sally wiped her nose on the back of her hand and reached for a stack of menus. Not that anybody in Big Verde needed one.

Then she gasped at the sight of Carmen breezing in.

"I was hoping I'd still find you two here," Carmen said, yanking out a seat.

"Oh, my," Sally said. "Are you who I think you are? Well, of course you are. That's a silly question, isn't it? I'd heard you were in town. Can I get you some coffee? A Danish maybe?"

"Both of those things sound delightful," Carmen said. "And do you have anything weird for me to try?"

"Um... weird?"

"Yeah," Carmen said, shrugging her shoulders. "I'm kinky that way."

"I have some goose jerky."

"I'm down for it," Carmen said. "Bring it."

Sally hurried off.

Jessica shifted in her seat. "Listen, Carmen, Casey and I are talking. This is kind of bad timing."

"So I did a thing," Carmen said, ignoring Jessica entirely.

Jessica rolled her eyes. "Tell me there's no restraining order. Was it one of those twins?"

Carmen laughed. "This has nothing to do with them."

"Oh. Well, then maybe it can wait—"

"I bought the Village Château restaurant. Well, part of it. The chef, Frederick, is in on it too. He wanted to buy it but didn't have the resources. I'm the majority owner. We're going to call it Le Château Bleu and we plan to fuse French and German—"

The words Carmen was stringing together finally formed themselves into sentences in Jessica's mind. "Are you serious? You bought the restaurant at the Château?"

Sally came back and set a plate down in front of Carmen. It looked like dehydrated dog poop, but it was set on a fancy doily. "You've got to hold it in your mouth for a few seconds to soften it up."

"Looks delish," Carmen said.

"My son, Bubba, made it."

"Carmen!" Jessica said. "Did you hear me? Did you really buy the Village Château?"

"Not technically. Closing date is a few weeks away. But it's happening."

Jessica's brain was on overdrive. She knew where this was heading, and it was too good to be true. She glanced at Casey across the table, and he was grinning and wiggling and appeared to be about ready to pop out of his skin.

Carmen picked up a piece of jerky and eyed it curiously. "We'd like a manager on the premises as soon as possible, of course. Current owners are cool with it. It's going to be a big transition. Lots to do. Because I have *huge* plans and we're going to have a lavish and extreme grand opening. I'm talking celebrity guest list. Big Verde won't know what hit it."

"A manager? You need a manager?"

"Yep. Do you know anybody who might be interested?" Carmen's eyes twinkled, but she managed to keep a straight face as she stuffed the jerky into her mouth.

"Careful now," Casey said. "That's going to expand."

Carmen, cheek bulging, gave him a thumbs-up and mouthed *I'll miss you* to Jessica. At least Jessica thought that's what she said.

Beneath the table, a big boot rubbed against Jessica's ankle. Casey raised his eyebrows. "Well? What do you say, Jess?"

She gazed at Casey, noting the slight wrinkles around his eyes.

They hadn't been there when she'd left twelve years ago. She took his hand and traced some light scars, wondering what had caused them. She'd missed parts of his life. Major parts. But the expression on his face, so hopeful and anxious, belonged to the boy she used to know.

Casey squeezed her hand. "We have our whole lives ahead of us, Jess."

He'd said the same thing on the night they'd promised to be together forever. It was true then, and it was true now.

"Oh, Casey," she said, choking back tears in disbelief. "I think I'm finally coming home."

Casey leaned over the table to kiss her, and when their lips met, applause broke out in the Corner Café.

Home was where her cowboy was, and he was in the best little town in Texas.

About the Author

Carly Bloom began her writing career as a family humor columnist and blogger, a pursuit she abandoned when her children grew old enough to literally die from embarrassment. To save their delicate lives, Carly turned to penning steamy contemporary romance. The kind with bare chests on the covers.

Carly and her husband raise their mortified brood of offspring on a cattle ranch in South Texas.

You can learn more at:
CarlyBloomBooks.com
Twitter @CarlyBloomBooks
Facebook.com/AuthorCarlyBloom
Instagram @CarlyBloomBooks

Find happily ever after with more sensational western romances by Carly Bloom!

ONCE UPON A TIME IN TEXAS SERIES

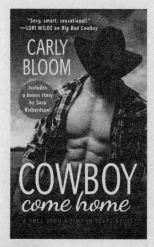

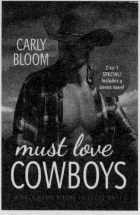

Available Spring 2021

Looking for more Western romance?
Take the reins with these cowboys from Forever!

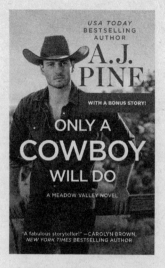

ONLY A COWBOY WILL DO
by A.J. Pine

After a lifetime of helping others, Jenna Owens is finally putting herself first, starting with her vacation at the Meadow Valley Guest Ranch to celebrate her fortieth birthday. Colt Morgan, part-owner of the ranch, is happy to help her have all the fun she deserves, especially her wish for a vacation fling. But will their two weeks of fantasy lead to a shot in the real world, or will their final destination be two broken hearts? Includes a bonus story from Melinda Curtis!

Discover bonus content and more on read-forever.com

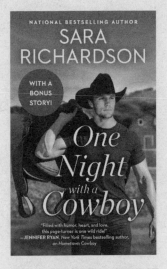

ONE NIGHT WITH A COWBOY
by Sara Richardson

Wes Harding is known as a devil-may-care bull rider—but now, with his sister's pregnancy at risk, Wes promises to put aside his wild ways and take the reins on their ranch's big charity event. Only he didn't count on his co-hostess—and little sister's best friend—being so darn distracting. One kiss with Thea Davis throws his world off-balance. But with her husband gone, Thea's focused only on raising her two rambunctious children. Can Wes convince her that he's the man on whom she can rely? Includes a bonus story by Carly Bloom!

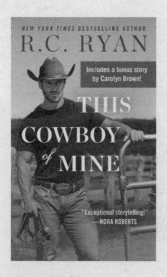

THIS COWBOY OF MINE
by R.C. Ryan

Kirby Regan just quit her career in Washington, D.C., to buy her family's Wyoming ranch. But when a snowstorm hits while she's out hiking in the Tetons, her only option for shelter is a nearby cave. She didn't realize it was already occupied...by a ruggedly handsome cowboy. Casey Merrick doesn't mind sharing his space with a gorgeous stranger, as long as they can both keep their distance—a task that begins to seem impossible as the attraction between them heats up. Includes a bonus story from Carolyn Brown!

BLACKLISTED
by Jay Crownover

In the small Texas town of Loveless, Palmer "Shot" Caldwell lives on the edge of the law. But this ruthlessly hot outlaw follows his own code of honor, and that includes repaying his debts. Which is exactly why icy, brilliant Dr. Presley Baskin is calling in a favor. She once saved Shot's life. Now she needs his help—and his protection.

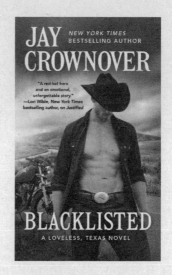

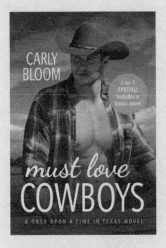

MUST LOVE COWBOYS
by Carly Bloom

Alice Martin doesn't regret putting her career as a librarian above personal relationships—but when cowboy Beau Montgomery comes to her for help, Alice decides to see what she's been missing. She agrees to help Beau improve his reading skills if he'll be her date to an upcoming wedding. But when the town's gossip mill gets going, they're forced into a fake romance to keep their deal a secret. And soon Alice is seeing Beau in a whole new way...Includes the bonus novel *Big Bad Cowboy*!